THE TRAIL WEST

Aaron whirled around. "Repair that wagon, rebuild it if you must. Get that wheel off. Oner, choose four strong mules to replace those horses..."

Adam shook his head. "They can't go on tonight. They're shocked, exhausted. They need days of rest and they'll then need men to help them across the Chattahoochee."

"Adam, are you crazy? Rest here, in an Indian campground? Don't you understand? They're moving north. By tomorrow whole tribes could be here. They move out tonight, and so do we." He leaned over Zilpah. "Let that boy rest until the wagon's ready."

Adam stepped forward. "We can't move out tonight, not with Rebecca ill."

"Not this time. I am not listening. Anyone who stays, stays alone. They'll have to go on without help. We've blazed the trail."

"I'll take six men in the morning, get them across and up the grade. We could be back by..."

"You'll take them as soon as the wagon is ready. I stand responsible for my family and my people. I give the orders. I will not be crossed, Adam."

SOUTH WIND

Esther Jane Neely

LEISURE BOOKS **NEW YORK CITY**

Previously published work included in SOUTH WIND:

Grasshopper, Grasshopper: Arizona Quarterly, Winter 1961

The Song of Ruby Ella: The University of New Mexico Review, Volume XXXV, Number 3, Autumn 1965
  The Song of Ruby Ella copyright © 1969 by E. J. Neely

The Big Road: The University Review, Volume XXXII, Number 3, 1966

Onward to Tellahavee: The New Renaissance, Volume II, Number 4

Doodle: The Mississippi Review, Volume IV, Number 2, 1975

A LEISURE BOOK

Published by

Dorchester Publishing Co., Inc.
41 E. 60 St.
New York City

Copyright © MCMLXXIX by Nordon Publications, Inc.
Copyright © 1983 by Dorchester Publishing Co., Inc.

All rights reserved. No part of this book may be reproduced or transmitted in any form or by any electronic or mechanical means, including photocopying, recording or by any information storage and retrieval system, without the written permission of the Publisher, except where permitted by law.

Printed in the United States of America

To Joe, with love

"We human beings tread a razor's edge of destiny—one misstep being fatal..."

—Jon Syme, 1542-1590

THE PEOPLE OF SOUTH WIND

Aaron Brewster	*Young planter*
Ruth Brewster	*Aaron's wife*
Aaron and Ara	*Aaron and Ruth's children*
Adam Brewster	*Aaron's younger brother*
Rebecca Brewster	*Adam's wife, Ruth's sister*
Adam and Ben	*Adam and Rebecca's children*
Brewster slaves	*Trunk, Zilpah, Jeddy Black, Oner, Laban, Nahor, Lutie, Aretha, Laurel Hill, Jethro, Joshua, Peleg, Serug, Simeon, Milcah, Sarai, Tamar, Zibeon, Leah*
Eli Salem	*Storekeeper*
Jules LeFleur	*Adventurer, privateer, carpenter*
Marie LeFleur	*Jules' wife*
Jacques LeFleur	*Jules' brother, handler of Baratarian goods*
Antoinette LeFleur	*Jacques' wife*
The trader	
Pete, the trapper	
Abram	*A slave rescued by Adam Brewster*

THE PEOPLE OF NOONDAY

Abraham Brewster Cork	*Son of Abram; an itinerant preacher*
Rosenberg	*His friend, a police sergeant*
Lelia LeFleur	*Descendant of Oner and Amelia LeFleur*
Clay Justice	*Descendant of Adam Brewster*
Raven Black	*Descendant of Jeddy Black*
Doodle	*Of unknown descent*
Lutie Mae	*Doodle's wife; descendant of Jeddy Black*
Adam Brewster	*Storekeeper, descendant of the Virginia Brewsters*
Aaron Brewster	*Descendant of the first Aaron Brewster*
Pinkney	*Aaron's manservant, descendant of Trunk and Zilpah*
Drew Brewster	*Possibly a descendant of Adam Brewster*
Sal Brewster	*Drew's wife*
Miss Olivia Flower	*Descended from Brewsters, married a LeFleur*
Arlie, Ruby Ella, Jesse and Madelaine LeFleur	*Descendants of Oner and Amelia LeFleur*
Brewster	*Abraham B. Cork's young nephew*
Terence Abernathy	*His friend*
Boyd Brewster	*Runs gas station*
Bimby Brewster	*Boyd's son*
Oriole	*A girl*
Bert Ainsley	*The outsider*

Book One

South Wind

Chapter 1

THE BLUE MOUNTAINS

Spring, 1804

The gentle wind-drifted spring rain touching the logs and shingles had already lulled Martha and the children into sleep when from the southeast road mud-muffled pounding of a single horse's hoofs beat annoyingly into Eli's consciousness. As the horse came to a sudden halt in front of his store, Eli drew reluctantly from Martha's solid form—but keeping his feet on the brick warmer—and leaned toward the window.

He squinted down into the shadows. A lantern faintly illuminated a dark horse and a rider wearing a large black hat and a sodden cape or blanket that draped down the horse, allowing the figures to appear as a formidable statue until the light moved, scanning the sign which read, "Eli Salem, General Store and Livery Stables."

Eli blinked. A lantern. Illness probably—in some planter's family, a frantic ride to the village for medicine. He stiffened. But there were no plantations out the southeast road, just deep woods for many miles, and rarely travelers at night when highwaymen lurked.

He waited breathlessly. He'd been held up and robbed twice this spring. There came no call. As boots hit the wooden porch, he snatched the top quilt, and searched at the side of the bed for his musket. Gun leveled, he leaned out the window.

"Yah?"

"Eli Salem?" instantly, a strange voice, husky, melodious, but with no trace of local accents and his ears had encountered many since his trader's cart trundled down the mountains from Pennsylvania into Virginia. "Eli Salem. Quickly."

Eli gasped. A French accent. A voice accustomed to issuing orders and being obeyed...

"Yah."

Tumbling down the dark familiar narrow staircase, Eli lighted a candle from the embers in the fireplace, and ran to the door. "Yah?" The definite scrape of a sword's sheath scared him almost to death.

"Open. I've traveled far with a packet for Aaron and Adam Brewster."

Eli's breath snorted noisily. A courier. Slamming the candle on a hogshead, he raised the heavy doorbar, and stuck out his musket.

"The Brewster plantation is many miles from here. Keep on the west road until..."

The palm of a ringed hand pushed the muzzle of the gun as the stranger shoved past Eli. The light from the ship's lantern of glistening brass glimmered on twinkling jet eyes and upon gem stones encrusting the sword sheath sticking out from a long fur-lined cape such as Eli had never seen. No mere courier dressed like that.

The black eyes flashed. "I've no time to search. My orders were to deliver it into your hands," slapping his dripping hat against the hogshead, splattering muddy water into Eli's face.

It amazed him that so elegant a man's teeth dared chatter. Hoisting his quilt, he put his musket on the counter, and darted to throw a log on the fire.

"You need a drink, sir, and food," he said, sliding the cold beef with a knife toward the stranger. He poured two whiskeys.

"I need a fresh horse and oil for my lantern." Accepting the glass, he bowed and placed a small leather-wrapped and thong-tied packet into Eli's hands.

Firelight flashed as Eli stared down. Gasping, he recognized the right-leaning, flowing script of Jules LeFleur, often on his books in the past.

"Hurry, man. My ship awaits at Norfolk."

Mouth open, Eli unlocked the strong-box, and stuffed the packet inside. "Ship? Is Jules...?"

"The *Gulf Wind*, out of New Orleans, returning from the African coast," the mustache twitched in a grin. "Jules is not aboard, much as he might wish to be."

Jules in New Orleans! "Dry your cloak," Eli urged, pushing the bottle closer. "I'll switch horses—an equal one. We've planty, all fast." Darting out into the rain, he restrained a chuckle. "I'll give him a Brewster horse. That would delight Adam, and Aaron would be furious. A Brewster horse carrying a courier for Jules LeFleur." Leading the exhausted horse into the stables, he did chuckle...

For a second the dimming lantern glow hung like a will o' the wisp, then evaporated into the dark dense woods. Clutching the quilt, Eli scurried inside to the fire. Never had he seen a man so debonair, with that impudent quality one would expect in a privateer—not that he thought the man was one. He hadn't disclosed his name. Sighing, he recalled the fine tight fit of the black suit, the magnificent cape, the strange wide-brimmed hat of short black fur. It was a dream...

Yet, still clutched in his hand was the gold coin the man had tossed. At the sight of the moneybag, Eli'd warned of highwaymen. The man had rocked with laughter that rattled the sword in the richly carved jeweled sheath. And the beef was smaller, and there was the packet. Glancing over his shoulder, he unlocked the strong-box, held the packet in his hands. Not heavy enough to contain gold or silver, yet it was thick enough to hold many paper notes. Well, at least Jules and Jacques LeFleur were finally paying to his sons the debt long owed Robert Brewster. Eli stood, elbows on the counter, remembering the LeFleur boys.

Upon finding the French boys, Jules and Jacques LeFleur, stranded at the docks of Portsmouth, England, and marveling at their courage to venture so far, Robert Brewster had paid the ship's captain their passage to the New World rather than have them become indentured servants. He brought them with his family from the port of Philadelphia into Virginia, cared for them, and being a fine carpenter as well as a farmer, taught them the trade. They learned it well, and worked hard, but they couldn't hang on to enough money to repay him before their adventurous spirits urged them onward. Instead, they borrowed from Robert for the trip west. Fantastic, those two married and settled—at least Jules was settled in New Orleans with a good business and a splendid home, the stranger had told him. And Jacques was a trader traveling between New Orleans and Spanish Mexico.

Eli shook his head. Spirited as fine horses, those LeFleur boys had been. He'd never forget their twinkling black eyes, the jokes they would... He gasped. Pounding his fist upon the counter, tears of laughter rolled down his cheeks. How he had bowed and scraped to that rascal he'd believed a courier! Jules LeFleur, who still owed him money, stood right there with rubies on his fingers... Eli's face flamed. He would never tell Aaron Brewster, not even Adam, although he could use a little of Adam's sympathy. Jules would laugh the whole way to Norfolk.

Glancing around his simple store, he shook his head. It was too much. When he left Pennsylvania he couldn't foresee that the wheels of his cart would wander no further than Appomattox County.

Sighing, he pulled shut the bedroom window. A cart tumbling over mountains was no place for a woman carrying a child. Seven children in that many years. Martha was so susceptible. He crept toward her warmth and comfort.

Early that next morning in the wet spring of 1804, Eli paced his damp wooden porch watching the west road for the Brewster wagon which could be easily recognized at a great distance: Aaron would be alone. When Robert Brewster lived he brought both boys and as many slaves as could squeeze in or hang on, as did most tobacco growers on the Saturday trip to town. Stretching his neck, he wished young Adam would come in today, yet he knew it would be Aaron.

The black team swept around the curve, their sleek forms shimmeringly outlined in streamers of sunlight filtering through the pale new green of the elms lining the road. Eli stopped pacing as he saw the proud-posed Aaron alone in the wagon. Leaning forward, he made out the stiffly handsome face, the fair short-trimmed beard. "Yah," he muttered meanly, "race your horses. Why must you do everything as if the devil chased you?" He shook his head. Such a fine father, Robert Brewster. How had he sired such as Aaron? Not that Aaron wasn't fine and honest. It was just Aaron's way that rankled him.

Turning, he hesitated, pondering if he dared conveniently forget his obligation and carry the packet out on Sunday and deliver it into Adam's hands, or at least give it to Aaron in Adam's presence.

The horses snorted as Aaron jerked the reins. Sighing, Eli darted inside to open the strong-box.

Aaron walked in, boot heels snapping.

Quivering, Eli reached under his apron and held out the packet. "Good morning, Mister Aaron, I was hoping you or Adam would come this day." Meeting the cold blue eyes he wondered that young Adam had managed of his own determination to father his two sons, or to slip in occasionally to order books. Adam had wanted to be a teacher, to go to school, but Aaron had chosen their beautiful girl-wives, the frail Rebecca for Adam, and the sturdy Ruth for himself.

Aaron glanced at the packet, and then turned to his list.

Exasperated, Eli pointed. "That packet traveled all the way from New Orleans..." he babbled on breathlessly, telling of the stranger, caught himself, and stood, mouth dry, waiting for Aaron to exclaim, to untie it; but Aaron placed it in his vest, and proceeded to order his supplies. Shriveled, Eli turned to his shelves. He'd seen the last of it. Once Aaron made his move, he never turned back....

From the instant his team swept from the store, Aaron's eyes gazed upon the solemn wall of the high-ridged blue-green mountains, aware of them, but seeing far beyond to the fabulous land Jules and Jacques had evidently conquered on money that should have been his years sooner. Twice he reached inside his vest to feel the thickness of the packet.

Unable to wait, although near home, but out of sight under a budding peach tree, he drew it out. It was addressed to him and to Adam. Hesitating, he stared at Jules's handwriting, then rapidly unlaced the leather thongs releasing a sheaf of parchment paper. Frowning, he flipped through pages covered with script, stiffened to stare at small maps drawn by Jacques. Shaking, he searched out the last page, read it, clasped it to his chest, shook it wildly at the mountains. He could hardly control his breathing. Never had such exaltation surged through him. Snapping the reins, he urged the horses homeward.

The small slave, Jeddy, waited in the circular drive. Pulling up sharply in front of the sprawling stone house built by his father and the LeFleur boys, Aaron waved the letter.

"Get Adam. A message from Jules LeFleur who is in New Orleans." Looking puzzled, Jeddy raced for the stables. Impatiently Aaron could see Adam still coddling the new mare and her colt. A fury burned in him that Adam would trade one of his fine riding horses for that mare.

At the sound of his voice his wife, Ruth, dusting flour from her apron, ran with Rebecca from the doorway. He felt the old tinge of pride at the sight of their shining light hair, the identical wide set green eyes with oddly contrasting black lashes and brows. He was again assured of his wisdom, grateful of their recommendation by the minister who reared them after Indians killed their parents. He could have searched far for better wives. And Adam's Rebecca carried another child...

Adam raced around the house followed by his son Ben, and Aaron's young Aaron, both little boys clearly Brewster. Aaron's small daughter Ara lugged chunky baby Adam. Trunk, greatest in size and strength of his negroes, pushed two slave boys to unload the wagon.

With more cheer than he'd known all winter, Aaron told how this letter arrived, how it traveled. While a breeze stirred his hair, he read down into their upturned faces. "'Thus,'" he concluded, "'it is our wish that the sons of our dear friend move west to share this wealth.'" He waited for the joy to rise into their faces, feeling heat moving up his own cheeks.

Adam glanced anxiously at Rebecca, in her sixth month with another child. Her wide eyes tried to read his brother's inscrutable face. He began to tremble uncontrollably for he knew the determination in Aaron's voice, the finality of his decision. He watched Ruth's hand slip out to clasp Rebecca's. Then he glanced back up at Aaron's straight back, his stiff face, and his hands clenched at his sides.

Trunk, who had traveled across an ocean, had escaped once from an indigo plantation and once from the turpentine stills of east Florida, who should remember that the fun-loving carpenters were capable of duplicity, but who had worked this same land for Robert Brewster and was wearied of struggling with the worn out soil, uttered a merry "Ho," and smacked the seats of the gaping Jethro and Joshua to start them unloading the wagon.

The children, who had stayed as well-mannered as if listening to Aaron's daily Bible reading which they may have thought they were hearing, now clambered up over a high wheel to search out the sugar candy always sent to them by Eli Salem.

Aaron, his eyebrows raised impatiently, thrust the letter down into Adam's upraised hand. "Well, Adam?" But Adam turned and ran back toward the stable. He would read the letter to Oner. Jumping down, Aaron strode forward to inspect his shining team. Over their backs, he allowed his glance to slide up at the blue mountains, his eyes narrowing, his exaltation flowing back.

Oner, who had traveled from Africa in the stinking hold of the same ship as Trunk and Zilpah, waited with the new colt. He'd been watching Aaron read and wondered at the reactions of the adults in the group.

"It's a letter from Jules and Jacques LeFleur." Voice quivering, Adam began reading to Oner. Halfway through, he glanced up. "If they're so successful, why didn't they send money?"

Watching for Aaron from the stable door, Oner shook his head. "Finish it, Mister Adam."

Adam turned back to the letter. Jules, operating a

builders' supply shop where he sold imported and New Orleans forged ironworks and hardware, had been visited by Jacques, now married to an Acadian girl. Jacques had acquired a fabulous Spanish grant to a rich area between the Red and the Trinity Rivers far north of a settlement called Nacogdoches "in that wildly spacious and beautiful country named Texas from the Indian word 'tejas' meaning friend." Remembering their debt, wondering about the fortunes of Robert's sons, they offered to share this great wealth if the boys would migrate west. "In my memory, Oner, Jules and Jacques were playful young adventurers, never serious, not dependable."

"Yes, Mister Adam, they were charming, but beyond building homes, they wouldn't know how to begin a plantation."

"Then that's why they want us. Well, we can hope that Aaron, given time, will recall the LeFleurs, and write that we prefer money."

He held out the letter to Jeddy who stood by. "Tell Mister Aaron I'll be in the stables if he wants me."

It was not until hours after dinner that Aaron sent Jeddy for Adam. Jeddy ran in, his eyes wide with excitement. "Mister Adam, Mister Aaron wants you."

Two chairs waited before the fire that shone goldly upon the brandy reserved for special guests. Aaron bowed, not mockingly, dismissed disappointed little Jeddy with a flick of his hand.

"Well, Adam, what do you think? You've had the day to ponder it."

"We would be wise to stay home, breed horses. There's a..."

Aaron interrupted. "And give them all to Eli?"

Adam waited, warily. If the new colt...

"Our land is worn out, Adam."

He'd argued crops with Aaron before, suggested new types of tobacco he'd read about with no more success than his early begging to be sent to school. He wanted to be a teacher. After Aaron brought Rebecca, he put his whole heart into improving the quality of their tobacco, but gave up when Aaron wouldn't change, and turned his attention to breeding horses. There was a good market for them.

"We could try one of the new varieties," carefully, feeling his way.

"It's the soil that's done for. No, we must sell out and go immediately, get settled in before winter."

Adam stared at him. "Immediately? We can't leave before the baby arrives. Rebecca isn't strong enough to undertake a long sea voyage with the danger of storms and pirates and privateers."

Pointing a slim finger, Aaron hooted. "Even if I get a good price for the plantation, even If I'd sell the slaves—and I won't part with one of them—I couldn't afford passage for our two families and animals and goods. We'll travel overland." Rocking back and forth, he placed his feet on the hearth. "As for Rebecca, our own mother crossed an ocean and traveled down here from Philadelphia."

"And did she not die at my birth?"

"But you live. Mother wasn't young. Rebecca is little more than a child." Aaron was far away, staring into the fire, a strangely satisfied expression on his face.

Adam leaned forward. "It was money father loaned Jules and Jacques. They could repay us."

"Land *is* money; better than gold."

"Then our land... We could switch to cotton."

"Our land is dead." Aaron's hands slammed down on the chair arms, his words echoing through the room and on and on in Adam's ears.

Adam went out into the night, walked beside the fresh turned earth. A horse whinnied in the stable. He could demand his share, borrow to buy Aaron's. He would breed horses, sell them. It was his chance to become...

In their bed, each holding a sleeping boy, he and Rebecca talked of Aaron's determination to go and at once.

Rebecca touched his face. "Ruth and I were frightened at first, but if our husbands decide, we'll go gladly." Her laughter tinkled. "To think we stayed away from young men because some wanted to go west, and others wanted to stay. We wanted to be together always, so you see, Adam, it doesn't matter if we go or stay, so we are all together."

"But the baby," he said. "You shouldn't travel..."

"Women carrying children have traveled since the beginning of time. It would be wonderful to see New Orleans."

Aaron listened as ashes drifted softly down the cold embers. Chilling, the silent house creaked. Taking a lamp, he searched out maps from Adam's bookcase, spread them with Jacques's sketches upon the table. Overland routes were many. They could cross their own rugged mountains to the Wilderness Trail, thence down the Natchez Trace, a dangerous trail, he had heard, where Indians were the lesser evil. Murderous thieves and villains had staked out that narrow, wooded way to commit heinous crimes against travelers. He could choose the longer route, up to Cumberland, across the hazardous Alleghenys to Zane's Trail to the Ohio, but this was not only prohibitive in cost of transporting people, goods and animals, it was dangerous: there were river pirates of the worst sort, and now swollen streams would be rushing into the Ohio and the Mississippi. He had to choose the cheapest way. Adam had no idea that the past three years had been financial failures, nor any dream of the money Aaron had borrowed on the plantation. So, in spite of possible trouble with Creek Indians or Spaniards, he chose the southwesterly, southward into Georgia, westward along one of the Indian trails through the new Mississippi Territory. He would buy the strongest wagons, supply every man with a gun and ammunition.

He would build an immense plantation in Texas. This would be something to make his father proud. Pressing his head in his hands, he remembered. He stood in the bedroom that was now his and Ruth's. His father's voice was weak and faltering from his long illness. "Perhaps it can't be done in one lifetime, Aaron. It's up to you and Adam. You are the end of the line. Build a fine family." Aaron pressed his father's head back into the pillows.

"Try to rest, father, later there will be time for talk."

Outside in that wild black winter night the sharp north

wind whipped ice-stiff branches to scratch the stones of the house. Adam, sitting close to the fire to read the fine print of a book, shivered and got up. He was twelve years old, tall for his age. He tucked the quilt around his father's shoulders, kissed his forehead. "We're going to get our snow tonight, father."

Aaron remembered that crystalline boy-voice, that quality of joy in the elements Adam and his father shared. "You'll be better. You said you'd feel well as soon as it snowed." He raised his head for Aaron's kiss. Tonight, all these years afterward, he still recalled his own cold lips touching that smooth young forehead, how he started to reach out to hold Adam because he was afraid. Even with Trunk asleep in the corner of the room, he was afraid. He knew death and feared it.

Their father tried to rise. "I've not left as much as I planned," waving an arm weakly to encompass the plantation. "Add to it. Find good healthy girls. Have sons." Weakening, the fever-wracked body shuddered. Aaron lowered him, kissed the hollowed cheeks now wet with his own tears. "I will, father. I will." Outside the wind blasted sleet against the house, a great crash of thunder shook the foundations, large flakes of snow began falling. Trunk stirred, shook himself, got up, almost filling the room with his immensity. Sobbing, Aaron ran to him. And he made the decision not to waken Adam.

Trunk went out into the storm, tolled the plantation bell. Zilpah and Oner prepared Robert Brewster for his last appearance to his sons, his slaves and his many friends. All through the night the mourning slaves hummed a tune of farewell remembered from their homeland.

Aaron sat that night beside his father. He was still there the next morning when Adam burst into the room.

"Father, here's our snow. You said..."

Aaron got up awkwardly to put his arms around his brother, to lead him outside. They stared across the whitened land to the high ridges glistening under the first rays of sun, knowing how much their father would have loved it.

Now Aaron stared into the dead embers of the fire. He

felt no love for the mountains. So much he remembered that Adam never knew. Aaron saw his mother lying in that same bed—an earlier time. He stood on tiptoe to raise her, to let her gasp for breath. "It's the mountains, Aaron. They choke me." After Adam's birth, after the slaves bore her to the place in the shadows of the mountains she hated, Aaron couldn't bear to look upon them.

After his father's death, as he stood with Adam, he loathed them. His eyes filled with the glare of sun on snow. He turned away for he had made a vow in the stormy night as his father lay dying. He knew his responsibility to young Adam and the slaves; all the dreams of his life that he had shared with no one—that one day he would cross those mountains to see the wide land on the other side—were ever lost. He choked back a sob and stood, hands clenched, and despised those mountains because he had built for himself a taller mountain, nameless, permanent, hemming him in, tying him to this land he had not chosen.

He stood up, collected Jacques's maps into his case. His back was stiff, his legs numb. Quietly he got his greatcoat, his boots and stepped out into the moonlight.

Beyond the stables the mountains were outlined, shadowy and still against the silvered sky. They were imposing no longer, not frightening. They could stand forever uncrossed by him for he would lead the way to the point where they diminished to trifling hills. They were no longer his barrier. In his mind he had chosen the strong wagons, the mules to pull them, the goods that would fill them, the route they would follow. The great blue barriers that held him were gone forever.

Chapter 2

FOUR WAGONS WEST

The colt staggered on wobbly legs to follow the mare. Grinning, Oner watched him. "Isn't he just what you wanted?"

Adam put his arms around the colt to steady him. "That's just the beginning. When Aaron sees him, he'll decide to raise horses. He'll see the folly of listening to the LeFleurs." As Oner's eyes saddened, Adam looked for Aaron's team. The stalls were empty. "When did he leave? Why, it's hardly dawn."

Oner touched his arm. "Now, Mister Adam..." shaking his head. "He left for Richmond just before I called you."

"Then he's going to try to sell out?" Oner nodded.

Aaron was gone for days. The letter, with its promise of wealth, tarnished the routine life on the plantation. The girls, Ruth and Rebecca, talked about New Orleans, and watched anxiously for Aaron's return. The slaves, murmuring excitedly, went on setting out the seedling beds. Adam spent the time rehearsing his arguments as he worked. He was sure Aaron wouldn't be able to sell quickly. In time he would see that it was best to stay home.

When the black team swept into the drive, Adam raced around the house, stopped behind an apple tree at the sight of Aaron's face.

"Ruth. Jeddy. It's sold. Our wagons are on the way from Richmond. Tell Trunk the new owner will finish planting. Jeddy, get everyone up to the house."

"Master Aaron, you sold us," cried Jeddy accusingly.

"Jeddy, a Brewster never sells a soul. Get," he said pointing.

Jeddy darted away, but flew back. "Master Aaron, do cows have souls?"

Dropping to one knee, Aaron drew him close. "Jeddy, all

25

our human souls go to Texas, but most cows must be sold. They couldn't stand the trip, and there are cows out there to be had, free. Weren't you listening when I read Jules's letter? But every man who owns a cow will get money to buy another." Flipping a coin, "You'll need this for sugar candy in New Orleans."

Turning blindly, Adam staggered through the orchards, ran across the naked fields to drop beside his father's grave. Resting his head on the stone, he stared at the mountains. Hidden beneath the trees were the trails he followed with his father. Now he would never take his own sons up there.

"It can't be. It is right that I obey my older brother, but I can not leave our home..." Staring blindly, eyes flooding, he held out his hands beseechingly. Why had Aaron never loved the land as he and his father had? How could brothers be so different? How could Aaron sell this land that was their heritage?

Staggering, Adam started back. The lowering sun caught the stones of the house where Robert's sons wouldn't grow up, the pink and white of the blossoms encircling it. He held out his arms, wanting to clasp it to him, to hold it always. Would the new owner hire him? It wouldn't be the same. Could he become an apprentice? What trade?

During the days of his frantic deliberation, he packed, accepting Aaron's decisions concerning what was to be sold, what was vital farm and household equipment, until he placed his books into one of the great wagons. Aaron removed them.

"Books are too heavy. New Orleans is a cosmopolitan city. You can buy others."

Adam knew better. "There is not one book store in New Orleans."

"How do you know that?"

"I have read it. Besides, most of these books were father's..."

"Toss out something you treasure less." He made countless trips disposing of goods and animals. He took none of the horses.

Oner told him the long distance to Texas would be hard on the colt. He owed Eli Salem for books. Slipping with it into the village, Adam questioned Eli about his route over the mountains from Pennsylvania.

"Treacherous. Aaron might be obstinate, but for Rebecca's sake, he was wise to choose the southwesterly. Adam, there is little hope of your being able to provide for your family here without land." His eyes squinched pityingly, and he turned to the colt. "You'll start a fine line of riding horses in Virginia. I'm proud to have it." Then, as if he couldn't stop talking about the trip, he looked westward, his eyes encompassed the mountains. "Yah, Adam, there's men would give their hearts to go with you. Don't be sad, lad."

Neighbors and friends began to call. Doubtfully, for they would leave all that was security behind them; fearfully, because tales of overland travel hardships and the danger of wild Indians terrified them, the girls talked with other women. Adam watched them, keeping his haunting fears to himself. By the time of the farewell gathering the children were wild with excitement; the eyes of most Brewsters and their slaves had already turned toward the golden glow of the westering sun. Adam almost forgot the LeFleur's tendency to exaggerate, their irresponsibility. Rebecca's gay chatter and Aaron's unusual high spirits swept him along. Yet, on the last morning Adam's footsteps through the quiet house echoed hollowly against a desolate emptiness.

Four great cumbersome, unwieldy wagons that swallowed tremendous spare wheels, extra harness contraptions, Oner's blacksmithing anvil, whole families and their goods rocked out of the circular drive, their ponderous weight seeming to press upon him.

As he stared back at the house, he counted their party. Souls: eight Brewsters. Trunk, Zilpah and Oner who had traveled together from Africa. Torn apart at a slave trading post on the east coast of north Florida, Trunk and Oner last saw Zilpah bound for the Carolinas. Trunk would not give her up. Adam had always marveled at the resolute search Trunk and Oner made through agonizing trials to find her safe in Robert Brewster's care. Trunk and Oner were not owned; they just stayed. They looked into Robert Brewster's kind eyes, and stayed.

Trunk and Zilpah's two small sons, Courtney and Pinkney. Laban and Nahor; their wives, Lutie and Aretha, five children. Laurel Hill, an aging female. George, Edward, Mary Anne—old slaves of his father. Ten very young slaves, males: Jethro, Joshua, Peleg, Serug, Simeon; females: Milcah, Sarai, Tamar, Zibeon, Leah. Lonely little Jeddy, orphan son of a dead slave girl. Thirty-seven souls bound for Texas. He thought of the miles ahead. England lay behind one of these souls: Aaron. African shores stretched far from many. Terror, heartbreak, horror, fields of indigo, great stands of pine, swamps, hunger stalked behind two. A lifetime in Virginia stretched behind most.

The four cumbersome wagons swallowed the best clothing of those thirty-seven souls. Four new grey kittens were concealed from Aaron in a box with the christening dress of a small black girl. "Dar'st I, Mister Adam? I love those kitties." One limp, panting creek frog was secreted in Ben's pocket.

Two small sacks of tobacco seed. Countless bags of flour. Barrels of apples from the summer-kitchen cellar. Extra wheels; parts. Guns and ammunition. Great coils of rope that came in the wagons from Richmond. The plantation bell Ruth remembered and sent Trunk running for. Dried beef, smoked hams, bacon, eggs. Cakes: farewell gifts. Great cans of grease and oil, lanterns, candles, pillows, feather ticks laid across barrels and hogsheads: the beds they would sleep upon. All these the wagons swallowed.

In the column followed the animals Aaron had chosen: one team jet black horses. Twenty-five fine Virginia riding horses. Countless farm horses. Forty-odd mules. Ten cows; two bulls. A well-chosen herd of swine.

All of the humans looked back, except one: Aaron, riding beside Adam at the head of the already stringing out column. Adam, throat constricted, chest aching, stared longingly at the stilled house, the empty fields, the quiet mountains, drawing them, etching them into his memory, for he would never see them again.

Behind him Ruth held the reins of the first wagon's four matched mules, her two children, Aaron and Ara, and a slave girl near her on the seat, her worldly goods at her back. Aaron had insisted upon the girls driving for part of the first day to take their minds off home and friends. Adam refused to allow Rebecca to drive. Leah held the reins. Wide-eyed Ben sat between Leah and Rebecca. At their backs, Milcah, a large-boned black girl seated upon the chest of Adam's books gently held little Adam, standing up in his cradle waving to Sarai who drove the third wagon filled with slave women and girls seated upon boxes, chests and bundles, and holding babies and small children.

The fourth and largest wagon carried the great weight of farm equipment, wheels, supplies, crates of chickens. Six strong mules were guided by Oner who stared backward over the cows tied to the wagon, back over little Jeddy and the boys with sticks driving swine, over the dogs, and over the head of Trunk, seated in immense dignity on one of Aaron's prized team and leading the other.

Stringing a line on each side of the train rode black men and boys on mules, farm horses and riding horses, many leading riderless animals. All of the men, and every boy big enough to hold one, held or balanced a gun stuck in his saddle. Jethro and Joshua guarded the first two wagons, ready to grab the reins the instant the road became rough or perilous.

The morning was fine, roads good for a short distance. By noon they were slapping and slogging through mud, rocking across puddles and deep holes. After the noon meal stop which lasted longer than Aaron had planned, Jethro and Joshua drove the first two wagons and Sarai had relinquished her reins to Peleg. By evening, two fine lines had formed between Aaron's brows. They had not made a quarter of the mileage he had expected. It rained in the night, hard. The earth was soft. Two horses pulled up stakes in the dark and wandered off. The column couldn't start in the morning until they were found. Aaron ordered a crew of boys to sleep by day and stand watch by night. He was learning.

By the time they crossed into North Carolina, which Aaron had expected to do days sooner, the rains were behind them. The sun rose up into a clear blue sky. Adam's heart wept at the familiar blue haze atop the mountains where great banks of white dogwood billowed up from bright spring green and the dark of evergreens. Up and down the hills flushed the same brilliant orchid-pink of their Virginia red-bud trees.

Meanwhile the men knew the hardness of leather saddles; women realized the firmness of wagon seats. The women in the third wagon busily stitched strong covers over pads of shortened bed pillows, and goose and chicken feathers flew back on the wind to settle upon dew-dampened wild flowers. And there were broken eggs, many, and at night women leaned over barrels to repack china and glassware, to sadly throw away fragments of once prized pieces.

One night they camped beside a river and were joined by a strange family of dark skinned people with many bright eyed children. Around the cook fires there was music and singing. Late into the darkness Adam and Rebecca lay listening as Trunk sang his ballad of the trip through the Georgia swamps. She placed her hand on his chest.

"Oh, Adam, I never dreamed traveling was so glorious. Every hour, every mile has something new and wonderful to show us."

He grasped her hand that was small as a child's, clung to it. "Then you are not sorry?"

"Sorrow is leaving those you love. We have all of our own with us. Ruth feared that Aaron would travel too fast and I dreaded the jolting, but he's been considerate."

"That you are safe, that you are happy—that is what matters to me." At her assurance, he drifted into exhausted sleep.

Rebecca clung to him bleakly, shivering, pressed her other hand to her lips to hold back her sobs. Ever since they pulled away from the drive she had watched his longing glances homeward. "Oh, Adam, I'm sorry. It didn't occur to me that you wanted to stay." Could they have persuaded Aaron? She recalled Ruth on the day Aaron read the letter to them. "You may as well sort your things, Becky. Aaron's made up his mind." Now, biting her lip, she looked back upon their terror when the Indians killed their parents, then the loneliness of the first years in the strange home of the minister who had taken them in.

"Adam, why didn't you speak up? The three of us—you and Ruth and I—might have..." She shook her head. No, that wasn't Adam's way. For weeks after they were married he clung to his side of the bed, his feet propped against the window sill. Sleeping little, afraid she would roll against him—the bed tick was soft and his weight twice hers—she held on to her side. The night of the big snow she waited, worrying. Finally, when she was sure he was asleep, she jumped out, ran around to brush snow from his icy feet, tugged until she had them under the quilts, and ran shivering to her side of the bed only to roll straight into his arms.

"Why did you do that, Becky?" he'd asked gently.

"I was afraid you'd take cold even though you said you always slept with your feet out the window..."

What children they had been then: she was fifteen and he was little past sixteen when they married.

Now, huddled in the wagon, she looked down at his sleeping face in the flickering firelight. "Adam, I'll make it up to you. We'll all be so happy out in Texas."

The first tragedy made itself known at dawn. Ben slept on his frog, squashing it. There was a quick burial, executed by Adam, a rushed search along the river bank for a replacement. Frogs were scarce that morning. A shy gypsy boy supplied a pleasant-faced turtle. In farewell, the gypsy leader presented Trunk with a stringed instrument, commenting that he'd shown talent. Impressed, Aaron gave him a pig for their meal. Rebecca watched Aaron take the old man's hand. He turned to the large gypsy family assembled for the farewell.

"You have fulfilled my own father's wish," he said gravely.

They stopped at friendly farmhouses to buy eggs, in towns

and villages where Aaron would stand, maps spread upon planks or benches while he questioned about roads. There were villages to pass through. People waved and called out messages of good luck. Stage coaches, caked with mud, swept past. Sometimes they would see weary faces brighten at the sight of their caravan, and handkerchiefs would flutter to be seen long after the dust settled behind the wheels.

There were Indian villages nestled in clearances beside clear streams. The Indians didn't kill them. Some waved. Some stared stonily. Some little Indian children ran from them in fright. At one dreadful river crossing many near-naked Indians appeared from nowhere to help balance the tall, tipping wagons. And quite often the entire train had to pull aside to allow the great swaying Conestoga freight wagons to roll past, spraying them with mud or dust. Often drivers would call out words of warning about sharp curves or treacherously steep grades.

North Carolina was in bloom. The days were fair. The children were sunburned and freckled; at times, chapped and chilled, but never happier. The eyes of the black children opened wider with each new scene. Seats and saddles were softer. Texas seemed closer every day. There were mountains to cross, and they crossed them. Aaron's great coils of rope made known their value. There were rivers to ford, and they did it, sometimes with extreme difficulty, many times with all hands that could reach the high wagons balancing them against tipping. There was mud and clay and sand to slog through. There were heavy rains. There were wildly beautiful fields of flowers, whole hillsides of blossoms. From one high road the world beneath appeared as a tapestry woven of pink and blue, with brown fields and islands of tall dark pines in raised stitches. Adam felt a contentment settling down inside his hurt.

Sunrises came earlier; sunsets filtered through blue haze. The moon was narrow, and then broad. One night it was round, and bright orange. The sun became warmer. The streams flowed faster. Settlements stretched out, became distant outposts to be watched for. Sometimes they traveled for days in deep dark woods so silent they could hear the tread of wheels, the padding steps of the mules, the jingle of harness, each sound echoing out across the silence of the woods. In camp at night the cook fires were surrounded by the blackest, deepest undergrowth they could imagine. Strange animal cries tore into the nights, stirring the restless dogs, frightening the children. Aaron increased the night watch. Guns that had lain forgotten were dug out. Slowly they crossed southwestward through South Carolina.

By now the children could recognize Creek or Cherokee villages, more numerous now. The mountains were shrinking. Sometimes trails faded off into woods to disappear causing almost impossible turnarounds. Back to a recognized point, they would start out again. Adam told Rebecca that trappers, traders, farmers all had different ideas of the best route west. From the hard Savannah River crossing, Aaron had planned to follow the famed Chattahoochee to a point where it was known to intersect an ancient Chickasaw trail used between Indian hunting grounds and the market for their pelts in Savannah. This was not always practical. Twice they became lost and were guided back to the river by friendly Indians.

The Georgians, few in this sparsely settled western sector, were friendly, begged them to stay in Georgia, give up that crazy idea of crossing Indian country, Indianland, The Creek Hunting Grounds, as they referred to the new Mississippi Territory waiting west of the Chattahoochee. The descriptions told by Georgians and travelers became so vivid and horrible that whenever people approached the caravan, Adam would chase Rebecca to their wagon.

Adam watched Rebecca and the boys closely. He had never seen Rebecca more glowing—tanned in spite of her bonnet. She blanched at the Indian stories, but he was proud of her courage, grateful for her health. But the lines on Aaron's forehead deepened. Most Georgians assured them that the old Savannah, or Chickasaw Trail was the fastest route to New Orleans: Aaron wanted to avoid Pensacola and Mobile. The days lengthened. He now had them traveling from daybreak to dusk.

There was clay now, or sand. There were strange tall long

needle pines so dark they seemed black at the top. There were bright green needle cypress with strange rough bark, round live oaks swinging weeps of grey-green moss, magnolia trees unfurling white-backed slick green leaves, saw palmettoes, squatty palmettoes, and cabbage palmettoes of an odd yellow green, sharp and permanent looking. The mountains had faded, dwindled in size, shrunk to hills, and their remembered grandeur increased with each mile that left them behind.

And there was sand. Progress was slow in deep sand; fine on shallow or wet sand. There were terrifying spring storms, torrential rains. During one storm some pigs got away to become lost in the woods, to meet with the wild razorbacks and make that class more palatable for travelers who might pass later. Still, the wagons made it south, not always beside the Chattahoochee, too often quite a distance east of it, with only two broken wheels. Adam recognized that Aaron had been wise to buy extra wheels, and to place Oner's blacksmithing tools near the tailgate of the big wagon.

But now and then, lurking in the woods, he would see a silent strong Indian stare at them, then dart behind a tree. He began watching for them, hoping he would not see them again, yet he would, and the hairs would stand up on his arms, and his throat would feel hard and dusty. He felt that he should mention the Indians to Aaron, but Aaron's eyes were straight ahead. The Indians had been friendly and helpful. There was no need for him to fret. Yet he did.

These Indians, definitely healthier than any they had passed, stronger, had burning eyes that he would remember far into the nights. Without mentioning it to Aaron, he made it a point to check through the train every night to make sure each man's gun was in sight. Some nights he lay restless watching Rebecca and the boys sleep, and he would suddenly break out in a sweat at the mere call of an owl.

As the settlements strung out, Adam believed that Aaron had been clairvoyant to buy heavily of extra food and supplies in Carolina and north Georgia. The food was holding up exactly as Aaron had predicted. They supplemented beef they'd been unable to buy by killing deer, wild turkeys, ducks and geese, all plentiful here.

Finally, on a warm spring morning they turned due west, and the sun was warm on their backs. Great forests of longleaf pine perfumed the soft south wind.

From the moment of their turning west leaving behind the frayed ends of the mountains, Adam found a new look in his brother's eyes, a distance-seeing gleam like that of a man finding his way out of a wilderness rather than entering into one, the look of a man realizing a dream come true. He wondered, reflected, remembered Aaron's new patience, recalled him waiting outside looking at the road they would travel while he walked alone through the empty house, and finally he knew, and was glad.

They rode closer together, and talked. Head high, eyes looking toward Texas, Aaron nodded.

"Perhaps we should switch to cotton. Jules wrote that Texas soil was just right for cotton." Narrowing, his eyes measured the distance.

Adam looked ahead. He could see his horses grazing in the long waving grass...

Chapter 3

FIELD OF BLUE LUPINE

Slowly, ponderously, too far east of the Chattahoochee, they rocked westward. For three days under torrential rains the wagons slipped and slogged through deep red clay.

During the next three days the trail was a straight line pointing due west, straight up steep hills and down deeply eroded gullies of boggy clay, over easy, gently undulating paths to drop down almost perpendicular cliffs. After that the path, which was all Adam could call the trail now, led through dense woods of the same tall dark pines thickly laced with budding azaleas, sweet flowering quince, red-bud, sharp palmettoes, interwoven by strong vines and honeysuckle alive with chattering birds and buzzing insects. A hot sky, rarely seen, was faded by the heavy moisture still sweeping from the south on strong winds. For more than a week meals were hastily prepared, quickly gulped soggy necessities, to be endured while swatting flies, sticky gnats and mosquitoes. Nights were humid, unbearably stuffy. Rebecca rested little, tossed fretfully when she did sleep. Adam watched for the strange brooding faces.

Ahead men and boys chopped and dug and cut through the tangled brush. Even so, canvas caught on branches. The discomforts stretched the distance to Texas immensely. For the present the aim of all humans of the caravan was that promised clearing where they could rest and dry out. There Aaron would perform his long postponed inspection of the slaves, a procedure handed down from Robert Brewster, and always looked forward to by the children who received sugar candy, even those who also got sulphur and molasses, or the dreaded castor oil. The slaves would bathe, line up before Aaron, Zilpah, and Trunk or Oner. They were looked over, thumped, questioned; ears, eyes, teeth, skin, limbs, feet and hands were inspected. Ailments and wounds were treated by Zilpah from a basket containing mysterious liquors, potions, lotions, teas, barks, herbs, powders, oils, cloth bandages, and strange little bags containing asafetida or weird objects.

Through the thicket they climbed, skidded, slid, rocked and hoped, but not in vain. On the fourth morning a small negro boy trudging behind a bush startled a magnificent, unbelievably white bird with long spindly legs. Adam watched the bird rise, and knew they were near the big river. The air felt like rain—they were now traveling through soggy clay a foot deep. He was sick with worry about Rebecca. They were all miserable and tired, but Rebecca was strangely quiet, pale.

The land flattened. The men ahead sent a runner back to tell them to prepare for roping: a sheer drop. They dismounted to rope the lead wagon. Women and children scrambled down from the wagons. Adam lifted Rebecca, touched her cheek with his hand. She answered with a wan smile.

Holding their skirts up out of the mud, the women stared wide-eyed and frightened as they watched the careful descent of the lead wagons, saw the mules slip and slide.

Mountains had been easy compared to this ordeal in clay.

Brakes screamed, screeched, held. Sweating men and boys strained. Mules, lathered hides steaming, stepped daintily, feeling their way, gripping footholds. One by one the four wagons were eased onto the steep cliff.

Peleg tore breathlessly up from the clearing crew ahead.

"Master Aaron, it's the Chatta'hootch, and she's flooding. There's no place to cross, and no turn-around."

Rebecca leaned against Ruth. Aaron took off his hat, and stared up the incline at the caravan hanging nose-down, every brake, rope, muscle and face straining. It was impossible to turn wagons there. He pointed.

"Get up top, Peleg. Get those cows and pigs out of the way. Tell Trunk to have every loose mule hitched to the work wagon's tail."

Peleg scooted. Aaron followed, ordering women and children out of the way, asking all wagon men to hold.

Adam stared uphill. He thought back. Seven wretched days since they passed a cross-trail, not one decent campsite, and Rebecca ill. The hanging caravan were statues ready to topple. Turn-around, even with Aaron ordering it, was impossible. They had to cross the Chattahoochee. Either way, disaster faced their whole group. Jumping on his horse, he headed for the river.

He faced the raging yellowish-brown-red waters that had been crystal clear up north where they had to leave its banks. It was five times broader and flowing swiftly. The flooded banks were solid brush stretching up steeply on both sides. He couldn't swim, but his horse was Virginia's finest. Back and forth he crossed, working downriver, sometimes in water so deep that only his head and the horse's high-tossed nose were free. Thirty feet down from the peering trail-blazing crew he found a level no higher than his knees. For the first time on the trip he was grateful for the height of the wagons.

He called back to the crew, "Clear the banks."

Terrified eyes stared at him, then uneasily upslope where Aaron moved among the wagons. One of the older men smiled, waved to him, and let out a merry "Ho," and started chopping. The deed was done. He had crossed Aaron for the first time in his life, and the men were with him. Drawing in a deep breath, he rode, recrossing the river until he had traced more than a wagon's width.

When he got back, the lead wagon was skidded crosswise of the trail. The big wagon, rear-hitched, was stuck axle deep. He rode up to Aaron, drew him aside.

"The Chattahoochee can be crossed thirty feet down."

"Are you crazy, Adam? We can't risk these wagons, our animals, these souls. I won't consider it."

Unflinching, although he quaked at the straightness of Aaron's back, the bitter glare in those eyes, Adam said, "It can be done. We've got to go on, Aaron. Think back. That trail was agony, and after these rains, it's worse now and clotted with our ruts. We'd never make it back."

His hands gripping the reins of his horse, white at the knuckles, Aaron stiffened his shoulders. "I won't risk one soul, nor our goods."

"Come with me, watch me cross."

"Adam, look at that wagon." He started away.

Reaching out, Adam touched his arm. "Aaron, it will be just like that the whole way back, wagons crosswise to probably turn over. We've been lucky. We've got to try."

The lines deepened in Aaron's face. He looked once at Adam, and turned back uphill.

Turning downward, Adam took the reins of the lead wagon. As hands balanced it, he inched cautiously down the crudely cleared bank. "Gee," he yelled shakily, while men steadied the high wagon in the turn. Undaunted by the racing currents, the mules scrambled, slipped, pulled until the wagon trembled, was jerked and then stopped in the brush of the west bank. Adam closed his eyes, and swallowed. He'd never known such fear. His heart had pounded almost out of his chest as he crossed with Aaron's own wagon. Now it stood alone across the river. He had no choice but to go back for his own. Leading another, he rode one of the mules back.

His wagon made the turn, a tight-faced Jethro at the reins. Jumping into the third wagon, Adam started behind it.

"Get aboard," he yelled to the clearing crew. "We've got that west bank to clear, then Mister Aaron will hold an inspection."

Wide eyes that had followed his course across the river now stared at the angry waters.

"Make haste!" For the first time in his life, in the life of any Brewster, he raised his arm with the whip, then dropped it, for the men and boys were climbing aboard. Clasping small children, frightened women and girls watched. Aaron, head tossed back, led his horse downgrade from the big wagon, and sat stiffly on the bank watching Adam's wagon tilt as Jethro swung upon the steep west bank.

When Adam got back across, the fourth wagon trembled down the steep and treacherously rutted, boggy grade, followed by boys riding or pulling cows. Inside the wagon, squealing pigs jammed against equipment and chicken crates.

Nodding to Serug and Joshua, Adam briefly held little Adam and Ben. Rebecca bit her lip. Choosing a broad-backed farm horse, he lifted the white-faced Rebecca, got up behind her. Shaking, Rebecca buried her face in his shoulder.

"The boys will be safe, Becky. Everything will be all right."

On the ground near them Ara began crying silently. Ruth snatched her up into her arms, straightened her small bonnet. Smiling tightly, she looked into her daughter's face.

"We're going to cross, Ara, don't be impatient."

"I'm scared," the child sobbed.

"We are all afraid, child. We have been afraid, but we have made it this far. It is better to go one in fear, than to turn back."

"I want to go home."

"Texas is our home," she said. "It lies across the river."

Joshua and Serug followed Adam, each clutching a boy. Aaron rode up to Ruth, his head high, and swept her upon his horse. Laban took up young Aaron. Ruth, her face white, slowly handed Ara into Nahor's arms.

"God be with you," a black woman called out, tears streaming down her cheeks.

The great last wagon, grunting and squealing, creaking and rocking and cackling was broadside of the east bank with Trunk, wide feet firmly planted, great hands gripping the reins of ten strong mules.

"Every man recross," Aaron ordered out. "Brace that wagon. Our lives rest in it."

"Gee," Trunk's voice rung out. The mules turned. On the bank Zilpah covered the faces of Pinkney and Courtney with her apron.

Rocking against a solid brace of horsemen hawside of the current, dragged by the stumbling, straining mules, the ponderous great wagon skidded up the west bank. A cheer went up. Old Mary Anne burst into tears and clung to the horse she would ride across.

Cows, mules, horses, women, children, men and wagons dripped red-brown water. Three chickens, crushed or drowned, were being plucked. Pigs were put down from the wagon to travel under their own power. The cows were retied to the end wagon. The clearing crew thrashed ahead, faces brighter.

"Aaron," Ruth said clearly, "Texas must surely be close. How well we've done."

His eyes weary, Aaron leaned against the lead mule.

His voice was hoarse. "Everyone walk until the wagons dry out. Adam, take Jethro and ride ahead. We need a clearing with a stream." In its tiredness, his voice had the throbbing quality of Robert Brewster's in his last years.

Cutting around the clearing crew, Adam and Jethro guided their horses around jutting trees. For miles, ducking limbs, they rode through tangled brush. Near the top of a winding hill they came upon a well-traveled, easily recognized Indian trace running northwestward. There it met the western trail, a cleared road with visible wagon tracks less than a month old. Adam got down and pushed mud aside to inspect the scratches on rock.

"Somehow we missed the main crossing, Jethro, but this is the road we've been watching for."

"Mighty thankful, Mister Adam. I like to died of fright on that river crossing. Seems like a man would have a ferry there." His eyes twinkled. "We were proud the way you handled it, Mister Adam."

"Thanks, Jethro. It isn't often that I handle anything."

"You're going to do all right, Mister Adam." He pushed back in the saddle. "Lordy, but I'm tired. How the women must feel. We sure need that clearing."

They passed beneath great spreading live oaks, ducked weeps of moss to a rise where stretched a cleared meadow, rounded and gracefully rolling with tall blue lupine. Encircled by the magnificent oaks, blooming dogwood, fragrant honeysuckle, the clearing was bisected by a clear creek flowing southeastwardly toward the Chattahoochee. Adam hesitated. Indian campground? He found no recent signs.

They galloped back to the waterlogged, straggling train. Ruth walked with the four Brewster children. Rebecca, eyes closed, rode the lead wagon, leaning against the hoop. Adam raced to her, took her hand.

"Oh, Becky, don't be ill. I need you so terribly."

She grasped his hands. "Thank God. I was so frightened. I haven't told you, Adam, because you knew how Ruth and I feared Indian attack. But I've seen them lurking behind trees for weeks."

"We can handle Indians. We have guns and ammunition. The important issue is you."

"I'm fine. The crossing upset me, and then Aaron sending you ahead. Now that you're back, everything's all right."

Aaron, pale, leaned down as Jeddy ran up to them, waving his stick to attract attention.

"Master Aaron, my cow's leg slipped into a wheel rut. The bone snapped."

"Tell Trunk to put her out of her misery, Jeddy. Fresh beef will be pay for your hard work."

"Master Aaron, we goin' *eat* that cow?" he asked, his wide eyes agonized. "Why, I walked that cow all the way from V'ginia. I know him like he was my sister." Meeting Aaron's stern gaze, he turned away, his small shoulders dropping disconsolately.

Aaron called after him, "The next calf born will be yours to raise." This was an honor bestowed upon slaves, rarely upon children. "We're going to make camp in a few minutes and hold inspection."

Jeddy's head twisted to one side doubtfully. "You carried sugar candy all this time, Master Aaron?"

"No, or you'd have had it before this time. Miss Ruth will make candy. I bought sugar in the last settlement. Do you remember when the Georgians were tapping those trees? You got your hand stuck in one of the buckets."

"Yes, suh. I licked my hand fo' days. It didn't taste like sugar candy," Jeddy said, grinning up at Aaron. Then he scurried back to his doomed cow.

The wagons were open, hoops showing, canvas flying. Wet canvas was spread over the blue field. Animals, tethered, were feeding. Women dragging soiled clothing and boys carrying huge pots and soap cans headed downstream. Ruth, Rebecca and the four Brewster children bathed upstream, guarded by Trunk and Oner. Beef was being readied. Two cook-fires burned. Aaron pored over his maps. Adam opened his book chest to air; found a dry quilt which he carried upstream with his fresh clothing.

He sat waiting under a great round oak. He was muddy, sweated and weary, but strangely uplifted. Through slitted lids, he watched Aaron whose once perfectly trimmed beard was spread and matted. What dreams had Aaron put aside? He'd never talked plans or hopes over with Adam, had not even discussed the financial condition of the plantation. He wondered if he had caused the formality, unknown in their childhood, to grow between them because he read so much? Aaron used to say he always had his head buried in a book. Had Aaron felt the too-great responsibility of running a large plantation for one so young as he was when Robert Brewster died?

Closing his eyes, he tried to dream of Texas. But the sun-warm trunk could be one of their own oaks in Virginia. A book would have been in his hands. *I'm sixteen now, Aaron. I would like to go to Williamsburg to study.*

His eyes met Aaron's. "I have chosen wives for us. You have seen the girls in church. The orphans raised by the minister, the ones whose parents were killed in Indian massacre..."

Aaron's hand touched his shoulder. Clean clothing over his arm, he waited while Adam stirred.

"Come, Adam, we're a disgrace to these fine Brewsters."

Their families stood behind him. Ben and young Aaron stood long enough to be seen, then raced away. Ruth and Rebecca wore green and white checked dresses Ruth had made the year before. Their washed hair, sun-touched, gleamed like gem-stone topaz, and hung down their backs, tied with green ribbons. Ara, a small duplicate of them, grinned at Adam. Ruth took her hand, picked up young Adam, and her eyes meeting his, spoke carefully.

"We're going to make candy while Rebecca rests. She is very tired." She stood waiting until Adam made Rebecca comfortable on the quilt.

Aaron's eyes followed the boys, a proud smile on his lips. "Another generation, Adam, and we will have fulfilled father's dream."

They walked upstream through a shadowed fernery.

"We'd better stay here in camp for some days. Rebecca is showing strain."

Aaron tugged his beard. "Perhaps we should." He placed a hand awkwardly on Adam's shoulder. "I hate to think where we might be now had you not braved that river."

"It would have only been a few minutes before you did the same thing I tried."

"I doubt it, Adam. I can be stubborn. It's . . . I'm afraid it's something a man is born with."

Splashing in the stream, Adam traced the beginning of an unidentified glow in his chest, a growing warming thing. He'd known for days that Rebecca needed to rest, but there had been no opportunity along that dreadful road. A great sigh of relief surged up through his chest. Within moments, he and Aaron, forgetting that Trunk watched closeby, began splashing water upon each other in their way of old.

Adam relaxed against the tree, Rebecca's head in his lap. A crestless jay scolded in the limbs, mockingbirds sang, a brilliant cardinal clicked among the leaves. The soft wind carried the salty scent from the Gulf far south. Beyond them, women leisurely spread washed clothing on the field. Men rested—word of a two-day rest stop had traveled fast. A great fire glowed beneath the long spit stretched across two iron spiders. Of the whole camp, only the dogs seemed restless and alert.

Rebecca stirred, looked up at him. He studied the violet circles under her eyes, felt the heat of her skin.

"I'm all right, Adam, just tired."

Pressing her close, he traced her brows with his finger. With a sickening familiar lurch he knew that he should have urged Aaron to wait in Virginia. He might have been able to convince him. Why didn't he try? For years he had let Aaron make all the decisions. Now he buried his face in her hair.

"We won't leave here until you are entirely well, Becky. Oh, Becky, for the rest of my life the one debt I owe Aaron is his gift of you. How could I have found you?"

A familiar bong charged across the green and blue field: Aaron calling the slaves to inspection.

"He could have waited," Adam said. "He is sick with exhaustion."

"A Brewster does his duty, Adam."

"An *Aaron* Brewster. Adam Brewster is going to stay with his beautiful wife."

While Rebecca slept, Adam cleaned his gun, his muddy saddle, his whip, all caked with drying red river silt.

The fragrance of broiling beef filled the air. There had been no noon meal.

His sons were asleep. They looked well. Adam studied their faces in the lamp light. Travel had not harmed them. Tenderly, he touched them. He and Rebecca lay beside them listening to the slaves singing around the fire while Trunk picked out tunes on the gypsy instrument. He was lulled into tranquility. The afternoon had been perfect...

The dogs began barking, cautiously, and then sharply. Leaping up, Adam yanked on his boots, his coat.

There came racing hoofs, voices: Oner, silencing the dogs. A clear ringing boy-voice.

"Hey, don't shoot! We're Georgians."

A trembling voice, a woman's. "Oh, thank God."

Adam ran to the wagon that had pulled up. It was already surrounded by slaves. The flare from the fire grotesquely outlined a jumble of women and children, eyes stark with horror, faces and clothing blood-smeared, mud-splattered, and streaked with soot.

He went to the boy who had called out. He was about fifteen years old. His hands seemed paralyzed on the reins. Gently, Adam released them, lifted the boy from the wagon.

"Creek," the boy whispered, but the word was already around them, cried out in the terrified voices of little children, in the tragic tones of the women. The emptying wagon was a makeshift uncovered vehicle thrown together of half-burned wood and unmatched wheels. There were no goods within.

Aaron rushed among the group, began questioning them. "They're famished, bring out food," he ordered.

The boy began talking, his face old and drawn. "They

attacked in the middle of the night," he said. "They came screaming and shooting, and throwing firebrands. My father ordered me to lead the women and children into the woods. When I got back every man was dead—my father, my grandfather, my uncles, and the fathers of all these children. Everything was burning... our shacks. We'd only been there for a few weeks, had just started cabins and a stockade." His voice rasped with the horror still in him. His eyes, facing the fire, were parched.

"Try to eat," Adam urged him, staring down at the torn hands. "Zilpah, this boy's hands..."

"We had a legal grant on the land. Three whole families, and ours. They told us in Georgia that the Indians would welcome us, would be friendly and want to trade. We never saw one until that night. My mother didn't want to leave home, none of the women did, but our men thought we'd all get rich."

Ruth was brushing an old woman's matted hair. The woman sobbed. "Our men wanted to get out there in time for spring planting. My grandson buried them all. He built that wagon. 'I'm takin' yo'all home,' he told us." Ruth patted her shoulder. "We have no homes," the woman screamed. "We sold out before we left."

"Us young'uns found them horses," one little boy put in. "While he was digging the graves and burying them, we scampered out into the woods and..."

"Now you children eat," Ruth urged.

Aaron was inspecting the wagon, the horses.

The old woman in Ruth's arms cried.

Ruth patted her. "Never mind, dear. We'll take you with us. We're on our way to Texas."

"Texas," the old woman screamed. "You'll never make it. You'll be dead and probably not buried, every one of you."

Zilpah, listening, her eyes immense, spread ointment on the boy's shattered and scorched hands.

Aaron came back to question the boy.

"What direction were the Creek traveling?"

"From Florida, I guess. They hit us from the south."

"Are you sure they were Creek?"

The boy nodded.

"How many were there?"

But the boy, exhausted, had fallen asleep in Zilpah's arms.

Ara, who had slipped out of the wagon, stood listening, her hands twisting her long flannel nightdress.

"I want to go home," she sobbed. "Father, take us home."

Trunk snatched her up into his arms and carried her back to the wagon, crooning, "Don' cry, little baby. Uncle Jacques build us a fine new home in Texas." Adam and Aaron's eyes met over the fire.

Aaron whirled around. "Repair that wagon, rebuild it if you must. Get that wheel off. Oner, choose four strong mules to replace those horses..."

Adam shook his head. "They can't go on tonight. They're shocked, exhausted. They need days of rest and they'll then need men to help them across the Chattahoochee."

"Adam, are you crazy? Rest here, in an Indian campground? Don't you understand? They're moving north. By tomorrow whole tribes could be here. They move out tonight, and so do we." He leaned over Zilpah. "Let that boy rest until the wagon's ready."

Adam stepped forward. "We can't move out tonight, not with Rebecca ill."

"Not this time. I am not listening. Anyone who stays, stays alone. They'll have to go on without help. We've blazed the trail."

"I'll take six men in the morning, get them across and up the grade. We could be back by..."

"You'll take them as soon as the wagon is ready. I stand responsible for my family and my people. I give the orders. I will not be crossed, Adam."

Striding to the circle of women and children eating around the fire, he pointed to the wagon.

"My brother and some of our men will get your party across the river and up the bluff. Adam, get some rest. I'll call you."

Jeddy shook Adam awake. "Master Adam, Master Aaron wants you now."

The mules were harnessed, ready to move out. Food and supplies were stacked in the wagon. Women, their eyes burning from exhaustion, dragged toward the wagon. Slaves carried sleeping children.

Rebecca stood holding Adam's hand while Aaron fastened a lantern to the wagon. The sleeping boy, wrapped in a quilt, was lifted into the back. Adam took up the reins.

"Our caravan moves westward as soon as the packing is finished, Adam. Turn back the instant this immigrant wagon is on top that Georgia cliff. We'll drop white rags for you to follow."

"No, Aaron," Rebecca screamed out.

"Get back to your wagon and rest," Aaron ordered. "If more than one person starts giving orders, we shall be lost."

Rebecca dropped back.

Every man had a gun in his saddle and a torch in his hand. One led Adam's horse, another led the Georgia horses. The night was black.

Chapter 4

PERDIDO RIVER, BOUNDARY LINE

The woods were aglow with a strange light, not dawn, behind them. It was too early, and not moonlight, but the eerie unreal dawn, the false dawn Adam had heard described by Trunk and Oner in their stories of Florida and the swamps of Georgia.

Behind Adam the negroes rode close, talking. Their voices carried up the still morning.

"Jethro, you give them women all that money Master Aaron give you at inspection to spend down New Orleans?"

"Sure, what I need money for with what I got? Trunk, he give that boy his cow money, said he'd have to earn himself a calf come Texas."

"That boy the deadest, sleepingest boy I ever saw."

"He sure surprised when Mister Adam woke him and told him we were in Georgia. You hear what he told him? He said, 'Your aunt got the reins. You let your hands heal. You got a man's job ahead of you. And you all get down when the mud gets deep. You walk, or the wagon will never make it.'"

"He give them money?"

"You know Mister Adam got no money."

"I didn't give them money. I might wish now I had. When Master Aaron gave them the mules, I said, 'Master Aaron, you need them mules bad.' But he told me they needed them worse. He made them keep their horses too. So I told him if we get west and he don't have enough, ask me back, and I'll give him my cow money."

"You boys hush. Master Aaron don't want Mister Adam to know he don't have much money."

"He don't know you give your savings last spring when the seed had the rot and he had to buy more?"

"Now you hush."

49

Then Trunk began singing. His voice reached out into the loneliness of the woods, soared into the mystic light, stirring birds to chirp. The boys hummed, an ethereal background to the tuneless words, touching an ache deep in Adam's chest.

As small boys he and Aaron would slip out of bed at night, and creep to the quarters to listen to the slaves singing. What had happened to them after their father's death? He could almost feel Aaron's firm hand leading him through the darkness past the stables to the quarters.

"Don't you ever tell father I bring you out here."

"I won't, Aaron, honest, I won't."

"If you do, I'll never bring you back."

How old had he been when his father gave him his first colt? Ben's age, almost six. Aaron walked beside the colt, bracing Adam. After he learned to ride well, he and his father raced. In the spring they roamed the foothills of the mountains, looking at the blossoms. Aaron was already working under Trunk in the fields, learning how to set out tender tobacco plants, learning how to run the plantation. They drifted apart. The rift widened after their father's illness. Aaron turned to Trunk, Adam to Oner.

Now, all these years afterward, he couldn't remember when the change had taken place, but Aaron was different, cold and distant. In his efforts to bring back their old relationship, Adam did everything Aaron told him to do.

"How come we stop?"

"They gone. This is where we camped. Mister Adam..."

"He knows. Don't worry him. You boys help watch for them white rags Master Aaron said he'd drop."

But the path lay clear in the strange light, deep ruts where the wagons had rocked in turning. Adam looked sickly at the mist hanging over the stream, shuddered at the scent of their deadened fires. If they were back home in Virginia, they would all be asleep. In the morning he would touch Rebecca's cheek, watch her open her eyes. Why hadn't he fought Aaron about leaving?

"There's one Master Aaron's marks. You think we should pick it up on account of the Creek?"

The strange light faded. Blackness deepened around

them. It was four o'clock. The party had a five hour start. They moved slowly, feeling their way, grateful for the white markers.

The true dawn came up grey, with increased winds carrying a chilling moisture from the south.

Trunk rode up beside him. "The way the clouds been riding mean rain, Mister Adam, big rain. I can smell it, and I don't like it."

"I don't either, Trunk."

And he didn't like the pace Aaron evidently was driving the caravan. Ruts visible now showed the swerving of the big wagons. His face pinched in fear at the thought of Rebecca hanging on to protect the baby she carried. Now, in fear and anger, he galloped, and no one stopped to pick up the markers.

The rain caught them, or they caught up with it. It was there without warning, drops, slashing in sharp gusts, drenching them. Eyes strained to the trail, they splashed through sheets of it, every man chilled to a teeth-chattering depression.

Adam saw a pig mistily outlined ahead, and called out.

The wagons were stopped. Almost all humans were under cover, crowded together eating a cold meal in the wagons.

Alone in their wagon, Rebecca clung to him.

"Aaron thinks I have fever. He made Ruth take the children into their wagon. He told me to sleep, but there couldn't be any rest for me until I knew you'd made the river crossing, until I saw you again."

His heart chilled as he saw the sickness in her eyes.

Zilpah crawled into the wagon. "You sick in your stomach, Miz Rebecca?" Rebecca nodded.

"Fever do that." She gave medicine in measured sips. "You got pains? It ain't time, Miz Rebecca." She laid her ear upon Rebecca's abdomen, held it there for a long time.

"Mister Adam, this rain just kills all sound. You send for me if she doesn't rest."

Adam watched the old black woman crawl slowly down from the wagon, saw her puzzled, inward-turned eyes and fear, deep fear.

They moved through torrents under a sky so black and dense it was impossible to determine night or day. On the first rest stop, he saw Ruth and the children staring out from the end of the wagon, their eyes wide and frightened.

Rebecca slept in his arms. He hoped his body softened the jolts which were many.

Finally the pace slowed. It seemed they climbed. There was no skidding, and the earth beneath the great wheels became firm.

He dozed. If Rebecca moved, or cried out, which she did often, he would wake up with a start.

The pounding of the rain on the canvas softened, died out. The wagons moved slowly. The air lay heavy, oppressive; the dampness was unbelievably penetrating. He wrapped another quilt around her, and hung one across the front opening of the wagon.

Jethro, at the reins, turned around. "You need Zilpah, Mister Adam?"

He shook his head. He felt himself drifting into deep sleep, and fought it. At some time he was aware of Jethro and Joshua talking, heard Aaron's and Jethro's voices beside the wagon, and Joshua's from the wagon seat. He knew they were changing crews, that he should relieve Aaron, but he was afraid to leave Rebecca. Holding her in his arms, he rocked back and forth, remembering his terror for her when Ben was born.

"Oh Becky, Becky, don't let anything happen to you."

"You hear anything, Joshua? Jethro told me she moaned awful."

"Zilpah, has Miz Rebecca got that terrible fever we heard about over in Georgia?"

"I wish I'd stayed back in V'ginia, and right now Master Aaron could go for the doctor."

"Now, Zilpah, you doctors all of us."

"I never doctored anything bad," she whispered. "Master Aaron's scared. He told me to tonic Mister Adam good."

Hands shaking, Adam tugged on his boots. The forms of

Zilpah and Joshua loomed dimly up out of a thick fog that concealed the mules ahead.

"You rested, Mister Adam?" Zilpah asked. "I'm goin' to stay with Miz Rebecca. You go eat. The cook fire's up at the end. Then you takes over so Master Aaron can rest. He about to fall in his tracks."

Feeling his way, Adam could see only the wet earth under his boots, a sandy, reddish clay. Incongruously grotesque shapes loomed—cows, horses; the third wagon; swollen and enlarged, circular trunks of trees that rose silvery and majestically into white nothing. Sounds were deadened to a soft cacophony of tree frogs, grunting pigs, whispering children, horses whinnying, the doubtful cheer of a cardinal, and in the background, twittering of small birds, and finally, muted voices. The cook-fire grew up out of the fog like an eclipsed sun.

The men hunkered around the fire and stopped talking. Their faces were grave. Trunk pulled a tin cup from the edge of the embers. "Zilpah mixed this for you." He followed the bitter potion with a cup of steaming coffee.

Aaron, grey and drawn, held out the maps. Adam looked in the direction he pointed. "We were moving due west..." Holding his cup in both hands, Adam knelt beside him. Aaron had worked southwestward all night, had crossed three trails.

"I'm not sure of this route, a traders', probably, if we're lucky, to Pensacola, or better, Mobile."

"You wanted to avoid Pensacola, we heard Indians got guns there."

Their eyes met. "We did not have illness then."

Adam and Oner walked, leading their horses. The trail was packed firmly by matted pine needles in which they could discern clear, small hoof-prints edged with the red claysand.

Oner got down to examine them. "Those little horses traders use, loaded down, I'd say. The prints are deep. But it could be Indians."

The trail was also exceedingly narrow. Boys rode on all the wagons to push back heavy branches, to release caught canvas. Clumps of azaleas and dogwood bloomed with a weird phosphorescense in the fog. They dragged on, silently except for the foot-falls of the animals, the tinkling of harness, the padded rumble of the great wheels. All of the wagons were closed against the gloom. Now and then one of the boys sent by Zilpah would tell Adam that Rebecca still slept.

Adam worried with the map. Trappers in Georgia told them they would pass outlying homes, even small villages that had sprung up around farms. At a well-marked crosstrail were tracings of many Indians moving northwesterly. He hesitated. This could be the route into Spanish Florida, but they'd been told that Spanish trails were fine shell roads. He'd been considering riding alone to Pensacola to bring a doctor back. Oner feared Florida, fretted about the Indian prints.

"There will be doctors in Mobile. Master Aaron preferred Mobile."

They passed by the cross-trail. Within an hour, Adam was distraught. The trail narrowed. They lost the traders' prints, if they were that. They were in a forest. The air, heavier and oppressive, heated fast. Drivers and riders removed coats. Wagons were opened, allowing fear to come out and be seen. The sultry trail followed a stream flowing southwesterly. By noon they crept along its east bank. Adam couldn't find it on the map.

They still walked, carrying whips as well as guns. Snakes abounded. Millions of insects buzzed, stuck to their skin. The humidity rose. They moved on soggy earth into a canebrake, startling grey and white waterbirds that darted, rattling the cane.

Walking ahead, Oner shouted. At the stream crossing was clearly a traders' route. The muddy path, crossing theirs, was pocked with small hoof prints. Stooping, Adam picked up a cork and smelled it. Rum.

He called a stop for the noon meal, wanting time to decide: Mobile or Pensacola? Fretting, he tore back to the wagon, sent Joshua out to eat. Inside, he found Rebecca desperately ill, raving and tossing in Zilpah's arms.

Their position was halfway between the 32° and 31° parallels, beside an unnamed river which on the maps joined the Escambia at the Spanish 31°. He walked briskly through the trail, chose a fit horse, saddled it. He would get to Mobile alone, and start back with a doctor to meet the caravan.

Two slave boys rushed from the woods into which they had just stepped. "Mister Adam, Mister Adam, an Indian watching you!"

Heavy-eyed, Aaron leaned against the wagon. Men scattered for guns. Women rushed children to wagons. Pigs were slammed into the chicken crates. The wagons began to roll across the shallow stream. Aaron was at the head with Trunk. Adam dropped back.

Jeddy, astride a cow, wore a string of bright blue beads. "Looka here, Mister Adam. See what I found..." He held the bottom of the strand. They were threaded on a fine leather thong.

"You find them back there, Jeddy?" Jeddy nodded. "That's probably what the Indian was looking for, Jeddy."

"I guess so, Mister Adam," reluctantly lifting the beads over his head. "Yo' ain't goin' to hunt him, are you, Mister Adam?"

"You haven't even seen me, Jeddy, understand? Now you switch that cow and get her moving until I can see you safely up against that end wagon. You hear?"

"Yes, sir, Mister Adam."

Adam waited until Jeddy was with the men, then swung his horse around, racing back toward the cross-trails. He left the path and carefully walked the horse around and around in the brush, through the cane, circling both trails. Headed northwesterly were recent prints of many small horses. If there were Indians, and they intended attacking the wagon train from the rear, he had to know it before he left for Mobile. Following the tracks, he whipped his horse frantically.

Around the bend, trotting briskly under odd, three-bundle loads covered with hides, were a dozen small horses, all in a line, followed by a young Indian boy with a stick. Adam let out a yell, and held out the beads. Grinning, the boy slipped them over his head.

From the front rode a stocky man thickly bearded and outrageously garbed in skins. He clasped Adam's hand.

"You crazy fools. You'll be lucky if you don't break all your wheels." His dried skin squinted into cheerful lines. His voice, rich and deep, familiar with its Pennsylvania Dutch accent so like Eli Salem's, scolded. "This boy, out hunting our meal, ran back to tell me you have fever, and were hurrying to Mobile. Mobile's thick with fever, worst epidemic since it killed off all them girls. I figured to head you off at the Perdido." He cocked his head. "Are you sure it's fever?"

"We can only guess that it is. My wife is very ill."

"Then let me go back with you. I've seen it, and plenty."

When they joined the train, Adam took the trader to Aaron, who welcomed him. The trader unfastened kegs that hung from the neck of his horse and handed one to Aaron.

"Taffai, a mean rum. Pass it around to your men. It's said to fight off fever."

The negroes edged in.

"Go ahead. I don't expect pay for it."

Adam tasted it, handed the keg back to Aaron who quickly gave it to Trunk.

Children crowded around the young Indian who handed out trinkets. The men moved back to the cook fire.

The trader held a soiled and tattered cloth map near Aaron's. "That unnamed creek was Cloud Creek. Now here is the Perdido. The doctor is here," he said, "at Mims Crossing on the Tensaw."

"Would you guide us there?"

"Gladly. I was headed for Pensacola, but met traders leaving as the town is jammed with Indians after guns to chase off the emigrants pushing them from their land. I said I'd take my hides on to Mobile, but they warned me of fever. I thought about going on to Georgia, but I figured I'd have a better time in New Orleans." He tipped back the second keg, and wiped his mouth. "No," he assured them, "it's not much extra trouble. And I like company. This doctor at Tensaw, a fine surgeon, moved out of Mobile years ago to join a colony of Indian-countrymen, rich traders, above Mims. Mims is as good a ferry crossing for me as any. Now let me see the sick girl. I've seen fever, and plenty. It doesn't sound like it to me."

Breathing easier, Adam led the man called Dutch back to his wagon where Zilpah questioned him about the number of hours it would take them to reach the Tensaw crossing and the doctor. Rebecca relaxed into a sleep shortly after Zilpah had prepared a new potion along the lines of the trader's suggestion. Adam held her, grateful to Jeddy and the blue beads.

Men with lanterns led the way across the Perdido which was wide here but not deep. For miles they rocked, splashing and tipping through marshes of tall cane. Adam didn't sleep, nor did the drivers, nor the men leading, nor the riders with guns across their laps, but Rebecca slept on, deep in an unnatural sleep.

At dawn they stopped on a rise. Aaron and the trader sat at a cook-fire, deep in conversation. Uneasy, Adam joined them. Jethro, who had been listening to the two men, motioned Adam aside. Behind his eyes lay a pleading.

"Mister Adam, Master Aaron wants you to ride up with the trader. I'm to drive your wagon now."

While the trader told him of the Tensaw settlement, the wagons lagged further and further back. Adam glanced around worriedly. The trader talked on.

"Now if your midwife is right, your missus is lucky to have made it this far, and to have a fine doctor in the neighborhood."

Adam stared at him, shuddered in fear he'd tried for days to suppress. Zilpah had never told him that she thought...

Dutch was shaking his head. "Your brother drives a hard bargain, but we agreed on a right enough price. Your wife won't be able to travel for a long time. Now, lad, don't look so troubled. Your brother is wise. The settlement can't accommodate all of you for a long stay. He has the safety of the rest of the family and all those slaves to think of."

Jerking around, Adam looked back. Aaron had rearranged the order. Jethro headed the caravan now, four cows tied to the wagon. The slave wagon followed. As the wagons moved slowly, men transferred goods from the great wagon. Aaron's wagon closed the caravan.

Adam stopped his horse. "God, man, he hired you to guide the rest on to New Orleans?"

Nodding, the trader took his arm. "It won't do any good to argue. He's a firm man," he said. "Your wife has got to get to the doctor. You should have known that a trip like this would mean..."

Adam stared at him, started to say something, then closed his lips. It had been the time to say it back in Virginia when Aaron insisted upon leaving immediately.

They reached a swampy area almost hidden in tall cane. On a rise, roofs of crude long log structures surrounded by a stockade appeared. Passing below the settlement, they came to the Tensaw.

Men approached from the large log ferry. With a raised hand, and a roar of greeting, the trader headed them away from the lead wagon, now drawn aside. He took Adam's hand.

"Don't be stunned, lad. Some things have to be done. I'll be back for you and your lady on my next trip. By that time she'll be able to travel. Good luck now, and give my regards to the doctor."

"Thank you, sir. I'm grateful that I found you."

As the trader rode away, Aaron, sitting stiffly, drew his horse alongside Adam's. He held out his hand.

"I'm leaving slaves and supplies. Don't feel that I'm deserting you and Rebecca. Men will guide you up to the doctor's house which is some distance from here. I wish you both well."

Adam stared beyond Aaron to the wagons. Ruth leaned out the side of her wagon, then jumped down and ran toward the isolated wagon, clasping little Adam and dragging Ben by the hand. He tried to listen to Aaron.

"The trader is in a hurry. We have two wide rivers to cross before dark."

Reaching Rebecca's wagon, Ruth shoved the children inside, and crawled up.

"The Tensaw and the Alabama. It is not easy, Adam, to leave you and Rebecca."

Now Ruth was being helped down from the wagon, and Jethro handed the children down to her. Taking the boys, she ran back to her own wagon.

"You must send word by every traveler so that we know how things go with Rebecca."

Ruth had reached her own wagon and was handing his boys up to waiting hands. Adam clung to his saddle for support.

"I suggest that you do not say goodbye to Adam and Ben. They have been riding with Ruth. They will not miss your wagon until we are so far from here. And don't worry. I'll keep them happy in Jules's home, happy and safe." He drew on the reins. "If word comes from you that Rebecca is unable to travel for some reason, we shall have to go on to Texas."

Adam found his voice. "My sons stay with me."

"No, Adam. I am doing this for the welfare of the children. Believe me, it isn't easy for me to..." placing his hand on Adam's shoulder, he leaned closer. "You've been under great strain. We all have been. This is desolate country here. I would not consider leaving Brewster children in such a place. I am not acting rashly. I've considered this ever since we left the Perdido."

Adam turned away.

Aaron's hand gripped his shoulder firmly. "After you are composed, you will realize that this difficult decision was the right one, the only possible one I could make under these circumstances. I can't leave Brewster children in a country terrorized by wild Indians."

Adam snapped the reins. "You should have thought of that back home in Virginia."

"I am thinking only of the children. You and Rebecca will be safe here in the doctor's care. As soon as she can travel the trader will guide you to New Orleans. Should the doctor decide she can't leave until after the child is born, or should she die..."

Adam slashed out with his whip. A flash of shock and pain crossed Aaron's eyes as the whip struck his face. Turning, his glance both arrogant and triumphant, he raised one arm to point. Ruth's wagon was small on the broad ferry halfway across the Tensaw.

Chapter 5

TENSAW

Ruth, her tear-stained face composed, handed little Adam down into Adam's arms.

"Aaron thought he was doing right, but bless you for not failing Rebecca. She will understand that I had to go on. God be with you all until..." Blindly, she turned, clutching Zilpah.

Clinging to young Aaron's hand, Ben waited his turn. Ara, her face drained and taut, hung back.

Zilpah leaned down. "I'll die until I know I done right by Miz Rebecca, Mister Adam. You write soon as the doctor tell you. Master Aaron says no family darst be separated, but..."

Jeddy shoved through. "Mister Adam, take me," he pleaded. "My soul and body belong to Master Aaron, but my heart belongs to you."

Ben stood half-turned looking at young Aaron, and was then lifted by Labon and placed carefully on the horse behind Adam, where, his arms cinched around Adam's waist, he sobbed.

His throat tight, Adam looked upon their faces. The ferryman uttered a string of oaths. "Shove off," he ordered the horsemen holding the lines of the ferry in the middle of the river.

Adam turned his horse. There was the soft swish of water under wood as the ferry moved westward, the dreadful mourning of the slaves standing with Ruth and her children.

Young Aaron's clear voice called, "Write to us at Jules LeFleur's."

Aaron waited on shore. Riding out into the river to meet them, he reached over and stuffed a small leather pouch into Adam's pocket.

"I can't leave you without money. That's half." Blood dripped from the lash mark on his cheek.

Too heartsick to look at him, Adam turned away.

"The slaves and goods have been divided. It isn't that my heart is not with you and Rebecca. It was my duty to get all the rest to safety from this wild land. Remember that, Adam, whenever you think ill of me."

Adam dug his boots into the horses flanks. His wagon carrying Rebecca, was half way up the cliff, followed by the slave wagon. He turned toward them, only in a small distant reality aware of the lamentations among the slaves waiting beside the great wagon at the ferry slip.

Trunk ran after them, grabbed Adam's hand. "I'll stall him in New Orleans, Mister Adam, if I have to hide half his slaves."

The doctor looked overtop small glasses. His face was grave. "Mr. Brewster, there was no saving the baby girl—she was long dead. Through some drug administered by the black woman, your wife was in a comatose stage and perfectly operable."

"Rebecca is all right?" his voice dead.

"There is great infection. Only time... It's a miracle she's alive now. I'd like to talk to your midwife."

"She's gone. They're all gone except..."

There was no priest nor preacher upon the Tensaw, but a man named Conterey, who knew the Bible, came from his home south and west of the Alabama to help when there was need. He was here at Mims Crossing waiting until his own wife gained strength for the long trip home. The Contereys had lost a son.

Women, smiling to encourage him with their stories of their own difficult times and eventual recoveries, brought eggs and pies and cakes. Men came bearing game and fish. Near naked Indians and halfbreeds brought dried corn to Oner, waiting with little Adam and Ben in the wagon beside the doctor's tall cypress stockade wall.

A lanky, too-thin, homely man with deepset eyes carried to Adam a small box he had just made. Inside lay a baby's white christening dress and a Bible.

"Conterey, Mr. Brewster. My wife who is also under Dr. Dejeune's care, sends her sympathy," he said. "This dress belonged to one of our little girls. My wife would have you use it."

Named Ruth, wearing the Conterey dress, the baby was placed in the box. Oner carried it to the small grave.

Conterey read the service, his mournful face and voice further saddening the slaves, the elegantly dressed Indian countrymen and their wives, traders, ferrymen, negroes, halfbreeds and Indians gathered in the graveyard.

Eyes upward, the Virginia slaves hummed their song of farewell. A formation of wild geese crossed the sky. One small white feather fluttered down to be caught by Zibeon, who ran with it into the Dejeune house.

Early phlox and great branches of pale rhododendron were laid upon the tiny mound. Every word, every sob entered into Adam's consciousness to be recorded, yet he stood tearless, to grope finally for Oner.

Oner pressed his arm. "Mister Adam, let's just be glad we don't bury Miz Rebecca."

With every passerby Adam dispatched letters to Ruth about Rebecca's improvement. Word of the party's safe arrival in New Orleans gave him the courage to tell Rebecca they had gone on. He stood over her, looking down at her white face, the thin hands.

"Didn't you think I knew, Adam? Ruth would have been with me." Her hands clasped his. "It's all right. Don't look so fearful. You and the boys are with me. They're safe." But her eyes had lost the laughter he had always known. Even when he told her that the trader would come for them...

"As soon as you're strong enough to travel." But she had turned her face to the wall.

But the blossoms had fallen, spring storms quieted, rivers slowed, wild birds had ceased to pass overhead. Her strength had not returned.

The days became hot. Conterey, getting a late start with his planting, needed help. Adam and Oner talked it over with the restless young slaves who then volunteered to go with

Conterey to that unknown land beyond the Alabama.

Once a week, Adam and Oner, each holding a boy on his horse, rode to Contereys' with word of Rebecca, or news of their friends in New Orleans. Often they would wind around a bend of the west bank of the Alabama, cross over rolling grass fields to enter a ferny shadowy forest of virgin pine. Following a narrow Indian trace, they would stop at the edge of the woods to look down upon a foaming white stream racing southward. The stream was lined with great oaks, sycamore, magnolia, interwoven with wild grape vines. Opposite rose the line of western hills—perfect afternoon shade, Adam would think. Ideal for tobacco. He would gaze silently at the lovely spot.

When he read the letters from Ruth with news of their friends in New Orleans, he would sit down on the ground wherever the negroes were working. In his mind, he would always see Aaron reading Jules's letter down to them all from the high wagon. At other times he refused to think about Aaron. Letters finished, while the boys fished with Oner and ate picnic lunches packed by Iris Conterey, Adam studied the tall grass, the southeastward slope that was meant for the cultivation of tobacco. He would sit for hours thinking. The Indian countrymen raced horses. Men came from as far away as Mobile and New Orleans with horses to enter into the races. Yet not once did he talk with Oner about the tobacco or the horses.

How do you recognize what is your own? Sitting there, yearning for home, knowing there was no home to go back to, no way to go back, he would look upon the western hills and dream of home. Sometimes he would imagine that he could breed horses to sell, and he would make enough money to go back and buy the Brewster plantation.

He had just left Rebecca with the girl Milcah and walked out on the doctor's porch when the trader arrived. They sat on the steps. The Indian boy stood at the stockade gate with the line of small horses.

"I hate to tell you this, lad." He reached inside his vest for an envelope addressed in Ruth's handwriting. "They were ready to pull out for Texas when I went by. Aaron was having one hell of a time rounding up the slaves, had to call out the city guards to find the last two—that big one called Trunk, and a mite jamed Jedd." He put his hand on Adam's shoulder. "Now, lad, don't..." Aaron had paid him to take their party to New Orleans. Since Rebecca could still not travel, he would head out for Tennessee. His sacks were filled with trinkets to trade for pelts with the friendly Indians up there. "I'll be passing through in the fall. You'll be ready by then." With a quick handshake he was gone. Half-sick, Adam watched the small horses trundle off.

Ruth's letter was blurred by tears. When Aaron learned that Rebecca was not able to travel, he wrote Jacques who had arrived to guide them to Texas. All were well, and Ruth was expecting. Aaron hoped to have them installed in homes before winter, and before the baby arrived. They would travel by the Acadian country route where the party would rest at Jacques's home while he and Aaron went on into Texas.

The small leather pouch Aaron had given him at parting was hard at his side. His hand closed over it. He had never opened it. Slowly he walked to the wagons. Oner and his boys were staying over at the Contereys'. Iris insisted that the boys were company for her lonely little girls.

So they had gone on to Texas, and he faced the task of telling Rebecca. Above him the sky hung like lead. He sat down on the wagon seat. Staring, seeing nothing, he dug that last dreadful day out from the deep place where he had stored it. Painfully, agonizingly out of his memory he dragged back his last moments with Aaron. He was deeply sorry, sick for his act against Aaron. He cried it out into the grey morning, sobbing deep in his chest that Aaron had never written.

Crawling heavily down from the wagon, he walked back to the doctor's house. Rebecca slept, her hand clasping the small box that had been found to hold the treasured white feather that had fallen from the sky the day her child was buried. Backing out of the room, he put the letter in his pocket. His hand closed over the leather pouch. Now a fine rain sprinkled the cane brake, slipped down the stockade fence. He climbed back into the wagon.

Pulling the strings, he opened the sack, held the money in his hand, sat remembering. The high cost of the strong wagons. The supplies and equipment Aaron had bought. A weirdly-lighted morning came back—*"I said, Master Aaron, you need them mules bad." "I'll give my cow money." "Yo' boys hush, Master Aaron don' want Mister Adam to know..."* Poor proud Aaron.

Resting his head against the wagon hoop, Adam stared at the small amount of money. He'd long known there was no going back, no returning. Everything that was theirs, except the graves in the shadows of the mountains, had been sold or uprooted and carried away. He had Rebecca and the boys to care for, Oner to pay, the slaves to feed. He knew Conterey was now keeping them occupied clearing land he wouldn't use.

He considered their worldly goods: ten fine Virginia horses, one of which was already promised to the doctor who chose it instead of money. He wanted a fast horse, and now exercised him regularly toward the day when the next race would be held. There was great need for good riding horses on the Tensaw. He'd had offers for all of them, but would part with no more. Twelve farm horses, fifteen mules, four cows, one bull, a dozen chickens, one dog, two fat grey cats with a Virginia heritage, farewell gifts smuggled into the wagon by a small negro girl leaving for New Orleans. One solid Carolina turtle. They had eaten the pigs. One small sack of tobacco seeds, only one sack of flour, two extra wheels, spare parts, harness, ropes, and the old plantation bell that had been placed in the slave wagon, guns and ammunition, farming equipment, a chest of books, clothing, household articles, a few pieces of furniture, a barrel of dishes, and the two wagons. Oner, who hadn't been paid since they left Virginia. Slaves: Jethro, Joshua, Peleg, Serug and Simeon. Milcah, Tamar, Zibeon, Sarai and Leah.

The slaves were young and healthy. To his perplexity, since no preacher had come through, they had paired off in their loneliness. Oner sanctioned the coupling. They were all of pure African blood: better they choose among themselves.

Every time he crossed the Tensaw, he asked the ferrymen if they had carried or heard of a preacher coming through. Fretting, he inquired of the Indian countrymen who laughed at his seriousness. Few couples on the Tensaw, he was told, ever had the benefit of a marriage ceremony.

He sat through the night while quiet rain fell upon the canvas. Much time must pass before Rebecca dared travel. He looked back on the first terrible weeks through which he made the decisions, often after talking with Oner—but in the end, he made them. He recognized a newness in himself, a buoyancy he had attributed to his great relief that Rebecca lived and the news of the party's safe arrival in New Orleans. But it was more than that.

Now he had to provide for his group. To do so would eventually mean parting with the horses, the cows, certainly the small amount of money since supplies on the Tensaw sold at exorbitant prices.

Toward morning, as the dawn mist rose over the dense arborescent forest of rattling cane, while blackbirds swayed the grasses, he thought of that gentle land and the singing frothy white creek west of the Alabama. The sun lay a sultry red on the flat horizon to suddenly colour the sky a brilliant crimson, to turn minute bubbles of dew on the cane and grass into diamond dust. Yes, he knew he had no desire to move on west to come once again under Aaron's guidance. Something immense swelled in his chest, felt that it must burst out. When Rebecca was herself again, upon seeing the land, she would love it too.

Saddling his horse, he set out to find the Indian countryman known to own the lands west of the Alabama.

When he went to tell the slaves over at Contereys', they stood in a clump staring at him, blinking. Finally, when it was apparent that none of the boys would speak, Zibeon did.

"You mean we'll never see Trunk and Zilpah again. And little Jeddy will grow up without us."

"No. I'd hate to think that myself. I love them all too. We must stay here until Miss Rebecca is strong enough to travel. We've been marking time. Conterey, in exchange for your good work—and he says he never had better workers—has given you homes and food. We must not impose upon him now when his work is finished. We'll do our own work, build homes, have gardens. You can fish and hunt. Then..." He trailed off. Aaron would have done that, and he flinched at the thought, but what he had said to them stirred them, and now they were glancing away toward the hills and the land he had bought, and their eyes were bright.

Serug and Simeon began laughing. Serug tapped Simeon playfully. "Now you find out why we needed only such a small sack of tobacco seed. Jest you wait."

Joshua and Jethro were already at his side. Joshua looked at Adam, his mouth working. "Tell you truth, Mister Adam, I just couldn't think of belonging to Master Aaron again. Now don't you be hurt. We all been happy here. Free like."

Jethro, who had been unable to say the words, kept nodding his head. Now he said, "Yes'suh. You just lead us over there." Standing tall, he flexed his muscles.

Leah stood aside from the others. Adam smiled at her, and held out his hand. "What is it, Leah?"

"Mister Adam, I jest wondering. Maybe someday we all go back to Virginia."

"I'm holding that same dream myself, Leah. I... I never wanted to leave home."

"I'm happy to hear you say that because I thought I was differn'. Why, I wake up mornings and I think about the big house. I always wanted to grow up to work in it, and here..."

"We don't have a big house. We'll build one, Leah."

There was no doubting the joy among the slaves. Except Milcah, who stayed on the Tensaw to nurse Rebecca, the girls began a late garden with seeds and young plants thinned out of Conterey's gardens. The boys began clearing the land, used the bald cypress for the tall stockade encircling a large area of sycamore, magnolia and poplar Adam chose for shade. It was as if the stockade wall gave them a security they had now known since the reading of Jules's letter and the import of its contents spread through the slave quarters. Now they sang at their work, happy to be left together in such a paradise.

Oner and Conterey supervised the building of the slave

homes, all of fine pine logs, each with a stone fireplace, fashioned in the Mississippi Territory dog-run style, low, sturdy, with an air-way between the kitchens and main rooms. Back home they had used one large kitchen and Zilpah prepared food for them all. The girls examined their kitchens with glee.

Sarai stuck her head out her own window. "What we goin' eat off, Mister Adam?"

Conterey laughed, leaned on his shovel. "Soon as the house is finished, Mister Adam and I are going down to Mobile. We'll stock up."

Zibeon shyly help up a plate and bowl that Peleg had fashioned out of wood. "He good with he hands."

Conterey and Adam were working in the immense potato cellar, helping the boys line it with stones. Adam wanted it large enough to hold all humans in case of Indian attack.

The main house was constructed in the same dog-run style. Firewood was cut and stacked. Chickens supplied by Conterey were installed in their runs, horses in the fine new stables and cows in barns, and still Rebecca hadn't been told. She believed they were still clearing land at Contereys' for their keep and was glad.

She had accepted Ruth's word of their moving on in silence. Gradually, as her health improved, she talked more and more about going on west, about stopping off for a long visit with the LeFleurs in New Orleans. Marie LeFleur wrote to her often with invitations to come as soon as she could travel. Marie's little daughter, Olivia, looked forward to seeing the boys. Ruth's letters were evasive, hinted of the crowded quarters, of her own discomfort in the humidity of southwest Louisiana, but much of the kindness of Jacques's beautiful wife, Antoinette, who was teaching them all French. Aaron's slaves, she wrote, spent their time fishing, waiting for Aaron's word that would send them into Texas to begin clearing land and building homes, but for some unknown reason, Aaron had gone with Jacques to Mexico City. She had had no word from him in months.

It was that letter that told Rebecca that there wasn't room for them at Jacques's home. She adjusted her planning. They would wait with Jules and Marie, whose home was spacious and elegant.

Adam would sit quietly listening to her, his heart pounding almost out of his chest, yet he couldn't bring himself to tell her. He would lie awake long into the nights trying to imagine her reaction to the step he had taken, the long step that made her own plans and hopes lost, at least for the time, he would tell himself. He promised himself she would have her visit in New Orleans, and later, on into Texas. Beyond that point, he would not let himself think. Never once did he try to visualize Texas nor what life there would be like. Except Aaron, none of their party had yet seen it.

Back in the tree-shaded area inside the stockade wall, Oner went on making furniture: for Rebecca, a beautifully carved four-poster bed with chest to match. The boys' bedroom was finished. Adam would often walk into the room and stand looking at the two sturdy desks and chairs, the double deck bed. He would go into the big room where Rebecca's dainty chair and desk waited, and into the immense kitchen where Oner's gleaming dining table with matched chairs stood.

On a trip into Mobile with the Contereys, he found an exquisite French mirror to hang above the chest Oner had carved for Rebecca. He told her about the trip, how strangers came up to admire his horse. He even ventured that if they stayed on their horses would find a good market. She changed the subject, and questioned him about Mobile, comparing it with descriptions of New Orleans taken from Marie's letters. There was about her now something evasive. She would talk about Ruth only up to a certain point, then stop. She never mentioned Aaron's name unless to read it from Ruth's pages whenever she read her letters to Adam. It was as if each of them held the thought that had Aaron not hurried them, had Aaron waited until their child was born in Virginia, none of this would have happened. They would all be together. But they didn't talk about it.

She was up part of each day now, and was able to go walking with him back and forth along the wall surrounding the doctor's house. Twice, he had taken her to Mims Crossing. To his horror, she had expressed a dislike of the log structures, and would compare them to the fine home back in Virginia.

"We lived in a log house when the Indians attacked. Ruth and I have hated log houses, not been able to look upon them ever since. I suppose you think women are odd creatures, Adam, and perhaps Ruth and I are different. We can't seem to forget how mother screamed, how father tried to save her. And Indians, Adam, every time I see one I almost faint with terror. Oh, my dear, I shall be so happy to move on, to get out of here, away from that!" She pointed to the stockade fence. "I detest it and what it stands for. Truly, I think it is that that has made my recovery so slow. I've felt confined by it, shadowed by it."

Heart tearing, Adam tried to calm her. "Surely it is because of your illness here, and the reason for it. Once you are better..."

She whirled around to face him, her eyes sparkling. "I'm better now. I keep trying to convince Doctor Dejeune that I am able to travel, far better than I was on the long trip out here. Soon, Adam, I promise. It must be dreadful for you here, and all this waiting. Oh, I can hardly stand it until I am with Ruth again. And New Orleans. Marie will never know how much her letters have meant to me. I live for that. To see New Orleans. How wonderful it will be, Adam."

He nodded. No wonder Milcah persuaded him to wait longer before he told Rebecca. "I just don' think you should shock her yet, Mister Adam. She got other plans. Talks about them all the time. And she mentions Miss Ruth just about every minute. She'd like to be out there when the baby comes. She don' want her alone out there and having a baby," Milcah had said.

"And our wagons. I don't know why you moved them on to Contereys'. I've been lost, knowing they were no longer there. They were my link with Ruth, with home, with everything familiar. And the boys... Not that I'm not grateful to Iris for caring for them, and they do love her classes."

Iris Conterey had set up a classroom for the four children, and was teaching them to read and to draw.

"Little Adam isn't getting much out of it, but Ben is reading now."

"You bring them in so seldom."

"It's a long trip." He had spoken sharply. What had happened to him? He'd been making excuses to her ever since they started building and planting, and to the boys too. He told himself he was holding it all back as a surprise to his family, yet in his heart he knew he didn't take the boys there because he was afraid they would tell Rebecca. Something cold flowed through his veins, settling in the vicinity of his heart. He shook it off. Rebecca would be happy when she saw the lovely spot he had chosen, the beautiful new home that was her own, not to be shared with Aaron and his family.

"Don't look so serious, Adam. I meant that I feel I hardly know my sons. That will soon change when we resume our trip."

He stared at her. That's what this had been to her, a waystop on their trip to Texas. And to him it had become home. Even now, walking beside Rebecca, knowing how she felt, a strange glow warmed him at the thought of the land that was his own, not half Aaron's, and the home that had never been anyone else's but was his, planned by him. His own sweat had gone into it. He had worked side by side with Conterey and the slaves. It had become a creation grown out of dreams. Of course she would love it. Women were flighty. She'd been very ill. Doctor Dejeune had explained to him that Rebecca might not be herself for years, that the shock of having the rest of the party leave them behind because of her illness had been greater than her physical fight with the dreadful infection. Shocks were harder to overcome than illness. She had sunk into so low a depression that he himself deplored her recovery after the little trader was known to have gone up into Tennessee, Doctor Dejeune had told him.

"Her condition is delicate," he warned Adam. "I would not consider letting you tell her you are planning to live here. Why, man, she hates the place. I've never known anyone to take so fierce a dislike to the land here. She complains constantly that she can't breathe, that the stockade takes her breath. That can not be."

And knowing all that, he had gone ahead.

"I must get back to the boys, Rebecca."

"You always say that. When the boys were in here last Ben said you spent most of your time with me. I'm beginning to suspect you have a squaw like some of the Indian countrymen. That wouldn't shock me. Adam, don't look so furious."

Parting with her was strained. Something had grown up between them. He turned at the stockade gate, and waved. She called from the steps where she stood with Milcah.

"When you return, I shall be ready to leave for New Orleans."

Behind her, Milcah's hands flew to her face.

Adam rode the long distance across the Alabama. He was like a man in a stupor. He hadn't even smiled when the Tensaw ferrymen joked about his hunting for a preacher to marry his slaves. When he reached home, Oner was watching for him. As his horse reached the top of the hill, Oner ran into the yard and joyously rang the old plantation bell that he'd found one morning while unloading the wagons. Half sick, Adam raised his hand to wave. In the short time he had been gone the big house had diminished, the slave houses were mere log cabins, the gleaming golden stockade wall had become a high fence to hem in Rebecca.

On a cool October day, with Conterey and Iris waiting apprehensively at their own place, Adam and Rebecca rode side by side.

"You'll never know the feeling of freedom, Adam." She waved her arms into the air and he had to grab her reins. "I hated to say goodbye to Doctor and Madame Dejeune who have been so kind to me, but I hope you have the wagons packed. I won't want to visit long at Contereys'."

The sky was a cloudless blue. The pines were sweet and dark. The brilliant red of fall-turned sumac lay rich against golden poplars and the bare sycamores. Adam's hands were wet on the reins as they drew near the edge of the woods. They passed from the forest into the clearing, stopped on the brim of the hill. In the valley below waited the stockade, the homes and stables. On their left lay the slope with seedling beds ready for spring planting. Across from them, rising up from the stream, the western hills glowed in reds and yellows against dark pines. They sat quietly. Apprehensively, he watched Rebecca. Her eyes glowed at the sight of the hills.

"How lovely. It reminds me of home. Iris didn't tell me how pretty it was." She glanced down. "Oh, it isn't the Conterey's place. It's a new fort." Staring at the wagons, her hand crept to her throat.

Seeing them, Oner rushed out to pull the bell cord. Milcah, who had ridden ahead with Jethro, stood looking up, her body tense.

Adam saw Rebecca's throat constrict. She didn't wave to the group below. Her gaze turned upward to the western hills, a long look. "It's ours, isn't it, Adam. You wanted to surprise me. You wanted to have a home ready when I got out. It is very lovely, and I thank you." In her voice hung a deadness, a lifelessness. Before her illness her every word tinkled. The joy was gone.

Iris gave Rebecca flower seeds collected all summer from her own gardens, and small fruit trees to be set out, and jars of canned berries and fruit and vegetables. The seeds she handed out to the slave girls. Listlessly, sitting on a chair near the storage cubbyhole, she marked the date upon the jar labels and handed them one by one to Sarai to place on the shelves. Sarai took over the meals, the cooking. Rebecca planned them. She sewed and wrote letters. There was about her a quiet calm. She was far away. She would stand in the doorway watching a faded sun die in the west. She spent the winter teaching the children. The Contereys came to visit. Friends they had made on the Tensaw came over. When on a clear day Adam would ask if she wanted to visit at Mims Crossing, she would answer that she never wanted to see it again. She did not ask to visit the small grave.

All that winter slaves pulled great stumps from the

hillsides. Adam held a daily Bible reading, a monthly slave inspection as his father had done and Aaron after him.

Adam's first colts came in the spring, but he took no joy in it. Men came from all over the territory to bid for them.

Rebecca's interest was centered on the mails. Letters from Ruth told that they still waited in Acadia. Ruth had had one letter from Aaron still in Mexico City where he and Jacques tried to get backing to overrule the law that slaves could not be taken into Spanish Texas. She lowered the letter she had been reading to Adam.

"How like Aaron to act before asking. If he had asked before we left Virginia, we would still be home, all together and happy. Perhaps we can all go home, Adam."

He dropped his face into his hands. "Why can't you be happy here, Becky? We have our own with us. There's no room for us at Jacques's. They're crowded in like pigs, and you know it. And what have we to go home to? no land, no home..."

"You'll prosper. We can go. I shall write it to Ruth in my next letter."

The winter brought letters and gifts from Marie LeFleur. Jeddy scrawled a note to enclose in one of Ruth's letters. He had his first calf. When Robert, Ruth's child was born, Rebecca read her letter to them all. "Boys, you have a new cousin. One day you will see him."

Adam walked to the window as he would do many times in the years ahead. He looked out across the barren snow-covered hills where the bare black trees stood starkly against the heavy sky. He had built for himself a barrier and in spite of Rebecca's hopes, he had the feeling he could never climb over it. The effort and his failure had been too great. The weight of his failure hung heavily upon him, and he looked darkly into tomorrow and tomorrow and tomorrow, year into year, years into decades... With a cry he ran out the door and walked around and around inside the stockade. Was there no way out?

Chapter 6

WHITE FEATHER CREEK

"You got that latch fastened, Miz Rebecca?" Oner's tense voice outside the stockade gate sounded far away.

"Yes, Oner. Be watchful. Iris and the young ladies won't be afraid with you and Peleg." The girls were terrified, she knew. Conterey and Iris wouldn't have a peaceful minute until they were safe again inside the Brewster stockade. How many times since the terrible massacre at Fort Mims?

"You rest. Finish your letters. No doubt we'll post 'em in New Orleans before many weeks," Oner called out.

Rebecca sighed. How many times had she heard that in their ten years on White Feather Creek? How many times had she planned and packed, then had to unpack? This time they would make it.

Adam rushed to the door of the house, sweated and disheveled from his frantic packing in the August heat. "Becky, that gate bar's too heavy for you. Why didn't you call me?"

She went to him, reached up to touch his frown lines with her fingers. "You were busy." You've had a busy ten years, she thought, and hard years. And he didn't want to leave, she knew that. Poor Adam. He hadn't wanted to leave Virginia so long ago, either. She followed him inside.

"Do I have all of your treasures now, Becky?" He held two small ebony framed tintypes made at the time of their wedding in 1797. A small jewel box rested on top of the chest. She opened it and the hot breeze ruffled the white feather.

"Could we go up there once more before we leave?"

Wiping his face on his sleeve, he leaned down to kiss her. "Mims Crossing is no place for you now. You'll need your strength for the long trip." He picked up the money box. "If anything should happen... Now, Becky, don't look so frightened." He put his arms around her.

She flushed, ashamed that she couldn't stop being afraid, couldn't get over the shock and horror of the Fort Mims massacre last year. They'd lost all their friends, Doctor and Madame Dejeune, everyone except the Contereys, who'd come to them for protection rather than risk the long run through Indian-sieged land to the Tensaw and the Fort Mims stockade.

"I just wanted to show you where I'm packing the strong box. If I forget, tell Ben when he comes in from the fields." He placed it in the last case of books, wrapped a scarf around the frames and the jewel box, laid boards across the top and began hammering.

She wandered around the room checking the stacks of good clothing they would need in the fine LeFleur home in New Orleans. Picking up the pale green velvet gown Marie had sent years before, she walked to the mirror Adam had ready to crate.

He touched the velvet. "The color's perfect. Don't think I'm not glad you're finally going to wear it. It's just..."

"I know, dear. I know, but it isn't as if we were going humbly, to accept charity. That land is your inheritance from the debt the LeFleurs owed to your father the same as it was Aaron's. And you've saved more money from your horse breeding and sales than Aaron has ever seen." She yearned to tell him how proud she was of him, how amazed Aaron would be if he knew Adam had bred the Virginia horses, sold them on the Tensaw, in Mobile, and many had gone clear across the Territory to Natchez. How hard he had worked to do it all—she didn't know how they could have managed these ten years if he hadn't. Prices of the few staples they had to buy were four times that paid in Natchez, and, in the years he'd had good crops, the tariff at Mobile had swallowed the profits. But Adam disliked praise. He had changed in many ways over the years. The year he had built this place she had thought he was getting like Aaron, but she had been wrong. He had been wise to build here. Whatever would have become of them in Texas? Live in a wretched dugout in terror over Indian attack the way Ruth had? As much as she despised the stockade, they had been safe here.

Adam watched her go outside to sit down at the table Oner had arranged for her writing materials away from the noise of his hammering. He was almost finished. One wagon had been filled last night to make room for Conterey's furniture. Since he had to part with his home, he was glad Conterey would live here.

Resting against the stacked book-boxes, he opened the Bible and took from it Aaron's letter, the only letter he had ever received from him since they parted ten years ago on the Tensaw. "Adam, as Ruth has written many times, your share of the land awaits you. Your home is under construction." Aaron had had his own Indian troubles, and got a slow start with the two trips to Mexico City to clear land titles and get permission to take slaves into Texas. While his party waited in cramped quarters in Acadia with Jacques's family, Aaron and Jacques had fought off Tonkawas and Mexicans while they cleared the land, living in rough-hewn underground dugouts that received little improvement when their families were finally moved into Texas. Those must have been bitter years for Aaron. Had it been pride that kept him from writing to Adam to claim his land before decent quarters were ready? "It is good to get above ground after living in the dugout for so long. Ruth tells me you think the soldiers have the Creek subdued. Don't be smug, Adam, or careless. We learned of Indian treachery as you did after the Mims massacre. How horrified we were when that news came until we got Rebecca's letter saying that you and the Contereys felt more secure in your own stockade and would not travel to Fort Mims or Fort Stoddart. Now that a home awaits, it is your duty to remove the Brewster family from that war torn area. I have written Jules and Marie to expect you. New Orleans will be a pleasant rest stop. Jacques's son, Anatole, will guide you here. Your brother, Aaron Brewster."

Adam smiled. How like Aaron. He also had to smile at the postscript in Ruth's handwriting. "Your land is three miles from Aaron's."

He stared out the window and up over the hills. In spite of

the Mims massacre, he still felt secure in their stockade. During the years target practise and marksmanship had become routine precaution, even for the women. The smallest child was trained to hide at the first sign of danger. When the men worked the fields, or woods, Peleg stood constant guard. If Rebecca's health had been better, or if she had ever settled in and considered this a home and not just a stopping off place, he wouldn't be packing. She had never ceased yearning to move on to Texas, not just to get there, but to be near Ruth. He couldn't believe the change in her since he told her they would go. And the slaves were overjoyed to be moving back among their old friends. His sons were excited, especially about going to New Orleans. Of course, he wanted to see them all too, but his real happiness would be in seeing Rebecca happy. It would be good to be close to Aaron again because once long ago they shared a relationship—not equal to the deep love and strong bond between Ben and young Adam. Yet, he knew he would never on earth have agreed to go had he not been financially independent of Aaron.

Walking to the back window, he glanced upslope where Ben and Adam and the slaves rapidly cut the last tobacco crop which would be stored in the drying wagon Oner had finished building last night. He planned to sell it in New Orleans. Returning, his footsteps echoed hollowly through the empty house, stirring a haunting, almost forgotten time, touching a desolate emptiness within him, causing him to shiver although it was hot. He stood looking out at Rebecca, trying to throw off the dreadful feeling of doom that he attributed to his love for this land. He had no earthly desire ever to leave it.

"Tell Jeddy," Rebecca wrote, "that we are proud of his success, and look forward to seeing his fine herd. Oh, Ruth, how long, how very long I have waited for this time..." Pen raised, she glanced upward beyond the stockade which she had despised yet been thankful for, and allowed herself to look with peace upon the western hills. Never so long as she lived would she forget the coldness settling down over her that long ago October afternoon. Instinctively, before she recognized the plantation bell, before Oner ran outside to ring it, she had known. All the pieces fit together. Adam's excitement, his unconcealed joy that seemed more than happiness over her recovery, his poor, cut hands that showed labour he denied; yet she had sat frozen on that horse staring down at the log cabins, aware of Adam's breathless fearful waiting, wanting to comfort him, to praise him, but unable to tear herself from that terror uncovered by the sight of the stockade.

She had seen another cabin in another valley. Their parents worked in the fields beside the woods. She remembered the Indians surrounding the field, the terrified shriek, the wild cries of the Indians. Ruth grabbed her. Horrified, the small sisters crouched in bushes while their home was plundered and burned. She remembered friends coming—they had seen the smoke. The safe town. The kind churchman. His ailing wife. All through their school days he wanted to take his wife to her family in Philadelphia. He would talk about the girls' futures.

She and Ruth turned away from young men because some young men looked westward, and others wanted to stay in the town. The girls never wanted to be separated. When Aaron came with his offer, it was an impossible dream come true. They could be together always in a settled home. Ruth was seventeen. She learned to love Aaron, and to obey him. Rebecca was fifteen. She loved Adam with her whole heart the moment she looked into his gentle eyes. Gratefully, the old minister rushed his wife to Philadelphia. Long after they moved into the stockade, she wrote to Ruth, "I love Adam to much to hurt him. If God wills it, when he tires of this venture, we will come." Now, after long years, they were going. Smiling, she dipped the pen.

Ben glanced down the field, saw Oner and Peleg leaving. He punched Adam with his elbow. "Oner's on his way over for the Contereys."

Adam groaned. The Conterey girls, fine playmates as children, were stretching into lanky, homely duplications of their father. Adam called them the gloomiest girls in the Territory. Worse yet, the girls considered his sons their property. The first thing Oner said when he knew they were finally going to Texas was, "That's a long run just to get away from two girls."

Ben was dying to get to the river again. He had been twice to Carter Ewing's plantation near Natchez where their father sold race horses. He was looking forward to New Orleans, but he wasn't too set on Texas. He remembered his uncle, and held a vivid picture of the farewells at Mims Crossing on the Tensaw. What he really wanted to do, and would have done long ago if it hadn't meant leaving his young brother behind, was join Jackson's Volunteers to help pay back the Creek for the slaughtering of their friends and neighbors in the Mims massacre. He hoped that he and his cousin Aaron could fight together after they got to Texas, if the war continued. He had followed the newspapers brought up from Mobile, had suffered when the *Wasp* was lost, but his real anger had been aroused when Tecumseh and his brother, the Prophet, visited Creek villages in the territory imploring them to drive the white settlers from their hunting grounds, to give up farming, to take up once again their own people's arms, the hatchet and the bow. And the Creek were doing it.

Young Adam wished they had been able to get away before the Conterey girls got there to sniffle and probably bawl. He was finally on his way to see Olivia LeFleur with whom he had corresponded ever since he learned to write. Even Ben didn't know that he had saved her letters from the first scribbled notes to the elegantly slanted writing of her Catholic school training. His mother encouraged writing to the LeFleurs. Every year she had expected them to be passing through New Orleans. As long as he could remember she had talked about the trip to Texas in such a way that his skin would stand up in bumps. In his heart, he yearned to see what lay beyond the hills. Some inherent feeling of movement stirred within him when he looked into sunsets. He wondered why it was that men seemed always to want to move on westward. Ben dismissed it as a natural desire born into man because the earth turned in that direction. A shadow crossed his hand. Looking up at the peaceful sky, he saw a buzzard floating. He leaned down to cut a leaf. Near him, Milcah's baby began to cry. Milcah touched it with her bare toe.

"Hush, little baby, don't cry. Uncle Jacques's got a fine big house in Texas."

They were moving down the side of the hill. Sarai lifted her baby, moving it down the row. Jethro and Joshua picked up the song. The rest of the slaves began humming as they cut the leaves. Other children, whispering, played under the great leaves.

The buzzard floated by. He was glad. It gave him a funny feeling, had ever since the Mims Massacre. Then it seemed that every buzzard in the world was circling their area. He wiped his sweating hands on his pants to remove the sticky viscid juice of the leaves. They moved downslope out of sight of the stockade. As he leaned over to cut a leaf the stillness was shattered by the roar of his father's musket. Sarai grabbed the babies and ducked under the tobacco. The children scattered to disappear in the leaves. At Ben's instant bidding, Milcah grabbed Adam and threw him to the ground as Ben and the four men snatched up their guns and tore down through the fields.

"Milcah, let me up. If it's Indians, I'm a better shot than father, whatever Ben chooses to think."

Milcah was unrelenting. The sounds of gunfire filled the air, quieted. There came Ben's tug on the plantation bell, a sharp dreadful toll. At its sound, Milcah released him. Grabbing his gun, he raced down the steep grade, the women and children behind him. Opposite, to a wild cacophony of cries, a band of Indians on his father's horses rode over the hillside. Smoke billowed from inside the stockade fence. He stumbled down the hill. Ben grabbed him, turned him away and then buried his own face in his hands, but Adam had already seen his father lying in the doorway, his smoking musket in his hands, a hatchet in his head. Jethro was covering his mother with a quilt. Dumbly, he picked up his mother's scattered pen and papers. Milcah uttered a moan, then whirled in to help carry water from the stream. Ben raced into the burning house to toss out his father's most treasured possessions, his crates of books.

The grief-stricken slaves dug two graves under the trees near the stream. A stiff-lipped Ben, just sixteen, read services from their father's smoke-tinged Bible. The Contereys, faces mirroring their horror, stood sobbing. The slaves hummed their strange sad tune of farewell. Oner wept bitterly, beat his hands upon a tree.

"I should have called Mister Adam to fasten that gate. Miz Rebecca never did do it right. I shouldn't have gone..."

That afternoon he fashioned a box, and rode away. He was gone for days. He returned to dig a third grave and place the box therein.

The slaves finished harvesting the tobacco. While the wagons sat packed and waiting, Adam and Ben helped rebuild the damaged house. Work moved slowly; trees had to be felled. Fall came, wild birds flew over. Winter set in, wet and dreary. A terse letter came from Aaron, ordering young Adam and Ben to bring their slaves and move to Texas immediately. Ben wanted Adam to stay with the Contereys while he joined Jackson's forces fighting the Indians. The Contereys urged them all to stay. By the time the rebuilding was finished, Jackson had subdued the tribes. Ben bought back from Conterey ten of his father's horses.

Milcah wove a wreath of bittersweet, and placed it on the stone marker Oner made for the graves. On a wet chill morning in December of 1814 the wagons rolled out of the stockade, moved slowly down the bank of the creek, crossed it to turn west.

Chapter 7

CHALMETTE

Ben felt Jethro's hand touch his shoulder. "Let me take the reins, Master Ben. You rest."

"Why, I heard them Conterey girls wailin' for miles," Jethro said hopefully, glancing at Oner hunched on the wagon seat, but Oner stared on into some unseen black depth.

They rode in the third and last wagon of the small caravan. Ben summed them: two sober white boys, tall for their ages; one black freeman; slaves: Joshua, Jethro, Peleg, Serug and Simeon, strong, ebony-skinned men from some unknown tribe of great physical endurance; straight features, clear black eyes, good stature and possessing intelligence and wit. Female slaves: Milcah, tall, raw-boned, jet black of some gentle race; Sarai from the same tribe but of a happier nature; Tamar, light brown; Zibeon, silky brown; Leah, almost blue-black, from unknown African tribes, young, healthy, strong, capable and loving. Their ten children.

He studied the material worth of his group: ten fine riding horses bought back from Conterey; twelve mules; five farm horses; a too-small herd of milk cows; one bull; a few pigs; a crate of chickens, and five grey cats with a distant Virginia background. One wagon of household goods, furniture, four crates of books, a few pieces of farm equipment. The drying wagon filled with tobacco. The small sack of money from Conterey for the property. Enough to start a farm somewhere. Did he have to obey his uncle's orders? How much land could he buy with the money from Conterey?

En route they met and traveled with a band of Andrew Jackson's Tennessee and Kentucky Volunteers, exhuberant but exhausted after chasing the Creek, and moving westward under orders to protect the city of New Orleans from a fast approaching British fleet. The group straggled through a cold rain into the Lake Pontchartrain area late in December to learn the immense proportions of the British fleet and the grave danger to the city. The officer in charge advised Ben to take his group north to a mission in Baton Rouge.

At the mission Ben arranged the wagons on the land assigned to them. Ordering big fourteen year old Adam to stay until his return, Ben started to ride south with his gun. The priest called after him. "Leave your horse, son, a faster, safer journey can be made on the river. Down that hill. Any boat." The small round man danced to keep his grip on the struggling Adam who was determined to go with Ben. Joshua and the rest of the slaves surrounded the little Jesuit.

"Father Diaz, I demand to go with Master Ben." The others joined in the fracas, yelling.

"Keep them here, Father Diaz," Ben called out, "they're family men." Standing there, one foot turned toward the river, he remembered his father's search for a priest to marry slaves. Going back, he inched his way through and whispered into the priest's ear. Adam caught his arm.

"Ben, you wouldn't go without me. I'm bigger and stronger and a better shot than most of Jackson's men we traveled with."

"Lad, you are indeed, and just what I need here at the mission," said the priest. Buggies from New Orleans and river plantations have been pouring in for days. There are children, young ladies and women to be fed and protected should the British get up the river." He faced the negroes. "Can you handle arms, men?"

Oner, who had been standing aside silently, nodded. "They're trained Indian fighters, sir, every one of them."

"Just what we need here. Why, men, I'll bet the six of you can protect this whole mission full of people."

Adam stopped struggling and looked with interest back at the buildings.

Shivering in the biting wind off the river, Ben leaped aboard a flat-boat. In the confusion—the docks were jammed with men, the river full of boats—he thought he saw a familiar bulky figure tear down the bank and wade out to catch his moving boat. He tried to see above the milling scores of cold, chapped faces, but was shoved down with his back against a raised shed, wedged between a sleeping Kentuckian with a long gun sticking up from his bent legs, and the smallest, dirtiest, weasel-like man he'd ever seen. A grubby hand shot out from the furs and skins he wore to grip his hand in a clasp that would have decked him if he hadn't been down.

"Pete," he gruffed, "trap my own spread upriver beyond Natchez," he said jerking his silver fox hat. "You?" Fixing right on Ben his bright blue eyes that looked like Indian trade beads, he leaned back waiting.

"Ben Brewster, from east in the territory." He found himself telling this old man about Adam who wanted to fight too, about his parents and the massacre, the farm he'd sold to the Contereys, the trips he'd made with his father to Natchez to sell horses, how much he admired the town, the river, the plantations.

Nodding now and then, shaking his head, muttering sympathetic sounds, the trapper listened. From somewhere down in the pile of fur that he was, he pulled out a jug and offered it.

"Wish I was your age, son." He stopped to take a drink. "Liking this country like you do, having those slaves to clear land. But since the territory opened up there's few fine spreads with river frontage left." He leaned over to gaze into Ben's face. "River frontage is the most valuable land around here, you know that, don't you?"

Ben nodded.

Satisfied, Pete leaned his cap against the shed. "All clear title my spread is, and the most bee-ute-te-ful bank of the Miss-ipp. Tell you what, after we get loose of them British, you bring your whole gang up to see my land, spend some time with me," he said. "After that, any boat can ferry you on across. It won't be far to your rich uncle's from my landing."

"I'm afraid Uncle Aaron isn't rich."

"All Texans is rich," he said solemnly.

A spider spinning, Pete wove the fabric of his spread. "You never saw an equal patch of earth." Graceful as two doves, his hands encompassed his land, "Closest to Heaven, on one of the old wide bends of this great river, nice rich lowland, not cliffs like where a man might need to track half a mile for a look at his river, but land low enough to be safe level above the flow and allowing a grand view. Live-oak trees wider than this shed in trunk alone, long moss, grey as an old squaw's hair, and all dotted with mistletoes, and climbed around by honeysuckle."

The raw odor of strange liquor crossed in front of Ben's nose as the old man raised the jug.

"I've cleared it only as much as I needed to get the view from my home which lays the length of this boat from the river. In spring that earth is thick velvet carpets of the richest purple violets God ever made. Did you ever smell a field of violets?"

"Yes," he said wistfully, leaning away from the jug.

"Now, lad, see what I'm showing you: here's this sable river flowing wide. Here's this bed of flowers. Here's the live oaks dipping moss into the water. Can you imagine what a fine boat dock a man with a little money and some slaves could build there?" His birdlike hands fluttered, showing the dock.

"Now, here's my house. Here around it are twelve of the biggest magnolia trees ever seeded by God above." His hand, pointing out God, shot upward almost skinning Ben's nose. The old man tossed back his head, and Ben saw the brown stumps of teeth. The blue eyes shone. "Now travel back apiece, say ten feet. I got that much cleared—took me nigh two year with the trapping I had—thick with rich furred animals my land is, and then all the trips floating my hides down to New Orleans to nearly get murdered by thieves on the way back. You got to hang on to your money in these parts. Now, here begin the woods. Gum, sycamore, wild plum... Son, you ever taste a Chickasaw plum warm off the tree? Well, come spring you'll see them plum trees in bloom, see the red-bud and the wild cherry, and a golden forsythia a planter give me to put beside my house. I'll tell you, when a trained woodsman like you gets back in there to what I call the bottoms—that's where the river flowed a long time back before it wearied of that bend and straightened itself out some, there are the straightest cypress trees, and I've counted them—you can tell by the leaves—twenty kinds of oak. Why, I could've sold off that lumber for a king's ransom with all the building going on by planters up and downriver, had I help. Now cleared, all that wood sold off for high prices, that land will grow cotton so high a picker might accidental get a cloud, that land," his face wasn't an inch from Ben's, "that land is rich delta soil, thicked-up by hundreds of years collection of silt from all up north and dropped in the bottoms there."

His eyes misty, leaning his head against the shed, he mourned, "Was I young again, and didn't have to trap for my meager living; had I help, that's what I'd do. I'd be a cotton baron, build me one of them," he pointed out a great white mansion rising from clustered live oaks across the river. Sighing, he drank deeply, and wiped his mouth on his sleeve.

"But let's think about you, son. You never been in New Orleans. Depending on how soon we get to fighting, I'll show you the town." He slapped his knee. "Got much money?"

Ben shook his head. He'd given it to Father Diaz to care for. "Friends, though, of my father; Jules LeFleur."

A mouthful of liquor shot past his face. "Jules? Why I know Jules and Jacques like I know where to slit a skunk's hide. I just saw Jacques's boy, Anatole; got on the boat ahead and I'da rode with him, but I had to line up to fill my jug. Anatole carted Jules's wife and daughter up to the mission. Many a fine fox I've traded Jules for traps. He really shows off that beautiful Spanish wife. Last year I gave him thirty perfect beaver pelts for his little girl, Olivia. The women are high-class. Jules now," he rocked with laughter, "Jules is as common as me; got more friends around the river than any man I know." He leaned close to hiss into Ben's ear. "You ever hear of Jean LaFitte's Baratarians? Well, son, most of them and Jules are like that. I know for a fact he traveled on his ships for years. A perfect pirate if ever there was one. He and Jean LaFitte are like that." He pressed his hands together. "However, Jacques's a regular warehouse of contraband Baratarian goods, carries a wagon load out through the Acadian country into Texas, and I'll bet down into Mexico. Kinda awful to think of them Spaniards having to buy back their own goods stole off their ships by pirates, isn't it?" he said winking.

The boat bumped. Jumping up, Ben saw tall masts. Great sailing ships such as he'd never seen in Mobile lay at anchor in the river which was a solid mass of flatboats jammed together. He and Pete walked over them for a half mile before leaping into the sticky mud of a New Orleans levee street. When he looked around, Pete was waving to friends.

"Ben, Ben, wait!" He knew that voice. Whirling around, Oner caught him.

"Oner!" he cried joyously, his voice cracking.

Pete took Oner's hand, and having met his match, let go. "Come on, let's make the fur fly before the fighting starts."

Bells rang, men shouted, horns tooted: "This way to enlist in the service of our country," was repeated in many languages, ringing out above the melee.

So cold he was almost frozen on the river, now Ben flushed with the excitement of the harbor, the fine brigantines, schooners, all manner of riverboats and flatboats maneuvering for landings, all jammed with men and guns. Crowded together were faces of more colors and features than he had realized covered the earth; tan, red, brown, white, some bearded, some mustached; sun-tanned, windburned, all yelling bizarre words.

They passed into the market where hundreds mobbed trying to buy food and drink. He saw lightcolored negro women in bright calico dresses and warm shawls, their heads tied in handkerchiefs, selling pralines to shy, glistening-eyed Acadian boys. There were near-naked Indians, unarmed and not trying to kill anyone. There were women in gowns of velvet and wraps of thick furs rushed past the mobs in buggies by drivers who shouted oaths to clear the way. There were red-shirted flatboat men, guns shouldered, yelling and cursing as they trooped through the mire. There were soldiers and guards in fine uniforms, muddy to the hips.

He was enthralled by the beauty of the Church of Saint Louis, the greatest he'd ever seen, the Cabildo with its arches, the wildly interesting Spanish buildings with lacey iron grillwork around the balconies. A memory came back of one of Marie LeFleur's letters to his mother in which she described the ironwork Jules sold in his shop.

"Oner, we should try to find Jules before we get into it."

"I'll lead you to Jules's shop," Pete offered, "and then we'll see the town. If he's there, he'll lead the way."

Munching bread and fruit Oner had bought in the market, they slipped and shoved their way through sickening-smelling slime to a shop near the levee. It was closed. A note in Jules's fine familiar lettering was nailed to the door; "Gone to chase the British; back in a few days."

A short, stocky and utterly filthy man rushed up to Pete, snatched his jug and was in the act of slamming him on the head with it when Oner held his arm. Pete looked up and the two men roared to each other in a strange manner of friendship with much cursing.

"Last I heard you were in jail, you old..."

"Jackson set us loose. We're joinin' the fight. Come on."

They were shoved along in the mob to the recruiting office. Within hours they were marching across wet fields under the orders of a frustrated young officer who was trying to teach them how to march past General Jackson in a soldierly manner. It was too late to teach any who didn't already know how to fight. It was near the end of December 1814.

After two days hard drilling in a chill drizzling rain, the mire was kneedeep. Ben was hungry, exhausted, and his feet felt as heavy as hoofs. Oner marched, his gun shouldered. Pete ran to keep up. His Baratarian friends who had been released with him from jail joked, roared and cursed the young officer. Their small company consisted of ten flatboat men who seemed never to tire, three tall Kentuckians in leather coats, six handsome boys from Tennesse in homespun, five too-young Acadian boys who marched close together, their almost identical clear eyes clouded and fearful, but their heads held wonderfully high, the Baratarians and other men freed from jail, about ten negroes of varying degrees of color, a lawyer who had been up north and missed his own company and who still wore his fine traveling suit, a boy who left his wagon mired down in the city square, farmers, fishermen—men and boys from all over the river, the levees, the distant farms and fields, the city, the slum and the pirate boats.

Governor Claiborne who was young and handsome with straight eyebrows meeting in worry, with curls on his forehead, dressed in a fine uniform with a high collar, white ruffles under his chin and golden shoulder epaulets, rode out to inspect the troops the day before they were to march before Jackson. But at noon of that same day word spread that the British had landed at Gabriel Villeré's plantation. General Villeré escaped through a window and raced from Bayou Bienvenue to warn Jackson who was gathering his scattered army.

Their company ran all the way into town. The young officer then held them to be last in line of march past their ailing general. Pete exclaimed, "Hell, commander, I know him; he lives right upriver. One look at this rat-taggle company of ours, and he'll turn tail and go home."

Leaning on his gun, Ben listened to the lawyer name the proud companies marching toward the fields of Chalmette. Not many to face Britain's ten thousand crack battle-trained troops—800 United States Regulars soaked and in all stages of uniform, soldiers to their chattering teeth; more than 500 Tennesseans with their long rifles, under Generals Coffee and Carroll; Beale's Rifles, merchants and professional men; the 365 Orleans Battalion of Creoles; over 200 free men of color; Hind's glorious Mississippi Dragoons; Pierre Jugeat's Choctaw Scouts...

"Forward, march!" The little-drilled group, muddy, hungry and shivering, straightened shoulders, raised their heads and marched past Jackson. Ben was so thrilled he almost collapsed into the mud. This was what he'd been straining to do for a long time, but it was Indians he wanted to fight. They kept right on marching past Jackson and onto the plains of Chalmette.

And he was scared. He was also overwhelmed at the rumors flying through the troops. Sir Edward Pakenham, brother-in-law of the Duke of Wellington, who might have sailed from the same port his grandfather and Uncle Aaron left so long ago, was in charge of the crack British troops.

Now that he was right in the thick of it with the fighting going to start any minute, he wished that he had held Adam's hand, warned him before they got to the mission that he was going to get into it, might be killed. He should have said, "Now, Adam, you're fourteen, and you've always wanted to go on west. You take the slaves..." It was too late to tell Adam anything, and he didn't know that Oner would follow him. He should have known.

He went there to get into the fight he'd been itching for, but he didn't need his gun for his first work. Oner maneuvered him and the Acadian boys into helping build a barricade, digging mud, stacking soaked bales of cotton, piling great layers of logs to support them; nor for his second job of carting drinking water to the men of batteries three and four under the stern command of Dominique You and Béluche, Baratarians whom Pete told him were close friends of Jules. He got to know them, to quake under their oaths. Even realizing they were pirates, he couldn't find them any different manner of men than trappers and traders he'd known most of his life near the Tensaw. And he honored them, for they were without fear. They couldn't wait for the battle to start.

The British wheeled twenty four cannon into position opposite their fourteen cannon. Dominique and Béluche destroyed all of the British cannon, losing only three of their own, and over the cannon roar, the field was filled with Dominique's cry, "Protect our country against the invaders!" It was the most powerful voice Ben had ever heard.

Between lulls in the battle, Ben told Oner about Pete's spread upriver. He still hadn't fired a shot. His present job was described by Pete as "powder runner," but the powder was wet, and they had to wait for a fresh supply. Christmas day came and passed. He thought of Adam, and watched Pete and the Baratarians get roaring drunk.

On 8 January, the British infantrymen advanced with short muskets bravely into the fire of the fine long rifles of the Tennesseans, and were mowed down. Within a short time word spread that the British ships were moving out. The Baratarians were disgusted. And, since they had no one else to fight, they fought uproariously among themselves.

Ben and Oner lost Pete in the cheering throngs on the way back to New Orleans. Oner was dying to see Jules.

"He was just a lad when he and Jacques left the plantation in Virginia, and it isn't as if we had ever been close, Ben. It's hard to explain. Like seeing someone from home, I guess."

Ben nodded. Oner had been lonely since Adam Brewster had been... Even now with the memory of his father lying there on the steps of the burning house still vivid in his mind, he couldn't bring himself to say the word, not even in his thoughts. But he understood how Oner felt about Jules. His feelings, like Adam's, were mixed. Deep in their hearts he felt that both his father and Oner blamed Jules for the great and terrible change in their lives. His father had often said, "If only Jules had not written that letter." That letter, with its promise of wealth and adventure, had been delivered when Aaron Brewster was in the depths of despair over the fortunes of the failing plantation. He had grasped the chance to move west, and in so doing had changed the lives of all the Brewsters and their slaves. His father had never ceased yearning for home as his mother had yearned for her sister.

Ben tried to imagine what his own life and young Adam's would have been had they not come west. His memory of the plantation and of Virginia was faint. Oh, he remembered the great house, the hills beyond it, and when he thought of it, he always thought of blossoms. He did remember Eli Salem who always gave them candy when they went to his store, and sent it with Aaron when he went in for the weekly supplies. He recalled the long trip west as being the most exciting adventure of his life. No, he had no hard feelings against Jules. In fact, what Pete had told him about Jules and Jacques had only added more to the glamour of the

LeFleurs' legend. Glancing at Oner, he wondered if he should tell him, and decided against it. Each man chose his own way of life, or should, his father had often said. As for the LeFleurs actually being pirates or privateers... It was still too new a thought. He couldn't understand his Uncle Aaron living with Jacques all these years and not knowing, if it were true and not an exaggeration of Pete's. He smiled to himself. Pete did paint a colorful tale of all he told. And he'd had lots of experience probably, sitting around campfires with other trappers and woodsmen.

By the time they had shoved their way through the wild and cheering and drunken throngs of New Orleans to Jules's shop and found it still locked and the sign still in place, Ben was having chills, and sickening waves of heat. They hunted for the LeFleur house, but gave up to wander through the melee and finally reach the docks and board a slow-moving keel boat.

On the way upriver he pointed out the white mansion to Oner, and told him of Pete's dream to raise cotton. Oner listened to his description of Pete's spread with a strange far away look in his eyes.

They arrived at the mission to learn that Father Diaz had baptised every one of his slaves and their children, and on Christmas day presented them with beads and Bibles. Joshua and Milcah were firmly married, as were Jethro and Sarai, Peleg and Tamar, Serug and Zibeon, and Simeon and Leah.

"This here is what we get for not going with you to New Orleans, Master Ben," Jethro mourned. "I been looking forward to that promised trip to New Orleans for so many years I'm beginning to think I ain't ever going to make it."

Oner laughed so hard at the groanings of the proud-eyed young negroes that he had to wipe his eyes.

"These little children have so many new names we'll have to get you to read them to us out our Bibles so we know who is who before we call them, Master Ben," Joshua mourned. "Mister Adam? Why, we hardly seen him at all since you left. He and that Miss Olivia LeFleur who come here with her mother out riding somewhere."

Father Diaz tumbled out to meet them. "Come, come, boys, let them get inside. They both look sick." He sniffed. "I believe they would enjoy bathing, and having a hot meal." Rustling and jingling in his habit, he led them into a long corridor of the mission and to rooms.

Intending to bathe, Ben rested his head for a moment on the clean pillow of the cot. His eyes burned and his throat rasped. When he woke up, Adam was standing over him.

"You are certainly one fine mess to present to the elegant LeFleurs." As Ben jumped up, he grabbed him and held him. "I'm almost blubbering. I was so afraid something..."

"I know, Adam. I know."

While he bathed, Adam told him about finding Marie and Olivia LeFleur.

"I didn't know what back-country boys we were until I saw them, Ben. You won't believe anything I tell you—it's all too fantastic, so just wait until you meet them."

The woman and the girl were all that Pete and Adam had told him, beautiful as paintings, fragile as Dresden, exquisitely gowned and furred like the women he had seen riding in carriages in New Orleans. Mobile had never prepared him for women like this, nor had his trips to Natchez. He sat entranced, listening to their gracious, gentle and cultured voices. Both were fair-skinned and dark-eyed. Marie, the mother, looked little older than Olivia with her sparkling dark-lashed eyes, her graceful hands that reminded him of his mother's.

It was not until Olivia had dragged Adam off to see the steady stream of boats moving upriver from New Orleans that Marie moved to sit beside him on the bench. She took his hand.

"Your grief is ours, Ben. Jules has been stricken by the tragedy, so much so that he was trying to get his business in order to travel to you boys, to bring you to New Orleans when the word that the British were planning an attack reached us. Your mother's letters to me were the joys of my own life. When the word came..." She drew a lace handkerchief from her sleeve and dabbed at her eyes. "I can not believe it, even now. Why, oh, why didn't your father

95

move out of there after the dreadful Mims massacre? Jules, who had been urging him for years, increased the pressure after that. We were so sure you were coming..."

Ben looked away. His mother and Iris Conterey were women who did not shed tears easily. He felt unprepared and inadequate to offer her solace.

"Mother never gave up planning to go to Texas, and our stopover in New Orleans was the dream of her life."

She glanced up swiftly, her eyes flashing. "We must take our dreams in our own hands, Ben. Your father stalled, made excuses. I think he did not want to move on to be with Aaron. Forgive me. I have no right to criticize him, nor to judge him. You must understand that through our letters your mother became as close to me as the sister I never had. We wrote as we would have talked had we been together. She was the one person on this earth who sensed my loneliness after Olivia went into school. Jules is away so much. It may be hard for you to understand that wives do not all have a close family association that your family had living a frontier life. I would urge her to come for a visit, to come alone by stage if Adam..."

"You were good to her. She treasured your friendship and looked forward to your letters. And when that green dress came... Well, you can't imagine the happiness it gave her."

"I am so glad to know that. It was my own design, made up by the modiste who makes all of our gowns. I saw the velvet in her shop. You see, Ruth had described Rebecca to me. Aaron had told that Rebecca was smaller but of Ruth's beautiful coloring."

"It was a perfect shade for her." He did not tell that his mother saved the dress for New Orleans and had never worn it.

"I think what drew me close to Rebecca was that I recognized, understood her need to be near her sister. I grew up in a convent, and knew loneliness. And Ben, although I do not say this to Jules, and probably should not say it to you, I have carried your whole family upon my conscience all these many years. Do you understand my reason for this?

Did your father ever tell you how it was that they moved west?"

He nodded.

"I am glad that I do not have to tell you. When you meet and know Jules and Jacques with their adventurous spirits, their vibrant, yes, and exciting viewpoints on life, you will understand why Jules would not heed me when I urged him not to invite your uncles to move on west. I became an orphan for a similar reason. My own father brought us out of Spain for this new world upon the urging of his brother who had come here. The ship on which we sailed was boarded off Florida by merciless pirates. Few survived. I, a small baby, was brought to New Orleans by a gentle priest who had hidden me under his robes. I told Jules, 'Do not insinuate yourself and your opinions into the lives of others, or you will change their destinies.' He laughed at me. I should not tell you this. He said they owed Robert Brewster's boys a chance to move on as Robert himself had once done, that hidden beneath their cool exteriors there had to be some of the spirit that fired Robert Brewster. He found in Aaron exactly what he expected, a latent but firelike spirit. I see it in him. He reminds me of a wild horse who must run."

Ben nodded, remembering his Uncle Aaron.

"With Aaron, Jules was lucky, and he was right, but I fear that your father..."

"My father felt that he had found his own where he settled. He would have preferred remaining in Virginia, for home was deep within him."

She hung her head.

"He loved horses, and enjoyed his work. He took pride in showing them, and in knowing of the races they won."

"Then he did know a little happiness? I have been so tortured..."

"Much happiness, I assure you. I will always think of him comfortably settled after a hard day of work in a chair by the fire and with a book in his hand. You sent many fine books to him. They are out in our wagons now. But tell me, did not the uncle who had sent for your family ever find you?"

"Never. Word was sent out by the priests, but no trace of him was ever found. He disappeared off the face of the earth."

"So somewhere in this broad land you have relatives that you have never known."

"That has been a part of my loneliness." Resolutely, she put down the bit of lace she'd been torturing in her hands. "That was the common ground Rebecca and Ruth and I walked. As little girls in the parsonage they used to run to the door at every knock and scrutinize the face of every caller, believing that someone of their own was coming for them. I do it still. I look into the face of every old man who passes on the street and I wonder if he is my uncle. Now, Ben, I have been cruel. I feel that I have made you suffer when I wanted only to tell you how deeply grieved I am over the loss of your parents. You don't look well. Why, your skin is hot."

Outside, the sound of hoofs pounded up the drive, and Marie jumped to her feet to look out the window. Snatching Ben's hand, she pulled him to the door.

"There is my beautiful Jules! Do hurry."

Ben stood watching as Marie ran to the man who stepped lightly out of the fine carriage. He looked upon this man whose name he'd known all of his life, whose handwriting was more familiar than his uncle's, and whose letter of long ago had changed the lives of all of the Brewsters of Virginia. Marie tugged him forward.

"Here is Adam Brewster's boy Ben for whom we have waited so long!"

Jules took Ben's hand in both of his. As they were the same height, Ben looked into the twinkling black eyes so like Olivia's. This tall, dark-skinned and mustached finely dressed man with his elegant fur-lined cloak and jeweled sword-sheath in no way resembled the carpenter-apprentice described so many times by his father and by Oner.

Olivia and Adam raced across the wet grounds to the carriage. Oner, who had just walked out the mission door with Father Diaz, rushed to embrace his long-lost friend. Jules insisted upon going immediately to the wagons to greet the slaves he felt he knew from Rebecca's letters.

When they were settled inside, Jules, like Olivia, swept them along with his enthusiasm.

"I certainly will not take no as your answer. We have waited too long. You must all come down to New Orleans for the celebration."

"I wish we could, Jules, but we have a long way to go. We're moving upriver to ferry across at Vicksburg."

"I will not hear of it. Besides, Marie tells me that you are not well. The instant we get into New Orleans, I shall have my personal physician look at you."

Ben thought about the tobacco wagon; he needed the money it would bring, and New Orleans was his best chance to get a decent price for it. And the slaves had waited many years for their passing-through New Orleans. In truth, he was in no hurry to see his uncle. And he did not feel well, not up to the long trek to Texas.

Father Diaz promised to have his stock cared for, and placed their wagons in stables just vacated by carriages returning to New Orleans. And so, dressed in the best they had, they jammed into one wagon with the tobacco cart trundling behind. In the coach ahead he could see Adam talking with animation to the LeFleurs. Huddled sickly down in a quilt beside Oner who drove, he looked back into his memory and wished this were an earlier time.

Chapter 8

THE CANTINA

Companionably, Aaron and Jacques rode side by side down the dusty trail to Loredo.

A short distance behind them and guarded by three grey eyed Acadian boys, trundled the wagonload of goods that Jacques would sell in Mexico. Glancing back at it, Aaron tossed back his head and laughed.

"I swear to God, Jacques, if I'd known back in Virginia that you and Jules were blasted pirates, I might have fainted. Certainly I would not have come halfway across the country to associate with you."

Jacques's eyes laughed. "And now, even with your precious nephews on their way here to Texas you wouldn't stay home even though Ruth urged you to do so. And I know your reason. But I was not fooled by you. I took one look at you in New Orleans and I said to myself, 'There is a man I will have as a rival for the courtesies extended to me by the lovely and generous Spanish girls below the border.' And I wasn't wrong. You bedded the very one I'd been looking forward to for months."

Aaron nodded, remembering, and smiled.

"And you claimed she was the first outside of your marriage bed. Come now, man, admit it, aren't quite a few of those not so black children yours?"

"No, Jacques. I grew up under my father's principles. I do not bed my slaves, nor shall I."

Jacques shook his head with mock seriousness. "I do sometimes wonder where you got the impression you have of Robert Brewster. There never lived a man—except Jules and myself, of course—who enjoyed life to the fullest as did your father."

Aaron's head twisted on his neck as he studied Jacques's

face for a sign that this was another of Jacques's jests.

"Believe me, many a trip we made into the bordellos of Norfolk. He was highly respected and welcomed."

There had been a time when Aaron would have yanked Jacques off his horse and beaten him within an inch of his life for that remark against his father, but now he mused. His own hot blood fired by their trips into Mexico had to come from some source. If he were completely honest with himself, it gave him pleasure to think that his father enjoyed a life beyond the plantation.

"Eli Salem could have told you. His store is the courier's stop, and news of new arrivals of girls in the port cities always showed your father that there was need for more plantation equipment, and off we would go, riding the hell out of his fine horses. Why did you think he raised fast horses?"

"Jacques," Aaron could hardly speak for laughing, "next to Jules, you are the most demoralizing man on the face of the earth. And, the most refreshing. You put new vigour into this quest."

"I had not intended leaving so soon with the houses still unfinished, but after you wrote to Adam and Ben, I knew they would obey your summons. It occurred to me that in setting a fine example for them, you would feel obligated to live by those standards and thus put an end to our ventures. I admit I could go without you and will many times, but it is not the same down there without you. I have ceased to be a wonder to the Spanish, but you with that imposing structure of yours stir them beyond imagination. The reason I make sure you dance with the one I shall bed is..."

"That's quite enough, Jacques, and I am not too sure it is true."

Still, he was vain and Jacques's praise of his prowess pleased him and had often urged him on to even greater conquests. The challenges were not the border girls, but the high class, well raised Spanish girls in Mexico City. They excelled even above the fine quadroon beauties he'd visited with Jacques in New Orleans.

Now he frowned to himself. If he figured timing correctly,

from Ben's letter, the group would now be moving into New Orleans. How old was Ben? He was himself now thirty six years old. It was hard to believe this was 1814. Ben would be sixteen and young Adam, fourteen. They were grown. He had been thinking of them as children. Thank God they had Oner to guide them... In a flash he saw his brother Adam on the long trek into the Mississippi Territory. The only fire Adam had ever shown was the day he crossed the Chattahoochee. Aaron had felt pride for Adam then, even if his bravery before the slaves had put Aaron in an uncomfortable position.

Jacques had never owned slaves and could not understand that a master had to stand high in their esteem. Aaron had not ignored many a shapely figure or an inviting smile entirely because of high standards, but he had known from the hour of his father's death that those people were in his hands, on his hands, and the responsibility had hung heavily on him. Had he bedded one of them, as Jacques so crudely put it, he would never again have been able to receive their respect, yes, and their allegiance. Now his hand crept to his cheek, felt the raised scar left by Adam's whip. God, he could have killed him then, would have had he not controlled himself with all his strength. He remembered thinking, "Which is worse, to accept this cruel blow manfully, or to strike back and knock the young fool off his horse?" His better judgement had won. Manfully, he had turned over to Adam more than half of what he had received for the plantation. He had permitted Adam to ride out into that river before the eyes of all of his slaves and retrieve his sons. Doubtless, that had been a mistake, although he believed he had gained more respect from the slaves by his act. Later, he should have returned and forced Adam to move on. He could have then insured himself that Adam gave Rebecca more sons instead of hiding behind his books. Well, he had a second chance now. He would see that Adam's sons married strong healthy girls, and his own father's dream would be fulfilled. Ah, the plantation he would have on that rich black land! Even now, sitting his horse crossing this dusty plateau near the Rio Grande, he could feel the moist soil crumbling in his hand.

"It sure will, Master Aaron," Trunk had said, wagging his huge head. "It will grow cotton higher than those live oaks and soon. Just let us get at it."

"The land must be cleared first, and the homes built."

"Yes, sir," he said, eager to plunge into the soil.

Together, standing near the cypress swamp, they had planned a system of irrigation ditches that would enrich their land when east Texas dry seasons tortured the lands.

"I thought that Acadian country the wettest, most rich country I'd seen, but this sure beats it, Master Aaron. Well, a shame we lost all that time. I like to had to beat the boys to stir them out of that paradise when you finally sent word for us."

It had had its compensations though. The slaves had propagated. He couldn't count the little ones toddling around that would be eager pickers when the cotton was ready.

Trunk had been dead set upon going back across the river to lead Adam's party forth. Trunk was a fool about Oner. Whether or not he cared about Adam, Aaron admitted he did not know, but Trunk and Zilpah acted like lost souls after they had been parted from Oner at the Tensaw ferry crossing.

How a man's steps are influenced by others. Had Adam not found that wretched little trader, the party would have moved on into Mobile where doubtless Rebecca's child could have been saved. It would have saved Aaron years of worry and grief. He had spent the first years in that dugout in a depth of despair, thinking over and over what his father would have thought of his leaving Adam in that wretched, isolated and utterly defenseless country and surrounded by Indian nations on the north, east and west. Of course that miserable trader had assured him that Fort Mims and Fort Stoddard were well manned in case of Indian uprisings. God, what he had suffered when he heard of the massacre! That word spread. Isolated Fort Mims caught off guard at noon, one thousand Creek warriors. He shook his head. He didn't realize that Adam's spread was so far away, nor that his "stockade," as Rebecca referred to his fence in letters, was sufficient protection against the red devils. Well, it hadn't been. It took but a small band to kill Adam and Rebecca. The fool probably had his head buried in a book. Indians were clever. He had warned Adam in a letter not long before. "Don't be smug, Adam," he had written. Had Adam listened to him, he would have been long gone from there.

Still, he had to confess to his conscience that with one thing and another he had been slow in preparing for Adam and his party and had not urged them forth. Certainly, if he had, Adam would have come, and would be alive now.

With a shake of his head, Aaron tried to put aside the fearful picture of Adam and Rebecca lying dead in that yard back in Alabama, but the image had not faded. He had seen too many of the dead left behind right here in Texas. And he'd paid them off. He had ridden hell for thunder after many a fleeing maurauder and seen him die. But that hadn't helped in any way to remove from Ruth's mind the terrible blame she had placed upon his shoulders.

When the news came that Adam and Rebecca were dead, Ruth had looked at him once, and turned away. That scathing, burning look had stayed with him. It was as if a part of her had died. He could not understand why she blamed him so entirely. Where had he gone wrong? He had to get Brewsters out of that wild Indian land. He had had to go on. He had no choice, none whatever. Still, deep in his heart, in some hidden recess that he could no longer reach, lay a memory of a boy who ran his errands, who looked upon him as some kind of God, and he had loved him, truly and deeply. He would take his hand and lead him back to the slave quarters to listen to the singing. Adam had been a sweet and pliable child. The change had come shortly after that cold bitter winter night when Robert Brewster died. With his death, the full responsibility of the plantation and the slaves had rested upon Aaron's shoulders. He had done his best, but the land had been worn out when he took it over. No, regretting was all very well, but with the problems he had had to face in his youth, and without guidance, he had done what he had to do. He would not accept the burden of guilt, and one day he would wipe that blame out of Ruth's eyes. A man could not live and prosper with that hanging over him night and day.

When Jules's letter had been placed into his hands that morning in Eli Salem's store, Aaron had felt elation. He had thought it was money owed Robert Brewster, and that he could pay off his debts, which were many. When he sat on that wagon seat and read the letter, and studied Jacques's maps that were enclosed, his elation had known no bounds, for the way had been prepared for him to cross over the barriers, the mountains that had hemmed him in, and the barrier he had built for himself upon his father's death. Aaron had not one iota of regret for his decision that had been instantaneous. He had been horrified to learn that he could not bring his slaves into Spanish Texas, but that blow had been lessened by his first trip to Mexico City with Jacques where they had been greeted like traveling kings. He knew the permission had to come from Spain and would be long in getting there. He admitted to some distrust of Jacques when his land title was not clear to the Texans, but that had meant a second trip to Mexico City, an extended and blissfully pleasant visit.

Upon their return to Texas they had traveled up to their grants. Seeing it for the third time, he had been enchanted by the sheer beauty of the land, the rolling hills, the great live oaks, the opulence of the growth of the wild greenery, and the promise of water from the swamp. He and Jacques had fashioned a boat of cypress and paddled deep into its bowels where only the wild cries of birds and the occasional leaping splash of a fish broke the deathly stillness. It had reminded him of Trunk and Oner's tales of their pilgrimage to rescue Zilpah. He and Jacques had returned from that excursion and strolled down the great swath of tall pines to plan the laying out of a plantation and a town, a town he hoped someday would be a city of his planning. When Trunk, with his negro sense of the dramatic, had arrived, he stood in that long lane of pines and said, "Master Aaron, this is the Evening Road."

Aaron had laughed. "You're not that old, Trunk. What

then shall we call the plantation?"

Twinkling, Trunk had not hesitated. "Noonday."

Noonday it had become, not that they had much to show for it yet...

Their horses were stepping gracefully down the bank to the brown, flowing Rio Grande. Jacques chuckled.

"I wondered when you would come back from that battle you're fighting. Aaron, friend, learn one more lesson from a Frenchman. Conscience is very fine, if a man can afford it. Ah, there is Loredo, filthy, dusty, and..." He kissed his fingers, and flung them outward toward the sprawling border town.

As they swept up to the door of the cantina, a buxom and dark-eyed woman strolled out to meet them.

"Welcome, Senor LeFleur, Senor Brewster!"

Chapter 9

SOUTH WIND

Desolate, and frightened in spite of Olivia's attempts to cheer him, Adam hunched down in the elegant brocade chair. From behind the closed door of the next room Ben, delirious with fever, raved that Jules was a pirate, which was embarrassing with Olivia listening. Straining, Adam tried to hear what the doctor was saying to Jules.

Across the room Olivia squirmed in her chair. "Adam, it isn't yellow fever. Mother has seen enough of it to know. And Doctor Pierre's taken care of all of us all of my life. He'll tell you, then we can go." Jumping up, she ran to kiss his forehead lightly. We've waited forever for this. Petit Garçon's down there with the carriage." Tugging his hand, she pointed out the window. "There's all New Orleans waiting. I want to show it to you."

Easing out of the too-small chair, Adam stood at her side. Even with Ben so ill he couldn't take his eyes off her. Her head didn't reach his shoulder. Sunlight caught red and blue glints in her hair, like a blackbird's wing in the rain. "Why didn't you grow more?" he asked. The Conterey girls were almost as big and strong as he and Ben. She was dainty and fragile looking. "You're fourteen. You should be..." he held out his arm to measure.

Stretching up on her toes, her head almost touched his arm. "I'll grow a lot before I'm sixteen." Pleading with her tantalizing eyes. Not once in all the years they had corresponded had he imagined her beautiful. Sweet and charming, yes, but not this exciting girl who made him feel taller than his six feet and grown up already. He cleared his throat.

"And when you're sixteen?" They'd been over this routine up at the mission in Baton Rouge.

Her eyes lowered. The thick lashes lay like small black wings on her cheeks. "When I'm sixteen, I'll marry you," she said softly.

Now he became very righteous and stern. "We'll have to clear up this pirate stuff Ben has been raving about. I can't," he began his father's imitation of his uncle Aaron. "I can't have Brewsters marrying into pirate families."

Her eyes became fierce. He clung to her hand, sorry he had jested.

She jerked away. "My father is the finest and most honest man in New Orleans! You'll learn. Most businessmen and even planters upriver have bought Baratarian goods for years. Besides, you don't need to worry about the future. I may not marry such a stuffed head after all, but for your information, the Baratarian warehouses are no more. The guards destroyed them before the British landed. Oh, you're impossible!"

Backing away, she curtsied politely. "I'll tell Petit Garçon to put away the carriage. Coffee will be served downstairs when the doctor comes out. Do make yourself comfortable."

He watched her run lightly down the tile stairway, one small hand trailing the wrought-iron balustrade, then ran to the window to see her talking with Jules's shriveled little driver.

He stared out over the town. New Orleans, the magic name that made his skin tingle when his mother talked of their stopover on their way to Texas. A city of trampled mud streets, narrow; a close jumble of strange buildings with metal balconies; the tall spire of the Cathedral where one day he would travel back from Texas to marry Olivia. Would his mother have been disappointed in New Orleans? Glancing around this elegant suite, he could imagine her turning to look at her reflection. She would have been wearing the pale green velvet gown, and would have seen herself in that elaborate gilt-framed mirror. She would have loved it, had they come long ago. He glanced backward, eastward, and wished it were another time.

Olivia ran back into the house. Would Ben go on to Texas when he recovered? Last night he had shrieked at Oner,

"What kind of man is Uncle Aaron that he would live on blood money? For isn't that what pirate gold is?" Jules had thrown back his head and laughed. Marie LeFleur had turned white. Oner had blinked questioningly and tried to placate Ben who had no idea what he was saying.

He whirled as the door opposite swung open. Doctor Pierre stepped out smiling. "It is malaria, I am relieved to tell you. When Petit Garçon came for me, he assured me that there was a yellow fever case here. After just finishing fighting a war, however short, we have many injured and dying, and a yellow fever epidemic was unthinkable at this time."

"Is he terribly ill?"

"Yes, but he'll survive, and with the medication, be well in a short time."

Adam stuck his head inside the door. Oner looked relieved. Jules, still smiling over Ben's outrageous shrieks against Jules's character, took Adam's arm.

"An old friend of your father's is having coffee with us, Carter Ewing from Natchez."

Adam knew the name. Ben talked about him often, about his racetrack that he'd seen when they sold horses to Ewing.

Carter Ewing expressed his deep regret that Ben and Adam had lost their parents.

"I regret, too, that Ben is ill. He's a fine young man, and always welcome on my plantation. I hope to be able to extend my invitation to him before I leave for home. I'm in town briefly to buy hardware and grillwork for my new home."

"I suppose you planters will miss Baratarian auctions," Jules mused with an eyebrow cocked at Adam.

"We certainly shall, and now with this slave shortage..." the planter shook his head.

Olivia discreetly lowered her cup to look at Adam for the first time since they parted at the top of the stairway.

Bright sunlight slanting out from the buildings caught the dust particles swirling from the horses' hoofs. Ben's face flushed with pleasure.

"It will be wonderful to see Mr. Ewing. I'm so glad you met him, Adam."

A small, furred man tore out from a group on the corner to race up to the carriage. "Ben! Ben!"

Petit Garçon stopped the horses.

"Ben, how I searched for you and Oner after the war ended the other day! Did Jules tell you that I sent you word that my spread is up for sale? I'm traveling upriver to trap the far northwest with old friends I found during the fighting. You must stop off to see it on your way west. There's no one I'd rather have on my land."

After dinner that night Carter Ewing and Jules checked the location of Pete's spread on their maps. They found it good. During that week they helped Ben close the deal, delighted to have them stay on their side of the river.

Ben wrote his letter to Aaron three times before Adam approved it. Anatole would carry it to Texas. It was brief, stating merely that they were not coming on to claim their father's land, they loved the river country and would raise cotton on the land they had purchased. Only two river crossings and the trip by wagon would separate the families.

During the letter writing, Oner stood staring out the window at the lowering sun. Understanding how it was with him, Adam pressed the older man's hand. It was all right. They would stay. Ben was well again, and this was what he wanted. He was happier than they had seen him for a long time.

What a long trek upriver it was. Wet, briar-scraped, muddy and weary they found the marker that Pete had placed when he went upriver with his friends. Adam stared at the horrid mired cabin, at the jungle of vine-wrapped trees to be felled, at the lake where the river had swept in to cover the entire front area of the land. But Ben stood, eyes glowing.

Oner looked from one boy to the other, then touched Ben's arm. "It'll be fine, Master Ben, just fine."

To Adam the only thing fine about it was that he was closer to Olivia than he would have been in Texas.

Ben's land lay north of Natchez, south of the loess cliffs of

Vicksburg. Pete's description of the bottoms had been exact, but it was a long time before they could begin clearing to plant. Shelters for humans and animals had to be built, trenches dug to drain the land which fortunately tilted back toward the bottoms. Pete had used his cabin to clean pelts. Adam and Ben backed away from it and knew that as far as they were concerned, it had no value. While the land drained, they built cabins. Men, women and children began the long task of building up the levee, a rampart of felled trees, logs, roots, branches, rocks, stones and even the evil-smelling cabin, all solidly packed with pebbles and earth. A gigantic task.

By then it was too late for them to plant. Carter Ewing came up. He was a naturalist. He told Ben which trees and bushes to preserve for landscaping, what to send upriver to the Vicksburg saw-mill to be saved for Ben's first house. He helped transplant red-bud and flowering plum, taught the negroes the edible fish of the river, but the sweet cat was already their favorite. Before the chill of the next winter they were out shooting deer, racoons, rabbits, squirrels, and even an occasional wolf that threatened the stock. Nothing was wasted. What couldn't be consumed was smoked for later use. The women made warm linings and coats of the pelts. Snow was rare, Carter Ewing told them, but the chill dampness along the river penetrated.

Little Jessie, son of Milcah and Joshua, salvaged Pete's rusty traps. Fascinated, he cleaned and oiled and repaired them. He and Adam set them out. They learned how to cure furs, and Adam sold them up in Vicksburg for shipment down to New Orleans.

All through the first winter everyone big enough worked in the bottoms. Women transplanted plum, wild cherry laurel, herbs and roots of Milcah's choosing, for she had learned at Zilpah's knee, blackberry, dewberry, horehound, ginger, sassafras and glistening holly to the space alotted behind their cabins.

Mattresses were made of moss. Choice magnolia, cypress, pine and oak were saved. When there was money the logs were hauled up to Vicksburg for milling. In January early vegetables were planted. By spring they had learned to rub oil on red-bug bites. On a trip to Vicksburg Milcah learned from a Chinese storekeeper that sulphur powder rubbed on the body and worn in shoes discouraged red-bugs and scorpians. They were all young. This was new country to them, but they were learning.

That spring the flood waters stayed below their levee. A wharf was built, gardens planted, a field of Indian corn. When the cottonwood trees bloomed in March, the first cotton seed was put into the ground.

Ben decided they should stay on in the crude cabins to spend all spare time clearing on into the bottoms. Carter Ewing told planters along the river of their fine wood. It began to move away from the wharf almost as fast as they could cut it. Money was known again. It was their own, earned by the sweat of their bodies from their own land. And it was good. Ben was exalted. He had fretted about his father's horse money lost in the fire in Alabama, for they had needed it badly.

Ben laid aside the necessary amount for staples he had to buy. "Look, Adam, I can pay Oner part of what I owe him."

"That's good, Ben, but I think Oner would be much happier if you gave him time off to go to Texas to visit Trunk and Zilpah. He's homesick for them."

Ben looked up aghast. "But I couldn't get along without Oner. One day when we are settled and all going well, we'll all go to Texas to visit." He looked across the river. "Now I can understand why Uncle Aaron has never had time to visit us. A man building up a plantation has no time for gallivanting."

Enchanting September. They all trouped into the bottoms to pick the first cotton crop. Adam felt the first soft bolls in his hand, and it was like holding a fluff of cloud. There was more joy to raising cotton than tobacco, he decided, remembering the sticky juice that seemed never to leave his hands. But they were new at it. The cotton didn't look like much, baled crudely and stacked on the wharf waiting for the boat to take it into Vicksburg for ginning, but Ben was proud.

The boatman brought letters, many from Olivia, one from Jules in that slanted script so familiar to them all. Jules wanted to bring up fixtures and hardware that he had been saving for their planned house. Ben's heart had been set on a white and pillared mansion such as Pete had shown him downriver, but it was the dog-trot style they finally decided to build Pete's magnolia trees, two flatboat lengths from the river on a rise with a splendid view of the bend. They planned two long rooms running parellel to the river with porch, floor to ceiling windows facing it. The back rooms were set aside for kitchen and pantry use. Beyond the airway would be two bedrooms. Adam chose not to look at the river and the west.

Jules came up and helped them lay the foundation, but Ben wanted to build the new slave houses first. All that winter houses identical in plan, each with a stone fireplace, were built. They stood all in one line so that anyone facing down saw small porches over and over and over one after the other.

Jules had been long gone. The fine hardware he brought to them lay covered in a shed with the boxes of their father's books and all their goods from Alabama. It was time again to plant. The rains were heavy. Ben had an attack of malaria, not as bad as the first, but so bad that Oner made the boys move out of the drafty shack into his new house. It would not stop raining. The river swamped over the levee, seeped toward the fine cypress floors of the new houses. The ditches were cleaned and draining attempted, but still the rains poured on. They raised the levee, reinforced it. Planting was late.

Now Jules came back to help build the house, for he was first a carpenter, and second a pirate, and third a gentleman but most important, he told Ben, he was a friend. But Ben was alarmed by the flooding. He wanted safer stables for the horses. The land was wild; fox and lynx had been caught in Jessie's traps.

Finally, in November 1818, their first house was finished. On Thanksgiving day, Adam and Ben began unpacking the crates and barrels and hogsheads that had not been opened since their father nailed them shut back on the White Feather Creek. A great fire glowed in the kitchen where wild turkeys roasted on the spit. Women made berry pies and sweet potato pies. The fragrance was maddening. Outside, little boys scampered up oak trees for mistletoe, and little girls carried in red and golden leaves and great armloads of bittersweet.

Ben sat on the floor beside the warm fireplace pulling up boards his father had nailed into the book crates. As fast as he unpacked the books, Adam wiped from them the accumulated mold, and placed them upon the unvarnished but hand-rubbed shelves. Unfolding a faded scarf, Ben held out ebony picture frames. The boys studied the aged tintypes, their parents' wedding pictures.

"What do you suppose this is?" Ben held out a small box that had no weight whatever. Carefully, he lifted from the cotton a small white feather.

Milcah came in from the kitchen. Wide-eyed, she stared down at it.

"I often saw mother holding that box," Ben mused.

"That feather dropped from the wing of a wild bird passing over when Master Adam was burying your sister that was born dead on the Tensaw. He named the crick he built on after that feather. While your mother lay sick in that bed at Mims Crossing that little feather was all she had to comfort her."

Looking down, Ben gasped at the sight of the strong box. Milcah and both boys stared at it. It was grating with rust. Ben took out his knife and worked at the edges. Milcah trounced back to her pies.

When Oner came in with an armload of bittersweet, Ben and Adam were staring into the strong-box full of money.

Oner smiled, and shook his head. "Master Adam would be happy to see that. It's his horse money. I thought it had burned in the fire or been carried off by the Indians."

"It was packed with his books." Laughing, Ben held out a

handful. "Now, Oner, I can pay back all we owe you."

"And if you can spare me, and little Jesse can get shed of his traps, I'd like to go to Texas to see Trunk and Zilpah."

Ben chewed his lip, his eyes pinched. "No, Oner, wait. We'll build a real house, a fine one, and invite them all over here."

They spent Christmas in New Orleans. After much deliberation, Ben and Jules decided upon a rambling Spanish style two-story with large airy rooms, arches, beamed ceilings and balconies. Adam and Olivia found hand-carved double doors from a Spanish house being demolished. Jules returned upriver with them and stayed to finish the house Ben named South Wind.

The plantation, South Wind, prospered. Inexorably, as relentlessly as the surging currents of their river, the years swept past. Adam's restlessness increased, for he wished to marry Olivia. He stood looking out over the river. Every year since 1818 he had told Olivia it would be this year for sure. He was like Oner and his dream of going to Texas. Each of them put off their own dreams because Ben was ill, Ben looked bad, Ben needed them: he was working too hard. Adam tried not to worry him, or to upset him.

Now, in this wet spring of 1823, the heavy rains had waited to fall in torrential cloudbursts, accompanied by wild tornado winds. By early May, great currents rushed down the river, hurrying it beyond its normal sluggish flow, swelling it out over the banks, washing out the levees.

It was June before the storms let up, but the river flooded on. They worked by day, by night with torches on tall poles, digging, carrying trees to build up their levee, but from the lowlands above and below the plantation, their ditches filled. The houses stood in a broad, moving lake. The heat came, humid and oppressive. Ben was hollow-eyed, exhausted. Adam begged him to rest, urged him to let him take him to the doctor in Vicksburg. Ben refused. Two nights later, he collapsed. Adam and Oner carried him into the house. Adam sent two boys on horseback to Vicksburg for the doctor, but the road was a quagmire and the river impossible for travel. Adam walked the floor, wringing his hands.

In torment and anger and frustration he said Ben's name over and over. What had driven Ben to work as he did? Let the river take the place; it had been working at it ever since their first year there, moving in, taking a bite, drawing back, flowing peacefully only to rampage into flood when they felt secure.

Ben's breathing was difficult. He held his head high while Milcah let vapors of steam from a kettle pass his face. Nothing they could do helped. Ben never rallied from his coma. When Milcah turned to him, Adam screamed out, ran to the wall, beat on it with his fists.

"Oner, no, not Ben! God, don't let him be dead!"

Oner dragged him down to the kitchen, made him drink strong whiskey. "Mister Adam, you're on your two feet. From now on to God knows when you gotta stay on them, go on the way Ben would have you do."

"I should have made him stop... Should have taken him up to Vicksburg."

"It isn't your fault. You did what he wanted you to do, worked to try to save the land he loved."

All through that tortured, endless night they worked to hold the levee. At dawn the flood waters spread wider and wider. Oner and Adam sat in exhaustion to stare across the rimless, reckless torrent, to stare at the negroes still leaning to the hopeless task.

A great surging anger tore up through Adam; he wanted to tear out the levee, made the river take South Wind the way it had taken Ben.

"Oner, why didn't I beg him to go on to Texas that long ago day? He'd still be alive if we had gone on."

"He wouldn't have gone, Adam. This was his... what he wanted."

"What drives a man, Oner? I've never felt that unrelenting drive to do anything."

"If you had, you'd have been just like him, or like Aaron. A man follows his will, Adam, and Ben's was to build a fine plantation, to raise cotton."

"Well, he did it, and for what? And now we must bury him in this... this mud."

The river withdrew, quietly, calmly, little by little, and the banks lay massed in a deep carpet of violets so fragrant that the scent was wafted aloft on the breeze. Oner and Adam looked back upon the vast purple carpet as the flatboat taking them to New Orleans for Adam's wedding to Olivia made the bend.

Chapter 10

RIVERBOAT

The golden lamp-glow of Natchez reached out across the sable river, faded beyond the bend, and then only darkening silhouettes of trees reflected against the violet evening. Oner felt a sharp sting of pain, for the evening brought back a morning long ago when he had led the grief-stricken Adam out to a flatboat to go down to New Orleans to marry Olivia, and now here he was aboard this shining new palace afloat. Music from the salon flowed into the rhythmic plash of wheel-turned water. The murmur of voices from the dining room became lost in the plaintive, poignant cry of the steamboat's whistle.

"The last sentence, again, Oner. It's almost dark," Olivia pleaded, holding the French textbook close to her chest.

He took one more look at the strange words. "Je ne regarde jamais les femmes," he said, watching her lips forming the words. "Miz Olivia, upon my word, I was never meant to speak French. You don't think Amelia is going to expect me to, do you?"

Her laugh rippled lightly, a warming sound after her terrible mourning since Jules's death.

"No, Oner. I just wanted your proposal to be romantic, if you wish it to be. It need not be at all. Amelia knows you are doing this for Camille's sons, my father's sons, Oner, so they can bear his name, so I can have them at South Wind to care for them."

"Don't suffer yourself so much, Miz Olivia. I understand."

"Now, you know the plans? Petit Garçon will meet the boat at dawn to drive you. From the church you are to take a hire-carriage. Wait at Amelia's home until I send for you."

He nodded. "I'll have breakfast aboard until Petit Garçon

returns to take me home. We will start for South Wind as soon as I have mother's things packed. I don't want to be away from Adam any longer than is necessary." She looked at him pleadingly. "All mother needs be told is that Amelia will relieve Sarai of much of the cooking. True, unless you wish it otherwise." Her gaze dropped from his face.

"I'll see, Miz Olivia," he said quietly. "I'll see." He straightened. He'd been hunkered beside her deckchair looking into the book she held between dainty white kid gloves. He tried to remember the French words.

Closing the grammar, she stood up, fluffed out her cape, shivering. He hesitated. He ought to tell her how much he had told Adam, that he hadn't been able to leave without giving him some warning.

"I just might bring home a wife, Mister Adam."

"Why, Oner, you old devil! So that's the reason you've been so pleased to make all those trips with Olivia." Shaking his hand warmly. "If you do, first-house will be yours." They stood looking at Ben's pride of long ago.

"She has two boys, Mister Adam," he said. If Adam knew he was marrying Amelia who had cared for the boys since Camille and Jules had died in the same epidemic, he didn't know what Adam would do. Adam never got over his shock of learning that Jules had been a privateer. No, he couldn't tell Adam the whole truth. Nor could he tell him that his name would soon be changed from Oner Brewster to Oner LeFleur so Jules's boys could bear his name.

"Why, Oner, that's wonderful. Then you shall certainly need first-house."

It hadn't been easy not to be entirely honest with Adam. Now he looked at Olivia.

"You get in out of this dampness, Miz Olivia. Mister Adam trusts me to care for you." He winced for the things he was going to do. He felt they were against Adam and all that he stood for, but he had agreed because Olivia had no one else to call upon in her need. As Jules lay dying, she had promised to care for his sons. Camille had died two weeks earlier. Amelia, Camille's youthful mother, cared for them. Olivia tried to stretch the money Adam gave her to run her mother's household into enough to feed Amelia and the boys. Marie LeFleur was too ill to be left alone. The trips back and forth had been wearing on Olivia. When Adam suggested that she bring Marie to South Wind, Olivia thought there would be money from the house sale to put the boys into a school, but there was no money left when she paid Jules's final debts. Jules had made money and gave it away. Oner had learned about him during his trips to New Orleans. Not a day passed that someone didn't come by the house or the shop when Oner was clearing it out expecting the money that Jules always gave or loaned.

Oner looked down at Olivia. It was a mystery to him how so fragile a form could fly about the plantation, manage the big house, teach lessons and the Bible to the black children and to most of the grown negroes, to their good natured chagrin. Joshua called her the "teachinest, Catholicist woman in the world."

Now her small gloved hand lay in his like a gardenia.

"You were wonderful in Natchez, Oner. It was lovely of you to be baptised, to change your name, to make this sacrifice for me."

"It's all right, Miz Olivia. I just missed being baptised by Father Diaz back in '14 at Baton Rouge when I went on to New Orleans with Ben. I've just delayed that part for a while."

He didn't want her to know how hard it had been for him to agree to change his name. He had always been proud to be Oner Brewster.

A vision of the warm-eyed radiance of Amelia made his act insignificant. Never in his deepest dreams had he imagined having a talented, dazzling woman as his wife. Her background made the quandary he had been suffering since Olivia asked him if he would, if he could go through with it. Sensing this, Olivia stressed that the arrangement need never be more than the ruse it was to allay any of Marie's suspicions should they arise.

She pressed his hand. "You do understand how it was with father, don't you, Oner?"

She looked out over the water.

"You understand about women like Amelia and Camille? It's a custom, like meeting at the market for coffee to discuss trade. Amelia knew no other life. She raised Camille on the same high standards of conduct that her mother raised her. Father saw Camille with Amelia at a quadroon ball. She was one of the most beautiful girls in New Orleans." She looked down. Oner pitied her. She had always had to protect her father's honor. Handsome, debonair, light-hearted Jules. He remembered how she had stood up to Adam for him long ago.

"Now just you stop fretting. I already know Amelia to be a gracious and lovely woman, and the finest cook I've known. No offense to Sarai."

"No wonder Adam adores you. Now, propose beautifully."

"Je ne regarde jamais les femmes," he repeated solemnly.

"Oh, Oner, you're so good. Adam would never have survived Ben's death without you. Goodnight, rest well."

Holding her elbow, he led her to the door of the women's corridor. "Bon soir, Madame Brewster."

Her eyes glistened in the light from the lanterns. "Lovely, Oner. Bon soir, Monsieur LeFleur."

He winced, and her hand flew to her mouth.

"Oh, Oner, we have exchanged names!"

He walked away, head bowed.

The night was chilling, black. The south wind was dying. Soon northwest winds would blow October into November.

Oner sat on the deck, leaned against the wall under the window behind which Olivia would sleep. String music from the salon throbbed into him, as from some far distance, reaching an unknown hurt. He was going to have a woman—beautiful, educated, intelligent.

He pulled his coat close. He'd never known a woman. He'd lived within himself from a child-slave torn from his mother's arms, dragged to a ship, shackled to the deck, was befriended by the girl Zilpah, the boy Trunk, sold with Trunk in Florida, escaped from two masters with him—slipped through deeper darkness than this night knew before he was eight years old.

He still remembered Robert Brewster lifting him. "A little more food, Oner Brewster, and you'll be a husky boy. The plantation needs a blacksmith. You'll make a fine one. You're free. Neither you nor Trunk will ever be slaves again. I have never been an advocate of slavery, yet I have slaves. Men are a confusion within themselves." Later, as he grew a few years older, he was to hear the story of how Robert Brewster brought those dark-eyed boys from the harbor in England, paid their passage and brought them with him into Virginia to save them from being indentured servants. Yes, Robert Brewster loved freedom.

Where had the years gone? Had he actually been needed as he felt needed? *Hail Mary, full of Grace. The Lord is with thee*... Awkwardly, he made the sign of the cross. He was going to be married. He couldn't believe it. Marveling, he held the beads the priest had given him.

The river was back in its course, flood waters receded, levees repaired, broken trees cut and sawed... how many times since the spring of 1815? Oh, Ben, how did you know it was your land? How did your father recognize that stream over in Alabama? The look had been identical, unmistakable...

How do you know what is your own?

Sometime in this dark night he would pass that big white house that Pete had pointed out to Ben. The sight of it rising up from the black trees would tear his heart. He couldn't forget Ben. He couldn't get over Ben dying. He lived it over and over within himself.

Stirring stiffly, he wiped his eyes on his coat sleeve to stare at the white mansion arising in wavering magnificence into the morning mist. Soon the steamboat whistle would jar awake Petit Garçon, the wizened child-man who had been Jules's trusted carriage driver. He would stumble from the carriage that was still grand to the wharf and squint through slitted, tired lids.

He stood up, walked around the stern, and raised his eyes to the black western sky.

"Trunk, oh, Trunk, now I'll never get to Texas, never."

The whistle echoed sadly.

Chapter 11

TAWNY RIVER

Adam opened his eyes slowly. Olivia had closed the draperies at dawn when she slipped from the room to steer the whole plantation along its journey to noon when Aunt Ruth and her youngest, Cecile, would arrive at the dock. Uncle Aaron, for the second time in a decade, was sending them with Trunk and Zilpah to safety from war-torn Texas. He had missed their first visit. They arrived at the same time his company landed in Mexico.

He stretched his leg which still gave him trouble; he had taken a Spanish ball in that skirmish. He had his friend Grey Rider, Captain of the Vicksburg ferry, had enlisted together. This time Ri's sons were over there fighting. Thank God David, Charles and young Adam weren't old enough to go. Damned wars. It seemed as if they would never end. Sometimes he felt that he was tumbling down the years of wars.

And the years were going fast. It seemed only yesterday that Olivia had arrived home from New Orleans bringing Marie. And Oner brought his beautiful new wife Amelia and those strange black-eyed boys Louis and Bertrand. Now Louis was practising law in New Orleans and Bertrand was in the import-export business. Amelia had been a blessing to the plantation and to Oner. She had given Oner three children—the exquisite Madelaine, and Honor and Albert, the pride and still unbelievable delights of Oner's life. The mystery of it all had been why Oner changed his name from Brewster to LeFleur. Adam, looking at those wiry black-eyed boys had figured it out once long ago, but Olivia had been so happy to have them up here that he kept it to himself. A man's decisions were his own, and anything Oner did had to be to a strong purpose. Jules was in it somewhere. Every time he looked at Louis, he remembered Jules.

He placed his hands behind his head leisurely and smiled at the sound of Olivia's and Marie's voices down the hall in the linen room. Marie talked excitedly in French. Evidently they were choosing table linens. Olivia's laughter tinkled. He lay listening to the twitter of children playing around the picnic tables Oner had finished yesterday and placed on the lawn. His own last child, Ruth, sounded as if she bossed whatever game the children played. From the kitchen unbreakfast-like scents drifted; cakes. Crab bisque, he could almost taste it, creamy and tangy in Amelia's flaky pastry shells; turkeys and hams roasting, Sarai showing her art, not in competition with Amelia whom she adored, but to please Trunk.

Reaching down, he lifted his leg. He and Ri had been going to "see Texas." He'd been carried home in a litter instead. Now he considered the possibility again. He could work up something about taking Ruth and her party home once things quieted down over there. He'd never given up wanting to go, never settled in here at South Wind. Why, I'm like my mother, he decided.

He was warm. Bracing himself, he reached the drapery and flipped the end of it over a chair. Heavy oppressive air crept into the room. Blasted fog hung over the river. It must not be as late as he thought. He glanced at Marie's porcelain clock that she'd insisted they have in their bedroom. Nine o'clock. Ri's boat would arrive by noon.

A hand tapped the door knocker. Oner pushed a dainty French tea-cart inside. "Amelia sent up your breakfast."

"Doesn't want me in the way," groaning at the sight of Milcah's liniment bottle sticking out of Oner's hip pocket.

Oner pushed the cart to the side of the bed. Sitting on the edge of a chair, he poured Amelia's deliciously aromatic and thick coffee into hot milk and handed the cup to Adam.

"How's the leg?"

"Better."

"When you finish, let me work on it. You'd be proud to

walk without your hobble stick when they get here. Course, you might want to limp worse so Miss Ruth will start in on their dry climate being good for you like she does in her letters."

"Still itching to go, aren't you, Oner? Well, so am I. We would have made it in '40 if it hadn't been for that hurricane."

"Yes. I almost had Amelia talked into it then, but she's like Miss Olivia. They both say they belong on this side of the river."

Heads bobbed as Adam passed the quarters. If he went across the river with Ri to meet the wagon, they'd all want to go. They couldn't wait to see Trunk and Zilpah. But there wasn't room on the boat for all of them. Moving carefully over the damp floor of the dock, he sat down on a wrought iron bench just as Ri's boat slipped up out of the mist.

"Hey, Adam, you're not going to miss seeing them this time. Going along over?"

"Thanks Ri. I'll wait here. What's the word?" Ri's sons had volunteered, left in July with Jefferson Davis. The last letter was written when they were being drilled on Brazos Island. It was now almost September.

"Up Vicksburg we hear Davis is giving them hell. Wish you'd go along across."

A warm gust from the stoker crossed over Adam as the boat headed out into the invisible river, the whistle sounding.

The picture he had of Aunt Ruth was a composite made up of remembered words of his mother's and Ben's, her letters to them in Alabama and to South Wind. Olivia said their own little Ruth now tearing down the bank toward him was her image.

"Aren't they here yet, father?" Wiggling, she crept close. Her eyes teased. "Cecile and I don't have to go with mother and Aunt Ruth to Alabama, do we?"

He'd planned three trips for the women to keep their minds off the fighting in Mexico. He knew Ruth yearned to see where they had lived on the White Feather Creek, and

Olivia was anxious to see Louis and Bertrand in New Orleans, and all had been invited to the Carter Ewing plantation downriver.

"You'll miss a lot if you don't go. Unless you want to stay here and assist me in slave inspection."

"Father!" Aghast, she turned away at his teasing. Olivia always took her indoors when inspection started. And he was stalling. The inspection was long overdue.

"You could hand out Doctor Craft's Tonic."

"I overheard mother tell Grandmother Marie that you should stop giving that to young girls."

"Oh, you did. Say, here comes Ri."

The whistle sounded. The boat loomed up, wavery. On deck he could make out a wagon and a team. Laughing and sobbing, the negroes tumbled down the bank. Oner took Adam's arm. While those on shore waved and called out, the forms on deck sat erect, a picture painted upon a cloud: grey mist, grey wagon, dark team, an immense man holding the reins, a diminuitive brown woman in a shawl, a woman and a young lady in grey sunbonnets and shawls. Men raced to help lead the team off the boat. How austere they all looked, how proud. Aunt Ruth, her bonnet stiff in spite of the fog, took Oner's extended arm.

"Adam. Oner," her calm voice embraced them. In her composed face he found his mother's grace, her same clear eyes, smudged by black lashes and brows, deepened and sorrowful. Dark haired, black eyed Cecile laughingly snatched up little Ruth, and ran, hugging her, up the bank to Olivia. A fleeting memory rose up of another river, another time, as Trunk, arms outstretched, eyes streaming tears, strode toward him.

The fog-enclosed kitchen was warmed by the voices, the sound of the names familiar only from Ruth's letters: Ara and Antoinette had taken their children and many slaves into the Acadian country. Marie and Aunt Ruth talked of New Orleans, of Jules and Jacques and days gone by.

Trunk, hunched over a cup of Marie's special coffee, talked softly of his Uncle Aaron. "He's known clear to the Llano Estacado as the white man with the scar, the most feared, dreaded Indian-killer of Texas, famed for tracking down Indians known to have killed white settlers if it took him years to do it." Adam's heart went up to those high plains he would never see. "He's a running man, Adam, full of bitterness, a man unfulfilled, untamed, with eyes always westward, revered by settlers, admired by all men, envied by many. We'd best get the Alabama trip done with before the war ends, before Master Aaron gets here, because he would have them leave within a day—not that he doesn't hold love for you, but... he can't show love. He loved your father. He thought he did right, Adam."

"Somehow I never visualized him like that. To me, in the only memory I have, he was stern and stiff, not at all like my father."

"No, he was never like Adam. He is not home a day before the light fades from his eyes. He's gone before I wake up. He comes home browned almost black, his fine white hair and beard, and those great white eyebrows covered with the red-brown dust of far west Texas, his eyes squinched to slits, ready to go again. His very soul seems to cry out, 'kill, kill,' until he can avenge the murders of your parents. What? Blood money worry Aaron Brewster? Why, Adam, his eyes were like stars when he came back into Acadia from Mexico City that first time. And when Anatole came out there with your letter that you and Ben were going to stay on this side of the river he repeated what Ben said when he was sick in New Orleans. He tossed back his head and laughed..."

Long after Oner came to take Trunk and Zilpah to the feast Amelia had waiting, Adam wondered what his uncle asked of life when now even the high plains hemmed him in.

Late that night after the house and grounds had quieted, when only the soft strains of Simeon's guitar and of voices singing reached them, Ruth Brewster and Adam sat talking.

"Although my heart cried for Rebecca, I wasn't sorry your father settled in Alabama. We were all so jammed in at Antoinette's, so wretched. And the years, Adam, before we could go on into Texas. Rebecca was so sensitive, I don't think she could have borne up under the trials. And it was rather dreadful our first years in Texas in the dugouts. Aaron wanted them to come, wanted Adam to claim his share of the land, but his pride... Oh, Adam, don't ever be prideful—not that I think you would be—but his pride wouldn't let him send for you all until Jacques finished a fine house for you. It's still standing, good as new. We house guests in it when we have overflow... There is so much I want you to tell me about Rebecca..."

Their words flowed on. She sat holding his hand. "And to think that I haven't set eyes upon you since that day your father took you from my arms on the Tensaw ferry. Why, you must be almost fifty years old."

"I'm forty-seven, Aunt Ruth."

She smiled, rising. "And I am very old tonight, my dear Adam."

Weeks later he watched the party leave for a visit with the Ewings. Ruth, rested, with her hair arranged by Madelaine, wearing a soft green traveling suit made over from one of Marie's, was beautiful as his mother had been, but stronger, and of a different courage.

By September Charles, Adam and David were in school in New Orleans. He wanted them home; but Olivia insisted. The long winter dragged into spring. In May, while Olivia and Ruth and the children were visiting again with the Ewings, Ri whistled at the landing. Adam knew it was good news when he saw his face.

"Adam, my boys' enlistments are over. They're safe! They're coming home. I'm going down to New Orleans to meet them. If the crowds along the banks equal those of our times, God knows when they'll get home if I don't go for them."

"I'm going with you."

In the fall of 1847, Adam and Trunk stood on the levee watching the muddy river sweep past. The war with Mexico was over.

"We'd best get that Alabama trip over with, or Master Aaron will be here."

"Yes, I haven't hurried Aunt Ruth into it. She wants to go, just to see it, to visit their graves, but she hesitates."

"If it's all the same to you, I'll see to the wagons."

"Better take a carriage or two, Trunk."

The dark eyes lighted. "I've been wanting to ride one of your horses. They remind me of the strain your father raised."

"Direct descendants. And I want you to take some back to Texas."

After the party left for Alabama the next day, Adam looked over the plantation. He wanted everything to be to Aaron's liking. It was unmercifully hot, but he knew he had to hold slave inspection. He'd put it off for so long now that the negroes had forgotten about it. It was too hot to hold it in the large building that served as workroom, storeroom, commissary—whatever the need was. His father used to hold inspection right out in the fields or on the lawn inside the stockade. Ben was the one who had insisted upon holding them indoors.

He hardly knew how to begin without Milcah; he should have held it before she went with the women to Alabama. Jethro and Joshua carried out the big table, Milcah's medical bag and the big crates of Doctor Craft's Indian Herb Medicinal Tonic, and the unlabeled bottles Milcah filled with some concoction she got back in the bottoms from an old freedman.

Slaves, washed and wrapped in towels or sheets, started down to the table. Considering how many went to Alabama, there seemed an awful lot of them. They kept shoving Jeffy, Jethro and Sarai's youngest son, to the front. Glancing uneasily down at Jeffy's swollen jaw, Adam reached for one of the unlabeled bottles. It would be inhuman to take that boy's tooth out without giving him some medication. Come to think of it, he'd never pulled a tooth that wasn't loose. Jeffy's infected tooth was firmly stuck up into that sore jaw. Wincing as he examined it, and a little nervous since he wasn't used to holding inspection without Milcah, he handed the unlabeled bottle to Jeffy, and let him take a long swallow. The boy's face brightened. Adam poured a little into a glass, sipped it, and sputtered. He tried it diluted with water, and it was still stronger than anything he drank on the rare occasions with Ri, or at the house when they had guests.

He opened the record book, dipped the pen. *Jethro.*

With a worried glance at Jeffy, Jethro moved to the table. Fine specimen, Adam wrote. Proud of it, too. *Removed splinter.*

He wasted minutes sorting through Milcah's ointments, wondering which she would use, and studying the big tweezers he'd used to pull Jethro's splinter to determine their strength in yanking a firmly set tooth. Teeth were slippery even when they were loose. He glanced down at the book. He hadn't finished Jethro's entry. *Paid: one calf and clothing allowance.* All he'd been hearing since the Mexican war ended was, "We wants to look nice for you when Master Aaron arrives." Aaron had certainly built up a reputation among the slaves.

Peleg: deep chest cold again. He couldn't be faking that wheeze. "Go to bed," handing him a pint. Then he wrote, *Dosed good with castor oil.*

Serug was too thin. He handed him two bottles of Dr. Craft's, and one unlabeled bottle.

Simeon. Remembering the fallen tree, he motioned Rip to get the package from the kitchen. Digging into Milcah's instruments, he found one that looked right to remove the blackened toenail struck by the tree.

"Hold your foot with both hands, Simeon. Press it against the table," fortifying himself with another sip of the liquid from the unlabeled bottle. "Close your eyes. No, I know you haven't, but I've never pulled one off, either. There." Simeon gasped softly. Slapping a pad of dripping turpentine on the toe, Adam handed him the odd-shaped bundle.

Simeon touched it. "Oh, Mister Adam, a new 'jo!" His banjo had been smashed when the tree came down.

The pen scratched on. *Simeon, color bad. Afraid to dose with castor oil—bulging intestine. Took off big toenail.*

Studying the pliers, he laid them aside; could grip a tooth. Refilling his glass, he handed the bottle to Jeffy. The problem was whether to jar the tooth loose—maybe pound it? That would hurt like the devil. Jeffy, who had watched the toenail operation apprehensively, now studied Adam and the pliers, his head cocked to one side. Adam watched him take another long swallow, and decided he'd better have another, too. He tried to recall how Milcah held a head when she pulled a tooth. Giggling, and carrying the bottle, Jeffy followed Simeon away.

Jesse, he wrote, *received from Jesse six bits for the strongbox.* Jesse had been saving ever since their fur trapping days. *Jock, son of Joshua and Milcah; dosed castor oil; and paid for shingling Leah's chicken run.*

"Master Adam, can I marry Madelaine?"

Adam studied Jock's serious face. He'd have to keep an eye on Madelaine while Oner was in Alabama.

Garrett, son of Jethro and Sarai; finest human specimen on the plantation. Ax wound healed. Shame that boy never saw Madelaine's eyes following him.

"Jeffy?" taking another sip, he glanced around, found Jeffy leaning comfortable against the tree near Simeon who tuned the new banjo. Aware of the sidelong glances from the men gathered around Simeon, Adam took another sip. Devils: usually after inspection they raced to dress to go up to Vicksburg and spend their money. Simeon's soft voice caressed the morning:

"Don' look to the tawny river..."

Now why did Milcah have to go to Alabama? Sighing, he poured a straight shot of this bottoms-potion. It wouldn't have hurt one of his sons to stick around and learn how to run a plantation.

Zib, son of Serug and Zibeon. He looked up. "Oh, Milcah doesn't give you that sized cup of castor oil? Well, show me the cup she does use."

The women were starting down. Usually by this time the men were dressing. They were all going to stick around to watch him pull Jeffy's tooth. Glancing at the group, he saw Jeffy singing, a sweet, far-away expression on his face. He felt a little that way himself.

The first thing he wrote in the women's page of the ledger was: *Pay Milcah extra upon return; she's earned it for helping with inspection.* Come to think of it, she had done all the doctoring. All he had ever done was look and thump.

Sarai; dropped kidney. "Sarai," he asked softly, "have you ever pulled a tooth?" Shaking her head, she hurried off to do the kitchen work.

"Zibeon, have you...? Yes, Milcah always..." *Two bottles Dr. Craft's,* he wrote, *clothing allowance.*

Leah, paid egg money.

Aretha, wife of Jessie, daughter of Simeon and Leah, baby due soon. Four bottles Dr. Craft's. He counted on his fingers. Milcah would be back in time.

Michelle, unmarried daughter of Joshua and Milcah, leaning back and rubbing his chin as she grabbed her sheet and wrapped it around herself.

"I want you to put that money away for me, Master Adam. I'm not going to Vicksburg. Amelia's teaching me to make my own dresses." Too bad Bertrand didn't look around last time he was up here, Adam thought, his ears buzzing strangely.

Ruby, unmarried daughter of Jethro and Sarai, three bottles Dr. Craft's. Who gave her those earings?

Sassie, daughter of Jethro and Sarai, gave yellow hairbows, two bottles Dr. Craft's. He glanced up. "Do I have what? Now what made you think I had a sore tooth?" shoving his glass to the back of the table.

He glanced over at the tree. Damn those negroes; they were going to stick around until he pulled Jeffy's tooth.

Sarah, daughter of Jethro and Sarai, move up to the adult list. He handed her four bottles Dr. Craft's.

Tibatha, daughter of Peleg and Tamar, he wrote, and handed her four bottles Dr. Craft's. "Straighten up, Tibby."

"Yes'suh. Does babies just come to growed people?"

Adam nodded, reaching for his glass. With a wide sweep of his pen, he wrote across the page, *Stop giving Dr. Craft's to girls.*

"Rachel, you do? Which one?" Reaching in, he rocked the tooth. Taking off his coat, he placed one arm around the girl's head, picked up the implement that had worked successfully on Simeon's toe. Nothing to it. The tooth came straight out. Relieved, he took a long drink. "No, Rachel, I do not have chest congestion." Frowning severely, he gave her red hairbows.

Dressed for Vicksburg, the women began bringing down the babies. Behind them, hat on the back of his head, Jethro strode to the tree, plucked Jeffy from the crowd, and carried him to the table.

Jeffy giggled. "You don' have to pull that ole tooth, Master Adam. I wanta sing." Rolling over in Jethro's arms, he hugged him. Jethro's mouth was set.

With immense dignity, Adam picked up the short strong pliers, and taking a deep breath, placed them around the tooth, closed his eyes and drew back. A crunching sound made him sweat. Now the men were gathered around, looking over his shoulder, faces set seriously. He replaced the pliers, felt around them with his fingers, then yanked. He looked inside Jeffy's mouth. Reaching in, he lifted out the tooth and handed it to Jeffy who studied it proudly. As the men passed the table, each one reached down for another bottle of unlabeled tonic. Wiping his face on his sleeve, Adam closed the ledger.

Inspection over, jammed slave wagons rocked out of the bottoms. Adam sat out on the dock. The sweet chords of Simeon's banjo stirred him, disturbing a peace he'd managed long ago to lay within himself. Simeon's voice, pulsing with longing, fell softly upon the stillness:

"Don' look to the tawny river; Texas is ever lost. Don' look to the yaller river, 'cause you'll never cross." Sobbing in the voice. Damn Simeon's hide. Hellbent to go back to Texas with Aaron. "We jest wants to see it, Master Adam. Jest wanta see Texas." So do I, Simeon. Turn your back to the river, Adam. You choose; you lose to gain. Olivia belongs to this side of the river...

He could see the river flowing under the dock. It was tawny, golden in the sun. A yellow river flowing peacefully, or rushing to drown out the plantation. A tawny temptress to entice, a cruel siren to allure and sweep away the fascinated; a cruel killer. He stared at the graveyard under the Chickasaw plum trees, enclosed by the wrought iron picket fence. First Ben, then three little boys who played too close to the levee.

He strolled up through the grounds, seeing it as Aaron would, as he had seen it himself so often coming upriver to the docks. Ben's dream had materialized. The big house, with its Spanish arches, wrought iron balconies, flowing, hanging flower baskets, stood elegant under the great live oaks and magnolias. Trimmed cherry laurel hedges grown tall hid the bottoms where cotton had flourished or failed, depending upon the years. The levees and docks were almost always new, washed out and rebuilt, higher every year.

In front of him, silhouetted against the lattice-work of the summerhouse, Madelaine's graceful hands worked with Marie's hair. How good she was to Marie. Olivia often remarked that Madelaine inherited Amelia's beauty and grace, and Oner's gentleness. Her eyes were a mystery: liquid, luminous, blue-grey flecked with black and brown. He glanced at the sun. On Saturdays Amelia served luncheon on the terrace near the summerhouse. He hadn't heard the bell. How quiet was the plantation. Tree limbs wickered. The river sang on softly, so softly he could hear the plink of oak limbs in the water.

"I'll run for Master Adam." Peleg's voice came from the quarters.

"I'm here, Peleg."

"It's Simeon, he's takin' on awful bad."

"Not his toe?"

"No, suh, it's his insides..."

All the rough way to Vicksburg Adam cradled Simeon in his arms.

"When Aaron comes, we'll all go to Texas for a visit."

"I jest sang that to tease you."

Leah sat outside the doctor's door while Adam listened to his opinion.

"No, Captain Brewster, it certainly had nothing to do with the tree accident. That tumor in his colon had been growing for a long time. I doubt if he..."

Adam and Leah sat on in the hot room. The slaves he had rounded up had finally gone home. Simeon opened his eyes.

"Leah, honey, give papa his new 'jo." Lovingly, his hands touched the strings. "This got better tune than the old one that got broke."

Adam walked out into the night, stared out across the river that stretched endlessly in the moonlight. And that was another thing—they were all getting old, all of them who had come from Virginia, from Alabama. He hoped Aaron would hurry. Simeon wanted to see him just once more before...

Chapter 12

WHITE MAN WITH SCAR

The lines between Aaron's heavy white brows deepened as he rode beside the crooked Virginia-rail fence, so new he could smell the pine. Drawing his horse up sharply, his mouth spread in an unaccustomed smile as he recognized Jeddy's Jacques-taught hand in the burned lettering of a sign swinging over the tall gate, "Noonday Plantation, owner Colonel Aaron Brewster." He nodded. His sons had beat him home or Jeddy wouldn't have known.

Tearing out of the cowbarn, Jeddy opened the gate. "Oh, Gawd, Master—*Colonel* Aaron, I was never so glad to see you in my life!"

"What the hell did you do, Jeddy, fence all of Texas?" Jeddy stood grinning, his eyes moist as he looked over the new uniform, the clean, trimmed beard and mustache, the smile. "I been riding this fence for miles."

"I wish Miz Ruth was home to see you."

"Looks like you were trying to fence me out, or was it in, Jeddy?" For years Jeddy had been begging him to stay home with Ruth, to let the younger men chase the Indians and fight the wars.

"No, sir, jest trying to keep the cows in. With near everybody gone..." he said wistfully.

Jeddy had wanted to go with him. He had had to put it to him straight. "It's your herd, Jeddy, your life's work and savings, and my land and horses—all our homes. It's up to you. It's as big a job to stay here to protect it as it is to fight." All Texans expected Indian pillage while battles raged to the south. He saw tragic signs of it all the way home. He glanced at the houses, the barns and stables.

"No Indian trouble?"

"They stole ten of my cows, then I started hanging your name all over the place. Not one Indian since."

"Jeddy, you know damned well those Indians can't read. Cut 'em out of my herd. You fence the swamp?" The negroes feared the swamp. He blamed it on Trunk's weird songs.

"Some, along the outer edge. Plenty water in the lake."

He jerked around to look at Jeddy. "You fenced around the lake?" When he left Jeddy had been ready to buy his freedom. The land that was to have been his included half the lake, crossed the road with the pines down to the monstrous tree a small wide-eyed Jeddy had inadvertently named. When he had first seen it he exclaimed, "Gawd, what a great live oak!" Down the years in Noonday it had become known as "God's Great Live Oak."

"Sho." The dropped eyes, the shy smile were reminiscent of a younger Jeddy.

"Where are my boys?"

"Young Mister Aaron's already gone uprange to check on the horses. Royal, Robert and Rayford left with Jacques for Acadia with the thought to see their families, set a spell, and then..."

"I know, go on to New Orleans. Well, they earned it," shaking his head. God, how proud old Robert Brewster would be of his sons.

Jeddy took his horse. Aaron strolled down the fenceline, leaned against the rough wood so redolent of the pines...

He was proud of his sons, happy they were not like him. Black-eyed Cecile was another matter. He hit the fence with his fist. All right. She'd paid him back. She had her pound of flesh. He sighed into the fast-cooling evening. Somewhere beyond the hills west of the lake a thunderstorm formed. The darkening water and the reflections of the black pines shivered, licked by the quickening winds. Great black thunderheads rolled and tumbled across the broad troubled sky.

"Can I be satisfied now? God knows I've fought enough." He stared beseechingly upward at the sky.

He had traveled far, far west, back and forth across the Pecos more times than he could count, chased Tonks clear to the staked plains, ambushed and wiped out the devils; trailed Apaches—Mescaleros—to the Rio Grande, lost them in the pass to the north, found them by their hunger smoke high in the bare mountains; fought the Cherokees under Houston; raced furiously after the Comanches headlong into the Battle of Plum Creek avenging in a small part the ruthless killings in the valley of the Guadalupe. Alone... how many had he chased alone? How long since he had followed five murderous savage creatures to the Clear Fork of the Brazos?

It was 1847. Sixty-nine years old. Fifty years since he married Ruth; thirty-four years since Adam and Rebecca were murdered. Young Aaron was forty-eight. That would make Adam past forty-five. God, how he hated to face him. It was the one thing in life he dreaded. Without seeing him since the Tensaw, Aaron knew he would look like his own brother.

Gigantic streaks of lightning flashed down the sky, showing it a pale yellowed grey-green, and a cold wind swept over him as hail fell somewhere upon the prairies beyond the hills.

He hit the fence again with his fist. If he could go in tenderness to Ruth waiting at South Wind. If he could find some way to wipe from her eyes that expression, still unchanged since the day she got word about Rebecca and Adam. She had collapsed before she heard his words, "It was my brother, too, not just Rebecca." He stared up at the sky.

"I thought I was doing right, don't you see, Ruth? I wanted you and Ara and young Aaron safe..."

Why is it I can say this to the sky, and not ever to Ruth? Did she hate him? Can you hate a man and still, at almost fifty, bear him a tender child like Cecile? He struck the fence again, a crushing blow. Would he wonder every time he looked into Cecile's black eyes?

How long must a man regret? How many times he had walked alone deep into the nights, black nights where no star glimmered, wild nights when snow slashed him, when swift winds whipped him, high, blue-black nights so clear stars were within reach of his hand, hot blistering nights under searing winds from the Mexican plateau—walked, wishing he could undo what he had done.

How many times did he stand alone hundreds of miles west of Noonday and loved ones and beat his chest in agony of remorse? Why had he left Adam and Rebecca behind? Why hadn't he turned back after he got Ruth and his own children to safety? He hadn't worried too much about it when he was younger, when he and Jacques were tearing off to Mexico, but as he got older, his guilt had increased, suffocating him. His hand traced the scar down his cheek. That was not his reason.

How many times had he said to the wind, to the night, to the sky, "Adam, I deserved this scar. Adam, I'm sorry. Forgive me." But never to Adam. He could have written it to him. But he hadn't. Why not? Was he too proud to tell Adam at first that the land grant was worthless, that he had to go to Mexico to beg for the land? That he had had to go back to gain permission to bring his slaves into Texas? Had he traded his brother's life for pride? Or had his enchantment with Mexico been his reason?

What forms a man? What molds him? How did he become what he was when the letter came to Virginia from Jules all those long years ago? What made his heart race wildly at the dream of coming west? How did he become what he now was? An inherent trait? Jacques said that. Weren't his dreams his own? Why did Robert Brewster cross an ocean? Why had he, Aaron, wanted beyond all else in life to get around, across, away from his great blue barriers? It was not for the riches that he read of in Jules's letter that made his eyes feverish. Somewhere back in his heart he had always known that Jules and Jacques were scoundrels, unprincipled pirates. He had not been in the least shocked to learn what they did for their livings.

And what had made him leave Ruth and her children with strangers, which Antoinette and her people, however kindly, were then? Afterwards, Ruth, it was always the Indians, or the wars. Do you understand? Can you understand? God, how he'd fought. As if a devil chased him....

"Colonel Brewster, I got a meal ready."

"Goddamn it, Jeddy, call me Aaron like you always do. How'd you find me?"

Gently, Jeddy took his arm. "I said to myself, Master

Aaron, he goin' down to the cabins. He gonna get messed up with nigga' liquor, and he goin' to ruin that fine uniform he had made jest to impress Miz Ruth and young Adam over across the river."

"You don't talk like that, Jeddy."

"No'sir."

"Where you going, Jeddy?"

"I thought I'd amble down to 'cadia, see if Laurel all right."

"If you were really interested in Laurel, you'd have married her years ago. Serve you right if she's married to some Cajun when you get there. No, you saw me headed out south instead of straight out for Louisiana, and you figured..."

"Yes, sir. I looked into your eyes and I figgered, 'Master Aaron, he headed down the Evening Road now, he almost seventy. He goin' back all the way to Alabama to tell Mister Adam and Miz Rebecca that he gon' walk that Evenin' Road straight, and make Miz Ruth happy. He gonna..."

"You figured that out?"

"Yes'sir."

"Jeddy, sometimes I wonder I don't kill you."

"Yes, sir," he said softly.

"You figured that I'd stop off in Acadia long enough for you to crawl in with Laurel, then we'd have a stopover in New Orleans and on up to Alabama before we hit South Wind."

"Yes, sir, I figgered that."

"Well, Goddamn it, Jeddy, either I talk in my sleep, or there's something to that voodoo stuff."

"Yes, sir."

"It's a damned shame a man can't think his own thoughts without some nigger reading them."

"Yes, sir," he said sharply.

"Damnit to hell, Jeddy, ride up here beside me so I can look at you."

"Yes, sir."

They stood in front of the irongrill gate staring into the

140

patio that once was Marie and Jules's. "Could be yesterday, couldn't it, Jeddy? I wish it were. You know that, Jeddy?"

"Yes, sir."

"Where did you and Trunk hide that night I was trying to round you all up to go on to Texas?"

"You mean when we come across the territory?"

"You know very well when I mean, Jeddy."

"When we followed that funny little trader with all the little horses with their funny sacks? And that little Indian boy with my blue beads?"

"Jeddy."

"Yes, sir, I sure do remember that trip."

"I asked you where you hid."

"Trunk never told you?"

"I never asked him. He's bigger than I am, but I could lick the hell out of you."

"Yes, sir."

"Goddamn it, where *did* you and Trunk hide?"

"In your wagon."

"You mean to tell me you were in my wagon the whole time?"

"No, sir. Not the whole time. *First* we were in your wagon. When we knew for sure you were goin' on without Mister Adam and Miz Rebecca and Oner, we tore down to the church, that one with the tall spire."

"We looked in there."

"We snuck out while you were lookin', and run like the devil for that cemetery behind the wall."

"The Saint Louis cemetery?" Aaron threw back his head and laughed. "God almighty!"

In Alabama the sumac was turned. Up and down the hill between the scattered black pines and the yellowing sycamores great blotches of reddening bittersweet sparkled in the morning sun. They crossed a stream, a frothy creek, white with foam. Only the birds and the soft stepping of their horses and the occasional lowing of cattle stirred the peaceful quiet.

Aaron saw the hillside first, bright yellow in dried corn

stalks, once billowing with the dark green of tobacco. Part of the stockade still stood, used now as a horse corral. Tops of fine stables could be seen. The long house and outbuildings, now white-washed, brought back remembered sentences from Rebecca's letters; *Surrounded by these poplars Adam kept for shade.* The poplars were gone. Live oaks shaded the house. The garden lay blooming in tall stock and drying asters. Rose bushes dotted the yard.

A tall, bony woman stood in the doorway. Aaron removed his hat. Jeddy stepped back.

"I'm looking for the Conterey house, ma'am."

She stepped out, a homely woman, one who had never been pretty and knew it.

"I know you, sir. You could be none other than Aaron Brewster. You have your brother's look, though many years have passed." Her tone was soft, reflective. "Miz Brewster said if her party lingered too long I should expect you. My father..." She stared at him. "What's the matter, sir? Are you ill?"

Aaron wiped his brow. "I didn't realize my wife was here. We came straight from Texas."

"My father took Miz Olivia and the girls with the slaves to Mims Crossing on the Tensaw. Miz Brewster didn't wish to go. If your boy will take your things inside, I'll show you to your wife's room. It was once Rebecca's."

She placed the lemonade pitcher in his left hand and two cups in the other. "Can you carry it all? Just follow the stream. The graveyard is under a large oak. My mother and sister rest with your people."

Ruth sat on the ground under the tree, her head resting against its broad base, her eyes closed. Her hair shone, had been arranged differently. She wore a fine green suit of a fashion he'd never seen. How well she looked; how peaceful.

"Ruth, Ruth darling..."

Her eyes opened slowly. "Oh, Aaron, I'm sorry. We have stayed much longer than we'd planned. The countryside is so beautiful." She reached for the pitcher. "Did Adam come down with you?"

She poured with the grace he had always admired.

"Jeddy and I came straight from Noonday. I have..."

Her eyes looked down at the lemonade. "I understand, Aaron. Now," she said, "let me look at your new uniform. How fine you look!"

"You look different, younger."

"Rested, don't you mean? I've had a long vacation."

"We need a holiday together. You could do some shopping in New Orleans."

Her surprised eyes met his. It had been a long time since he'd asked her to go somewhere with him. "Olivia must get back."

"If you want to go back to South Wind, we could take the steamboat up from New Orleans." He knew he was stalling. He suspected that she knew it too, but her eyes shone.

"I adore the steamboats. Adam sent us down to visit the Ewings aboard one. And I did so enjoy watching them pass the plantation."

"Ruth," his head resting in her lap, his voice tight. "Can you forgive me?" Finally.

He felt purged, renewed, emptied.

One March 1848
Noonday

Dear Olivia, Adam and children:

How often we think of you all, and remember our wonderful visit. It was good to get your letter. I fear that I have some lonely days ahead. In fact, I'm thinking that I shall accept your kind invitation to return soon. My sons, and Aaron, are wildly discussing the discovery of gold in California. The girls are reconciled to having their husbands leave, but I find it difficult to see Aaron go at his age, even though he assures me that he is just going to see California, and will return soon. Trunk and five young slaves plan to go with the men. You should see the wagons packed and ready. How very reminiscent of our trail wagons of so many years ago.

Should Aaron decide not to go with the boys, I feel

sure that Trunk will not go either. In this case, and dear ones, I pray it will be this way, perhaps Aaron and I will come soon, bringing Trunk and Zilpah. And Jeddy, if I can pry him away from his herd. Aaron regrets that we did not after all make it upriver from New Orleans.

Can you imagine how much I miss Cecile? I am delighted that she chose to attend the school you attended, Olivia. And, for many reasons, I'm frankly happy that she has become Catholic. She is very much in love with one of the fine Acadian boys who visits here with Antoinette's family. Had Aaron not stayed home with me, I could not have borne up under the strain of her leaving at the same time the boys Jacques and Auguste traveled to Virginia to school, and Ara's whole family moving to Acadia. What a changeling year this has been for me!

Ruth laid her pen on the blotting cloth and stared out the window at the half-finished addition Jacques was building on the house at Aaron's request.

"But Aaron," she had remarked, "with the children gone, we need less room, not more."

Was it pride? Had he compared the exquisite home of Olivia and Adam that Trunk had been so enthusiastic about with their plain farm-type two-story house built above the original dugout? He should be proud of it. She was. She looked up at the beautiful beamed ceiling, at the chalk fireplace. After their New Orleans trip, Aaron wanted fine new furniture, paintings... He'd insisted upon buying an amazing assortment of useless but decorative items for their home. He had just given her a large amount of money to buy new furniture while he was in California, even suggested that she take Olivia to New Orleans for a holiday and shopping. *Oh, Aaron, if only you knew how satisfied I am with the plain old table Laban made, and with the fine heavy chairs!*

If only you knew how much I want you to stay home. What if you become ill on that long journey? There were great wide spaces to cross, unwatered deserts between Texas and California. Their route was planned out across the

Texas plains to El Paso, westward across the newly acquired territory, across that spaceless desert, up the Pacific coast to San Francisco, inland to the gold. *Oh, Aaron, we don't need gold. When Jeddy gets back with those fine wild horses, you'll have planty to do taming them. Stay. Don't go, Aaron. Let the boys go. They've worked all their lives doing your work while you chased Indians and fought wars. Now you stay home.* But she wouldn't say the words to him, she could only hope. She could only look at him and hope, and not let him see the hopes, the dreams she had allowed herself to dream since that day in Alabama.

Wiping away a lonely tear, one of few she had ever let herself shed, she picked up the pen. Outside a tremendous uproar startled her, and she stood up listening.

Jeddy had been gone to far west Texas with many of the neighboring ranchers to collect stray and wild horses. Aaron had asked that Auguste, who had his father's keen sense about horses, ship many from Virginia to improve his herd. Horse sales had improved agreeably since the war. And cows were moving too.

She sat back down to add this new excitement to her letter:

Jeddy is back, I believe from the commotion outside. How I wish you could see our strange western cows—so stringy and tall, with great horns. I would never in the world say this to Aaron, but when I look at one, across a fence, believe me, I often think how like him they are around the eyes, some unexplainable expression—untamed, unbound, ready at a gust of wind to follow it.

I hope this finds you all well and happy, dear ones. Tell Leah I think of her with compassion many times during my days. Simeon was always one of my favorites. Poor Simeon. Alas, so many of us are aging. Who will be next, I ask myself. Our own cemetery is growing too rapidly. Let us hope that your magnificent river remains within its banks this spring...

Aaron's voice ripped in through the window. "Jeddy!" She couldn't tell if his voice was raised in anger or surprise, but upon the bellering of wild cows, she ran to the door.

Laughter, thank goodness, great guffs of laughter.

"Get those damned skinny cows into the corral, Jeddy, before they trample those children! Jeddy, get that big one out of Ruth's flowers!"

Ruth gasped. The yard was full of wild lanky Texas cows, pushing and wedging and gouging toward the corral, trampling hedges, her little patch of grass, her sweet williams and all the rabbits had left of her delicate phlox. Sighing, she did have to laugh. The big awkward cows, so wildly beautiful, so untamed, and being pushed by little Jeddy.

His hand on the gate, Jeddy stared accusingly at Aaron and then to the packed wagons, his voice, every line of his body vibrating.

"Master Aaron, you goin' with the boys? After what you promised me?"

"Goddamn it, Jeddy, mind your own business!" Aaron shouted harshly, then accusingly. "Just for a little while. The boys can stay on to hunt gold. I just want to see..." His eyes were slits. His gaze traveled beyond the low hills, westward.

Jeddy's hand fell from the gate. He stepped forward, and put one hand on Aaron's knee and one on his saddle.

"Don't go, Master Aaron. Don't go. Miz Ruth so happy, so satisfied since you stay home."

The wild cows shuffled nervously, jamming and milling toward the gate. Aaron's horse danced. He reined in tight, and leaned down. "Damnit, Damnit to hell, Jeddy. I'm going to California!"

The gate crashed open. Ruth screamed. "Aaron!"

Jeddy grabbed for Aaron, tried to snatch him from the air as he was thrown into the path of the stampeding wild cows.

Jeddy's scream was a shrieking, dreadful cry, forever unforgettable.

"Oh, Gawd, I done killed Master Aaron! I done killed Master Aaron! I done killed Master Aaron!" And it rang and rang on in her ears, while she held her hands over them and screamed.

"Jeddy, it wasn't your fault. It was an accident."

"He didn't want them wild cows. I did. He sent me for

horses. I was scoldin' him for leavin' again." Oh, the awful sobbing. The silent crying. The dark night. The wild storm. The lashing wind. The great jagged darts of lightning through the rolling black sky, the terrible earth-shaking thunder. Aaron would have loved it.

One brilliant flash outlined a small figure running crookedly toward the swamp.

"Jeddy," Laurel screamed. "Jeddy, come back!" Ruth screamed, running after him.

Chapter 13

CROSS OVER THE RIVER

Adam slept fitfully. He would sit up with a start, hear the pounding rain, the rolling of the wind-lashed trees. How many days since the new ferry operating from the Louisiana side fought across the rushing current bringing Aunt Ruth and Trunk? Six days and six nights of crazy wild daggers of lightning, rumbling thunder, sporadic hail, steady downpour, the unceasing wind. On the fourth day the fine dock built after the flood of '51 cracked, split to sweep away. He couldn't rest, even though it had been seven years since the river had washed up over their high levee.

Olivia slept peacefully. He was grateful. The past years had been hard on her. It hadn't been easy for him to see Marie slip patiently into death, to make that bleak and sorrowful trip to New Orleans. And they had held each other long into the night after Charles's letter came from Charlottesville. He loved Virginia, and had accepted a teaching job. Weekends he visited his cousins Jacques and Auguste who had stayed on there to buy the old Brewster plantation where they raised horses.

Adam tried to remember his home back there, but found he could not sort out his own faint memories from the descriptions Charles had written. Charles was collecting material from old Brewster neighbors and townspeople, some of whom remembered the wagons rolling out of the circular drive to cross the Roanoke, the Bannister, headed out of Appomattox county. Charles planned to write the history of their family and slaves. He hoped to travel west on his next vacation to talk with Aunt Ruth and those of the group who were still living. He asked Adam to inquire if his cousin young Aaron Brewster would part with grandfather

Robert Brewster's ledgers. Auguste said they were still in the home in Noonday.

"Father, surely you remember some details of that long and arduous journey the family made in 1804? Write to me of it, and about Alabama, all that you recall. I'll stop there on my way to Texas." The plans of youth, the dreams. But he wrote to Charles, long letters with many scratched out words.

"Why don't you bring mother for a visit? Jacques and Auguste are trying to persuade Aunt Ruth to come. Don't you want to see the house where you were born?" *Yes, yes, Charles. I long to see it all...*

"There is much talk here of the slavery problem." Charles enclosed a clipping from the Richmond Enquirer, written two years earlier by William Fitzhugh as an editorial in defence of slavery, and a note: "Father, please return this. It's from my file." File? Adam began trying to make his letters neater. Would Charles one day shudder to read his illegible, fading letters?

Poor Charles. It's too late for you to talk with Simeon, Laurel Hill, to George, Edward and Mary Anne—too late to ask questions of your Uncle Aaron.

Actually, Olivia had been closer to David. It had almost killed her when he accepted a position with a Chicago law firm, and, when the announcement came telling of his marriage to a Chicago girl, Madelaine had to fan Olivia and administer brandy. "Adam, why would David marry a stranger when all of these beautiful daughters of our friends from here to Natchez swooned at one glance from him?" David was handsome, tall, blonde, with a fascinating combination of old Aaron's arrogance and Jules's charm.

It was easy-going young Adam, now working in the New Orleans cotton brokerage, who would one day come back upriver to take over South Wind. He wouldn't mind the sweat-soiled ledgers. Young Adam adored the slaves, but he didn't believe in slavery. "I would set them all free, father, pay wages. Those who would go, could go."

How many would leave? Adam often wondered.

Troubled by his sons' opinions, he kept up with the

incendiary documents streaming down from the north, followed every printed word of Jefferson Davis, went up to Vicksburg and over to Jackson to hear what he had to say. His own friends, also planters, talked at parties, at the cotton gins, at the races in Natchez. Some had paid passage to ship slaves back to Africa.

One planting season he brought it up in the fields. Joshua and Jethro stared at him as if he'd gone mad. "Master Adam," accused a young voice, "yo' gon sell us down the river?"

Olivia worried about their daughter Ruth's husband Regent whose plantation lay north of Natchez. "Adam, he's too fiery. Any day I expect him to start shooting northerners." Once, at a party, Regent read aloud William Grayson's poem, "The Hireling and the Slave," Grayson's answer to Harriet Beecher Stowe.

Adam fretted through the night of that party, and spent the next day at inspection and in checking the slaves' homes. Ever since, when he saw a troubled face, he questioned the slave. Oner shook his head. "Mister Adam, they've been to New Orleans, Natchez, Vicksburg—they've seen freedmen making their own ways. They see the good jobs Amelia's sons have. We've all been close. If they wanted freedom, you'd know it."

Still, he would ask himself: what are they really thinking underneath, inside, behind the smiles, deep in the songs they sing so yearningly, so poignantly? They were all so good, so kind, polite, seemed so contented and happy—yet he was troubled.

It was almost morning. The French porcelain clock on Olivia's table ticked on sightlessly. Downstairs, from that far greater distance, the big clock struck four. It was 30 March 1858. He pulled the velvet quilt around his head and tried to sleep. The trees felt the side of the house. Deep sweeping gusts of rain lashed the grillwork, washed over the balcony.

At the sudden frantic ringing of the plantation bell, he threw back the quilt and raced to the window. Weirdly outlined by the lanterns they carried, forms raced toward the levee.

Olivia sat up. "Oh, Adam, not the levee again!"

He kissed her. "Go back to sleep."

"How many times?" he asked himself. How many times had the levee gone out since Ben died?

Wet world of April. The rains had finally stopped falling. The sky, lead grey, hung low, shrouding the trees, the new levee, the still-raw edges of poles where the dock broke loose and was swept as a leaf by the torrent, but the flood gushed onward and outward. The main current swept with the now-familiar roar; the ever-sprawling brown-water rift bit deeper into the new rampart of logs and mud and limbs and leaves and old clothing being topped by driftwood pulled from the current with long boat-hooks.

Trunk sat on the wrought iron bench behind Adam, one of many brought up from New Orleans long ago by Jules, once used on porches, now kept on the river front. It was a Sunday place nowadays where the slaves sat with dressed-up children to watch the steamboats pass.

"Lawdy, Mister Adam, I never imagined you all had to fight this mighty river every spring." Gently laying his banjo on the seat, he got up. "Let me snag awhile."

Oner pushed him back down. "You keep on singing, Trunk. The boys work better. If it gets worse, you can help."

Trunk struck a delicate chord, and drops fell from the oak limbs above to shimmer on his hair which was whiter than a just-unfurled cotton boll. "You all really want to hear these songs? Clear back to Jeddy?"

"Clear back to Jeddy, Trunk." Adam leaned far out to snag a floating log which the boys pulled in.

"Let him sing after he drinks this hot coffee." Milcah began handing out cups from the tea-cart two children had eased through the mire that smeared the grass. "Old men got no business sitting in this dampness."

Balancing a cup, Adam sat down. "We haven't had to fight it every year. We built a good levee that first year that somehow held through the spring of '16. '23, '24 and '28 were bad ones." He sat remembering May of 1840.

Oner shivered. "The one I want to forget is the cold one.

'40, January and February. I thought we'd never get warm."

"Lawdy."

"And all through March up to May in '50. We almost didn't get the cotton in, eh, Mister Adam?"

"Wasn't that the year we bricked in the ditches?"

"No, sir, that was '51, the year we had two bad ones: February and March. Late May we got the bricks and the boys dug ditches almost to China."

"Lawdy." Trunk stared at the river. "It's powerful. The years we could have used some of that water in Texas."

Oner picked up his shovel, and placed the banjo across Trunk's knees. "Give us Jeddy, and we'll heave the mud."

Milcah scolded. "Don't you children sit on that wet ground. You crawl up here near Trunk, you want to hear the songs."

Like timid does, like wide-eyed baby owls, children emerged from behind trees, from behind one another, and crept closer to this gigantic and gentle venerable balladman they'd heard about all of their lives, but who had never come over from Texas since they were born.

Trunk, his shoulders still massive although he was almost eighty, sat hunched on the bench, his distant eye westward, his seamed face set in sweet sad memory. He struck a melancholy strain:

> *They run off into the swamp,*
> *did Laurel and Jeddy Black,*
> *while baby Raven sobbed,*
> *wantin' his mama back.*
>
> *Raven's mama ran,*
> *black shawl over her head,*
> *searchin' for her Jeddy—*
> *the others gave up for dead.*
>
> *Laurel set out to hunt him,*
> *with a yaller torch held high,*
> *searchin' the white cypress tunnels,*
> *on the night Master Aaron died.*

Milcah stood with her hand on Trunk's shoulder. "Poor little Jeddy. I can never forget how heartbroke he was when you had to shoot that cow beyond the Chattahooch."

"Oh, Lawdy, how long back!"

The children looked mystified. Giggled. None of them could even imagine shooting a cow.

Slave women, slipping up softly to stand behind the benches, hummed. Trunk said the tuneless words, the banjo sobbed, the river raced on, men and boys shoveled mud. Adam, long boathook in hand, stared westward beyond the broadening flood.

"Master Adam, quick. It's a dawg." A small raft loomed up out of the mist. A sleek black form crouched low upon it. Adam's hook struck wood, held.

"Get him off, Jesse."

Jesse sprawled headlong into the rushing water, clasping an arm behind him until a human chain formed from the bank where Oner gripped the last boy's legs.

"He shackled. Chained to a door."

Oner backed, and got a footing. Hand over hand, men against the torrent, the door was handed bankward until Adam grabbed the black form. Horror crept up around his heart. He could feel his face draining.

"Lawdy," Trunk leaned over him. "It's a child, a slave child." He touched the small body Adam clutched.

Oner grabbed a massive sledge hammer. "You look away, Mister Adam, but hold him best you can."

Adam felt the mighty blow to the chains. Above the rush of the river, he heard the cracking of wet wood, the snap as the massive chain link fell apart, and his own sobbing. His overflowing eyes met the dulled, agonized black eyes, saw them close for the second of impact, saw the mouth draw back from ivory teeth in a grimace of agony. He felt the sigh as the released body crept closer to his warmth. One swollen arm crept around his neck, and a piece of still-dangling chain hit his shoulder. The other arm crept around, slowly, questioningly, doubtfully. The wrist shackles clanked together at the back of Adam's neck. The small face quivered, and the eyes filled. The boy laid his head on

Adam's shoulder. Terrible wracking sobs shook the naked body. Milcah ran forward and wrapped her shawl around the boy.

Oner was still standing holding the sledge. "Mister Adam, best I crack them shackles now. He'll swell worse."

Milcah examined the boy's legs. "Best wait until the swelling goes down."

The slaves crowded around.

"Shovel!" Oner yelled. "You boys want your houses to wash downriver tonight?" He snatched up his own shovel, singing out, "Build up the levee."

"Sing, please, Trunk," a frightened child-voice quailed.

Trunk, his eyes pinched, picked up the banjo.

> *Amazing grace! how sweet the sound,*
> *That saved a wretch like me!*
> *I once was lost, but now am found,*
> *Was blind, but now I see...**

Trunk and Oner's eyes met across the river mist; it was another time, long past. Milcah saw the look. Children saw the look and wondered, for their lives had been short.

Sobbing and limping, clutching the child, Adam ran past the eyes of his slaves up the long carpet of mud-trampled violets to the porch where Olivia and Aunt Ruth strained to see.

Aunt Ruth came in softly, and stared down. "He's dying, isn't he, Adam? If only the doctor would come."

Still seated beside the great four-poster, Adam slipped his hand between the white sheets to rest it again on the thin, ribbed chest. He couldn't stop crying; it was all too much. The fury up north about cruelty, the pictures of crouching, frightened slaves. He'd seen New Orleans and Mobile slave markets long ago, yet he never really believed, had never actually seen slaves suffering, and now it was here in the big house, in his own guest room. A scarred, starved body, a

---

*Amazing Grace, by John Newton

well-shaped black head small upon the embroidered pillow slip. A faint life fading.

"If anyone can get through to Vicksburg on these washed-out roads, Garrett can. He's riding the best horse on the plantation," he told her wearily.

"He must be baptised," Olivia insisted. "Since it's impossible to get a priest, I've sent Jeffy for that preacher back in the bottoms."

Adam straightened. "You're right, Olivia. We've got to do something. Milcah, get whiskey. And call Oner." Examining a swollen ankle.

Aunt Ruth looked away painfully. "I told you those shackles were cutting off his blood."

Adam rubbed the leg. "If only he had some fight. If he'd just fight. Boy, we don't want you to die. You've got to have a strong will to live."

Aunt Ruth leaned toward Olivia. "Do slave boats really still go upriver? Joshua said that child had been chained to deck-wood, that he'd come off a ship."

Adam looked away. He knew it was a deck hatch. He'd had Jesse standing by all day with the boat hook. He was sure a boat had broken up in the night. He'd heard rumors. Had he ignored them? Other planters talked of hearing cries in the nights, hinted that slave-traders still smuggled humans upriver under cover of darkness. The very idea of it had tormented him. Now he knew it was true.

Dropping to his knees, he clasped the child. "Now, boy, you'll never be a slave, never be mistreated, not as long as I live, never know more sorrow if I can help it." Placing his hand on the black head and the other on the Bible that lay on the table, he looked upward. "My world has been too narrow, but God willing, I christen you Abram Brewster Cork, freeman."

"You got the whiskey, Milcah? You try that little spoon."

"But his teeth clenched. You think he got locked-jaw?"

Adam tilted the small head. "Pour some in. Now, when Oner comes, you and Aunt Ruth go out of here, Olivia."

Oner backed away, pulling the table holding the heavy anvil.

"Leave it, Oner. The boys can move it later. Did you send Trunk to bed?"

"Amelia put him to bed. You want me to tell Miss Olivia and Miss Ruth that the shackles are off?"

Adam held the thin wrist. The small hand closed around one of his fingers, gripped it, and held on.

"Yes. And if Milcah's still waiting, tell her she can bandage now." The black eyes opened, and stared solemnly into his. He looked toward the levee where torches burned, where the work went on. "Tell them."

The doctor did not get there until after noon of the next day. He examined the boy, and turned to Adam, smiling.

"Why, Captain Brewster, this slave will live to be a hundred. Garrett told me how he floated in. We've heard of no more along the river, at least not yet."

"My boys have watched too. I'm grateful to you, but this boy is no slave. Do you have time to give my people their regular checkup while you're here?"

Aunt Ruth leaned back smiling. "Isn't mail wonderful? The children don't write often, but when I get a stack like this, I'm glad I've lived so long." She flipped through the letters in her lap. "Virginia, Texas, California and New Orleans." Her eyes narrowed thoughtfully. Jacques and Auguste clear back in Virginia, Ara and her family in New Orleans, young Aaron and Rayford in Texas. "You'll want to read this. Auguste's wife has written descriptions of the house. It sounds unchanged. They want me to come back for a visit. I may go someday. But for now I think my trip to New Orleans will satisfy me. Aaron says Robert and Royal are crazy to stay out in California, but their wives love it. He's happy to have Rayford to help with the horses. Auguste shipped the finest ones they've seen in years. Believe me, Adam, if it wasn't for Rayford, we wouldn't have cotton. Aaron's just like his father, horse-wild, but it has paid off, so have the cows."

She picked up Aaron's letter. "Jeddy's boy Raven is going

to be just like Jeddy. You knew Aaron gave him Jeddy's land and all the Jeddy cows. His grandmother supplies half of Noonday with milk. It would made my Aaron happy, if he knew."

Adam shook his head. "And they never found a trace of Jeddy and Laurel?"

"No. They searched the swamp ... I often think they still search it. Well, I must be getting ready to go. It's been good to be here, Adam."

Trunk stood beside Ruth on the new dock, one hand clasping Adam's and one holding Oner's. "You come on over to Texas, Oner. I'll try to wait for you. Mister Adam, I've been urging Oner and Amelia to move over with me."

Ruth touched his sleeve. "He'd stay here in a minute, but he won't leave me. I'm sorry we can't come back this way. I really must stop off in Acadia."

The great yellow water flowed peacefully again, exerted, and spent. The winds were stilled. The day was so quiet they heard the steamboat whistle out of Vicksburg. Everyone bustled around to make it to the dock to watch it pass. Adam held Abram's hand. He looked at them all. Some had been his father's slaves, went back as far as Virginia. And all of those young ones had come along, and then those little children, so many of them. And he knew all of their names, their aches and pains, their heartaches, and their loves. He even knew which one liked white meat or dark when they all had turkey. Jessica, daughter of Jesse and Aretha, granddaughter of Simeon and Leah, tugged at Abram.

"Come *on*, Abram. You said you wanted one of my kittens."

"Not now, Jessica," Adam said gently, "We're going to have inspection as soon as the steamboat passes."

Coming around the bend, the steamboat whistle sounded. The passengers scurried to their side of the deck to wave. All of the negroes waved back, some with handkerchiefs in their hands. Then it was gone around the bend and all that was left trailed in a long streamer of black smoke that Adam would forever after think of in connection with that day and what he knew he must do, had to do, a trail of smoke floating upriver, settling down over the plantation like a thin dim cloud.

Some cried. Adam tried to explain. "It isn't that I don't love you all or want you with me always. I don't mean that any of you need to leave South Wind or your homes. You belong here the same as Oner who has always been free. It's just that I want you to be free, to know you are free, to be slaves no longer for I no longer believe in the institution of slavery. Do you understand?"

"We never goin' have inspection no more?" a young voice piped up accusingly.

"We'll do everything as we've always done it. The only difference lies here," he pointed down to the ledger. "From now on you will be paid wages. You all have your own gardens, your cows and chickens. Miss Olivia will continue to buy eggs and milk from you as she always has. You just aren't slaves."

A young boy ran from the group. "I doesn't have to obey Master Adam anymore?"

"You'll obey Master Adam if I have to beat you bloody." A small backside was smacked.

Adam looked around him. The eyes of the older slaves looked no different than they had when he told them the big table was being moved back into old-house, not that Miss Olivia didn't want them to all eat together as they always had with him and Ben, but that she preferred a quiet meal at a smaller table.

"This has been hard for me to say, but I must. You have been given as much education as I ever had, and more, since Miss Olivia knew far more to teach you than I did. If any of you feel..." Unable to go on, he looked into their faces, blank, thoughtful, shocked, dazed, questioning, some crying. Children looked to parents for a hint. They didn't know whether to smile or cry. Behind them loomed their homes set under the Chickasaw plum trees, under the great shining-leaf magnolias. Behind him, behind Oner whose hand rested on his shoulder, flowed the soft-moving river, golden in the sunset of the western sky.

Afterward he wrote to young Adam:

Not one of them left South Wind. I can't say that this surprised me. No, I suppose that it did not. It has made me exceedingly happy. Abram is learning to talk, but slowly. His scars are healed. Trunk and Oner believed him to be straight out of Africa. They tried a few remembered words, but he knew none of them. Amelia tried some lingo from her Caribbean island; he didn't know it. It has been like teaching a baby. We have only his teeth by which to guess his age. He follows wherever I go, and little Jessica seems never to let go of his hand. I hope he is happy. He seems to be, in a sober way. That terrible sadness has never left his eyes. I wonder if it ever will. It haunts me. Your mother is well, more beautiful than ever. Do call Amelia's boys. Did you know that Charles rode up to Washington to see Jefferson Davis?

Always my love to you,
Your Father

1 August 1860
South Wind

And now a greater flood swept the land. Every word Jefferson Davis spoke or wrote home was read and re-read. South Carolina seceded. Less than a month later Mississippi became a republic. David rushed home from Chicago with his weeping wife Lila, the strange violet-eyed girl who cried all the time, and kept her two little girls in her room. David enlisted. Before the republic's eighty day span was over, Lila, in tears and furs, took the girls from Adam's arms and stepped aboard Captain Rider's boat to travel to Vicksburg where she would get a steamboat north.

On 18 February 1861, Jefferson Davis was inaugurated president of the Confederacy. Mississippi had joined six other cotton states in Montgomery.

By April, after Fort Sumpter fell, Mississippi boys were

already in Florida, Virginia and Tennessee. Adam raced to New Orleans to say a frightening farewell to young Adam in uniform, to Amelia's octoroon boys, Louis and Bertrand, leaving with him, to Ara's husband, and to Ara and her children starting out for Noonday.

Jacques and Auguste and Charles were fighting in Virginia. *Charles. Oh, Charles, where are you? Write to me when you can.* Rayford, Royal, Robert and every one of their sons big enough to put on pants rushed into the army, Aunt Ruth wrote. Ara had arrived to tell them that New Orleans was frozen in fear, and dreadfully unprotected. "Adam, pack up your whole family and slaves and come to Texas before the North takes the river, which they will surely try to do soon. Come. I'll send wagons and carriages through Louisiana to wait for you."

Adam and Olivia's daughter Ruth was desperate: Regent her husband was missing in action. Her slaves had run off. Adam, Oner and Garrett tore down the back roads to bring home Ruth and the children, passing closed and quiet plantation houses. Northern gunboats had been seen on the river. Mississippi families were broken and scattered.

They were packing when Ri brought a telegram from Vicksburg: David was dead at Shiloh. It was April 1862. And before they'd collected themselves, New Orleans fell under Farragut. Adam sent Garret to Vicksburg with a private letter for Ri. They were ready. The young negroes were dying to enlist. Adam advised them to wait until they saw their families safely off for Texas.

He watched his shocked Olivia roam the rooms of the house picking up things she wanted to save: a toy that had been David's, a packet of his letters, Marie's French porcelain clock, Jules's pen, his inkwell and the desk he had made for Marie before she was born. Abram pushed the desk out into the hall. She found Adam's father's Bible, and opened a molded jewel box that rested beside it. A small white feather ruffled in the breeze from the balcony window. Abram's eyes lighted. She gave him the box. With extreme care, he shoved it deep into his pocket.

Adam packed the old ledgers with his father's books, to be

saved for Charles, wherever Charles was. And he worked feverishly to finish the ledger which Olivia would take with her. He wanted it preserved for Charles, for Charles's manuscript. He wrote: *Crossed over with Olivia LeFleur Brewster: Joshua, 75 years old, wife Milcah, 70; Jethro, 72, wife, Sarai 70; Peleg, 73; wife Tamar, 67; Serug, 70, wife Zibeon, 65; Leah, 65, widow of Simeon. Jesse and wife Aretha; Jock; Tammy; Jeffy; Ruby; Rip; Cecille.* He wrote it all, all of their names and their childrens' names and the family connections so that one day each slave child would know his background. He didn't know which man or boy would enlist, so he put down all of their names and their ages, ending with *Abram, small foundling, age unknown. Stayed at South Wind with Adam Brewster, Garrett, Solom, Targ and Zibe.*

"Master Adam, Captain Rider's boat's out there. He says to tell you to leave lamps burning in the house, but everybody slip down in the dark. He don' have one light on that whole boat."

"Did you get the horses aboard, the goods?"

"Yes, sir."

"Did he see any gunboats?" Rider had spies spotted all the way from Vicksburg.

The black head jerked. "Some downriver."

Adam's heart chilled.

There was no moon, yet the sky held a strange glow; plantations burning south of them, or planters burning their cotton to keep it out of Yankee hands. The smell of fire hung over the river.

There were no lights on board. The fire in the stoker led the negroes down the grassy slope they knew so well, up over the levee their hands had built. Children's mouths were muffled with shawls, babies' with gentle hands. All children had been carefully counted, warned not to call out, nor to cry. Northern gunboats could be close.

Olivia clung to Adam. "Why would I leave you, Adam? Oh, why won't you let me stay? It is a cruel and inhuman thing you ask of me."

He looked back at the house, held her shaking hands.

"I'm crossing over with you to make sure the wagons are there. If I find anything you treasure, I'll bring it when I come." He put his hand under her chin. "Don't cry, dear heart. I know. I know."

What an oddly familiar sound their footsteps made on the floors of the quieted house.

"No, I forbid it! How would I know that Captain Rider got you safely back? Oh, Adam, forget South Wind. It is already lost. Can't you see that? Come with me. Your heart has always yearned for Texas. Come."

"I'll write every day that I can, Olivia."

"Adam, you're too old to fight even if your leg is better. You're..."

"Come aboard, Captain Brewster. We've got to get back across."

Olivia clung to him. The wagons and carriages Aunt Ruth had sent had waited for days. Slipping in darkness the group climbed aboard. Voices sobbed. Trunk whispered orders. Names were called out, voices answered. A dreadful fear hung over them all. They were leaving behind all that was familiar.

Trunk put his hand on Adam's shoulders. "You should come, you know that, Mister Adam. There won't be anything left of South Wind. Miss Ruth says to tell you not to be noble. Just come, all of you."

"I can't, Trunk. I can't."

"Yes, sir, Mister Adam. Don' worry. I'll care for them. Don' worry. Me and Oner. Oner? Oner, where'd you go?"

Adam stood on the deck. Carriages, wagons, horses and the shadowy outlines of humans stood silhouetted against the black western sky. Soft lamentations of slaves warned not to cry out reached him and the sounds touched a faint memory, an almost forgotten memory of another river, another boat, of a man on a horse deep in the river. From somewhere far off he imagined he heard a crystalline boy-voice call out, "Write to us at LeFleurs!" He wasn't sure. He wished that he could be sure. It would be something to write in his next letter to Charles, wherever Charles was, but it faded into memory, faded with the grey-black shoreline of Louisiana, drifted back into the darkness of forgotten times. And a hand touched his arm.

"Oner. I told you to go with Trunk. You are to look after Olivia."

"I know, Mister Adam, but I never planned it. I told Amelia when I knew we had to go. I said, 'Amelia, Ben wouldn't want me to leave Adam on the other side of the river.' And Amelia said, 'I know, Oner. I know.'"

Oner pushed forward a small, shivering form. "Now, what this one thought, I don't know. I found him hiding below deck."

Adam pulled Abram to him.

"Mister Adam, I can fight. I can fight as good as any grown man."

Adam touched the dark head. "You'll be burning cotton, feeding cows."

"I'll be helping Oner take care of you."

On 8 May, Farragut appeared on the river south of Vicksburg. There were rumors that gunboats waited north of the city. At South Wind they burned the cotton, packed supplies and guns, and leading cows, rode to Vicksburg.

For two months Adam, Oner, Garrett, Solom, Targ or Zibe took turns slipping down to South Wind for food, anything they could find, for more clothing. In Vicksburg there was continuous bombardment. They would creep along the back roads, sticking close to the woods. They would lead back cows, a few pigs, a chicken, and finally the last of the mules. A small ration was kept for their cave, the rest distributed to the troops and the hungry civilians.

While shells exploded around the hillside where they lived in the cave, while balls hit with dull thuds, Adam wrote to Olivia of their well-being, even when they were reduced to living on a terrible tasting mash made of cornmeal and peameal, even after they knew the taste of mule meat, even when they huddled together around little Abram to warm him and one another.

During those rare times when they weren't under seige the

boys hired themselves out to dig caves. Many of the townspeople were moving into the hillsides to become cave-dwellers of the loess hills above the busy river.

Through the long hours in the rifle pits, Oner taught Abram songs that he remembered. Abram was adroit at darting between balls and throwing himself headlong into a pit when a shell exploded. They all were.

Summer ended. Raw winter blew into wet spring. Adam thought they might slip home to plant a few vegetables, to dig up anything that might have come up. They walked from Vicksburg through the cold wet mud to South Wind. They stood side by side in the bottoms staring at the smoking ruins. Targ confessed that he'd seen troops stationed there on his last trip down. He hadn't wanted to tell Adam. Adam would not write this to Olivia, not even to Charles, not ever to Charles, for Charles lay buried in a land shaded from the western sun by great blue mountains. He wouldn't write it ever, or tell it, since no words equalled his anguish—not for South Wind, but for Charles, for David, for Olivia's sorrow. He stood with Oner, Garrett, Targ, Solom, Zibe and the quivering baffled Abram. The cold crept up through his worn boots, up past the old wound, aching him, up into his chest where it lay like a stone.

They went in. Adam pulled a branch of flowering plum and placed it on Ben's grave. The blooms were faded by the rains. There was no fragrance, and there was no fragrance from the fast-growing honeysuckle creeping around the trees reaching out toward the blackened, smoking, wet, charred ruins, only the heavy smell of burning. Turning, they went back to Vicksburg to fight on.

Late in July of that year 1863, Captain Rider took them in a makeshift boat to the shore of Louisiana. Vicksburg was lost. Ri's sons were lost. Charles and David were lost. South Wind was lost. An empty fear held Adam when he thought of young Adam fighting on in some unknown distant battlefield. Adam held Ri's hand in the darkness. The war was over for them. They were old now. Adam knew he would never recross the river.

Oner, waiting with the lantern, his eyes slitted, and gazing west, took his arm. With Abram's hand in his, Adam ran limping to catch up with the others headed west to Texas.

Chapter 14

THE LAST RUN

Young Adam's breath tore out of his agonized chest in great choking gasps. Half-blinded by tears and gunsmoke, he staggered against small trunks of young growth on the edge of the hill somewhere near Petersburg to slam straight into a great tree. With both hands he grabbed out at the trunk, let his body slide down until he rested on his knees. He could run no more. His heart tore at his chest, the pounding as loud as the dreadful and terrible bombardment he had run from.

He could hear others stumbling through the eerie smoke-filled forest, Confederates like himself lost from their regiments, half-dead with exhaustion and hunger, sick unto death with the stench of gunsmoke, fires and unburied bodies. Would he ever—if he lived, for he was going back as soon as daylight came to fight on—get rid of that stench? Would it walk with him, a specter following his steps for whatever days were left of his life?

What would his father think of him for running? His father, old and weary and still plagued with his leg injury, had fought on in Vicksburg. David had been killed in the first lunge at Shiloh; David would never on earth have run. And Charles, the scholar of the family, who had chosen to teach here in Virginia rather than return to South Wind, the least-likely soldier of them all, would never have run from battle even when they were so badly beaten. The retreat had been ordered. He heard it. They were running for their lives, he and these boys in the woods around him. But shouldn't he have stayed? Couldn't he have found another musket among all those dead and got in another lick?

Crying bitterly, he sunk deeper into the muddy earth, staring down into the weirdly colored night so like a burning town to be fled. He knew that somewhere out beyond the orange-red glare there must be stars, black sky and clear air. His lungs all but burst in his need. Then he heard the sudden pounding of horses' hoofs. His heart reared. His hand stretched out across the needles of the pine he rested against. He drew it back, remembering he had lost his musket in the blind fighting of the night.

His breath escaped softly as the sound of hoofs drew near. None of their men were mounted and riding with that assurance now. With some primitive strength roused by the natural urge of self preservation, he edged around the tree, crawling as he had so often on hands and knees. The pounding raced closer. The sound of voices rose above the hoofbeats. His trained ears caught the harsh accents of the North. He lay still.

A piercing shriek of agony tore the night. A hoarse voice cried out in glee.

"I got me another Reb."

"The way you thrust that saber, you mighta broke it. See if he's got a musket. Quit fooling with Confederate money; it's no good now. Give me that watch."

"Hell, you take 'em all. I want some souvenirs too."

"Come on, you guys. We're not on a souvenir hunt. We're out for stragglers."

A laugh went up incongruously in that hideous night. Adam could hear twigs snap here and there near him in the woods as other boys crept away from the glare of lanterns and the uneasy stamping of hoofs as horses waited. He wished he could reach out and touch the boys trying to slip away into the thicker woods.

"Yeah, stragglers, and what do we find? A nice little nest of grey stragglers instead of our own."

"They ain't stragglers. They're what we might be tomorrow—wounded boys."

"We're supposed to round them up and take them back."

"I ain't heard about no bounty for carrying in half-dead men."

"They aren't men. They're just boys like us. We should carry them."

"Carry a Reb? You'ins are so soft I don't know. I swear I

don't know how you got through this much of the war, or will get through more."

"There won't *be* much more. From what I hear Richmond's about to fall, and we got Lee on the run now for sure. Next thing is to find Johnston down in Carolina, then we can go home. That's the only reason I signed up for this detail. I want to get home with all my arms and legs."

"You always get the news, don't you? How many times have we been told Richmond had fallen? Every time we head into a battle."

Their steps scrambled through the trees, past bushes. Adam looked around for something to grab. He had no strength to crawl. He'd lost too much blood. And it sounded as if there were four. Near him a soft Southern voice cried out, "Let me alone. You can see I can't walk." A moan followed a soft crash and a slap of the saber against a trunk.

"God, you didn't have to do that! You could see he was finished anyhow. I'd let them alone. They're half-starved. What a rotten war. That poor kid. Did you have to do it that way?"

"That poor kid might have got you. See that musket?"

"Pick it up and come on."

"Gimme that lantern. I've got to find some boots. I haven't found a whole pair all night. Now look at that bright eyed boy over there. Here you are, sonny. Now you weren't about to throw that canteen at us, were you? Now, that arm won't ever throw anything again."

An agonized piercing shriek cut through the night. Adam looked at his own hands. If he could make it to those bushes... Too late; the lantern light touched a budding laurel above his head and he knew it searched his tattered grey uniform. He lay limp, his breath held until his lungs almost burst.

"Here's another one. God, look at the blood! I don't want to touch him."

"Get his musket. Make sure he's dead."

"For God's sake, don't do that."

There was a scuffle near him as a sharp saber tip jerked across his back and was jammed into his hip and yanked out.

The agony was too sudden for an outcry, and he had learned not to cry out. He knew he was fainting and tore his eyes open for one last look of his lifetime at the budding laurel bush. His body was roughly jerked around, his pocket yanked off as his wallet was taken. For one moment he stared up into the lantern light and saw four dirty and unfriendly faces looking at him. Except for one whose eyes looked war-weary and sympathetic, the eyes were bitter; war eyes. A heavy boot struck his face and as welcome oblivion was sweeping over him there came a great burst of shellfire that lit up the woods. There came a simultaneous yelp from the group, the racing of feet, the sudden jingle of harness and sabers and then retreating hoofbeats padding down the soft muddy earth...

He felt hands turning him, touching him. Very slowly he opened his eyes. He was aware that he had never expected to open them again. Certainly not into this bright sunlight filtering down through the trees from a clear blue sky.

"You gone be all right, mistah, soon's I get some water down you throat."

Adam felt the trickle of warm liquid in his throat and fought the terrible gagging and heaving in his chest. He looked deeply into a black face, into bloodshot old eyes, down over rags that somehow had been wrapped around a black chest. The canteen was lowered as the man waited. Adam tried to sit up and the pain in his hip was unbearable. Hands gently lowered him but kept his head high.

"Now you jest quiet down like. Don't call out. You be all right once we get working on those hurts. That's a bad old hole in that shoulder."

A picture formed. A memory forgotten. That's when he dropped his musket. A ball had torn into his shoulder. That's when he had started running into the night, running toward the dark shadow of a hill against the sky. He shuddered in memory of the horsemen of that night.

Slowly the old man got water into him. A filthy piece of hardtack was placed between his teeth.

"You bite hard on that but don't swallow. I been working

to get that ball out your shoulder. You the only one alive on this whole hill. I been working here two days huntin' and findin' our boys. Lee, he in a mess. We gotta get you well enough to get down there."

Adam nodded. The old man talked constantly while he dug. Strange odors wafted around Adam's nose nauseating him. He tried not to get sick. The old man sat down on his hunkers and looked into Adam's face.

"You gettin' color now. How you feel?"

Adam tried to get words out, but none came. What met his eyes was so utterly fantastic that he thought he was going to laugh, that he would have to laugh, for what he saw formed a picture he would remember for all of the days of his life: the old man in rags and tatters worse than any of the soldiers. A worn and weary bright-eyed mule hung from end to end to side with canteens, many covered with dried blood. Muskets, sabers, gun belts, strange bags made of rags and belts, torn and filthy blankets, slabs of bacon, ears of corn long dried. The man followed his gaze and he smiled toothlessly.

"I be a travelin' man. Got rations too. Feed you as soon's you can hold it."

Adam cleared his throat and let the hardtack he had been sucking finally slip down.

"Thank you. I know I would have died here if you hadn't found me."

"Oh, that's all right now. I been findin' boys ever since fightin' started here in Virginia. One battle after another battle. I found my way around. Easy, long as they fight near the hills. My, but that was one terrible battle three-four nights ago! That when you got it, likely. Wonder you didn't die 'fore I got here. I had to go clear down to the train to steal rations."

Adam closed his eyes. The train would be the Southside Railroad at Petersburg that was bringing food for the Army of Northern Virginia—what was left of it. Had Lee reached it after all?

He asked the old man.

The old man shook his head sadly. "No, he sure didn't.

Them Northers took off with it, run it down the line. I found it."

Adam nodded, then they both started as shells began exploding somewhere down in the clear morning.

The old man shook his head again. "Seems like a shame they have to fight on Sunday, and this Palm Sunday, too. A body would think men would have enough grace to lie down and rest of a Sunday. The Lord would like that. Not that He'd 'prove of all this fightin' anyhow. I thought He'd protect General Lee who fought so gloriously. Now he all hemmed in down there. Oh, my, the battle they gonna fight soon as them Northers get lined up! They been linin' up since early dawn."

He saw the horror mount in Adam's face and smoothed over his words.

"Course, Lee and them boys can fight their way out of this. You feel like you can crawl a little bit? I take you over to the edge of the woods and you can look down..."

A clear bugle sang out across the morning. Painfully, Adam turned and began crawling on hands and knees.

The old man braced him against a tree and they lay side by side staring down at the battlelines drawn up, etched upon the morning. Blue cavalry with sabers flashing in the sunlight, rows and rows of them ready, and Federals in blue, waves and waves of them marching, flags fluttering in the spring air. Sickeningly, he picked out the small band of men in grey, their colors flying valiantly. It was almost as if there was a flag for each man instead of one for each regiment. Where were the rest of them? He knew General Lee had wanted to move on to meet up with Johnston, but he knew in his heart thousands of them had been taken prisoner that terrible night he ran. And what were left now were surrounded and more Federals were still coming, marching in perfect formation, rows and rows and rows of them. Would they never stop coming? Would it never end? The South was hopelessly outnumbered now. Sobs choked him and he dropped his head into his arms.

"You hurtin' pretty bad, boy?"

Then they heard it, the stirring call of bugles clear upon

the air, and in his stupor he tried to rise, to answer the call. Crying, he waited for the attack, for the sounds of charging cavalry, the distinctive rattle of artillery, the bombardment of cannon but no sound broke through the immense and terrible silence. Stiffening, he waited, listening.

"Looka there. Looka there. That way."

The old man lifted his shoulders and twisted his head around and pointed.

Out from the Confederate lines tore a minute figure on horseback to race straight into the Federal lines. He carried high a white flag.

"We callin' a truce," the old man said stoically. "I gotta feelin' we're licked right here at Appomattox Court House. Yes, boy. I got that feelin'."

Adam could not accept a Union victory. His confused mind traveled back into the ditches they had dug, the trenches... too many boys never made it out of them. It had cost too much. Another paroxysm of agony tore through him. David. And where was Charles?

"Don' you carry on so, boy. All fightin' is victorious. Don' matter in the far end which side wins. Don' think I'm sayin' our side don' matter. What you gotta 'member the rest of your years is that the North had 'vantages. Now we gotta work to build back this laid-waste land, this once beautiful land. That gonna take more work than diggin' ditches. And it's plantin' time."

Adam forced himself to sit up to stare into the old face. His own father might have said those words.

They waited. There were no more shots. They lay there on the hilltop staring down onto what could have been a painted picture of armies ready to go into battle. The river and the streams and the once-desired end of their own immediate rainbow, the railroad, lay sparkling in the sunlight. There were no more shots. It seemed no one moved down there. They stood or lay or leaned against horses or artillery or cannon. Then, soundlessly up here so far away, a few horses cantered up to a small frame building.

It was dark when the old man rode back up into the woods. His lantern outlined his tear-streaked face. He told

Adam all that he had heard. General Lee had surrendered the Army of Northern Virginia to General Grant. This battle was over forever.

Adam spoke brokenly. "But Johnston is still in North Carolina. If I can get down there..."

"Don' you go eying my mule like that. I gots work to do here. And you gotta get your hip helped. Tomorrow I carry you down below to an ambulance. Get you to a hospital."

Adam shook his head. "I'd be taken prisoner. You carry me anywhere, you carry me to the Brewster Plantation. It's near here. I don't know exactly where, but it's somewhere west of the Appomattox Court House."

The old man leaned close and stared into Adam's face. "You one them missin' husbands? Glory! You mean I can go back to them nice women and give one of them a husband from the dead? That little fellow minding the forge where I tooken many a horse for shoeing gonna be so happy."

"No. I would be his cousin." Something warm rose up in his chest, something that hadn't been there for a long long time. Words of his father's came back to him: *Oner was the blacksmith. Had his own shop. He was never a slave from the time he wandered into my grandfather's plantation.* He was like a green leaf of a vine creeping quietly up from the ruins of a great and terrible fire. He was alive. He would live. Thoughtfully, he tried to move his stiff arm but the shoulder felt dead. Squirming, he moved his hip where the saber had been thrust into the muscles. He let the old man stretch the stinking blanket over him. He would heal. His body would mend, but...

All that fitful night he kept thinking that his mind would clear. Terrible memories would wake him and he'd jerk with a start, breaking out in horrible sweats. In one dream he was back on the burial crew he'd been assigned to, cleaning off the faces to gaze at them fearfully. Would it be Charles? During lulls, before he had lost sight of his regimental flag and become lost that first time after he came east, he had searched the markers all through the Shenandoah Valley dreading to find the name, Charles Aaron Brewster.

His father's last letter had begged: *Oh, Adam, find*

Charles. Tell him I've kept the ledgers. There may be old ledgers back there at the Brewster Plantation with Aaron's boys, Jacques and Auguste. How I wish I were with you to see the old house where I was born. The minute I heard you had been transferred back there my heart went home although I remember little. I was very young when my father and Uncle Aaron headed out for Texas. And on and on. That letter had torn him apart. But he couldn't quiet his own hope that Charles was still alive, in a hospital or a captive somewhere up in those vermin-ridden prison camps.

He had wandered around the country, falling in with this group and another. Battle fatigue, men said about him. One youthful captain looked into his eyes.

"I'd like to send you out in one of the ambulances—if they ever find us."

Fighting through a terrible sweat, he imagined the captain shaking him. When he looked into his eyes it was the old man.

"You awful sick, boy. Better let me get you down before..."

"No. My brother may be at the Brewster Plantation. I must get there."

The old man shook his head. "You got fever, bad. We gone have to slip through these woods now before clear light. Let me help you up on this mule. Oh, no. You can't walk..."

When Adam woke up they were passing down a lane of trees in full blossom. As the old mule pranced around a curve in the road pink bricks showed through the trees. The old man led the mule into a circular drive and began calling out, "Got me a sick man here. Anybody here?"

A door opened. Two women rushed out and Adam felt hands touch his face.

"This boy a Brewster from Mississippi. He tole me bring him here, but he near dead now."

He knew he was in a bed. Nothing had ever felt so soft, so warm, not in his memory. Someone, a small girl, it looked like, was spooning broth into his mouth.

"I'm not supposed to let it drip, Cousin Adam. Could you

try to sit up? You really are much better, you know. And the war is over. Did you know the war is over?"

Adam leaned on one arm and stared into wide green eyes, teasing eyes in a face far too old for its age and size.

The sun was warm upon him when Adam woke up. At the side of his bed stood Edward, a boy of eleven, the last male Brewster left at the Brewster Plantation. Edward's eyes twinkled at him.

"Wore you out yesterday, didn't I, Cousin Adam?"

"You did, but we got that big garden plot ready. Now if we can talk that Salem girl into letting us have seeds. Do you really think she has some?"

Edward frowned. "I heard that some were brought in. We'll have to try."

"We were lucky your mother and your aunt saved seeds to plant those beans."

"They had them hid, or we would have eaten them. We'll have beans, potatoes and tomatoes, if they take hold." He waited for Adam to pull on the pants the women had made for him of a pair of Auguste's that before the war had been fine and good and worn for parties. "Mother said you would head out for Mississippi soon. She thought you'd go as soon as you could walk."

Edward's eyes were bleak. "And I'll do as I promised. When we get word of Charles or our fathers, I'll write to you at South Wind."

Something warm rose up in Adam's chest at the thought of South Wind, home. But what would be left of South Wind now? He had had no mail since his regiment moved east. He knew they had written. It was just that he had become lost.

He followed his cousin quietly out of the room. Unknown to the women, he and Edward were going to the old Eli Salem store that his Aunt Ruth had told him so much about. It was also the post office, but he didn't let himself hope for mail even though it was weeks since he'd written to his father that he was here at the old Brewster Plantation, that Auguste and Jacques had never returned, nor had their older boys, and that most of the slaves had run away so that all that were left to try to bring back this once beautiful plantation were the two heartsick women, a small girl and this skinny boy. He told his father he could not leave until he had helped with the planting.

As they walked down the tree-lined road he saw for the hundredth time since he'd come here the terrible devastation left by foraging troops. At least the Brewster house had not been burned. So many had. So much futile, terrible burning. He swallowed gall as his anger rose up, and he choked it back. There was a job to do here. Then he had a long journey across the sad country to South Wind.

He looked down the road, remembering his Aunt Ruth's description of the caravan leaving so long ago. A shiver passed through him. Had they not gone, he would not be here, would have never been at all. His father would not have met Olivia LeFleur. He had never treasured life as fully as he did now he had survived the war. He would go home. He would rebuild South Wind. If Charles were truly gone, he was the only one left to do it.

Adam ran the last mile, the shoes a woman had given him in Alabama worn through now and sliding up and down his heels. He ran down the back road that was overgrown now and unfamiliar. He ran in terror, a desperate clutching in his chest, for the Ewing Plantation was burned and deserted. He stopped running in the bottoms and stood staring at the old shack where his father and the negroes would buy the tonic his father passed around at inspection. Then slowly, fearfully, for a silence hung over the land, he made his way through vines and thistles where once cotton had billowed.

He stood in the chill silence. It was almost winter here and beyond the vine-grown ruins the river flowed sullenly. Where had they all gone? Had they run for their lives when the homes were fired? Not one stood now, not old-house, or new-house, nor one of the slave homes.

A bird swept high and called. A mockingbird answered softly and wing-whirled over his head.

Fearfully, he made his way through the heavy undergrowth, the tangle of weeds and flowers now gone wild, to the old cemetery. With his bare hands he tore at the vines and bushes. There were no new graves. He sat down on a stone and let his eyes travel over what had once been South Wind. Could one man worn from war, worn in his heart from walking all those miles from Virginia to stop here and there for weeks to help women plant, to help build a shack of ruins of great houses, rebuild here? He stared down at his torn hands. Yes, one man could start small. Men and women were doing it all over the south.

He stood up. His knees were weak. He rubbed them, warming them against the chill damp from the river. He would walk to Vicksburg. Grey Rider would know where they all had gone.

Chapter 15

THE BLACK SWAMP

Abram walked slowly now. He was almost fifty, or so they told him. No one had ever been sure of his age when old Adam Brewster fished him out of the Mississippi River. He had a vivid memory etched forever on his heart of the gentleness of Adam's arms encircling him on that raft, that ship's door he had been lashed to through a night of horror that ended so many nights of horror in the slave ship where his mother had died in the hold crossing over from Africa. She had been torn from his arms and thrown overboard. He had screamed and screamed. Others around him screamed and lamented, sounds that all these years he had never forgotten, never would.

All through his growing up years under kind Adam's care, back in his mind the horror and terrors had stayed. People spoke of the sadness in his eyes. Well, many were still alive today, not slaves now but free, who remembered the stinking holds of the slave ships, many who had memories yet of Africa. He had but a faint memory. It was this black swamp that kindled that memory. Something of the vastness, the wildness, the unearthly stillness that would be shattered by the shrill cry of a bird. When they had first come here from South Wind the swamp had taken the place of the wide-flowing Mississippi he loved.

He sat down slowly, folding his legs under him, and wrapped one arm around the trunk of a great cypress that stretched upward toward the sky. He swiped at the tears on his face and stared up beyond the spindly top of the tree.

"Oh, Adam, are you up there now looking down at me here alone?" The Book Miss Olivia had taught him by promised that when a man died it was but a crossing over like crossing over a river. "Adam, I'll see you on the other side.

I'm just that sure that God lets us black folks come there too."

Now the great clogging of tears that had been in his chest since last night flowed freely. He had held Adam while the last breath slipped soundlessly from those thin lips. Only a minute before he had leaned down when Adam spoke his last words, a whisper, "Ben. Oh, Ben." He didn't tell young Adam nor Miss Sue Ann, for she might not know about Ben. He knew about Ben who had died for South Wind, for his dream, but somehow he had expected old Adam to call out for Charles. For all the years since the war he had looked for Charles, in that same way that until her own passing, Miss Olivia had waited for word from up Chicago about Lila, David's widow, and his little violet-eyed girls.

It seemed to him some people just never got over having someone they loved die and leave them alone as Adam had just left him. Olivia used to tell Adam that out of 80,000 Mississippi men and boys fighting in the War only 20,000 lived to come home and many of them not whole, but Adam wouldn't accept that Charles had been killed. He never stopped writing to him to that far away place in Virginia that Abram never got to see. They had often talked about someday Abram taking Adam back to see the plantation where he was born. But life had a way of going wrong and when it was on the down side people looked back and wondered if they had handled it well, if they had done right.

He supposed that he could have just started out walking with old Adam to get to Virginia, but Miss Olivia said they'd never make it. First, the land was so ruined, so poor. Wouldn't have been anyone along the way to invite them in or to give them a meal. Well, he didn't do it. He'd always be sorry, have that one regret.

But he didn't regret one minute of time he'd spent with old Adam, helping him, mostly listening. Old Adam became a great one to talk, to look back into the history of the Brewster family and retell the story of the long trek west heading for Texas.

As a young boy, Abram had thought their trek from Vicksburg to Noonday was long. Sadly, he gazed out over the swamp. This was the swamp they had seen when they came around the bend in the road that long ago evening. It was little Jessica who spotted them coming and came running and yelling "Abram, Abram! Oh, Mister Adam..." There they came. He could see them now. Seven abreast, weary shoulders straightening, Abram dragging the exhausted Adam by the hand, Oner LeFleur pulling him by the other hand, Garrett, Solom, Zibe and Targ, seven of them who had dodged balls and got in their licks at Vicksburg, coming in to Noonday where Adam had been headed all those many years.

An old woman he remembered from her visits with Miss Ruth to South Wind heard Jessica screaming and looked up from the line where she'd been pulling clothes down. Women scream so much. Zilpah had started screaming, "Oner, oh, Oner! Oh, now where's that Trunk!" Trunk had come running so fast out of the trees that they trembled.

The three of them, Oner, Trunk and Zilpah, stood in the road holding on to one another not yelling now, nor talking, just sort of murmuring and crying. Oh, the silent crying. All crying is not sorrow. He thought they would never let go of each other. People started running out of the houses along Evening Road and just stood there crying and watching those three who had waited for so long, and who God had let come together while they were still on this side.

They were all gone now, lying in that same cemetery where tomorrow they would place old Adam, but no one alive in Noonday then ever forgot that meeting at the bend of the road. They had stayed in that hugging until Trunk finally called out to the children who had crept silently up to watch those three shriveled, ancient people. The children jumped to attention, for Trunk was venerable, adored and respected, and fun when he sang to them or told them stories.

"You children, run up to Master Adam's and tell Miss Olivia that Master Adam here, come to his home that waited so long." For it was three miles from Adam's house to Aaron's house and boys were swifter of foot. "You take off fast as you can to Master Aaron's house and tell Miss Ruth her nephew is here from Mississippi." Then he threw back his great white head and laughed up at the sky. The children stared, puzzled, not seeing what was funny, then scampered off laughing and singing for joy.

When Miss Olivia came running, holding her skirts high with both hands, laughing and crying and calling out, her face nearly broke with emotion. They led Adam over to the house near the swamp, the house built by Jacques LeFleur for his father, the Adam Brewster from Virginia who never made it beyond a stockade wall in Alabama.

Miss Olivia looked young then in those years, tanned almost as dark as some of the negroes from working in the garden. They all worked, all that were there those war years. There hadn't been a man there, white or black, over fifteen or under sixty. Most of their black boys big enough to wear pants had gone off to Mississippi where the President of the Confederacy Jefferson Davis or some such man had promised to organize a negro army to win the war for the South. Nothing had come of it, a shame too, Trunk always said, because an army like that would have the stamina built up from years of working in the fields that would have won the war. All of them knew it, still talked about it.

Adam and Miss Olivia began watching the road with the others, watched for mail, prayed until that Catholic altar she brought with her from Mississippi almost toppled under the pressure and the crystal chandelier packed so carefully and hauled down the bank that dark and terrifying night they crossed over fairly shook. She wrote dozens and dozens of letters up North to Chicago trying to locate David's violet-eyed wife and his two little girls but it was as if the war had swallowed them. And to young Adam, wherever he was.

Abram didn't know how many letters he had carried out to mail to young Adam and to Charles even though he knew Miss Olivia believed the Army's word that Charles was dead. No word had come from him since he'd been transferred out of Mississippi although they all knew he had probably written.

Then on one cold blustery winter day little children saw this ragged, bearded blonde man come limping down the road and came screaming up to the big house. They all came running out. No one knew who he was then but they knew he was theirs and that he had come to heal someone's heart that was near broken. Oh, the silent crying.

One little child took his hand and said to him, "I don't know you, sir, but I'm right glad to welcome you to Noonday Plantation, home of the Brewsters and the LeFleurs." That greeting kind of took on and for more than half a century white and black used that welcome to friends and strangers coming to visit or passing through.

Young Adam Brewster had come home. Oh, he didn't know Noonday was home. His heart and soul belonged on the other side of the river at South Wind. He was hellbent and determined to go back there and rebuild that whole plantation single-handed if necessary. But he came home to Noonday to a greater need, for he was needed. He came home a broken man, a man who had left a lot of his blood and more of his mind back there somewhere on some terrible battlefield.

Sort of dazed when his father and mother begged him to stay around for awhile until his body healed, he worked in the fields with the Negroes. By that time men were straggling in; he wasn't really needed in the fields. Men were coming around asking for work. And work was hard to find.

But new industries were starting all over Texas, sawmills and plants and businesses. Eventually young Adam drifted off to work in a sawmill, for money was needed. That was the best drift his life had taken. In some town down south in Texas he met a girl who had it in her to heal a man's mind and his heart. When he married her, he became whole again and planned once more to go back to rebuild South Wind.

But her family and her heart belonged to this side of the river, and she stood firm about not going and he listened for he knew what he had found in her heart. Besides, he couldn't seem to earn quite enough money. Then, old Adam heard from Grey Rider about taxation and the dreadful Northerners who had swept over that sad, beautiful, devastated state of Mississippi...

Abram remembered the night the family had talked until the great orange moon sunk down behind the pines and reflected like a ball in the black lake. With tears streaming down his face young Adam came out to walk over to that lake and to stand, shoulders shaking, weeping, his hands outflung toward the water that lay peacefully, almost as if dead. That lake was in no way like the Mississippi so many of them loved and could never get over leaving. Abram saw him standing there. Somehow from the way he stood with his shoulders shaking, Abram knew that young Adam had trouble. As far as he knew all was well with young Adam's wife Sue Ann who would have a child soon. He knew it had to do with South Wind because when Jessica came home from helping with dinner at the big house she told him they were talking about old Mister Ryder back in Vicksburg and about the old home they all missed so much.

He walked slowly up to where young Adam stood crying, and put his hand on his shoulder.

"That moon could be one of our Mississippi moons reflected in the river, young Adam."

"Yes, Abram. Oh, that it were."

Abram stood silent while they watched the moon glide silently out of sight, allowing the stars to stand out against the velvet black Texas sky, allowing them to stand out in their own lights. Around them frogs croaked, a cricket here and there started to chirp, and out in the deep part of the lake, a fish broke the smooth surface and fell back with a splash.

"Peaceful, ain't it, young Adam." He said it softly, wanting to let young Adam see for himself that there was great beauty in Texas. He let his voice soften. "Sometimes I think the sky was never this big over there, that there's just something special about a Texas sky."

"You like it here? You don't talk as much about the river as you used to do." He was quiet for a minute. "I guess most of us have accepted this as home. How about your people, Abram?"

"Oh, we loves it, young Adam." At that moment his own heart almost tore apart for just one sight of the Mississippi, for just a few minutes of being able to stand beside it and listen to the deep never-ending sound of it flowing. In spite of a river's tantrums which would send it out of its banks and up over the levee, in spite of its greed to swallow little children who played too close to its banks and swam out into forbidden eddies, he had never stopped loving to listen to it.

Young Adam cleared his throat as if to finish off his tears. "After Sue Ann has the baby and is all right, I'll be going over there. Would you go with me?"

Swift as a hawk soaring, Abram's heart went lifting straight up into the black sky. For a whole minute he let himself believe, really believe that young Adam had defied them all and was going back there to rebuild South Wind and Abram would go with him and live out the rest of his years there beside the river. The minute ended. He faced reality. He could not leave old Adam forever. He could go over there with young Adam, but he had to come back to Noonday. His heart belonged to old Adam. He owed the debt of his life to him. And it wasn't all what he owed. He loved old Adam. He loved the time they spent together floating around fishing in the swamp, even just sitting listening while old Adam told and retold the stories of the Brewster family clear back to Virginia and the long trek west. He didn't know how many times he had heard about the terrible sound of the shot there in Alabama on the White Feather Creek. Down in his pants pocket, his hand sought out the small jewel box that he had kept and treasured ever since that dark night when Miss Olivia crossed over the river to come without old Adam to Noonday. His fingers closed over the box. The white feather that had tumbled down from the sky at Mims Crossing when old Adam's little unborn sister was buried belonged to him now. It was an heirloom and a heritage and made him one of them. By *them,* he knew that he meant all the slaves and the descendants of the slaves who had started out from Virginia and who had a heritage they were proud of, proud to talk about and remember.

Later on, his memory would return to this night when he stood beside young Adam, both with tear-swum eyes, and he would recall a vow he made to himself: when old Adam was gone, if God hadn't taken him too and until God did take him, he would carry on the job old Adam had now, that of telling all the children the stories of the Brewsters and the LeFleurs. Something like that gave a man a purpose in life.

"Yes, young Adam, if when you are ready your father is well and doesn't need me." At the very thought of going back, his heart swelled again and a great joy swept through him. "And there isn't one in Noonday that won't want to go."

Young Adam chuckled, a cheering sound. "I've thought of that. Father wants to go, and mother. But he isn't able to make two trips. Tonight he promised her that when money is more plentiful, he'll take her down to New Orleans, and that satisfies her. She can visit Jules and Marie LeFleur's graves. Women always want to see graves. Sue Ann's been wanting to go south to put flowers on her grandparents' graves."

"Women are soft-hearted creatures, young Adam."

Young Adam patted his shoulder. "Just women, Abram?"

Sue Ann gave birth to a boy named Charles Robert Brewster on a wild night when Abram had to hang on to Milcah to keep the old woman from flying away. Milcah told him afterward that it might be the last Sue Ann saw of her baby, that old Adam and Miss Olivia waited outside the door ready to grab and hold their grandson.

Adam and Abram went back, just the two of them, riding on fine horses with a distant Virginia background and leading two mules with their packs. It was as if they were leaving forever, the way everyone in Noonday stood on Evening Road to wave and to call out farewells. When Adam looked back upon their faces that early spring morning there wasn't a dry face, white or black.

They were silent on the new ferry carrying them across to Vicksburg, each deep in memories of other crossings. Abram stared at the new, strange and swift boats on the river. Vicksburg was in full spring blossom, more fragrant, more green than ever in his memory. This was not a happy journey for them, and they did not hurry, but rode silently through the cemetery that lay high on the loess hills. Abram showed Adam where they had lived in the cave, and told how they had slipped down the back road to dig up the last of the potatoes and hunt through weeds and vines for any vegetable that had come up. His throat constricted as he got to that last trip down when they had found the ruins of South Wind, and he could not go on, but it was to become one of the most vivid of the stories he would tell later in his life.

They went silently down that back road, reaching out to push aside a branch sweeping grey with moss, or billowing pink with blossoms, down into the old bottoms to stare at the ruins of the old cabin where an ancient negro had sold "tonic" that was in truth hard whiskey. The bottoms were overgrown with young trees and bushes and flowers with not one trace of the cotton known so well to them in their youth.

They made camp near the bank of the river not far from the old cemetery. Young Adam walked away and wandered among the ruins of the houses. Sensing his need, Abram stayed behind and while listening to the swift flowing river that he loved, he grabbed at the weeds grown high around the markers. Violets were everywhere, a carpet of purple he would never in his whole life forget. He picked great bunches of them and, tying each with string, placed one bouquet in front of each marker.

They stayed for more than a week making trips downriver to try to find some trace of the Brewsters' old friends, the Ewings, but the once fabulous Ewing Plantation lay as desolate as South Wind. New people in the area knew nothing about them, where they had gone nor how they had fared. It was as if the earth had swallowed them. Young Adam's face became more stern as the days passed, as he talked with these new people who lived along the river. Back at Noonday he had promised his father and Miss Olivia that he would take the best offer for the land, clear up the debts on it and return home. He didn't want to, but he did it. They went into Vicksburg and sold it for very little to a rich man who had come down from the north at the end of the war. They didn't want to go back down there with that strange hard man with eyes that glinted narrowly at them, but they had to show him the boundaries and dig out the markers. He was not a planter, and he wasn't going to live down there, he told young Adam. He was buying up land for speculation.

While he talked, his hard eyes searched their worn and shabby clothing, and he knew...

For years and years and years, for decades and decades afterward tears would form in Abram's eyes at the memory of young Adam's set face when he sold off his land, his home, his heritage, his dream, for young Adam had held a dream that one day he would return and rebuild South Wind. For decades Abram remembered how, after the man had gone riding back to Vicksburg, he and young Adam sat on the washed-out old levee staring at the river.

Young Adam's voice quivered with emotion. "We move on in life, Abram. We cross over our rivers, never to return. There is no returning. Life flows on like a great river."

Earlier in their visit they had remarked how the river had changed its course, how it had eaten at the levee. Now young Adam stared at the river.

"If we did come back, if we had been able to come back to stay, nothing would ever be the same again. We have a chance in Texas. We have rich soil there too." He stood up, his eyes looking westward. Abram believed he would never again look back.

But Abram didn't know what was in young Adam's heart as he went about his life in Texas, building up Noonday the way Jacques LeFleur and his grandfather had dreamed of doing it. In his own heart, he never stopped missing the river, never stopped listening for it in the black slow-moving water of the swamp where he and old Adam lived out old Adam's last days.

After they got back from Mississippi he and old Adam fished and Abram talked about the new boats on the river, about how Vicksburg had changed, about how young Adam hunted for old friends. Just the talking kept old Adam busy and happy for months. There was just an awful lot to talk about a river. A man could go on for the rest of his life telling about a river the way Noonday folks and maybe folks up north talked and talked about the war. It was as if the war had ended last year instead of all those years ago.

Now, almost fifty years old, Abram stared out upon the timeless swamp. He supposed that in his old age he would talk about this swamp, tell how he used to carry old Adam down to the skiff and shove off with the pole and talk about the war and the Mississippi and South Wind and Charles and David and David's lost wife Lila and David's two violet-eyed girls that they'd never found, tell how young Adam made that trip up to Chicago to try to find them before Miss Olivia left them. He guessed that old Adam was the only person in the whole world who knew how much Abram loved the river. He knew why he loved it, not just for the beauty of its flowing but because it had brought Abram to Adam to be saved. To his dying day old Trunk never saw Abram that he didn't sing or hum "Amazing Grace" with his eyes shining as if he had seen a miracle.

Swallowing, Abram stared deep into the dusk. The rusty needles of the cypress had turned grey to the evening. A man could spend his life in a swamp and never know it all. Ever since the Noonday Plantation's beginning men and boys had spent Saturdays and Sundays and some of their best holidays going into the swamp to hunt for some trace of Jeddy and Laurel. Abram had his own thoughts on them. No trace was ever found, but he felt that since they had belonged together that they had found a place, built them a cabin and started a new life and that somewhere out in Texas or on across into Louisiana where he had been told this swamp went there would be descendants.

As the swamp darkened, he turned to look toward the lake and the tall pines and the low hills to the west.

"Weather coming in," he said aloud. He had wanted a beautiful day for burying old Adam, for seeing him placed beside Miss Olivia who had waited for so long.

He saw Jessica coming then, her hands folded under her apron. She was coming on firm and he knew by the set of her shoulders that she wasn't going to have any part of his staying beside the swamp mourning. She held her tongue until she got right up in front of him, her legs planted right in front of his face.

"Abram Brewster Cork, you get up out of that dampness

this instant! I got supper cooked. You're coming home with me tonight and for the rest of your life you are not going to leave. You can go on to the big house someday and get your stuff out of that shed where you been living these many years, but now you're coming home."

He knew she meant it. He let her take his hand and drag him to his feet. They walked across the field together and up Evening Road past the tall pines. He smelled the black eyed peas cooking and saw the white shirt she had made for him.

"You sit down at that table. Later on I'll show you how I fixed that old suit for you to wear to the funeral. That old Sunday suit of yours you were going to wear is worn through the seat of the pants."

"That just shows I been sitting in church absorbing the word of the Lord."

"I know how you sit in church. You sit there hoping the preacher will get finished so you can carry Mister Adam out to the swamp to fish. Well, I'm mighty glad this talk got around to the preacher because as soon as we finish burying Mister Adam, that preacher is going to stand on his two feet and marry us."

Abram chewed the rest of the peas that were in his mouth and nodded.

"Yes, Jessica, I think it is about time."

Book Two

Noonday

Chapter 16

ONWARD TO TELLAHAVEE
Fall, 1957

The rain had begun quietly and too late. Abraham Brewster Cork had already locked the door of his room in the boardinghouse, and handed the key to the silky black girl.

The girl held the key loosely in one hand, the broom in the other, abandoning the rusty screen door which slammed behind her as she followed him to the porch. "If you say you don't owe any back rent, I'll believe you because you're a preacher. If you do owe any, they'll catch you, old man."

She said the words with the same blankness of voice and eyes that enclosed everything she did all day until evening when her young man arrived; then she came to life and cared. He had seen that metamorphosis from uncaring to caring, empty to filled, ever since he moved into the boardinghouse in the beginning of summer.

Abraham had settled in the town on the outskirts of Little Rock for the summer to relieve the local preachers for whatever length vacations they could afford to take. Now summer was gone. In his pocket was a letter from Noonday, forwarded back and forth across four states to Arkansas, telling him of the passing of his friend and teacher, Salem Rowe, whose small church was now without a leader.

Clay Justice, writer of the letter and a reporter in the town near Noonday, wrote that Salem while ill made the whimsical bequest that Abraham consider settling, finally, to live out his years in the quiet community of his birth, take over the church where he had read the Bible with Salem. To this end Salem had bequeathed to Abraham his wading boots and dinghy. Abraham intended claiming his property and putting them to good use through winter into spring with his cousin Joshua and his friend Pinkney. Beyond that time he did not wish to venture.

Stooping, he unstrapped his large black umbrella from his suitcase and swung the hook-handle over his wrist.

"When she comes to start supper, I'll tell her." The silky girl let the key slide into her apron pocket, and stirred the broom in useless movements on the porch floor.

The boardinghouse keeper was down at the school watching. If he saw her, he would tell her himself. He intended passing the school on his way to the road in hopes that he could bid his friend police sergeant Rosenberg goodbye. He hated to leave Rosey. In a lifetime of wandering that young man was one of the closest friends he had made. They talked about almost everything since they had met in the late hours of a night in early summer when he went to the station to try to gain freedom for a young boy detained for a disturbance. He was going to miss walking down there evenings.

"Are you leaving because of the trouble at the school?" the girl asked dully, waiting for him to finish and be gone.

Stuffing the umbrella between his legs, he glanced up at her untenanted face; she simply remembered that the boardinghouse keeper was down there. Smiling, he shook his head.

In truth, this was his long settled pattern—southward with the ducks and geese, in front of the north wind, always following the flyways. East Texas was one of the finest, and Noonday lay in the middle of it. It was always good to go home, to be with his own, to be back where he had once been so happy with his father Abram. He had been gone four years and had collected much material for Clay's book on Noonday. He patted the pocket containing the letter, his distant eye already encompassing the duck blind he and Joshua would build on the pine-wrapped lake. The letter had followed him for months, but the undesirable pulpit would be empty and waiting.

He stood for a moment looking out at the rain, wondering if he should fasten his beloved canvas-covered duckgun to the suitcase or carry it under his overcoat to keep it dry.

He studied the wrapped gun, poked in the ends of the canvas. It really looked like a tight bedroll. It would not be wise, he decided soberly, for a negro, even a venerable preacher, to appear at the disturbance at the school with a gun. Pressing it to the side of the gladstone, he tightened the straps. He'd have to carry everything until he got a ride. Getting a ride was never easy, however long the miles, however weary he might be, and soaking wet he'd surely walk. After struggling into his long black overcoat, he raised his hand to the silky girl. May you be happy with your boy, he prayed silently.

"Godbye, miss. My thanks to you."

Lifting the suitcase and holding the umbrella high, he walked down the wooden steps into the rain.

"Goodbye, preacher." Without looking at him, she made a slovenly swish to scatter the small amount of dirt that had managed to collect in front of the broom.

He stepped resolutely out, a youthful gait for a heavy set, middle aged, white haired man wearing and carrying everything he owned in the world, except his wading boots and dinghy. He pondered his decision about leaving without waiting for another letter from his small nephew Brewster. As for the job in Noonday, Abram would have loved his taking it, would have wanted him to do it. He remembered Abram telling him of the building of that church.

The gladstone, of little weight itself, but gun-heavy, contained only his Bible and hymn book, his hand-written notes for Clay, the age-lightened Brewster ledgers he was bringing from the plantation in Virginia, two freshly laundered wing tip collars, four immense starched white cuffs, two frayed black string ties, a matchbox of assorted fish hooks, one spool of double tapered nylon flycasting line, only one clean white Sunday shirt, a small jewel box protecting a white feather, his sewing kit and the one sieve-like mended birdseye suit of bvds wrapped around his nicked straight razor and chewed strop and the box of Number 4 ch shotgun shells. He had put on his long underwear in advance of the trip.

You could never tell about late September. The nights in the open could be cold. He looked at the smudged sky. Tonight would be wet and cold.

As he walked he checked off his preparatory steps for the road. He had done almost everything within an hour after the mail arrived. He had gone to the post office and filled out a forwarding card, hesitated to consider waiting a day or two for another letter from his nephew Brewster who had written from East St. Louis that Leah, his mother and Abraham's sister, was ill, decided, and then dropped the forwarding card into the slot.

He had proceeded to the bus depot where he bought a one way ticket to the town near Noonday. The ticket, in an envelope bearing the address of the depot where it was purchased, was tucked next to the gun permit in his wallet. Except in case of dire emergency the ticket would not be used. After all the miles south had unfolded behind him, and all danger of being arrested for vagrancy were eliminated, he would mail it back for a refund. He had checked his vagrancy fund, a sum kept intact to bring forth should a constable or policeman ask if he had means or employment. The fund was safe.

He always walked with a determined gait. The rules of the road were many. He had learned young, right after he lost his companion Lavender, that a man who steps out as if his errand is important is rarely stopped.

The rain whipped against him, sounding out lonesomely on the umbrella. He listened to it, to the steady rhythm of his shoes on the wet pavement.

He stepped right out, in spite of aching bunions freed recently from the confinement of heavy shoes. Just before leaving his room he had slivered a leather circle from the side of each one with his penknife. He thought that he actually marched, that his procedure was soldierly—he'd spent four years in mess hall kitchens. Shoulders straight, stomach flat, firm; he knew it protruded roundly. Left, right; left, right. Count your blessings: Lord, I'm thankful I'm not in jail. I'm glad I'm not in the nuthouse. I've never killed another man. I've not committed rape—his mind paused while he pondered a point of law. The laws of the land were equally important as the laws of God, as he had learned to his great sorrow at the beginning of his lifetime as a wandering preacher.

He had committed the crime in this way: he was following a circuit, preaching every Sunday in a different and far distant church. He rode the miles sitting far to the rear of Lavender, a gift from Abram, the little orchid-grey mule who had become his beloved companion, had traveled with him for many years. They were crossing a high mountain pass. It was spring. White dogwood blossoms laced the edges of the woods. Mountain laurel, and great banks of rhododendron tinted the mountainsides. Into this fragrant, peaceful scene ripped frantic human screams. They raced up a path, and came upon a small log cabin. Inside, Abraham found a young and frightened girl giving birth to her first child. Her terrified ashen-faced boy husband was passed out cold on the cabin floor.

A very young Abraham Brewster Cork stooped to the job on hand, brought forth by breech birth a living child who had come too far ahead of the circuit running nurse. With shaking brown hands he had reshaped the small yellow-gold head before splashing cold water upon the face of the new father. Because the roads were muddy and almost impassable, because Abraham rode a mule and would be passing through the county seat, the happy couple asked if he would be kind enough to stop off to register the birth of the child.

At the county seat he fastened his beloved Lavender to a hitching-post, located the clerk and asked permission to register the birth. The couple had written their names and the infant's name on a slip of paper. The clerk copied from the slip, and asked what doctor or nurse had brought the child. Abraham told the clerk he had brought the child. He proudly related the experience, stood there telling the tale he would never again relate in his life. He stood in front of that clerk, stood there on his nicely-shaped slim bunionless feet, and was arrested for the unheard-of crime of unregistered midwifery.

He was put into jail to await a circuit running judge who would hold trial. Lavender was impounded in a yard in back of the building. From the jail window in the front of the building, Abraham pleaded with everyone who passed to go around behind the jail to offer some kindness, some affection to his little mule. He never knew if any kindness—a sugar lump, an ear-scratching, or a soft word—was administered to Lavender. Months passed. One terrible morning the jailor remarked, "Your mule died last night or sometime. Anyhow, he's dead."

It was during the time that the very young Abraham mourned the mule who died of heartbreak waiting for Abraham until those alert orchid-lined ears drooped in final dejection, and while he fulfilled the bidding of the unheard-of law concerning unregistered midwifery that he began writing down on tablets the stories old Abram had told him of the Brewster family and their slaves. He wrote them for the children of Noonday. Years afterward his friend Clay Justice was to borrow them to write the history of the town which was in no way famous, and certainly of no importance to the world. Abraham felt positive of this, yet Clay wanted to do it.

In spite of the drizzling rain a crowd still gathered on the sidewalks across the street from the school. The police, Rosey not among them, had strung ropes from trees and poles to keep the street clear. A reporter with a wet notebook was questioning a small cluster of excitedly gesturing housewives.

Abraham put his bag on the ground, and leaning against a tree, pulled a handkerchief from his pocket and across his face. The weight of the bag or the recollections, the long underwear and his heavy coat were too much in the humidity.

As he stood looking around for Rosey and the boardinghouse keeper, a familiar and dilapidated silver-grey car pulled to the curb beside him. A long ununiformed arm stretched across the seat to open the door, to flop Abraham's bag into the back seat. He leaned down to peer in, hardly recognizing Rosey out of uniform.

"I went by your boardinghouse. The girl said you'd

headed this way. You shouldn't be standing in the rain, and you shouldn't be here with that gun. Get in."

Delightedly, he grabbed his friend's hand. "Rosey, I was looking for you to say goodbye. I'm moving on. I was just wondering if I'd find you if I walked to your room."

"Well, pop, I'm leaving too. Come along to my room. We'll talk while I pack."

He couldn't get over Rosenberg's resigning from the force. He was headed out for California, had a married sister out there. They talked until Rosenberg was ready to leave. He insisted that it wasn't out of his way to drop down into Texarkana instead of his planned route through Oklahoma City.

It was dark when they left, and rain still fell. Abraham shook his head drowsily, trying to stay awake. The rhythm of the windshield wipers, the singing of the tires on the wet road, and the steady tapping of the rain on the top of the car mesmerized him into a state between tranquility and sleep. He missed something Rosenberg said, and pulled his head to one side listening as Rosenberg laughed. He looked over at his face, but was unable to determine humor or cynicism in the gloom.

"I thought I'd visit Ceil in California... Not for long. She has her own life."

Abraham thought of Leah, sick up in East St. Louis. He had honestly intended going up there before the letter came from Clay. Closing his eyes he remembered her unflinching sense of responsibility for Abram, how she stayed on at the cabin, youngest of Abram and Jessica's children, working in the cotton fields until, when she was almost forty and had a chance to marry that railroad porter from East St. Louis, Abram had chased her off. After her little Brewster was born, she took in washing until he was old enough to shift for himself, and then she got day work. The porter was long gone. Leah was determined that Brewster would have a chance in life that she thought he wouldn't get in Noonday. Abraham couldn't be located when Lelia LeFleur sent Leah word that Abram was blind and going deaf. Leah went down there, took him back to East St. Louis where little Brewster cared for him until he died. No one knew how old Abram was, but the Noonday Brewsters said he was over a hundred.

"I thought I'd just start out. I've been thinking about doing it for some time." Rosenberg was almost talking to himself.

Abraham was fully awake now, his conscience had seen to that, but he stayed quiet. It was good for people to talk things out, out loud. He did it a lot, walking in the woods or along a road, sitting in a church somewhere, or in a room, if he had one.

"Don't laugh, pop. I thought I might sell this heap out there, maybe up in San Francisco, and ship out. I was in the Navy once. Wish I'd stayed, but I got stuck in one place. I might join up again. I'd like to see more of the world. Just start out, no place in mind, take the first job on a ship. I don't have any ties, or strings, owe nothing to anyone alive." Rosey struck a match to light a cigarette.

There was something exceedingly bitter in the way Rosey struck that match with his thumbnail. It made Abraham remember one of the talks they had one night at the station. It was about Rosey's father who had been a maker of shoes. He might be referred to as an artist of that craft—he designed women's shoes. Once a shoe manufacturer in New England recognized some special merit in one of his samples and searched him out. They were living in some middle west town. The manufacturer sent his private plane. Rosey's father didn't want to go. He was afraid. It was all too fancy for him. They had been in this country fifteen years, most of which had been spent trying to understand and to make himself understood. They moved a lot, searching. Rosey, growing up at the time, was never sure what his parents hunted, but he thought his father's designs were wonderful. He talked him into going. The men were to meet at a fabulous resort hotel on a lake. Instead a telegram met the plane; the manufacturer was delayed, he would arrive the following day. Rosenberg was to wait at the hotel. He took a taxi out there. The instant he entered the spacious lobby something told him he should never have gone there. The desk clerk wasn't apologetic. He was emphatic. If Rosenberg had a confirmation, it was an error, the hotel was full. Rosenberg took a taxi back to town, got a bus home. It cost him a lot of money. There was a greater cost. The shoe manufacturer wrote intense apologies, but it was too late. Rosey's father died shortly afterward.

Abraham had never forgotten the picture that formed after the telling of it. He would never forget Rosey's father turning away from that hotel desk and walking the length of that hotel lobby. Uncomfortably, he moved his feet inside his wet shoes, imagined he heard water squishing. One of his bunions hurt terribly.

"I thought I might go around the world, see all those places you hear about. I might even see Paris. I've always wanted to see Casablanca, something about the name. Pop, I'd like to see how other people live, find out what they really think about one another. I feel as if I'd like to know, once and for all, what really is important, the person or the whole." He leaned forward to mash the cigarette into the dashboard ashtray.

Abraham shivered, searching deep. He remembered leaving Noonday long ago, moving on until he crossed the Mississippi. He wandered through Vicksburg, up and down the hills, trudged a back road searching for South Wind, watching for the landmarks known from Abram's stories and Pinkney's songs. The Brewster plantation? People remembered. He was told that young Adam had sold off the bottoms. "Well, there's an old graveyard near the levee, around that bend. The river's changed its course a lot since the War." He found the graves, cleaned around them, sat beside them all through a long night while he thought about things he'd heard all his life—of Simeon's banjo, of Oner and how he happened to marry Amelia. He imagined he heard the voices of slave children, heard them laughing. He tried to see the big house, first house, the cabins—nothing remained except the graves in that dense jungle of trees and vines. He listened to the wind in the trees, to the moving river. Toward morning, a raft of driftwood floated through the early mist. He had hurried back to Noonday, stayed with Abram, listened again to his stories, talked with Brewsters, LeFleurs,

Blacks—and they all loved to talk about it—and then he decided. He had to see it all, every mile of the long road back to Virginia. How long it had taken, and then he'd met Clay Justice back in Noonday, and started the long trek again.

He wondered if it was instinct; maybe people inherently searched. Maybe wandering was born into man, inherited from the nomadic tribes. Maybe it was as simple as that. Whatever it was, he believed it was rare that a man when troubled didn't think of moving on to change a condition, to try to find something better. Or was it dreams? Did men follow their dreams?

"Another one starting out on his own hegira. Who knows? I might even end up in Tel Aviv."

Tellahavee. Silently, Abraham savored the word. It was romantic, idealistic and must be very far away. Somehow it made him feel like crying. He cried a lot, out walking in the woods or along a road, in a church somewhere, alone in a room. He didn't know why he cried, some deep loneliness inside him, something unfulfilled, some unknown sorrow that men inherited. He wondered if other men cried at night because of their failures, their incapabilities, cried out of hopelessness. He wondered if other men cried when they prayed, or if they prayed. One never knew what another man did in his silences.

"Pop, I don't know why it was that I fell in love with a blonde grey-eyed Gentile girl. But I'd made the vow when mama was dying like she asked me to. 'I will, mama, I will.' You're a preacher, pop, is that a vow? Is it a vow to say 'I will, mama, I will' when she's dying and says 'marry in the faith, your father would have wanted you to.'? Is that a vow when she's dying and asks? Yet, I keep having the feeling that if she'd got well and met Polly, I could have talked her out of it. But I felt that obligation, that vow or promise, so I went away. I never even wrote to Polly. One time in the navy I ran into a guy from home. He said, 'Do you remember Polly, oh, sure you remember Polly. Well, she died.' I said, 'What'd she die of?' He said, 'I don't know. One of my sisters wrote it in a letter. Do you want me to write and ask her what she died of?' I said no, I was just wondering. The whole time I was in the navy before that I kept going over it in my mind, figuring I'd go back someday, see how Polly was doing. I ought to have married Polly. I wanted to. But, I didn't. Sometimes I get mad and blame mama, and then I remember the hell Polly's people raised."

Was it a vow, Abraham asked himself. Was it a promise? Did people take vows too seriously? Did Rosey's mama do the cruelest thing she could ever have done to two young people in love? Which did matter most, the individual or the group?

"I'd lie awake in my hammock and the ship would be swaying, and I'd remember how the trees swayed in the wind above us when we'd lie in the grass and plan. We were in love. We were going to get married, have kids. Want to know something, pop, the truth? Neither of us gave a damn what church our kids went to. What do you think of that?"

Abraham saw them then; the black eyed boy with the solemn expression—or were those eyes solemn then?—and the grey-eyed girl got up out of the grass and ran, her fair hair flying out in the wind, like he always pictured youth, running with the wind. He sobbed aloud, then coughed to hide the sound.

Rosenberg looked over at him. "Pop, you're cold. I didn't want you walking in the rain, yet I let you ride for hours in those wet clothes." He snapped on the car heater, and warm air swept around them.

They were going through a settlement. Lights flickered mistily back and forth like Rosey's ships signaling in passing.

Rosenberg braked evenly, swinging into a cafe parking lot. "We'll get hot coffee, something to eat." Racing around the car, he opened the door for Abraham.

Abraham looked out at him. Rosenberg glanced over the top of the lighted restaurant windows that flashed across his eyes. He slammed the car door violently.

It was still raining when Abraham woke up. The car was steamed over inside and filled with smells of wet wool, cigarette smoke and the greasy scent rising from the bag of hamburgers on his lap. Rosey had brought them to the car with the paper container of coffee. It was nine o'clock on the wildly racing clock on the dashboard. They'd been on the road over three hours. He sat up, glancing around. The car moved slowly. Street lights were frosted circles beyond the windshield.

"This Texarkana?" he asked softly, not wanting it to be.

"Yes. Listen, pop, are you sure you've got a place to stay? There's an inch of rain in the street. I sure would hate to have you start walking in this. I wish you'd just go on west with me. I'll bet you'd like California. We'd hit right out of here on 82, pick up 187 at Wichita Falls, get on 66 at Amarillo." He started singing, "'Get your kicks on old 66.' How about it, pop? You could spell me at the wheel."

"Thanks, Rosey. I've held you back enough. You'd have made better time through Oklahoma City. No, you just let me out." He wiped steam off the window with his coat sleeve, and peered out. "I'll find my friend's house." He crossed his fingers under the hamburger bag—he didn't know a living soul in Texarkana. But he chose a likely looking street. He didn't want Rosey to get too far off the highway. Picking out a shabby little deserted-looking house, he pointed. "There it is, sure enough. Dark though, they're in bed, or out for the evening."

The car stopped; the dashboard clock raced on. "Are you sure, pop? I don't feel satisfied leaving you here...the rain and all, and it being night."

Rosenberg carried the bag up to the porch and placed it against the wooden wall near the door. The headlights of the car streamed ahead down the street, glistening into puddles, turning rain into shimmering shreds of tinsel. There was the soft sound of the idling motor.

Rosenberg took his hand. "I hate to leave you, pop. Hope your friends get home soon."

There were many things to say, to answer. Rosey was leaving too soon. Abraham smiled in the dim light. Everything ended too soon. But it was all right about the answers. Each man had to search out his own answers. He raised his free hand in a hail.

"I hope you make it to Tellahavee."

Rosenberg laughed, that same indecipherable laugh, and squeezed Abraham's hand with an almost unbearable pressure. He saw Rosenberg silhouetted against the sky which was red with the watery reflections of the lights of the town and the highway's flashing neons. It looked like a burning town to be fled.

"I hope you get the church job if you really want it. You're pretty used to the road."

"Thanks, Rosey. I can always move on if it gets to feeling tight."

Rosenberg's footsteps made a hollow sound crossing the wooden porch and going down the wooden steps. The car door slammed, a familiar sound. The motor raced, the car moved, turning around. The lights passed over Abraham, picking him out and there came a soft bleep of the horn. Then the two streamers of light bobbed up and down, up and down on the rough unpaved street, darting this way and then that way as Rosenberg drove around the ruts filled with water. Then the tail-lights flashed red, turned westward and were gone.

Somewhere down the dark street a radio cried a sad song. The rain fell steadily on the galvanized roof of the small house. Ripped by one of the deepest, soul-searing stabs of loneliness he had ever known in his life, Abraham wished he could call Rosey back. He wished he had gone with him. He wondered why people waited until others had gone out of their lives to wish to call them back. He wondered why people couldn't see ahead far enough to know how they would feel after someone left.

He sat down on his suitcase. All departures, all leave takings, all goodbyes were hard, but it was more than that. He knew in his heart he would never see Rosenberg again. He hoped that Rosenberg would make it to his Tellahavee, wherever it was, however hard it would be for him to get there. Leaning back against the damp wooden wall of the house, he raised his eyes to the sky so weirdly lighted yet so strangely dark. He prayed that Rosenberg would find whatever he sought, and in addition, he prayed he would find someone sweet, someone fine to replace Polly, his lost love.

The wind was changing, coming in from the north. He felt the house shiver in the sudden cold, and got up to tap lightly upon the door. The house had a hollow sound. He was sure it was empty, but he went to the window, cupped his hands on the glass to peer in. Satisfied, he turned the doorknob gently. Inside he stretched out on the bare floor under the window, his head in his arms on a pillow of his folded coat. He lay there and cried.

Abraham felt the weak warmth of the morning sun. He was stiff and sore. The floor was still damp, but swift cold air sweeping in around the door and the loose-fitting window was dry and crisp. He became aware of the aroma of Rosenberg's hamburgers in the paper bag beside him. He lay there remembering. Probably Rosey was still driving, or right now he might be sipping scalding coffee in a roadside cafe far west in Texas. Rosenberg would think that Abraham was up and walking briskly toward Noonday.

Forcing open his eyes to blink into the brilliant clarity of a blue Texas norther, he found the high sky a washed morning blue with swift small left-over white clouds traveling south. He pulled himself into a sitting position, automatically straightening the tails of his frock coat out behind him, crossing his legs, and reached for the greasy paper bag.

Slowly chewing, he saw the dilapidated grey car shoot out from some unknown driveway onto the westering highway, the morning sun giving the car the shine of new metal, so that Rosey became a glittering silver streak headed west. Still watching the chimerical streak, he drew the second hamburger from the bag. A small folded piece of paper fell to the floor. He unfolded a greasy ten dollar bill and a note written on the cafe saleslip. *Good luck, pop. Rosey.*

He could hear Rosey's voice. "Pop, maybe this Noonday deal *is* yours. Get a store-bought haircut and a press and walk right in like you owned the place." Well, in truth he did own a dinghy and wading boots. Clay Justice had written that the whole congregation wanted him. He took out his wallet, removed a ten dollar bill from his vagrancy fund and replaced it with Rosey's gift carefully folded in the note. He knew he would never part with either of them.

Balanced carefully on the tailgate of an empty watermelon truck headed south, Abraham's glistening shoes swung free. The holes he had cut were hardly noticeable. He ran a finger along the fine new crease in his pants. At Evening Road, he gave the driver a hail, and marched across the macadam. The sounds of the motor died off in the distance as he stepped from the road upon fragrant drying earth meshed with fallen leaves of the age-old narrow trace walled in by red cypress and mammoth live oaks holding mistletoe. The sweet gums were turning. Dark shining leaves of magnolia and youpon made an arch trimmed with millions of red pyracantha berries and the brilliant red-orange of fall-turned sumac. He passed a new clearing with a comfortable grey plank shack, came to God's Great Live Oak. Stopping, he looked in at Black's house, at the old cow barn, the remembered corn fields; inhaled the sweet pine smoke rising from the chimney of the familiar corrugated tin roof. He hesitated, for Raven Black, the far descendant of Jeddy Black of Abram's stories and Pinkney's songs, was his friend. He hesitated, but the sun was dropping fast.

He broke out of the tree-closed trace into the stand of tall long-needle pines. The sky was immense and endless over fields of unpicked cotton hanging wet and silvery pink on black-brown leafless stalks. Running crookedly, the gladstone banging his legs, he crossed a field of wild grass turned rust red. Upon the lake's flat-silver surface lay shadows of the dark green pines. End to end streamed one shining ribbon of the same sunset Rosey would see.

Placing his bag on the ground, he stood listening as a chattering flock of wild geese rode in on the north wind.

Chapter 17

EVENING ROAD

He sat on his suitcase. Through the dense black pines the sun rested, an orange ball upon the hills, its gleam spreading out through the thin rows of curled evening clouds. On the horizon shimmered a pink mist. Suddenly, in the moment of dying, the broad western sky became the inner edge of a rainbow, dimming to orchid, to grey, like a fire dying out behind the pines. The hills were gone. All color was gone. Only the black barriers of pines lay between him and the west. A nighthawk swept high, called. Geese, settling, rattled the cane. His gleaming shoes sank into the cooling mud. Moving his feet to a grassy spot, he pulled his overcoat close. The water lay bluish black with an oiled green cast. The shadows of the trees and reeds lay dead black upon its surface. One star shone upon it. Looking up, he found its immense unblinking clarity.

This was the west his father saw that night he trudged into Noonday Plantation pulling the exhausted Adam Brewster. He imagined he saw them in the shadows, marching. They were marching; he could hear their steps, the rhythm, and from a deeper distance, he imagined a gentle roll of drums, the high plaintive pitch of a fife, because after all they were soldiers. They'd lost, but they'd fought. Wasn't all fighting victorious?

There they came, seven abreast, weary shoulders straightening, almost in, almost there, almost to the west Adam and Oner had been heading for all those waiting years... Adam Brewster, Oner LeFleur, Garrett, Targ, Solom, Zibe and Abram. Of them, only Adam and Oner were very old. One, Abram, was very young. The others were to run briefly into the arms of loved ones, to ride out again, to turn eastward, to slip in with Texans headed out to fight.

He heard their horses in the wind, racing through the dusty road, walking through brambles, pulling through mud, treading on drying leaves, dying leaves... Abram said there wasn't a man white or black over fifteen or under sixty left on the plantation.

The first Brewster to die in the war was David at Shiloh, at Pittsburg Landing, Tennessee, under General Albert Johnston, who also died. General Beauregard took the rest of that youthful Confederate Army of Mississippi into other battles. His name still lived today in Noonday in old men, in young boys. They were still naming babies after him the last time he was here: "I christen thee Beauregard Brewster Brown."

And then Charles. Oner had told Abram of Charles, of his clear blue-grey eyes, Brewster eyes with black brows and heavy lashes inherited from his grandmother Rebecca to encircle Adam Brewster's somber expression, and Olivia's sudden twinklings of gaiety. Charles Brewster, a gentle boy who, given time, would write the history of the Brewster migration, had died in Maryland, at Antietam, on the bloodiest day of the war. In his late years Adam refused to accept Charles's death. He continued to write letters to him in Virginia. How many letters had Olivia written to Illinois trying to seek out David's violet-eyed girls? But they were lost somewhere above the line. Of Adam's and Olivia's boys, only sturdy young Adam came on to Texas, to marry, to plant cotton he would have planted at South Wind had South Wind survived, to become the grandfather of Adam who now ran the store, and of Boyd, who operated the Noonday filling station where Joshua worked. Adam and Olivia's daughter Ruth remarried and her descendents were scattered all over Texas.

Of Aaron and Ruth's boys, Jacques and Auguste, who rode proud Virginia horses out of the circular drive of the old Brewster plantation in Appomattox county, parted forever. Jacques died in Pennsylvania, at Gettysburg. Auguste rode away from the Battle of the Wilderness near Chancellorsville, out through the dense forest to die at Cedar Creek in the last battle of the Shenandoah. Abraham had seen these battlefields, had walked the rows, had written names down on his tablet, had heard the silence while he sat wondering why it was so important to Adam that Charles's dream come true, why it had become so necessary to Abram that Adam's last hope be realized, while he sat thinking it all out, trying to comprehend the importance, the necessity, the reason for the conflict...

Young Aaron came back. His descendants lived here today. Aaron Brewster still lived in the old Noonday house built above the original dugout at the other end of Evening Road shadowed now by the modern apartments Drew Brewster had built. Enchanting Olivia Flower lived in the house Jacques LeFleur built long ago for an Adam Brewster who never got beyond a stockade wall in Alabama. Ara, the daughter of Aaron of Virginia, lived out her years in the Acadian country—still had descendants there. Rayford and young Aaron stayed on at Noonday, saw the lean years. Robert and Royal returned to California.

"I wouldn't be here to tell all this, son, if Adam Brewster hadn't stood on the Mississippi levee snagging logs with that boathook..." And, had it not been that Olivia insisted upon every slave child of South Wind learning to write, however poorly, who would have known where they'd all headed when they scattered? "You tell Master Adam I snuck in with Forrest's troops, got many a lick in to satisfy Mister David. Tell him I told you how the river looked. Better don't tell him I couldn't make myself let fly one ball at them negroes in the Union garrison." A treasured letter handed down, written somewhere west of Fort Pillow, in Tennessee, to Cecile, daughter of Rip. Rip's last letter came from Georgia. "You be sure to tell Trunk I swum the Chattahooch." How many years had Cecile watched the road. "I ain't worried, now the prisoners is stragglin' in." Abram said her eyes were still turned to the road when she died. Abraham had walked through all the Georgia cemeteries and never found a marker.

Honor, son of Oner and Amelia:
You tell Master Adam I found Charles's grave. Give him this man's name. I talked to him. If he still wants Charles moved... Tell Trunk I made myself known to

Mister Jacques and Mister Auguste's widows. Better not tell how starved they and the children are. I had my mouth set for some of that Virginia ham, but I didn't taste it. Tell pa I saw his shop; it's a fine shed. The boys here use it to shoe horses. All the horses left are fine, but not many... Tell Master Adam I was shown his grandparents's graves. They're still there. Tell him Eli Salem's great grandchildren run the store.

Honor came home. Children in Noonday were still christened in his name. Jessie, Jock and Josh came home. Jeffy and Edgar disappeared as if the darkness of night had melted them. Rachel had three letters from Albert. Long after the war a letter came from a nurse in Georgia addressed *Mrs. Albert Brewster LeFleur, Noonday, Texas.*

You wouldn't mourn if you knew how he suffered. He didn't want you to know. I have lain through many nights wondering what course I should take. Were I you, I would want to know. Albert had been shattered by the explosion of a shell. Abraham had found his grave. He had written of it in his notes for Clay. Young Peleg came back, running crookedly, limping, yelling, forgetting what his crutch was for, to wave it high in the air, to be caught in loving arms, to be wept over, fed, praised, questioned, and to talk about it all until the day he died, an old veteran. A memory now.

All through Abraham's childhood he had heard the stories of the end of the war, how they looked when they straggled in: white faces, black faces, brown faces; grave faces, scarred faces, bandaged faces, weary faces, horrified faces to light up in the joy of homecoming, to cloud over, to crinkle in happiness, to crumble in sorrow over bad news, to light up when medals came in the mail, to darken when final word arrived... Those were the feet that marched, or walked or dragged or hopped or ran back down Evening Road where the bare feet of their grandchildren and great-grandchildren still ran. Some came back on litters, to await artificial limbs, to whittle out a wooden leg that Oner would finish. Some dragged home to die, to briefly hold a beloved hand. Some were to reach out sightlessly to touch a remembered face.

Abram said there were busy years after the war. It was

true that a few sat around waiting for the promised forty acres and a mule, but after drifters floated into Noonday seeking work or to steal food, they got to work, began building homes on the land parceled out by young Aaron who had had to sell part of his father's plantation and by Old Adam who'd hardly had time to claim his long-due inheritance from the LeFleur debt owed his grandfather. Sawmills sprang up all over East Texas. In the slack months men sought work at them. Now and then one wandered off eastward, westward or south to the coast.

Of those who never got back from the war, how many graves had he been able to locate? How many white? How many black? How many unmarked as to color so that only the names remained? How many brass plates tarnished green to be polished for parade days back through all those states he had traveled? But what of the graves he never found? Did a white boy or a black boy of theirs fall at Chattanooga? Had any made it to Lookout Mountain, or Missionary Ridge? How he had wondered as he retraced those miles...

Abram said they had been baffling years for old Adam, years filled with sorrows past. While Olivia and Abram tried to lead him out of his darkness, he sank deeper, lost track of time, lived in the futile hope that Charles waited eagerly for his letters, that David still practised law in Chicago. When money got scarce, his young Adam went back to Mississippi, that broken devastated beautiful land, and sold off the bottoms for so little he felt ashamed to give it to Olivia. Abram stayed by old Adam until he wandered into his last shadows before he turned to be consoled by his waiting Jessica who so late in life gave him Abraham and later, Leah.

Frogs were singing, splashing the calm lake. Dampness from the mud seeped through his shoes, chilling him. He gazed at the sky. The star blinked, unanswering. Up on the road a lantern swung high over a white mule, mistily outlined a woman standing up in the wagon.

"Now don't you boys fall in. Remember, I promised Ivory. When you get them frogs, scatter to Raven's, you hear? Or you'll miss the food."

Two flashlights bobbed toward the lake. "Yes'm, Miss

Lelia." The brave flash of a light into his face. "That you, Pinkney? It's the preacher. Miss Lelia, the preacher's here! Boy, preacher, Miss Lelia just said too bad you weren't here to baptise Raven's new baby. Another girl. Are you going to take the place of the preacher who died?"

The lantern-lighted mule paused on the road. "You boys teasing me?"

Two flashes blinded him. "No, he's here, honest, look."

"Reverend Cork, you down there fishing already?"

With flashlights bobbing, the boys ran with him to the wagon. "How are you, Miss LeFleur?"

"Reverend Cork, I'm so glad you're here. This is Ivory Johnson's boys, you remember Ivory, porter on the Cotton Belt. Now, give me them frogging forks. You got traipsin' to do. You know what, don't you?"

Young Ivory nodded, his broad grin gleaming in the lantern light. The other boy looked puzzled, then brightened.

"You run home fast as you can. Tell everybody the preacher's here and we're going to Raven's," she spoke slowly, emphasising that they would be gone long enough. "Tell your Aunt Tulley that the new preacher would appreciate a nice clean jar and washbowl. You understand?" She reached into a pleasantly fragrant paper bag on the floor of the wagon and drew out two drumsticks. "Now, scatter, don't miss anybody."

Abraham could hear them pattering toward Noonday. Within an hour every single borrowed piece of furniture and utility would be returned to the long abandoned parsonage. Everything would be in its place. The two room shack would be swept and neat. There probably would be considerable overflow since it would be hard to remember exactly who had borrowed what.

"Don't you start worrying about your dinghy and boots, Reverend Cork. Mister Clay put them up in his garage and I got the key swinging around my neck on a string. He was just heartbroke you didn't get here before he had to leave. He said to tell you he'd be back around Christmas."

Abraham shook his head. He'd been looking forward to

handing Clay the borrowed ledgers and explaining that they must be returned to the old Brewster plantation in Virginia. She handed him the reins. The mule stepped lightly, the wheels trundled, a familiar sound. He drooped into the curve of a man leading a mule down Evening Road.

"Last year the cotton dried up. Year before that the seeds flooded out. Your paper wherever you were must have covered that tornado that hit Dallas. Joshua lost his house, his cat, everything."

Now he was stricken. "Joshua's in Dallas."

"Goin' on three years. Ever since Mister Boyd closed the filling station. You didn't know the station was closed?"

Joshua had always worked at Boyd's station on Evening Road, at the junction of Old Swamp Road. "Pokeen?" He was almost afraid to ask. Pokeen Black's Funeral Home and Record Studio stood across the street from the station, next to Adam's General Store and Post Office.

"Pokeen's busier than ever. Now don't you fret about Joshua. No doubt he'll come home the minute he hears you're home to stay. You *are* going to stay?" Digging down, she handed him a drumstick. "Things will pick up. That wet spring of '57 just made it awful for the Brewsters and the Ainsleys."

Bert Ainsley was an outsider, married one of the dark-eyed granddaughters of Jacques LeFleur. Lived up beyond the main road for years, and then lucked into oil. Everyone in Noonday thought Miss Ainsley urged him to buy cotton land to get him away from drink. He drank up the oil money. He was one white man with no respect whatever for negroes. Folks said he couldn't have sprung from anything except slave-traders. He had to bring his own field hands. No self-respecting local man would work for him if he didn't need the work. The women pitied Miss Ainsley so much they felt they had to help her out. Pinkney still worked for Aaron Brewster at the old house. Shame of the town were those modern apartments Drew Brewster built between old-house and the graveyard. Abraham heard her out; a lot she told he knew. He turned into the Black's yard.

A woman opened the door. "Well, Reverend Cork! We sure hope you're going to take Salem's place. Old Salem was so full of fire and brimstone that he forgot today. We need some today-preaching."

"This is Miss Johnson, Reverend Cork. Mister Johnson cleared that land above Raven's."

Abraham moved on in. Raven held out both hands.

"Raven, congratulations," he said. "Aretha, what a pretty child. Now with little Jib here you don't have to worry about not getting another boy. Raven, you still working way over in Dallas?" It seemed that every time he came home for a visit Raven's wife had a new baby, all girls. Jib had been a blessing.

"We had a real norther last night. Yesterday I stopped by to see Aretha, and that field was green as poke. Then that norther blew in, hail balls big as beau d'arc apples. Wouldn't surprise me it broke some windows in the parsonage."

Abraham smiled. He remembered the broken windows in the parsonage.

"You remember Courtney?"

"Pinkney's off playing somewhere. Joshua couldn't leave Boyd. Looks after him like an old hen." Oil lamps shone on their faces. They still didn't have electricity down Evening Road. This was Noonday. He could go into any house and find it just like this. They accepted life's gifts, its tragedies, and its laughter. Crowded in here were elderly men and women whose funeral services he would read, young people he would marry, and he'd baptise their children.

"There are fifteen unbaptised babies waiting for you."

"This young man has been waiting three months to marry this little girl."

"Reverend, would you like a slice of pecan pie?"

"How long since you've tasted greens cooked with salt pork?"

He was home. He felt as if he'd already stepped into Salem's shoes.

It was very late when the party ended. They rode toward Noonday under the clear black sky where stars blinked. His heart was warm with friendship, his belly almost beyond comfort with fried chicken, grits, corn bread, greens, pecan pie. His coat still held the fragrance of the wood fire.

"... Cary Mae died, you remember? Weren't you here when Garrett brought them all home for the funeral? Garrett never went back to New Orleans. Neither did Arlie. They're still working in Dallas. You'd know every one of Arlie's children by their eyes." A tone of pride touched her voice now that she spoke of the LeFleurs, her own people.

A lamp glowed in the old house that had been Salem's. The church was dark. "We just never got the wiring past the filling station, Reverend. Now that you're here, maybe we'll get it." She got down from the wagon. "Now you just sit there. Someone's still inside and you know how they'd feel if..."

Lelia LeFleur slipped up to the door and peered inside. "Come on in, Reverend. It's just Doodle."

A man leaned over the sink, priming the pump with water he poured from a gasoline can. "This is Doodle, Reverend. He came down here with the Ainsleys." Eyes raised, smiled, dropped back down shyly. A young girl ran in the back door, a quart bottle stuffed with straw flowers and drooping yellow zinnias held out in front.

"Doodle, they all frost eat, nothing fit for a preacher. Oh, Miz Lelia! We not quite ready. How'do, preacher." She curtsied quaintly, and there was a flash of a smile somehow familiar.

He held out his hand. "Now, let's see, you belong to..."

"No, suh. I don't come from none of yor people. Doodle and me, we come up from the swamp..." There was yearning in the fresh young voice.

Lelia put her arm on the girl's shoulder. "You belong to us all, Lutie Mae. Reverend, Lutie Mae and Doodle live behind you in Joshua's old house."

"You just want anything, you holler. Doodle and me'll hear you."

Doodle's deft hands had brought water up through the dry pipes, had filled all the returned lamps with kerosene, and replaced burned wicks. He smiled occasionally as he worked, as if he thought he was expected to say something but had nothing to say.

When they had gone Abraham walked around the two rooms. The feather bed was back, fresh mended sheets white as new cotton stretched tight under a quilt not long off a quilting rack. All of the furniture that he remembered was back in its exact spot. There seemed to be a lot of extra chairs. He placed his suitcase on one, lighted the lamp above the bed and carried it to the dresser.

He lay a long while listening to the night. Somewhere an owl questioned. Frogs. A mockingbird: they never did know night from day. A longing cry from a killdeer. The wind stirring. The great live oaks' movement, steady, sweeping, brushing, never still. He leaned out of bed and pulled from the window a rag that had been stuffed into a broken pane. The night swept in, sweet with the fragrance of wood fires, of cottonseed oil. He breathed deeply, peacefully.

The day was too early for light. Somewhere outside a cardinal clicked in the live oaks. Grackles and blackbirds creaked, like the rusted chains of a swing. Brewster had gone to a second hand store up in East St. Louis and found an old swing like the one Abram had been used to in Noonday, and with the sky hooks the man gave him, hung the swing in the hall outside Leah's apartment, facing the fire escape, facing the river, although he couldn't see it. Every morning Brewster, after he dressed Abram and fried his eggs and warmed his grits, led the old man into the hall and sat him down on the swing. There Abram rocked back and forth and dreamed. When the wind was right he could smell the smoke from the incinerators, and he would call Brewster. "That smell like cottonseed oil to you, nephew?" Brewster would look deep into the eyes that were unseeing. "No, sir, not exactly like cottonseed oil, and I'm your own grandson." Abram had called most of the children of Noonday nephew, girls and boys. Once Brewster took Abram over to the river and described the boats, the water, the color and the sound of its flowing, yelling at the top of his voice. A man, curious, came over to listen. Brewster told him how far back into time

Abram went and the man said he bet Abram would like a ride on the fine shining Admiral that sat waiting at the dock. The man paid for the ride. Brewster was so excited that he forgot to find out the man's name so that Leah could write her thanks to him. Abram couldn't understand how this river could be the same Mississippi he had crossed with Adam Brewster.

Abram had talked to Brewster in a voice now pitched high with age, talked ceaselessly, explaining, telling in the way he had told Abraham, and Brewster sat through those stifling summer hours, patiently holding the old hand, watching the loose mouth. After school on a winter's day he wound a scarf around the thin ropey neck, bundled the shrunken body into a heavy overcoat and led him out into the clean fresh air. Remembering, Abraham twisted his own neck painfully. His bunions ached fiercely, but he got out of bed, straightened the sheet, and went to his bag for his tablet. He had to write to Brewster. Maybe Leah was bad sick. Maybe they needed money. When he went out to mail the letter, he thought he would call Joshua over in Dallas. If Leah was bad sick, he might have to go up to East St. Louis. He wouldn't want to leave without seeing Joshua.

Chapter 18

NOONDAY

The lamp smoked when Abraham blew it out. An unreal dawn came slowly filtering whitely through the fog. The pounding he heard as he wrote to Brewster stopped suddenly. Soft voices crossed the mist. Back at the boardinghouse the landlady would be frying bacon; the sleek silky girl would be yawning. There came an odd knock on his back door, as if an elbow tapped it. He got up stiffly.

"Rever'nd? Lutie Mae said bring yor breakfuss." Doodle edged in, plate in one hand, coffee pot in the other. "You want I should take that letter for you? I gotta ride Lutie Mae up to Ainsley's and get on in town." Last night Lutie Mae had told him that Doodle did yard work up in the town beyond Noonday, but it would slack off since they had a frost that dried the grass. After that most work he would have would be raking leaves, carrying off folks bois d'arc apples, trimming back rose bushes. "I gotta, if Bessie starts."

The fragrance from the small blue granite coffee pot, from the steaming plate of eggs perfectly fried and waiting in snowy grits filled the room, warming it.

Doodle's shyly extended axle grease-covered hand took his letter by gentle fingertips and slipped it into the top pocket of faded blue overalls. The screen door closed softly, and reopened like a sudden thought. "Rever'nd, yor dressed. You like a ride into Noonday? Folks be mighty proud to see you." He glanced back at the fog. "If they can," he said.

The truck, Bessie, started, wheezed, died, started again, chugged, caught, jerked to lunge forward, throwing the three of them toward a dashboard handmade of fine wood.

"Doodle, he built Bessie, every lick of her," said Lutie Mae proudly. "He didn't mind I walk up to Ainsley's, but come night he had to walk up there to walk me home."

Doodle, she told, had not bought one single part for Bessie, but had collected junk from Boyd's deserted filling station, from alleyways and trashcans, from the dump in the town beyond Noonday, from back yards and back roads. When it was finished—all but the wiring, Doodle hadn't found headlights yet—he had started out again to find old yard tools which he had oiled and repaired. Last year when the work was bad, Doodle got work in yards in the town, and even in Noonday. Miss Flower sent for him often. Colonel Aaron Brewster, he sent Doodle flying.

"Doodle, he got the power of doing. Some folks got the power of learnin', some got the power of thinkin', but Doodle, he got the power of doing. Ain't nothing 'canikle he can't fix. Sometimes it takes him long, but he don' stop till it runs. I show you. You eat with us tonight. Miz Ainsley, she give me a clock. She say, 'Lutie Mae, what on earth you do with that old clock?' It ain't run since doomsday, but Doodle, he sits for weeks looking at them little parts, pieces, chewed-edge wheels, all rusty and worn, and then, just by trying, he got it clean and wiped and wound, and I heard it tick."

Doodle, mouth abashed, eyelids lowered but letting a prideful glint through, adroitly guided Bessie around the ruts and puddles of Evening Road past familiar grey plank shacks that loomed up out of the fog timeless yet almost unreal in the dreamlike morning. There was about Doodle a certain quality when he drove, a firmness, a fineness that seemed to shrivel when he stopped the car. Abraham looked around. It was a car, yet it had a truck back, or at least a wagon back with a long, beautifully rubbed chest that shone under the film of mist. In front of Adam's General Store and Post Office Lutie Mae shifted her folded apron and reached back to lift the lid of the chest to show Abraham Doodle's neat burlap-wrapped tools, the gasoline can that had to be filled in the town since Boyd had closed the station. Doodle ran around to unfasten the door that actually was a picket gate with a black rubber tire neatly nailed over top the sawed-off pickets.

When Abraham opened the door of Adam Brewster's

store, Adam looked up from the bundle of mail he was sorting. His glasses slid down the bridge of his nose as he ran out from behind the brass cage that was the Noonday post office. He grabbed Abraham's hands.

"Abraham, this is great! I knew you were on your way before I heard it last night. Two letters from your nephew were sent on from Little Rock. You sure get around, and you look younger than ever. You're going to be just like Abram. Yes, I'm sick about Boyd and Mil moving to Dallas. Three years and Boyd still doesn't have his own station. His health's bad. Mil wrote that she'd give anything to come home, but Bimby loves Dallas. If I had a kid like him, I'd disown him, but Boyd has his heart set on Bimby getting through S.M.U..."

"Joshua? never better. He wasn't home when the tornado struck. Afterward he moved closer to Boyd's station, got himself some good second-hand furniture on Second Avenue and a new cat. Old Aaron? More cantankerous than ever. I don't know how Pinkney stands him. He doesn't stand him for very long stretches, just rides off with his banjo on the seat of the wagon. Say, Aunt Olivia will be glad to see you. She loves to talk about the old days. She talked an ear off that young Yankee reporter. He was in here before he left. Said to tell you he'd be back by Christmas. Olivia swears that old wagon Pinkney has is the same one that brought her grandmother Olivia from Mississippi. Say, Pokeen's got a funeral lined up for you. Old Aunt Minnie passed last night."

Abraham nodded his head. Old Minnie was a direct descendent of Trunk and Zilpah, worked all her life for Rayford's granddaughters up to the last one who married Craft, a rich cotton broker.

"That Pokeen's said to be a second Trunk. No, I certainly will not let you pay for the call. I was going to call Boyd anyhow. Soon as I get this mail sorted, we'll put it in. It would do Boyd worlds of good to come over for the hunting season."

Abraham sat down to read Brewster's letters. Leah had been taken to the hospital for an operation. A tumor had been removed from her stomach. She had tubes in her nose and arms. She wasn't able to eat, but she held Brewster's hand and told him she was fine. Brewster wanted Abraham to know so he wouldn't worry. The welfare woman called the railroad. The railroad confirmed Brewster's father's death and a pension. He felt he shouldn't tell Leah his father was dead until she was better. Abraham held his letter to Brewster up over the steaming coffee pot, unsealing it, and added, "Brewster, if you need me, you put in a collect call to Adam's store." The money order he enclosed wiped out his vagrancy fund. He sat holding one foot in his hand. Dampness sure ached those bunions. He stared out at the fog. He ought to go up there, should have gone the instant he knew Leah was sick. A nauseous paroxysm shook him at the thought of Brewster waiting near the operating room alone.

Out in the fog boys and girls were running, books clutched to their chests, the sound of their joy filling the store. Brewster used to tear out for school after fixing old Abram on his swing. How long would it take the railroad to get the pension through? If they were like the army, it would be a year. Leah wouldn't be able to work for a long time. She'd hate being on the welfare. He saw the little one-bedroom house that had been Salem's and was now his if he wanted it, and tried to visualize the three of them living there. He glanced up at Adam.

"Ivory come in much?"

"Still gets his calls here." Adam stuffed the last of the mail into the slots. "Still no other phones in Noonday. I think he's on a run now. You want me to ask little Ivory and Johnny? They'll be in after school."

"Tell them I want to talk railroad business with Ivory."

"Now, Abraham, you're not going up to East St. Louis? Leah's all right, or the welfare people would send for you, and Brewster's one of the most capable boys I've known. He loved Abram." He looked out at the fog. "You didn't make it back, did you? Brewster was manly at the funeral. Took care of everything. Now, listen, Abraham, your people need you here. They've watched the road for months. They need a new church, and lights down the road. They want the road paved. You do anything, best would be to have Leah and Brewster move back."

Abraham felt the eggs and grits churning in his stomach. His belt tightened around his middle like a vise. He looked out at the road.

"Now, come on, cheer up. Let's get Joshua off that grease rack." He took dimes and nickles from the till. "You know, Abraham, it would help Noonday a lot if Boyd came back and opened the station. That boy who drove you down here is a mechanical wizard. He'd be having people bringing cars down from town. He got Pokeen's old hearse going. The other day my pop machine broke down. He sat on the floor, studied it, and had it running in no time. He ought to get Lutie Mae out of Bert Ainsley's house. Bert's a bad one. Biggest worry old Salem had. He's always tangling with your people, got more than one of them in trouble. Ask Aunt Olivia. She sees him heading for the swamp with his bottle, and chases off the children who start down there frogging. You remember Oriole, Abraham...?"

The sun broke through to spin lights on the dew-dulled orchid-painted hearse waiting in the curved driveway in front of Pokeen's. The mourning sound of a clarinet wailed from the windows. Pokeen sat on a stool in the main room swinging a long leg to the music as he stitched a frill to a purple satin lining of a narrow pewter-colored casket, whistling the tune blaring in from the record studio. Abraham touched his shoulder.

"Well, think of the devil! I was just going to finish this lining and stop off for you."

Pokeen had come back from Korea, studied embalming on a G.I. loan that he'd somehow stretched to cover the cost of a third-hand hearse, equipment and this house, once a LeFleur's home.

"Did Adam tell you little Aunt Minnie got her call last night? I swear she waited until she knew you were here. She's been watching the road for a long time. My niece Milly told me she said, 'You tell Pokeen I want the finest funeral my account will cover, but he can't preach it. I want the real preacher to send me off right.' She carried Aunt Minnie's checkbook over here. I don't understand why they can't take me seriously. I've handled all the services since Salem's, but not one of them suited the families. I can't say about the deceased." Sitting back down on the stool, he picked up the needle with the long purple thread.

"Aunt Minnie must have been eighty-five when Miss Craft—she was a Brewster—up in town found out Minnie'd never collected a penny of her social security. The Crafts have paid it forever. Miss Craft went to the office, got it straightened out, put the money in the bank and carried the check book to Aunt Minnie who couldn't read or write." Pulling the book out of his pocket, he handed it to Abraham. "As you can see, the amount was large. To Aunt Minnie, it was a million dollars. She went up town and bought fancy clothes, left on the bus to see her brother up in Buffalo, New York. When she got off the bus she wandered around asking people for the street written on the back of one of his letters. Finally a policeman read the address, turned the letter over to look at the postmark. 'Granny, I hate to tell you this address is in Buffalo, New York. You're in Buffalo, Texas.' He took her to the bus depot. The girl in town says she sold her a ticket for Buffalo, just exactly what she asked for. She came back and rolled straight into Adam for never telling her her brother lived up in Yankee country. Adam used to read her mail to her.

"After she got back, she decided to move into a better house. You remember she used to live back on the swamp. Miss Craft came down here to get her to serve at a bridge party right after Minnie'd moved. Miss Craft forgot to tell Mister Craft she'd moved. When he drove Minnie back, he got that big Lincoln stuck on old Swamp road. After he'd worked for a while trying to dig it out, Minnie leaned out and said, 'I doesn't live here no mo', Mister Craft. I don't know why you drove down here in the first place.' She couldn't tell him exactly where she did live now so he had to drive all the way back to town, get Miss Craft out of bed to ride along and show him. After that even though she wanted to keep on working, they didn't use her every day.

"One afternoon Miss Craft came and got her to work a card party. Minnie was going through a swinging door and broke some cups on the tray. Miss Craft yelled out, 'Oh,

Minnie, not mother's heirloom china!' Minnie gave her that arrogant stare. 'Oh, tha's all righ', Miz Craft, yo' jest write yo'self a check on my account.' She went to Adam one day last year and told him she wanted to settle her bill in case she died. She hadn't paid a nickel on it for as long as he could remember. He stopped keeping account long ago. He told her, 'Aunt Minnie, I don't have any idea how much you owe me.' " He made a knot in the purple thread, cut it on his teeth and fluffed out the ruffle.

"She drew herself up—you know how she could do it. 'Well, Mister Adam, you that poor a businessman, you jest write yorself a check fo' a hundred dollars, and calls it square.' He didn't know what to do so he wrote one for ten. She never knew the difference. You going with me to get Aunt Minnie?" Pokeen was ready to give old Minnie the best funeral service he had. When Abraham glanced down at the checkbook, he'd seen that old Minnie's balance was seventeen dollars.

Olivia Flower watched Abraham come down the road. Same old coat. His hair was whiter than hers. He wasn't old. She remembered his birth in 1905, when old Abram must have been in his fifties. She remembered Abraham as a small boy bringing a twig from which all but two or three bittersweet berries had been swept in his haste for a much needed penny. Now that he was back, Clay could get all that Mississippi side of the family straight. She classified Brewsters, LeFleurs, Blacks and all the negroes of Noonday as Mississippi, Virginia or Texas-born. Old Aaron was the one Clay should talk to. How one's own brother could be so hard-headed was beyond her. Personally, she was proud to read about her ancestors. Aaron took the Noonday historical articles Clay had got printed in that newspaper he worked for as an affront to his own poverty. Hell, weren't all southerners left destitute by the war? She wasn't too proud to admit she'd had a struggle. She inherited what was known as "The Old Adam Brewster House," built practically in the swamp for the Adam Brewster who never got beyond a stockade wall in Alabama. Her brother Aaron should have known she would have ditches dug. She'd been proud of her crops, too, although to plant she'd had to have that lovely stand of pines cut down. She glanced down at the lone tall pine at the far edge of her land. Aunt Madelaine, of the Mississippians, Lelia LeFleur's sister, still lived in that house there built for Olivia's slaves when she got here during the war. Why, hell, her brother ought to be proud they were so steeped in tradition.

All of Madelaine's and Lelia's nephews and nices had scattered to New Orleans, Dallas, Louisiana. She could recognize every one of them that came back to visit by their eyes, still called the LeFleur eyes—grey flecked with brown and blue and green, large liquid eyes of beautiful luminosity. Beautiful children; a good third of her flowers could be credited to them.

Well, someone had stopped Abraham to talk. She sat down to wait, rocking and sniffing the air, thankful the fog had lifted, grateful for fall coming. Thank goodness, now all those damned flowers could wilt. She kicked the penny-jar, a chamber pot, hurt her toe, emitted an unladylike word and sat there smiling.

She loathed, despised, detested, utterly abhorred flowers. UnTexan as it was, it remained the dreadful truth, and there wasn't a living soul she dared tell. She had become a Noonday institution—Carry a flower to Miz Flower, get a penny or a wish come true; or a kitten. Her yard, house and porch purred with cats. Sighing, she glanced around the shabby, pot-covered, termite-chewed porch, its once gloriously proud pillars standing as erected long ago by Jacques LeFleur. She had been a Brewster who married a LeFleur who for obvious reasons changed his ancestoral name to Flower since he had to live in Noonday. The institution she was began after Dubois, her husband, died. The negroes came bearing cakes and jellies and great masses of red-purple bougainvillea which was so lovely that year. In desperation she wandered the grounds after the funeral poking the branches in anywhere to get rid of them. The soil, so close to the swamp, grabbed the cut ends which sent down roots. Within two years the pillars had been climbed around presenting such a magnificent spectacle that a mysterious Negro story spread. She supposed it meant she had a green thumb, or Miz Flower brings us luck. At any rate, ever since, children in trouble or needing a penny carried offerings of flowers to her. The penny jar remained on her steps and the porch was solidly covered with flower pots, tin cans, old dishpans and kettles overflowing geraniums, African violets, rose trees, every kind of flowering plant known to man. She spent her time praying for rain with strong enough winds to blow the rain through the honeysuckle and wisteria and bougainvillea to water the plants on the porches or for a boy to water them. Dry years she was torn between hoping every azalea, camellia and all the other flowering plants would die, although she knew they would be generously replaced. What she needed was a yard boy who loved flowers enough to trim bushes and hedges, cut low limbs from the magnolias, flowering plum and red bud, who would go into that jungle of a back yard and scrape his way through jacob's ladder, fringed gentian, blue bonnets, swamp milkweed, bind weed, delphinium, dahlias... And now when Aunt Minnie's funeral was over, she could expect a lot of business. She'd finished filling the penny jar minutes after Tinny raced down there with the word.

Standing up, she held out her hand. Here came Abraham smiling with a limb of bittersweet under his arm. Reaching into the pot, she handed him a penny, and stuck the limb into the earth she'd cleared with her toe.

"Honestly, Abraham, honestly! Well, come inside. I've got the best elderberry wine you've tasted since you were here the last time. Come in. Tell me about it."

Chapter 19

HEAR THE TRAIN BLOW

Muffled by the pelting rain, the eastbound whistle echoed down from the crossing and on and on in Abraham's ears. He had heard the baggage express in the night, and sat straight up in bed to worry about Leah and Brewster. He should go up to East St. Louis. When he wrote Leah that a house would be provided as soon as Lutie Mae's baby was strong enough to ride in Bessie, she answered, "Abraham, what would become of Brewster in Noonday?"

Then last week brought Brewster's frightened letter. His mother looked bad, he didn't want to worry his uncle, but... The whistle sounded again, fainter, touching an ache deep in his chest. Across the room, his dusty gladstone waited.

He leaned forward in the soft feather bed to stare out at the rain that made a curtain on the glass so that he couldn't actually see Evening Road, but he knew how it would be after six days of November rains. Sticky and deep, so that no one would use it for auto travel for days. The wires were down. Brewster couldn't reach Adam's store if he tried. Raven was working at Carlisle's ranch near Dallas. Doodle was still in town hanging around the hospital where Lutie Mae's baby had come early, and here he lay, suffering almost beyond endurance with pain in his feet and scarcely able to stand.

Clay had written he was in Chicago on business. Boyd and Joshua were coming over when the season opened. How many times Abraham had stood in that doorway listening to ducks and geese going over. But it wasn't the same when you were troubled.

He looked out at the rain and satisfied himself that he had no way to get in to the depot, and that he certainly was in no condition to travel, and then he sent forth a prayer for his sister and Brewster. He prayed that some fine charitable organization, in fervent zeal to do good, would overlook the fact that there was an uncle and hasten Brewster into some fine school with opportunities so that Leah could know her wish. He then proceeded to justify himself further in his own eyes. He tried to concentrate on the good he had done in Noonday since he had settled down.

He had stopped roaming, not so much because he was tired of the ever-changing scenes of beauty and fulfillment, not to mention the delightful changes of diet due to the hospitality of his people to a wandering preacher, nor because of the increasing advance of years on his bones. A sort of weariness had overcome him up in Arkansas just when Clay's letter told of Salem's passing and Noonday's need of him. He had listened through many nights to the northering flights of geese during his first and second springs here. He had buried his head like a huge wounded swamp hog and come up determined to stay settled, to stop roaming, to do good.

He had tried to do good. Besides being busy with funerals and christenings he had, with the help of the whole congregation, farmed a large cotton patch donated by Olivia Flower. They had chopped one fine crop and the proceeds were safe in a moneybelt around his middle to be added to the box supper collection Clay was banking for him toward the new church. With Doodle and Raven's help he had repaired the church roof. With Adam and Clay behind him he had convinced the town to extend the electric lines beyond Pokeen's to the church. Doodle hadn't got the parsonage wired yet because the rains set in. He had bought an old restaurant fan and Doodle rebuilt it so that it brought cool breezes into the meeting room throughout the exceedingly hot summer. Recently he had found a wood stove to keep his congregation warm on the days when a norther blew in. All things considered, he felt that he had sacrificed his freedom to stay here, and he hesitated to make further encroachments upon himself until he knew for sure that his wandering spirit was satisfied.

Although Abraham had always considered his freedom most vital to his wellbeing, he had to admit that sometimes along the line of his itinerant preaching he had wished for a permanent home with a woman to cook the meals. He thought about it here when he'd tire of his own steady diet of grits and eggs plus fringe benefits. And he had to admit that he glanced over the single female members of his congregation and found Lelia foremost in his admiration. He had reason to believe she was interested in matrimony and available—unless some cotton picker moved in before he'd thought it all out. He shook his head sadly, thinking how in spite of his worries, his aching bunions, hunger had a way of making itself known so that his thoughts strayed from his problems to settle upon the box lunch he'd shared with Lelia not three weeks ago. Besides being a good cook, she had good humor and a strong constitution, and he believed he had heard that her mule was paid out.

Holding his red flannel-covered arms heavenward, he spoke. "Lord, send me a sign, so I know your bidding, so I won't fail you again and do wrong by Leah and Brewster." He dropped back into the softness of the bed, only to pop forward with an added thought. He'd like the misery taken away from his feet before Sunday. Exhausted, he fell back into the pillows. He'd forgotten to mention that after Sunday came Monday, the day duck hunting season opened.

Down Evening Road, on a hill in a large red brick house with white pillars that overlooked the town and allowed a glance down toward oak-concealed Noonday, Lelia stirred a rich chocolate icing preparatory to spreading it over huge layers of almost black devil's food cake, her bosom rising and falling with the notes of the song she sang, which she would have to remember to stop singing when Miz Abernathy got home from the beauty parlor where she was having her hair done for the party tonight. Her voice stopped abruptly, and a frown creased her smooth forehead.

"Get out of them bushes, Terence Abernathy!" she shrieked toward the window. Flinging herself forward, she took the handle of the wooden spoon and pounded on the glass. Not one but two faces arose from the dripping crape myrtle. The white one, Terence's, grinned wetly at her. The other, a dark face apparently in agony, pleaded with her, as any child in any way connected with Terence would.

"Terence Abernathy, get in here! Miz Abernathy will ship me to Africa in chains if she catches you soaked to the bone and muddy from head to foot." She turned to the other boy who frantically tried to gain freedom from Terence's strangle hold. "Let go of him! Boy, you don't live around here, do you?"

Terence pushed the boy ahead of him into the kitchen. "He's going to, Lelia. I'm walking him to his uncle's down in Noonday. He tried to call him from the depot but the wires are down."

"You're walking nobody nowhere, Terence Abernathy." Snatching both boys, she began removing their soaked coats.

"Who're you trying to call, honey?"

"His uncle told him to call Adam Brewster's store if he needed him."

The boy held his sodden cap in his hands, a little to the side so as not to touch her white uniform with his wetness.

"His uncle is the preacher," Terence said with one eye on the chocolate bowl.

She stood in frozen astonishment. "Oh, my dear! You're Brewster. Is Leah all right?" He nodded. "Did you sit up all the way from East St. Louis? You didn't sleep? And Leah's coming?" He nodded again. He looked done in. Now why would Leah come in on a different train? Well, he looked too tired to talk. "Bet you're hungry."

"*I'm* hungry, Lelia," Terence announced, "and I'll eat with Brewster. And after we eat, we'll please lick that bowl or else I'll tell mother that Brewster is the brother God sent to me."

Lelia cringed. She pitied Terence with all her heart because of his frailties and the allergies that kept him from enjoying the sweets he craved, but she knew blackmail when she heard it. He was a master of it. She had promised him she would pray he would get a brother, although Miz Abernathy would skin her for the thought. One more like Terence would lead them all to early graves, but she had run out of ways to get him to take his allergy medicine and had instigated the prayer session.

"Yes indeed, you may lick the chocolate bowl, and if you haven't had enough chocolate by then, I'll mix you up a bowl of fudge." Chocolate was his worst allergy, and he knew it. His sharp little eyes met hers. "Now get upstairs and out of those wet clothes."

Brewster made a dive for the door, but Terence yanked, and both boys disappeared up the back stairway.

She found the boy's traveling bag out under the crape myrtle, wiped it with a towel and placed it beside the stove. While the boys ate, she explained to Brewster that the rains had made a quagmire of Noonday roads and since she lived down that way, she would take him to his uncle's after the party. Although it was risky since nuts were another of Terence's allergies, she placed a sack of walnuts and a box of pecans on the table for the boys to shell. It would keep four small hands busy during the afternoon hours while she baked pecan pies. After she basted the turkey, she beat up a batch of oatmeal cookies, the only sweets allowed on Terence's diet.

She had everything finished and was carrying the boys' dinner trays to them at the table when Miz Abernathy came home. She smiled her approval of the oatmeal cookies on Terence's tray, kissed Terence and said hello to Brewster. Lelia often brought a child up from Noonday to play with Terence.

Brewster let out a sigh when she boosted him up into the top bunk of Terence's bed where he would sleep until she could get away. He had tried to leave three times but she explained the distance, and told him what his uncle would think of her if she let him walk through a storm.

The boys had been asleep for hours. Now beside Brewster's dry coat waited her own white plastic rain cape and a sack of food. Miz Abernathy always gave her left-over pie and cake she didn't dare keep in the house and Lelia would drop it off somewhere along Evening Road. From the front of the house came the delicate tinkle of demitasse cups that told her she could soon finish the dishes and leave. Suddenly, down the back stairway, came Miz Abernathy's shriek, "Lelia!"

Upstairs, she stared at the sight of Terence whose nose and cheeks were criss-crossed with great welts, whose lips showed white rimmed with crimson.

"That child hasn't had one thing he wasn't supposed to have! He had his allergy medicine, his tonic, his carrot juice, meat, vegetables and oatmeal cookies." Terence nodded his agreement, his eyes bland and innocent, and obediently pulled off his bathrobe preparatory to getting on with the next step, a hot bath and a sponging with baking soda.

"If he didn't have anything he wasn't supposed to have, then we'll have to start his tests all over again tomorrow," Miz Abernathy mused.

Nothing could make Terence happier than to go back to Dallas. The beady little eyes strained to keep joy from showing. During the next frantic hour, his welts diminished and he was drowsing comfortably when she put him to bed and carried Brewster out.

During that hour the rain had slowed and settled into a quiet drizzle. Hunger and discomfort awakened Abraham who crawled from the soft bed and went to the kitchen to look over the possibilities of a meal. He found some slices of cold bacon left over from breakfast and placed them between two slices of dry bread and stood in the doorway munching and wondering when his problems would end. The sky was clearing. He could wear his boots to the depot. He chewed slowly. Suddenly a strange light appeared upon the horizon, round and floating, an illuminated little orchid mule. He stood transfixed. Trembling, he felt the open road beckoning.

Lelia's little white mule plodded and picked his way through the mud and the Sunday and prayer meeting section of the road. Behind him, billowing out in the lantern's glow, Lelia's white plastic rain cape protected the sleeping Brewster from water dripping off the oaks. The reins were lax; Lelia rode humped and troubled. It didn't sound right,

Brewster coming alone, and Leah coming in tomorrow night. The only night train was the Cotton Belt Baggage Express. The wires to Noonday had been down for days. She went on to her other worry. She reset in her mind the kitchen table. Brewster sat here; Terence sat there. Then she nodded. Terence had switched the trays.

They met at the door of the parsonage, Abraham wearing boots to wade the mud, gladstone, umbrella and gun strapped on the side, and Lelia carrying the sleep-blessed Brewster and the large sack of party food.

"I brought your sister's boy, Reverend."

Blinking, Abraham dropped the gladstone to sweep Brewster into his arms. "I was just this minute leaving for..." He didn't finish the sentence.

"Let him sleep; he's worn out, sat up all the way. Tomorrow be sure he gets a big piece of that cake. He didn't get any for dinner."

Rain passed, and the next grey day dawned with a deeper gloom. Brewster told Abraham how he had tried to get him on the telephone, and how the neighbors had taken up the collection to pay the trainfare.

Noonday lay sleeping as Pokeen drove the orchid-painted hearse around the muddy ruts toward town. A few dim lights burned at the depot. There was only the stillness and waiting until the baggage express swept down the rails to stop near where they stood. Pokeen gripped Abraham's shoulder as Brewster whirled from the sight of the wooden box to clamp his arms around Abraham's legs. Pokeen and the baggageman slid the box to the mail truck. The train moved forward; the baggage car passed. The wheels roared as the speed increased. There came the whistle for the crossing. Brewster climbed up on the cart. Legs tucked under, he huddled, small and alone, his arms wrapped around a corner of the box and his head resting against it. Pokeen picked up the handle. The wheels trundled down the platform sounding out into the still night. Down the line the whistle blew for the Noonday crossing. As if he watched a distant scene, Abraham nodded his head. He would soon be back in Noonday, and he had a feeling he was there to stay.

Chapter 20

DEAD CRICKETS

Boyd Brewster lurched into the bus seat. The office building faded behind him.

"You avoiding the company doc, Boyd?" Doc Walls skidded his chair back. "Know what happens when he sees you? I'll be crossing the street to Baylor to look in on you. Look, Boyd, you've got sick benefits, hospitalization..."

Sick benefits wouldn't pay Bimby's school expenses. Bimby could have worked, saved enough. Not Bimby. He didn't know a Brewster Bimby took after unless it was Drew, and God knew Drew was less Brewster than any he'd met, coming down there from Chicago, putting Aaron through that lawsuit, getting the choice land Aaron had been able to hang on to. Drew had been stationed at an east Texas camp, had read that a David Brewster married a Chicago girl, went back and got a job in the Cook County Records Department and came back years later armed with documents necessary to convince the judge, who was a long standing enemy of Aaron's. The whole family knew Drew was a crook and a liar. Aaron was right to condemn Clay. That was the hell of having your family history exposed. But Bimby was too lazy to work like that even for money, and lazy or not, Bimby couldn't be that rotten.

They had that fight in the spring. "I didn't have a car, Bimby. I folded cardboard in my shoes to keep the mud out." "I can't help it, dad, the kids look at you funny when you get off a bus. Some of the guys have foreign jobs." Well, he just couldn't afford another car and he told Bimby so. "You take it until the end of the term. I'll want it next summer. Remember, no reckless driving, and take your mother to the store." That summer he asked him to take a job at the station. Bill would hire him. He could save toward next

235

semester's tuition, buy school clothes. "No, seriously, dad, I should do library work."

In May Bill told Boyd, "I could use that kid of yours at the station."

"Bimby's getting ready for senior year." Bill looked up, red-mad.

"You mean to tell me that lazy slob... look Boyd, you look bad. You tell him my kid's at SMU, too. He's carrying sacks at the grocery."

The bus had passed the fair grounds. He closed his eyes. Maybe Bimby would be a lawyer, but that would mean more years of his blaring records, blaring radio.

He saw the shopping center clock. It was noon. He pulled himself out of the seat as the bus slowed for Eastwest Highway. "Only a hundred today," the driver said. "I don't mind a hundred and ten any more than I mind a hundred." It had been a hundred and ten the day before.

Across Eastwest he picked out the bedroom window of their apartment. The venetian blind was tilted in Mil's signal signifying "Everything's fine." *Not quite, Mil. Not quite.* He crossed Northsouth Road. A dozen cars were lined up, three waiting behind the west pump. Josh was checking the tires on a blue convertible. He tapped his shoulder.

"Hey, where was you?" grinning. "The doc's? What'd he say?"

Boyd shrugged in a lie that he was okay. Josh looked doubtful. "You gotta take care, Mister Boyd, so we can go home and open the quiet station like we promised Abraham." All Josh thought about since Abraham was settled in with a nephew to raise was going back. It *was* the most beautiful station in the world. Oh, not the rusted pumps, nor the grey shack, nor the outhouses hidden in the great oaks, but the setting under the trees, and the peace and quiet. This corner had been driving him nuts for three years. Out of Josh's dreams came Boyd's own hopes. Go back. Mil wanted to. He picked up an air hose.

Josh knocked a black cricket from his arm. "You'll wish you hadn't told Bill you'd work tonight. Them crickets roll in soon as the lights come on." Boyd had hosed them out for three mornings in a row.

The phone bell shrilled through the discord of motors, pumps, voices, traffic, radios (ball game). "Phone, Boyd," Bill yelled from the station doorway.

He recognized Sal Brewster's voice. After Drew built the apartments for Aaron to stare at, he and Sal moved into a fine house in Dallas so Drew would be able to go back to collect the rents and not linger under the cold stares. "Same place, Sal? Boiling again?"

"No, it's the battery again. Hurry, can you? I've got the meat."

Drew's handsome wife, meat package in hand, stood in the middle of the space next to hers waving on other cars, saving the space for the pickup. He could see the water under her car. It had boiled. She'd circled, probably. The parking lot was too small for the shopping center and women circled constantly, hunting space.

"Drew says this car has to last us five years. What's wrong with it, Boyd? Personally, I think it's your batteries." Her eyes twinkled. He'd told her a dozen times the car wasn't built for air-conditioning. They'd had a unit installed. Almost every hot day that she shopped, the battery died. She didn't believe that the battery had anything to do with it. He thought Drew should buy a new air-conditioned car.

"Boyd, you know I stalled three times last winter. You said then the engine was cold."

He reached under the hood, started the motor. She leaned over him. "What I'm afraid of is sometime it's going to stall on the tracks."

"Why don't you use Eastwest?"

She looked at the stream of highway traffic. "In that? Drew'd kill me if I stalled and got a ticket."

"You wouldn't get a ticket for stalling."

She stared up at the hot sky, hugging the meat package. He had a notion to drive her down to the apartment to wait with Mil. It wasn't that Mil didn't like Sal. It was that she was loyal to Aaron and couldn't stand anyone connected with Drew.

"Get in, Sal. I'll follow you to the station, charge the battery some."

She swung up under the west shed, and stalled.

He picked up her meat package. "We'd better charge it full time. Get the rest of your groceries. I'll run you home."

"Thanks, Boyd. I'll wait. I have to stop for the laundry."

He started for the Coke machine. She ran after him sniffing the meat package. He pointed to the strip of earth beside the station apron.

She shuddered. "Crickets?"

Josh, rolling the charger past them, stopped. "Didn't you read about them crickets, Miz Brewster? Fort Worthers were asked not to drive except for vital business. Millions of them mashed on the downtown streets, slippery as glass."

She stood looking down at them. Some clicked faintly. Here and there an antenna fluttered weakly. To Boyd it was like looking at a pile of massed futility.

"I'll bring some lime tomorrow," Josh told him. "We used to use it in the outhouses, remember?"

"I believe that would do it, Josh," Sal nodded. "When I was a girl in Chicago, my father used it on dead cows." She pronounced it Chi-*kaw*-go.

Josh connected the charger. "Now, Miz Brewster, you go wait at the drug store. It's air conditioned."

"No, this time I'm going to wait to see what's wrong with this car. It's getting so I'm afraid to drive it." She leaned under the hood. "You put water in that battery just last week, Josh," she said accusingly.

Josh winked at Boyd. "Yes'm, I sure do remember."

"Are you sure there isn't a short in the lights? Or wouldn't that have anything to do with it? Look, could it be that water bottle that's supposed to wash the windshield? It never did work."

Josh fanned his hand out at the side of his seat to tell Boyd to go on inside. "No'm, that don't work off your battery."

Boyd went inside and picked up the slips from the desk. The truck was due any minute and he hadn't totaled yesterday's gas. Sal followed him in and sat down on the edge of the desk. Bill was at the cash register changing a ten. "My battery died again." Bill nodded, recounted the change.

"There's something wrong with that car, or your batteries."

Bill walked out and looked under the hood. "That battery's only four months old. I told Drew it was your air conditioner." Bill was always growling because Drew was too tight to buy a new car.

A horn bleated. Bill ran to it, then back in to count out trading stamps. An old car, boiling, with steam shooting out the front, rolled under the east shed. A large man jumped out, threw up the hood. One of the new boys approached cautiously with the hose, began playing water on the bottom of the radiator. The man yanked the windshield cloth from the boy's pocket and twisted the cap, working it up and down the way Mil worked the cap on her pressure cooker. The radiator hissed threateningly. Sal drew back from the door where she'd gone to watch.

"How do you know it won't blow up?"

"It won't," counting frantically.

Skeptical, but curious about the woman in the car who was apparently naked, she went back to the door. The woman was enjoying the boiling radiator, puffing constantly on a cigarette she kept in her mouth. When the hissing settled down, Sal walked past, glanced in at the woman, then around to look at the plate.

"Michigan," she announced, coming back inside. "Bet they wish they'd stayed where it's cool. Every car on the road is boiling today."

The new boy came in. She touched his arm. "See if they're traveling, or if they've moved here."

He looked at her oddly, shrugged, strolled to the car, looked in the rear window.

"No luggage, so I don't know. They've got an ice cooler."

"Probably full of beer," Sal mused.

The man held up two fingers. Sal leaned over the desk. "How does that boy know if he wants two gallons or two dollars' worth?" She walked back outside. The man opened the car door. The woman wore a brief strapless halter that kept slipping. As Boyd glanced out, she hiked it up with both hands. Sal came back. The sun was lower, beating on the glass. She studied the hot glare. "I saw an air-conditioned car with the back glass blown out. Do they blow out when the

239

car's cold from the air-conditioning and parked in the sun, or when the car is hot and they turn on the air-conditioning?"

Boyd's hand clamped on the slips. "It doesn't happen very often. Heating expands cold air. Crack a window when you park."

"Drew says I'm to lock the car tight. Too many stolen."

"People forget their keys."

"They have hooks to trip the engine. Remember when Drew and I visited the relatives in California?" Drew had seen to it to look up all of his new found Brewster relatives. "Cars were disappearing by the hundreds. Do you know what they found out?" He laid down the slips.

"Drew said they were using a wrecker, you know, like your tow truck. They'd pull up behind a car, hook on and away they'd go to the beach where they loaded them on boats and smuggled them into Mexico. Our cars are worth a fortune there."

The tank truck swept in off Eastwest. Josh hightailed to the top. Boyd counted frantically, still not coming out even. She watched Josh. "Why don't you send one of the younger boys up there? Josh is too old to walk on that truck. I wish Drew would let me hire him for the yard. He's so handy. When Drew was gone during that tornado Josh came out and helped me, even lighted the water heater again. I don't believe Drew would mind him. He told me not to hire any of those East Texas niggers."

Josh was standing straddled on the truck walk, joking with the driver. "Josh is younger than I am, and he likes station work. He's no yard man."

Josh came in for the slips. Her attention was riveted on the truck. "Those boys shouldn't be smoking around there with all that gas." Nervously, she edged around the door and opened the Coke machine to put a finger testingly on her meat. A young colored girl walked up to the machine, dropped in a coin and waited. When no bottle came, Sal reopened the door and handed her one. "They always keep my meat in the cold drink machine while they charge my battery."

The girl studied her for a minute, then leaned around to look in. "Well, I say. I'll bring back the bottle."

"Oh, that's all right, dearie."

Red-mad, Bill slammed out to her car, checked the voltage regulator. "Your amps don't register right. You need a new regulator."

"How much will that cost?"

"Thirteen-eighty."

"Almost as much as a new battery. Maybe I should take a new battery. You'd discount fourteen months. Why, it would cost me next to nothing. Well, go ahead, anything. I'll go get a cup of coffee."

The new boy made a dive for the men's room. Josh shook his head. "What's she always want to worry about money for? That big house, swell car, that whole block in Noonday. I thought they were rich. People in Noonday say..." He frowned as Bimby swept under the west pump shed, car radio blaring.

"Fill 'er up," Bimby roared, holding up five fingers. When the new boy waited to be paid, he yelled from the cold drink machine, "Boyd Brewster, junior." The new boy looked at Boyd as Bimby swung out of the station.

Sal came back, stood in the doorway. "Was that your boy, Boyd? Wish I'd been here."

Just last year Boyd's insurance with the company doubled. If he died there would be plenty for Bimby's last year in school, and for Mil if she could keep Bimby out of it. He wiped sweat from his face. If he laid off, went into the hospital... He looked from his face. If he laid off, went into the hospital... He looked toward their apartment. "I can pick out our bedroom window from the station, Mil." That started her signaling with the shade... Mil didn't like him to work nights. She said he didn't eat right, and it was dangerous for him to walk on Eastwest after dark. He wished he'd told her he was going into town to see Doc Walls. It would be easier to tell her if he'd prepared her. Maybe he could say he'd decided to go over to visit Adam. Take his vacation. She'd like that. He tried to see the window but the last rays of the sun blazed on the building. Behind him, Josh slammed down the hood on Sal's car, handed her the meat.

"If any of your friends come over from Noonday looking for work, Josh, send them up. With Drew gone, I need a yard man."

There was a lull. He thought he heard the steeple clock strike, and looked up. Lettering under the clock stated the words, "Night cometh," and when the wind was from the east its striking could be heard all over the center. It was seven o'clock. Bill switched on the lights. Out of nowhere crickets flew in. The train whistled from the trestle above Eastwest. The phone rang. Bill got it.

"Your cousin-in-law, Boyd, from the cleaners. You forgot her trading stamps. Save them for her." He came around to stand in front of Boyd. "What the hell's eating her?"

"She's lonely, Bill, the loneliest woman on earth."

She acts scared."

Boyd started out to a car. It hit him then. He lurched back inside, doubled and stood gagging. The new boy yelled for Josh. Bill reached for a paper cup. Josh pushed him into a chair. "You goin' faint, Mister Boyd? You sho' look sick."

He hung on to Josh's arm while the dizziness rushed through his head and the pain roared into his chest. Josh pushed his head down. He could see his own hands, grey-white and cold with a layer of sticky perspiration. Bill held out the paper cup of water. "Something you ate for lunch, maybe, or the heat?"

Josh shook his head. "It's them dead crickets."

Bill hung up the receiver, grabbed Boy'ds wrist. Once before, when a trucker got sick, Bill called the fire department a block away. The emergency crew made it in less than a minute. That time he'd heard the siren before Bill hung up. He heard it now. Mil would see it, and look out, see the flashing lights stop here. Boyd looked up at Josh, wanting to tell him to call her, to tell her not to be scared, that he'd be all right once he got a rest. A car rolled in under the east shed, radio blaring. If Bimby knew how much it would mean to Mil to have a little house back in Noonday . . . There was a cricket on Josh's shoulder. He brushed it off. "Don' you worry none, Mister Boyd. I'll bring that lime tomorrow." The black face beamed but the eyes held fear.

Sal leaned inside her kitchen door, keeping one muddy galosh outside. "Do they think it was a heat-stroke, Bill? Then he's all right? Well, I won't call again today. I just couldn't stop worrying. I couldn't get Mil, and he could be dead for all the hospital tells you. Thanks, Bill. Listen, Bill, tell Josh to tell him I called." She replaced the receiver, drew a deep breath, and plunged back out into the searing heat.

Startled, she looked up from the watering hose as the first crack of back-firing shot the quiet of the morning. She stared unbelieving at the blind, blank look of the vehicle struggling up the slight grade toward the house, to resolve that the thing was blind because it had no headlights. Even as the uninquisitive side of her mind distinctly and thankfully spoke the words, "a yardman with a truck," the questioning side of her mind asked "Where on earth did that terrible looking thing come from?" Her mind chose *thing* over *truck;* she couldn't possibly call it a truck. It came shooting and banging and clanking and creaking and wheezing, eased weakly, almost apologetically up to her curb where it died with a sickeningly final wheeze. As she looked frantically around for help in case she needed it, a long skinny black arm looking much more like a blacksnake than an arm shot out from the dim interior of the cab to reach down and lift the rope loop that rounded a shining white doorknob halfway down the door. No, she couldn't call it a door. It was a gate, a picket gate, once painted white. Now the pickets were sawed off level and a worn piece of black tire was nailed to make an armrest.

The gate flew open. An extremely ragged and very worried negro leaped out, raced to the rear where he slammed a piece of cordwood under a weary tire. As she ducked behind the gardenia bush she was watering, he sunk against the bleached wood siding of the thing. All manner of purpose seemed to have flowed from him. It was as if the death of the thing had been too much for him, as if he had been a mechanical part which had ceased to function with the other parts. He moved; tugged a handkerchief from a pocket and across his face. The movement seemed purposeless, as if he knew the action would accomplish nothing, that he was finished anyhow. He had a finished look. He was the thinnest full grown negro she'd ever seen. She had missed guessing Josh's age by ten years... Did Josh send this man? The responsive part of her mind questioned his sending this particular man, driving that *thing*. He looked done and dying. The sigh she heard above the sizzle of the hose under the bush sounded like a death gurgle. *Please don't let him die on me here all alone.* Drew was on a two month long business trip. Most of the neighbors, southerners, spent the hot months in Colorado or Yellowstone.

If he came to mow this yard, at least give him strength to do it. As surely as if in answer, he came back to life, raised his head which hung dejectedly so low his chin rested on the thin sunken sweatshirted chest, spotted the green plastic hose she had spread down through the lawn. Doggedly, like a sickly hound trailing crumbs to the ultimate crust, he followed the hose around the small live oaks, past the crape myrtle, and across the walk to the gardenia bush. He stopped. His eyes widened at the sight of her black rubber galoshes that she wore to water even when the temperature was a hundred and five, as it was now. They traveled from the boots up over the red shins sticking out under her blue jeans, then rapidly, wildly to stare in absolute horror into her face. A bone-thin hand flew to remove a moldy felt hat.

"Oh, pardon me, ma'am," his voice was as soft as warm air, "I didn't see you behint of gardenias. My car, that is, my truck," (even he hesitated to designate the exact title of the thing at the curb) "broke down. I thought maybe I could borry a little water from this hose to maybe get it goin' again."

"Certainly." Disappointed, she held out the nozzle.

He hesitated. "Pardon me, ma'am, but where is this place at?" He handed her a slip, a saleslip from Adam Brewster's store in Noonday. Boyd's name, the station address, Josh's name, and the name Arlie LeFleur and her address were written on the back. Beneath, in another hand was clearly printed "Drew Brewster" and their address. "I bin drivin' around and around like a swamp hog huntin' out." The new streets wound around wooded areas. Her neighbors' friends had trouble finding the street, and finding their way out.

Carefully, she asked him, "Did you want to see Mister Drew Brewster?"

"No'm," accepting the hose. "Up east Texas we got word to come to the cities for the interrogation. Mistah Adam he said Mistah Boyd would hire me to work on the cars. I druv to the station and a boy he wrote this address on here but he wouldn't tell where to find Mistah Boyd."

She put the slip in her bluejean pocket. "Mister Boyd had a heat-stroke. He's in the hospital."

"I'm right sorry, ma'am." His dust-tired eyes were on the hose. They stared at Drew's going-to-seed Bermuda grass. "Oh, ma'am, does maybe yo' grass need mown?" The most glorious discovery voice. For two hot weeks she had prayed for a yardman with any kind of transportation. Drew forebade her to meet one at the busline. Yard maintenance companies were too busy or wanted more than Drew would pay. The yard had brought new hope into the dejected face. There were times when a woman had to use her own judgement.

"Yes. The machine's in the garage. How much would you charge? We have half an acre."

"A dollar or two?" The maintenance crews charged twenty.

"I'll make it one dollar an hour. It'll take you all day if you edge and trim." He stared at her, then stuffed the hose into the gardenia bush. Within a few minutes she heard the power mower start with a whirling freshness. Drew spent twenty minutes warming it up. Marveling, she headed for the cool comfort of the air-conditioned house.

The *thing* fascinated her. While she sipped coffee at the front window, her mind pursued an investigation of its source and parts and accumulation. She traced his trips across dumps and junk yards, ferreted out the sources of the unmatched wheels and tires. Painstakingly, she assembled it from the parts she had gathered in her mind. The picket gate swung open. A young negro girl slid out, reached back across the seat to pick up a small grocery box. Walking with unimaginable grace, she placed the box in the shade of the cherry laurel hedge. Slipping to her knees, she began pulling weeds. She stacked them neatly, gliding along pulling the box.

Sal's first thought was that the box held lunch, but there was something so lovingly gentle about the way the girl handled it she decided that it contained a dog or a kitten. Since it didn't hold a lunch, she mused upon an attractive and appealing menu to offer the man and the girl. Mrs. Stanley, from New Jersey, who was spending the summer back with her people, once admonished Sal about giving her yardman ice water. "He's used to drinking from the hose. You'll spoil him. You may as well start off right." Sal nodded in the direction of the Stanley house where the grass had dried to a light tan. Mrs. Stanley was so afraid Sal would spoil him she hesitated to give her his telephone number when she left. Sal didn't call until the Stanley yard began to look neglected, and her own need for a yardman became desperate. A well modulated voice answered, announcing a law firm. "Could you call George Anderson to the phone, please?" "One moment, I will ask my wife about him." Sal distinctly heard the wife's answer. "You know very well George is still in jail." There came the sound of a man clearing his throat, then the beautifully toned words, "I am very sorry. That man is not quite available, ma'am."

She couldn't go on alone any longer. She had to have a yardman. She intended starting off in her own way, not Mrs. Stanley's. From the instant the girl slid out the door of the thing her mind assembled the man and the girl into "couple." Her mind moved the couple into the small compact house behind the garage. She placed them there despite Drew's objections to a couple living-in. Drew liked privacy; he certainly would not want a Noonday couple there. She had had a chance to bring a lovely Noonday girl back with her when they moved to Dallas, and Drew hit the ceiling. Also, he liked to do his own yard work when he was home. She traced a line in the dust on the venetian blind slat in front of her eyes. It was impossible to get a maid with a car. She had her order in at three agencies. With Drew gone, the yard and the house were beyond her catching up. Her skin was already burned to a frazzle, and her legs walked off up to her knees with all the hot hours of watering. The days were exceedingly hot. There was no rain, none at all. They had had a stretch of twenty seven days when the temperature stayed over a hundred. The hot dusty winds from the Mexican plateau prevailed. All over the area her neighbors' grass dried brown and stiff. Drew wanted their grass to stay green. He planned to put out rye for winter grass. He would want the rye watered.

The man walking behind the mower on the strip of earth outside the drive had changed. He was no longer a picture of forlorn dejection. He walked with an intentness of purpose. Behind him the grass flowed smooth and level, not path marked as when Drew mowed it. On the other side of the yard the girl had already worked the full length of the hedge and two flower beds. The weeds were neatly stacked at the curb.

Sal went into the kitchen where she added chopped hard boiled eggs, olives and pickles and pecans with mayonnaise to canned chicken. She washed purple plums and placed them to chill beside the dainty sandwiches in the refrigerator. While the food chilled, she allowed herself the pleasure of a scented bath.

When the man and the girl moved into the back yard, she stepped out on the patio with the lunch. The patio was in full sun; the heat hit her fiercely. It was ridiculous to expect people to eat there when she had an air-conditioner in the quarters. She took the tray there, turned on the unit, and opened the door of the neat, tiled bathroom.

The girl was pulling weeds around the violet plants Sal had brought from Chicago. There were no blooms on the plants, but as the girl raised her eyes, Sal looked into two purple-black eyes just as soft. The eyes met hers with an unusual directness. "Hello, would you like to wash up before you eat?"

The girl smiled and nodded, and picked up the box. When she stepped inside the room she held the box up in front of the unit and laughed. Sal looked in. She looked into a baby's face, stared at a wet mass of red rash. The baby gazed placidly up at her, and then laughed, reaching a hand up to touch her cheek.

"Pip Doodle, he never seen a white lady since the hospital," the girl hugged the box.

Sal gasped. "This child has ringworm." She could feel a hot spot on her cheek where the miniature hand had touched her. Drew would be furious if she got ringworm on her face. The girl shook her head, the velvet eyes quizzical.

"Doodle, he thought Pip Doodle had the prizzley heat."

"No, it's ringworm. The heat probably has made it worse." She tried to recall the name of a medicine but only words she'd laughed at when they first moved south remained in her mind: *Does the fiery itch of ringworm drive you wild?* The girl placed the box on the couch, arranged two places at the table. "You've worked out, haven't you?"

"Oh, yes'm, I worked for Miz Ainsley over to Noonday until Mista Ainsley took to drinkin' and took out after me. Miz Ainsley say, 'Lutie Mae, I'm tearing my hair. You're the best girl I ever had in the kitchen, but 'count of Mista Ainsley carryin' on so crazy-like, I'll have to ask you to go back to the cotton. Yo' send Aunt Carrie up fast. If Aunt isn't able, you send me the strongest, meanest-looking niggah out there. I'll fix Bert Ainsley.' Poor Miz Ainsley such a little thing to have so much trouble."

"I can see why she hated to lose you," she said.

"Mista Ainsley, he never did get better of the drinkin'. One year his cotton flooded out, next year it dried up. The preacher who died said it was retribution. When that preacher died, Mista Ainsley said *that* was retribution. Things got bad for us pickers. A man came into town above Noonday and told us we better get to the cities 'cause the integration done started. The new preacher, Rever'end Cork, he said, 'Doodle, you'd do much better to stay on here. Things will be picking up.'"

"Do you know what integration is, Lutie Mae?"

"Oh, yes'm, and I likes it fine, but Doodle, it scares him. I stamp my foot. I say 'Doodle, I don't care what the new preacher says, we gotta go on account of Pip Doodle so he don't grow up ignorant like you and me.' Doodle and me come up out of the swamp country. We didn't get enough school. We don't have background like the new preacher keeps telling the Noonday folks they got. We ain't nobody." She smiled sadly, showing even white teeth.

"Did all Mr. Ainsley's cotton pickers come into Dallas to be integrated?"

"Oh, no'm. Preacher talked a lot of them out of leaving. Some of them went over to Shrevepo't, some to south Texas—wherever they had folks. Doodle and me, we got no folks, but Aunt Lelia LeFleur gave Doodle her niece Arlie LeFleur's address. We goin' live down there in colored town and Doodle goin' work on cars when Mista Boyd Brewster gets better. Then we'll get us a fine house up here with a room like that," she pointed to the tiled bath. "We gotta go before dark too, 'cause the preacher kept Doodle too busy at the parsonage and he never did get to finish wiring Bessie."

"Bessie?"

"Doodle's truck. He built it himself. I called her Bessie cause Mista Adam gave him a horn sounds like a old cow but it don't blow on account of the wirin'. That's why we gotta get to Arlie's before dark. Bessie got no lights."

"It'll take your husband most of the day to finish the yard. I don't think it's a good idea to expose the baby to the heat until his face is better."

The eyes pinched. "You want us should leave Pip Doodle here accounta the fan? Nice as you are and much as I want Pip Doodle better of the ringworm, I just couldn't leave him."

"I wouldn't think of your leaving him. You could all stay here, live in the quarters until his face is better. You could help me in the house." The girl was shaking her head, looking wistfully at the small efficient kitchen.

"It's no use, ma'am. Doodle says livin' with white folks is the same as his havin' no other name except Ainsley." She glanced up. The man was standing there, moldy hat in his hands. With the machine stilled, it was as if he had turned off some part of himself.

Sal turned to him. "If you can start your truck, Doodle, you could put it into the shade." She pointed to the mimosa trees beyond the garage. "I'm going to run up to the shopping center to get something for the baby's face. You two enjoy your lunch. Do you want milk for the baby, Lutie Mae?"

Sal knew she was spending too much time wandering through the shelves searching for the exact medicine. And she stood too long choosing an assortment of minute jars of baby food. She enjoyed doing it; it was almost like having a family. But the sun was low in the sky when she drove up the hill to the house. The yard gleamed. Two sprinklers ran. The grey frayed ends of the *thing* stuck out from under the mimosa trees. Lutie Mae appeared to help her carry in the bags. They took the medicine to the quarters. The girl's eyes followed Sal's hand as she bathed the baby's face and applied the lotion. The baby stared up at her, not smiling, but not afraid until she applied the medicine which must have burned fiercely because he shuddered, his face puckered. Tears squeezed out of his eyes. He let out one searing shriek. Lutie Mae patted his head, began singing, "Don cry, lil baby, Uncle Jacques got fine big house in Texas." The man appeared in the doorway, his face withered in worry. A few minutes later Sal heard the spattering of the motor trying to make some contact to set the *thing* running. She handed the baby to Lutie Mae.

"I hate to see you leave."

"I hate to go, Miz Brewster. I had me a fine time, and Pip Doodle, he mighta died of the ringworm, but we gotta find Arlie's before dark."

Sal helped her out to the truck with the bag of baby food. When she handed the money up to Doodle, he smiled at her praise of the yard.

"Doodle, Lutie Mae has a card in her pocket with my name, address and telephone number. You have a job here and a home for your family any time you want it." He shook his head. "Well, if you need day work, you come back any time you can. I need someone to wash venetian blinds and scrub down the patio." As she told him, she doubted that he would ever find their street again.

She was eating a sandwich of the leftover chicken spread and watching the news on TV when the telephone rang. It was the police. A Negro couple driving a vehicle without lights after sundown had been stopped. Yes, she had asked them to work for her. They couldn't drive that vehicle out there without lights; would she come for them? Her husband was out of town; he forebade her to drive after dark. The policeman said he could put them up for the night. They could drive out there in the morning, but that vehicle had to have lights installed.

"Where will you put them up? In the jail?" He sputtered. "You most certainly are not going to put that couple with that sick baby up in jail!"

"Well, lady it isn't exactly like putting them in jail. It's more like providing a place for them to sleep."

"How did you get them down there?"

"Lady, we towed them down."

"Can't you tow them out here? If I send a tow truck, will you see that they come?"

It was past ten o'clock when the entourage arrived. Sal ran outside. Josh drove the bright red tow truck with the red lights on top. The headlights of a police car outlined an upended, cool, unboiling Bessie strung down the lift like a great dead cricket. Inside, shrunken, shriveled, almost green with horror, Doodle sat behind the wheel. Next to him, with the box on her lap, Lutie Mae stared straight ahead. Suddenly Sal remembered that back in her closet, in the clothes hamper, rested her blue jeans. In the pocket was Doodle's note from Adam Brewster with Arlie LeFleur's address.

Chapter 21

GRASSHOPPER, GRASSHOPPER

"Sunset and evening star, and one clear call for me,"* the undertaker read in quick woman-like tones, and from far, far off Arlie heard the call "Grasshopper, grasshopper," in the shrill mean voices of children, and in her mind she saw Garrett run from them, run with that painful hop caused by his one short leg. After that he was never able to believe that anyone could love him. After that he couldn't wait to get out of Noonday ... only thing kept him there was Moma. Such a little light-brown boy, Arlie used to think, so little to be hurt so soon; couldn't they have waited until he was older, bigger? Not that he ever did grow very big.

All day she had been seeing him small again, all day while she scrubbed Miz Toliver's venetian blinds and ran the sweeper, even when she took off her uniform and stuffed it into her paper sack and ran for the bus to get to the funeral parlor on time. She saw him that long-ago day carefully fold his suit and place it in a wrinkled paper sack and twist the ends up tight and clench one hand around the paper rope he'd made of the top of the sack. How old had he been then? That suit was given to him by the welfare woman for Moma's funeral. She closed her eyes and counted back. She'd been eighteen and Garrett fifteen, with all those little ones behind him.

She kept seeing him small; that was the reason the casket looked so big. She hated telling the funeral-parlor man on the phone that day to make it the cheapest service he had; even so it was nice, with the programs and all, and the record player hidden so the women were looking around for the organ. "I'll pay you ten dollars every month until it's all paid

---

* *Crossing the Bar*, by Alfred, Lord Tennyson

252

out," she told the undertaker on the phone that day and Miz Toliver said, "Now what are you buying, Arlie?" and somehow she couldn't tell her about Garrett. Miz Toliver had her own troubles trying to get ready to go back east where her husband was sick. Arlie looked down at the program.

"Twilight and evening bell, and after that..." the undertaker, who was nearsighted and wore heavy glasses held the book further from his eyes and his voice rose to a high pitch of anxiety as he found the words "the dark." It was nice that he chose such a sweet sounding poem to read, but Garrett would have liked something about trees or flowers, or maybe God.

She hated working on his funeral day. It wasn't right, but when you got five children all school age with clothes and shoes and food to buy and rent to meet, and now the undertaker to pay, you gotta work every day and get evening work when you can. Outside the window a siren wailed and back where the mourners sat a woman said a soft amen. Arlie glanced around. Few of them knew Garrett. Most of them were her friends, her own children and their friends, and the rest were strangers, all dressed in black, old people who lived near the funeral parlor and came when there was room, or a need for mourners. She nodded a thank you to the woman who said amen.

"I'll send you half of what money I make, Arlie. You keep them children in school and keep the girls from the cotton pickers like Moma kept you," Garrett said, twisting the paper sack rope in his hands.

Main things that had been on Moma's mind was keeping the girls from the cotton pickers until marrying time, keeping the boys out of jail, feeding them, keeping them warm, never really easy 'cause they didn't have clothes enough. "All you chilluns run in a bunch and keep the littlest ones in the middle and sit close in school..." She could see them all running, shivering down the muddy road, Garrett hopping with Cary Mae on his back. Cary Mae loved to ride on his shoulders, bouncing along, and it was warm there. School was important; Moma never got to school. The greatest marvel of her life was when Garrett could read the Bible to her.

"Ain't you goin' tell me where you goin'?" she asked him that day.

"I'm goin' down Naw Leans, goin' hitch me a ride on the strawberry truck, if'n they'll take me. If they won't, I'll walk." And his head came up on the word "walk" like it always did.

And he did send money, never very much, a dollar here, five dollars there; yard men didn't make much. Always stuck the bills in envelopes, they never knew what money orders were then; they were all so dumb and countrified.

There, he did say something about God. Garrett would like that. The Pilot was God. Well, he was there now, she guessed, right in front of God. Was he asking, "God, why did you make my one leg shorter than the other? Why, God? Why couldn't I have at least started out with them both the same length and then, if that be for me, let one of them shrink?" He'd often asked her that.

"Don't have no preacher, Arlie; I've always had my own way of talking with God." He whispered the words, his voice already gone to the cancer. He was arranging flowers out where he worked. She went out there to see why he hadn't called or come in; little Jem had been asking about Uncle Garrett. Garrett had been sick for weeks; the white folks sent him to the doctor and they shot the X-rays all through him and showed him a picture of something grown beyond fixing. So he went back to work. Now there was a man for God, worked his life with grass and trees and flowers; loved everything alive; helped Arlie raise their brothers and sisters and then, when she'd gone to New Orleans with that cotton picker and he went off leaving her with five of her own, Garrett had started helping again. Then when Cary Mae took sick up to Dallas, he'd somehow managed to pay busfare for all of them, and they'd never gone back to New Orleans, never had money enough. She got on with Miz Toliver, and Garrett got on as gardener on that big estate. It took him almost five years to pay out what it cost to have Cary Mae buried out to Noonday, in the cemetery at the end of Evening Road where Moma and the rest of the family were laid. Somehow she should've tried to carry Garrett back there instead of putting him all alone here in Dallas. She could've paid it out, just like Garrett did for Cary Mae. She could have borrowed money to carry them all out on the Noonday bus. Maybe they'd just stayed on in Noonday; big city no place to raise up children. She looked over to Ruby Ella, near grown.

"How you like this arrangement, Arlie?"
"Oh, it's lovely, Garrett." She'd looked at the round bowl of flowers he had ready to take into the house. The center was a circle of bright flowers, yellow calendulas, he told her, rimmed with a fluffy wide ring of tiny flowers like lace.

"Looks just like a fried egg," she'd told him, and he studied her face, and she looked right back at him steady because she always thought fried eggs were pretty.

The undertaker moved silently around back of the casket and changed the record. Ten minutes of silent meditation and prayer with music, the program said. She didn't know the music. Oh, Lordy, it was sad. She should have asked for a hymn the children could hum. They were squirming now, trying to see Uncle Garrett inside the casket. She should have brought something for Jesse to hold. He was squeezin' one hand wid he other hand... There, she knew better than to talk like that, think like that. It was all this going back in her mind. Miz Toliver been teaching her how to think right words, to say right words. Best thing she liked about Miz Toliver was she knew Arlie could think.

Bless Ruby Ella, she was holding Jesse's hand now and patting it; she did look almost grown in that black dress. And Jesse, Jesse looked like Garrett when Garrett was small. Why was she always seeing him small again? She could see him the day he found the dead grasshopper on Evening Road, dead and dried and brown as clay and he held it in his hand and studied it for a long time, and she went up to him. "Do grasshoppers always fold they arms when they die?" he asked her, trying to hide the fact that he'd been measuring the grasshopper's legs to see if one was shorter than the rest.

And she suddenly had that joyful thought. "Garrett, you plays hopped-scotch better'n any of the boys." His eyes got wide and his mouth came open, and he turned and ran from her. And he never would play hopscotch any more.

Soon she would have to stand up and walk down to the casket and pull that cover up over Garrett's face like the undertaker told her she was to do before he shut down the lid... There, he was playing a hymn they all knew and the children were humming:

Sweet wind, south wind,
Carry me home...

That was Moma's favorite hymn. Moma and Garrett used to sing it out chopping cotton. She could see Moma with her long skirts tied down by that rope and hear her high-pitched voice ring out over the field...

The music died softly out and the undertaker came toward her motioning and she knew what she must do. A siren wailed again, further down the street, and she heard the rain crow cry up in the tall long-needle pine, and she saw Garrett hopping down the dry dusty road holding the paper sack stiffly in one hand, bouncing and hopping, and the dust followed him until he disappeared around the bend of the field where the cotton had dried up. A sob rose inside her and she gasped, "Oh, Garrett, I'll carry you home," out loud into the room in a shrill voice that rang and rang in her own ears, and far back in the room the mourner wailed, "Amen."

Chapter 22

LONG ROAD TO NOONDAY

Lutie Mae examined Pip Doodle's knitted tam, and straightened his blue sweater, the blanket, tugged at her own skirt while Doodle carefully parked Sal Brewster's big pale blue Cadillac, brand new and air-conditioned. He wouldn't trust the lot attendant. They waited for the light, crossed, and began the walk down the city sidewalk to the big court house.

Doodle was death afraid of the police. He wouldn't have agreed to come if she hadn't convinced him that Arlie would never be in jail if he hadn't lost her address, and she wouldn't have been if they had been on hand to help in her time of need.

"Now, Doodle, let me do the talking." Having bailed out Bert Ainsley so many times she felt experienced.

"I let you talk the last time we was here and look where we landed."

"Where you ever had it so good? Drivin' big Cad'lac. Wearing a suit Mistah Brewster might kill por Miz Brewster fo' lendin' it to yo' to make impression when he gets back." Drew Brewster was six weeks overdue. "'Sides, Arlie wouldn't be here if..."

"I know."

"If you talk, 'member all Josh and Miz Brewster tole you. Josh will get here in the morning with the bailman. Lelia 'ranged for Pokeen to pick up poor Garrett. Everybody to meet in front of Miz Brewster's house. No doubt she got that part straightened out now." They had left Sal at the door of the juvenile home where Arlie's children had been kept since her arrest. "Now, 'member, Doodle, Arlie's children going to be well cared for in Noonday by their Aunt Lelia." She pronounced the words slowly as instructed by Sal.

"Where Miz Brewster get all this knowing about getting people out of jails I don't know," Doodle fretted.

"She smart, besides, Mistah Drew Brewster worked for big Cook County Records Department and you know more people get arrested in Chi-caw-go than anywhere else in the world." Miz Ainsley had given Lutie Mae a day by day rundown on the court case in the county seat beyond Noonday while Drew proved his claim for Aaron's land.

"We come to see Miz Arlie LeFleur." Doodle poked her in the back. She was supposed to emphasize "Missus," and had failed. "She's in here for stealing money." The policeman handed her a pencil. Doodle took Pip Doodle from her arms.

"Are you relatives?" over the rim of his glasses.

"No'suh."

"Friends?"

"No'suh, not exactly. We don't know Arlie—Missus LeFleur, but we good friends of her aunt, Miz Lelia LeFleur, in Noonday, who's going to take care of Arlie's children 'til she gets out of jail." With Doodle punching and the policeman's gaze steady on her, she lost her way. "Mistah policeman, Arlie never stole nothing in her life. Them checks was left in the cream pitcher for her pay while Miz Toliver went back east. All she did was borrow her own pay ahead to pay the undertaker so she could carry her poor brother over to Noonday and bury him, now..." Doodle nudged her.

"Well, just sign here if you want to see her." He waited. "Well, tell me your name. Spell it. Okay, now put an X beside this line." He pointed. Doodle handed the baby back and slowly wrote out his own name.

"You wait in here. She'll be out." He held the door.

Lutie Mae walked in and sat down.

"You was supposed to tell him Josh and Miz Brewster guar'tee bail money."

"Not now, Doodle. Mix Brewster said to tell Arlie that. The man with Josh does the talking tomorrow. We're supposed to make Arlie feel good, tell her about the fine funeral arranged for Sunday in Noonday, and that she can go to it. Tell her that Miz Lelia's going to care for the children..." She jumped to her feet as a woman came through the door and held it open.

Arlie looked like a younger Lelia LeFleur, Lutie Mae thought when she saw her, much thinner, but with the same soft tan skin, identical great blue-grey eyes with the LeFleur brown and black flecks, the same brilliance, as if she was ready to cry, or just had been. She looked at them, a dazed and puzzled expression forming.

"We come to 'stend our sympathy about your brother." Lutie Mae rushed into her rehearsed speech, remembering to finish her words as Sal Brewster had been teaching her. "I'm Lutie Mae Ainsley. This is my husband, Doodle, and the baby is Pip Doodle." She turned down the blanket so Arlie could see Pip Doodle's face now healed of the ringworm and smiling as his little hand reached out toward the warder's keys swinging nearby. "We live here in Dallas, but we come from Noonday. We know your Aunt Lelia."

Arlie nodded and dropped into a chair and put her hands over her face. The warder closed the door as Lutie Mae rushed to Arlie.

Arlie was so sweet-looking Lutie Mae couldn't bear to see her cry. "Now, Arlie, don't cry. Look here at Pip Doodle laughing for you." She chucked Pip Doodle into Doodle's arms and placed her own around the girl. "Oh, Arlie, what made you do it? You knew Pokeen would come for Garrett; he never cares if he gets no more than diggin' money." Doodle edged up against her. "Doodle, quit punching me."

"I never knew Pokeen. He was away so much."

"How come you didn't call Josh when you needed money?"

"I didn't think of anything except it was late. I jumped on the bus and went back out to Miz Toliver's. I knew if I got there before she left, she'd lend me the money, but she'd gone. I had my key. I went into the kitchen and sat down. She'd left the checks like she said. I was to cash one a week, pay the yard man. I knew she wouldn't care."

"Then how come you're in jail?"

"The woman next door saw the kitchen light, saw me running for the bus. Miz Toliver had given her a key, and asked her to check on the house. She went in and found all the checks gone, and called the police. They arrested me in the grocery store right in my own block. I'd just cashed them.

I begged them to leave the boys with Ruby Ella. I told them if I could reach Miz Toliver back east she would tell them it was all right."

"Miz Brewster who I work for says they can't punish you until somebody accuses you."

"The neighbor accused me. The checks were advance dated. My groceryman said he'd hold back on them and cash one a week. I didn't think it was so wrong."

When they went out, Doodle fussed at Lutie Mae. "Yo' was supposed to make Arlie feel good. 'Stead, you left her in a flood of tears."

"She was cryin' for happiness 'cause she knew we was goin' to pick up her children, and 'cause you promised to move her things over to Noonday in Bessie."

"She didn't quite seem to understand Bessie."

"I made it plain when I told her Josh was going to pack everything real nice for her and store it over there."

Sal Brewster switched out the light in the guest room and pulled the door shut behind her, and leaned against it. Such darling little children. Drew would kill her if he came in tonight and found the house jammed with Noonday negroes. She flounced away from the door, and went to the kitchen to make coffee. For some strange reason she couldn't care very much. What cotton picking business was there in Mexico City? He'd written that he had to be there much longer than he had expected. "Would you want to move to Mexico City, Sal?" Oh, he was having hallucinations. She was so far south now she was sinking. That letter came the day she drove that damned stalling car down and traded it in on the new one. She'd hit the bank account hard, but how was she to know the apartment rent checks weren't being deposited?

Sipping coffee, she stood at the front window gazing out at the wide sky. What's the matter with me? I didn't want any part of Texas in the beginning. God, how I hated the thought of coming back. The heat in that little town. Shake out my skirt before I put it on in the mornings. Look into my shoes, pull the sheets off the bed and shake them then lie there wondering if I'd wake up with a scorpion on my nose, or be jabbed awake by a centipede.

But now in the nights when she stood alone looking out at the immense black velvet sky, at stars glittering out of its depth, she felt a new stirring. She could sit in front of the TV weather map and not yearn when snow fell on Illinois. Oh, you lose yourself in Texas. Why couldn't Drew settle down? Shivering, she wrapped her arms tightly around her chest. Why not face it, Sal? You've guessed. You guessed a long time ago. Now someone else was wise to Drew, and Drew knew it... The wide sky didn't answer.

It was up there: black, peaceful, permanent, serene. She'd known little peace, certainly never permanence until she dug up the violets on the farm that had been her father's, the farm Drew sold to get enough money to float the loan to build the apartments that were supposed to get him in solid with the Brewsters. She put the violets, damp and wet, into a plastic bag where they rode to Texas. She was down on her knees planting them when the Illinois earthworm nosed out of the black dirt around the roots. "Did you have a nice trip?" she'd asked. Drew would have thought she was crazy to talk to a worm. Lonesome as he really was, he couldn't recognize it in her. Why couldn't he line up his needs with hers? Drew, who needed so terribly to belong, who worked like a fiend to prove he belonged to the Noonday Brewsters, never would. Rejected, he tried to make the money he thought would give him a place in a lonely world. Why hadn't he seen that she wanted children? That they could make their own family, be a family? But he went off, still seeking what he already had in her if he had looked, leaving her caretaker, maid, yardman of his house until she snagged poor Doodle and Lutie Mae.

Tossing, she slept restlessly. The fragrance of coffee on a tray beside the bed awakened her to see Arlie framed by the rose-violet dawn in the window behind her.

"Lutie Mae's feeding the children, Miz Brewster. Doodle's here with my things. It must have taken them most of the night to pack them. You all so good to see me through..."

"Hell, Arlie, what else is there if we don't help one another?"

The morning showed a scattered sky. Somewhere over

Dallas a shower fell. Over the house the sun specked, and then dropped behind a cloud, and flickered. Clouds were moving fast. There was lots of wind, little winds that scurried. Sal loved the sky like this. She tilted the venetian blind. The *thing* was parked nose down the hill. Behind it, in Boyd's car Josh had borrowed sat the bondsman. Josh and Doodle were working under the *thing's* hood when the dreadful long purple hearse crept up the grade, turned in her drive and backed to pull to the curb in front of the *thing*. She turned from the window to tell them, but one of the children had already seen it. Arlie and Ruby Ella were helping the boys into their coats. Ruby Ella was the most beautiful child she'd ever seen, with those waist length braids, her paper-sack color skin and those luminous eyes like Arlie's. Her teeth were perfect enough to be hung as examples in front of a dental office. The little boy, Jesse, clung to Ruby Ella. There were three other little boys, all in steps. Nice looking children. They had been so horrified to be shut up in the detention home that they couldn't even talk when she went for them yesterday.

Lutie Mae came into the room, pulling on black gloves. "I've changed the beds, Miz Brewster. I'll do up that laundry fast when I get back."

"You did fine, Lutie Mae. Don't worry. Just be sure you come back."

"I'll be back fast, Miz Brewster. I've had me a good time." Her laughing eyes met Sal's.

With a lonely feeling, Sal stared on out the window. A huge preacher and a little boy got out of one side of the hearse, and an immense man out of the other. Where were they all going to ride? Doodle was coming up to the house.

Doodle shook his head. "Miz Brewster, it just won't go."

Sal got on the phone. "Yes, Bill, it won't start. Sure they could leave it here, but it's loaded with everything Arlie has in the world ... I'll appreciate it. Will it matter if it's gone all day? The funeral's today."

"Oh, I can always close the station." He hung up.

Bimby drove up in the red tow truck. Now the procession

lined up. The purple hearse with the huge man, the preacher and the little boy in the front seat. The tow truck with Bimby at the wheel, and Arlie's three little boys jammed in beside him. Josh at the wheel of Boyd's car, the bondsman with him. Arlie, Ruby Ella and Jesse, Lutie Mae, Doodle, Pip Doodle, all to get in that car. Grinding out her cigarette, she called out to Doodle.

"Go get the car, Doodle. I'm going along." Running, she grabbed her purse.

The purple hearse rolled down the hill, the bright red tow truck dragged the upended *thing,* all Arlie's possessions tied down, Boyd's car with the children spread more evenly. The big blue Cadillac. Many eyes turned to look upon the strange entourage speeding through the towns, down the macadam past the black earthen fields. The speed didn't slacken until the turn into the tree-lined road she remembered.

A wagon pulled out from the first farm. Lutie Mae whispered to Arlie. "That's the Johnson's wagon. They're new over here."

They were riding at a funeral pace now. At the great live oak, a pickup truck drew out to travel behind the wagon.

Lutie Mae leaned to Arlie. "Raven Black's family, Raven and Aretha." She named them all, like calling a roll. Jones. Honor and Sarah. Sol and Jinny Brown. Another truck. Aunt Minnie's niece—you knew Aunt Minnie passed? Simon and Celia. Tammy and Jeth. Rachel and Sammy. The tow truck turned off. "There's your Aunt Lelia and Aunt Madelaine. That Miz Flower with Mister Clay Justice." Did Sal's heart pound? Don't see me, Clay. I can't face you...

"Oh, there's Mister Adam. His whole family. I didn't think he'd remember Garrett." Arlie was looking out now with interest. After her van had turned down the road toward the tall lone pine, she had shrunken down into her seat.

Lutie Mae stiffened. "Ruby Ella, you look hard at that man on the corner. That's Bert Ainsley. You ever see him, you run. Ask your Aunt Lelia. Ask Oriole."

"Yes'm, Lutie Mae."

The graveyard lay at the end of Evening Road, at the oak

263

lined curve where the town began, where the apartments incongruously turned the street of fine old houses—Brewster and LeFleur houses—into anachronisms, the apartments that should never have been built.

Clay walked around the group to stand beside her. Sal watched him come. How many years back? The hot courthouse. The overpowering scent of gardenias, magnolias, oleander blossoms; the paper fan she waved in front of her face. "You must be from the north too, miss?" She had glanced up into his violet eyes. She had been seeing his neatly cut blonde head all week. He sat taking notes seriously, even more seriously than most reporters would have, she remembered thinking. He seemed to take unusual interest in the case, watched everyone closely, studied the bitter Aaron, leaning forward to hear his harsh words. He had watched every move of the Brewsters, but mostly, his attention was rooted on Drew, examining him. It made her so nervous that she stayed in the hotel room, sweltering, for a whole day, and rushed back the next day to sit right down next to him, on his tablet. She took off her gloves. "Yes, Illinois. I guess you're a reporter."

He'd stared at her rings. "I don't know why I didn't know who you were, but I didn't."

"Yes, I'm Mrs. Drew Brewster."

Now she held out her hand. "Long time, Clay. Where are you paying your rent these days?" She hadn't meant to ask that. He had moved into one of Drew's apartments. He liked the air-conditioning.

"Mailing it to your new agency. I've been away."

"Where?"

"Chicago."

Why so distinctly, Clay. "Oh." Of course. She should have guessed, should have known who was tracing Drew's movements...

"Dear friends," the preacher's compelling voice reached out across the uncovered heads. "We gather in this place where our people, our loved ones, through more than a century have been laid to rest, to return another brother to the earth that awaits us all, to the soil that will be his resting place until eternity..."

His seamed kindly face cried out to you. His somber eyes looked with appalling directness through you. He was tearing her apart. All around her people, black and white, sobbed, blew their noses and sobbed. Her own eyes filled... for whom? She wasn't sure, but it was good to let the tears flow, finally, to turn her eyes up to the wide Texas sky and cry... for Drew. Poor Drew who wanted so terribly to belong.

Chapter 23

THE SONG OF RUBY ELLA

The sky was as yellow as lemons. The wind had changed. The full, heavy branches of the great grey-green live oaks that lined Evening Road undulated toward the south for the first time since Ruby Ella came to Noonday. No longer did the south wind steadily, gently and so terribly quietly waft from the Gulf the unceasing, the endless drifts of screening mists.

The air had been hot and heavy and oppressive ever since Mama had to go back to Dallas leaving the children behind in the strange town to unknown to them, yet so known from all that Mama had told them about it. Now, although it was still hot, the air had a magical quality, a tinkling gaiety, like listening to a crystal pitcher as big as the whole world and filled with icy, sparkling lemonade.

She didn't know what it was. She was only aware that the wind was coming from the north, far far from the north, and that it was high, high and dry.

Whatever it was that she felt effervescing through her made her run, pulling Jesse faster than his chubby six year old legs wanted to go. He seemed almost to fly behind her, his bare feet hardly touching the dusty road that took them to their secret reading place beyond the cotton fields, clear out on the edge of The Great Cypress Swamp.

She knew that her exhilaration was due in part to the unread letter Lutie Mae had carried over from Mama and now swung in the big black shoulder-bag pocketbook Mama gave her before she went back. It was partly too because it was Halloween—not for her or Jesse, who was too little to go to the preacher's big frogging party tonight. She knew in her heart some of it came from the glimpse of the Yellow Peril, as everybody referred to Good-Time Joe's fabulous, shining, beautiful yellow convertible car, sticking out from behind Pokeen's.

Good-Time Joe was a record salesman from Chicago. She had talked to him only once. After that she had to store him way up there with her can-never-be-agains. The time she saw him was the morning after Mama left. That morning Aunt Lelia drove away to work sitting high on the board seat of her wagon behind the quiet and graceful little white mule. She and Jesse stood forlorn on the strange, warped porch of the unpainted broad-plank shack. With his hand squeezed unmercifully tight in hers, they watched until Aunt Lelia was out of sight. Above them the deadly quiet sky moved white with mists, moved endlessly like a silent curtain closing out all that was familiar, all sounds, all pictures. The home they had known back in Dallas was gone. Their furniture was stacked and covered in the shanty back of Aunt Madelaine's house at the tall lone pine where the rest of the boys were staying, clear out somewhere on another lonely road.

On that morning way back at the beginning, she stood on the porch unable to stop squeezing Jesse's hand. She knew she must be hurting him; he was standing so stiff and straight. She wanted terribly to lean down and pick him up, but she knew if she moved that action would cause something inside her to break. She knew she would scream out and sob for Mama and home and the boys. She had learned the night before that she had to be grown-up for Jesse.

In that night without Mama, after they had gone to bed, after Aunt Lelia's easy-breathing sounds began, she heard the immense and terrible silence of the place where Mama had left them.

All her life they had lived on city streets. All night long the sound of cars, of horns, of tires singing on pavement, of people laughing and talking and crying and singing and fighting, of radios and TVs and of trains, the wheels on the rails and the whistles had lulled her to sleep.

In that new quiet she became aware of the soundlessness, of the tightness of Jesse, still wide awake, although laid to sleep on a day-bed on the other side of the room. Into the immense quiet came the terrifying sound of an owl. The mournful cry reached deep into her loneliness. She could feel hot tears gathering in her eyes when Jesse started to sob. She rushed to him, grabbed him up in her arms, holding him the way Mama would have held him. Long after he went to sleep she lay awake. She recognized how she had to be from that time on, not just for Jesse who needed her, but for Mama, who had placed her faith and trust in her until she could come back.

Awake alone she heard a lonesome night train whistle echoing across the stillness. She had gripped her fingers into the palms of her hands.

She didn't dare cry the next morning when Aunt Lelia left for work. Jesse looked up at her from his smallness, his hand still pinched in hers. "Oh, Ruby Ella, let's not stand here any longer. Let's go see the boys. Mama said we could go any time we wanted to..." He'd been so crushed when there wasn't room in Aunt Lelia's small house for all five of them.

She ran inside to lovingly place the worn straps of Mama's big black shoulder-bag pocketbook over her shoulder. She and Jesse crossed the porch and went down the steps into the dust of Evening Road.

She knew only the general direction the boys had been taken. Aunt Madelaine lived in the house where Mama and Uncle Garrett grew up. She knew that the house stood high on stilts at the end of one of the many lanes leading from Evening Road straight through the cotton fields, separating the fields like lines. She knew it was way out in the land near the Great Cypress Swamp, that the rich black soil now planted in cotton had once been a forest of dark, long-needle pines. There still remained one wide swathe of pines cutting across the fields and the road to stand behind a lake. One straggler, a scrawny, immensely tall and bare tree stood near the old house. To Mama that tree, like the secret hiding place in the swamp, was a landmark reaching back into Mama's own childhood.

Ruby Ella, wearing Mama's pocketbook and holding Jesse's hand, set out that morning way back at the beginning to search for that tall lone pine that would lead them to the boys. They set out, dressed in their city clothes, and wearing shoes and stockings, walking past the other shacks set so far apart, one to each field, some clear back at the far end of the fields.

They explored each road. The roads were known by the names of the families who had worked the fields when they were all a part of the great Noonday plantation, but the names were known only to the people; the roads were unmarked. They searched for the LeFleur Road.

They walked in their strangeness, in their city clothes, past country children who were barefoot, shy, but not unfriendly, sweet but unquestioning and silent and therefore could not be asked directions by city children, new in experience and just starting out.

It was at that time, in the early morning's misty light, with the long, lonely shadows of the pines crossing in front of them, that she realized they were walking toward the macadam road to Dallas, the road down which they had come the day before. She was thinking, *Here we are, Jesse and I, and somewhere near here are the rest of the boys, and there is the road leading back home, but we can't go home.* Home as a word, as a place, no longer existed. Home that was made up of them, of Mama and their things, was gone.

It had been a small painted house, rented. Nothing of theirs remained in that house. It was awful thinking of that house empty. It was the most terrible feeling to think of the same morning sun that laid the pine tree shadows across the road ahead of them reaching into that empty house and not finding the table it always touched first. She could see the sun searching, becoming brighter and brighter, like a surprised person opens her eyes wider and wider. The sun wouldn't find them eating breakfast, laughing and happy, at that table. She could see the broad yellow beam coming through the window bare of curtains. It would pick out dust particles floating in that room.

She was seeing that yellow shaft of dancing dust particles cutting into that empty house when a yellow car, gayer than the sun, brighter and shinier than joy, streaked around a bend and swept down the road toward them, scattering dust and children and chickens.

To Ruby Ella, back there at the beginning, back there in that lonely early morning light, the first sight of that car was the City coming for them. She had an instantaneous joyful thought that Mama had somehow managed to send someone for them, to take them back, back home, back where they had all been happy together, back where they all wanted so terribly to be always.

Back then, staring at that yellow car, that city car, Ruby Ella recognized what it was that she had to fight, that Mama and the boys had to fight. It was change. Changes came to you. Somehow, no matter how deep it hurt, how awful it hurt, you had to face them, you had to meet them, you had to do what you had to do because once a change came there was no going back. There was no returning. No matter how awful you wanted things to be like they were before, they could never be again. Mama and the children would be together again after Mama had "paid" for Uncle Garrett's funeral, but it wouldn't be the same. Ruby Ella would be grown up. Worry and trouble grew you up fast.

When Good-Time Joe slammed on the brakes of that yellow city car that morning and ground to a dust-flinging stop in front of them, her almost-grown-up city eyes met Joe's city eyes in a glance that was recognition even though they had never seen one another before in their whole lives. He had clean, clear skin the exact color of blended coffee and cream; his neat hair and small trim mustache were jet black. His eyes, which were sparkling black, changed from showing recognition to disappointment, to apology. He smiled, showing even white teeth. "Oops, I thought you were Oriole and her little brother. You aren't from Noonday, are you? I come here often to see Pokeen. I sell him records down at the Record Studio."

"I'm Ruby Ella LeFleur. This is my brother, Jesse. We're staying with Aunt Lelia LeFleur. We know Pokeen. He drove the hearse to Dallas to bring back our Uncle Garrett."

"I'm sorry. I thought you looked sad."

"We're hunting for the LeFleur Road. Our brothers are staying with Aunt Madelaine LeFleur."

"Big brothers?" he asked oddly.

It was such a funny question that she laughed. "No, I'm the oldest. Jesse's the baby." Jesse slipped his hand out of hers and walked away, far to the side of the road where he stood with his head bent down.

"Then you're just visiting? You won't be here the next time I come through."

"We'll be here." Something cheerful, the first buds of hope effloresced up out of her gloom. "We'll be here for a long time."

Leaning out, he placed his hands on her shoulders to turn her around, and pointed out the tall lone pine way down at the end of a road. There was a fresh scent, like nice soap; she noticed it, but at the same time she drew away. He gave her a friendly squeeze before releasing her.

"I'm Joe Time, Ruby Ella. I'm glad you'll be around. Maybe I'll arrange to stay over some night. After you get to know me, maybe you'll go to the picture show with me."

It was too hard to believe. She closed her eyes, and then opened them cautiously. He was still there, his head ducked down, his eyes laughing into hers. She let her breath escape between her teeth, trying not to let him know how he made her feel. "I almost know you already," she told him.

That was the only time she ever saw Good-Time Joe. Now summer was almost gone, slipping away into the fastly fading past, and she was older. Worry and trouble aged a girl fast. She pushed her chest forward and looked serenely down at her almost-completely-developed front.

When Aunt Lelia got home from Abernathy's that night she had already heard that Ruby Ella was seen talking to Good-Time Joe. Ruby Ella had a cooking fire going in the funny old wood stove; the iron kettle, still half-full of blackeyed peas from the day before, was warming and sending fragrant whiffs through the screen door to the back stoop where she cleaned their shoes. She and Jesse were tired, almost exhausted from seeing the boys, going exploring along the edges of the pines, venturing near the swamp, and their shoes were practically wrecked.

Frowning, Aunt Lelia examined the heels of Ruby Ella's shoes. "You children best go barefoot like the country kids."

It tickled Jesse so much that he laughed. After he was put down to sleep, Aunt Lelia plaited Ruby Ella's hair. "Ruby Ella, there's a man comes to town, a city man called Good-Time Joe."

"We met him today. He's a lovely boy. He said maybe sometime I could go to the picture show with him."

Lelia studied the white eyelet top of Ruby Ella's pettycoat. "He isn't a boy. He's a man, and a practised one. Didn't your mama explain all the dangers? All the pitfalls?"

She nodded, and reached for Mama's pocketbook to show the inconspicuous black bead head of the long sharp hat pin Mama always carried to protect herself when she came home late from work. She took the bead of the pin adroitly in her fingers, pulling its length from the leather to show the protection.

Before leaving, Mama reminded her that the pin was in the pocketbook. Placing her hands on her shoulders, she smiled down into her eyes. "Don't forget, Ruby Ella, what you lack in strength and size, you must make up for in surprise." The sudden jab of a hat pin could make someone who grabbed you let go so you could run away. "Then run, Ruby Ella, run like the wind," Mama said, "and Ruby Ella, don't fall down. So you don't knock out your pretty teeth. So you don't get hurt." Then she started to cry.

Aunt Lelia didn't forget Good-Time Joe. After church the next Sunday, when the preacher and his nephew took all of her brothers fishing, she took Ruby Ella to a shabby little shanty beyond a flower-buried mansion on Old Swamp Road. A young girl carrying a baby ran from the porch. The baby's face was crinkled with pain.

"Oh, Aunt Lelia, the baby's no bettah."

Aunt Lelia took the baby, burped it on her shoulder, and handed it back to Oriole. "Poor little thing. Oriole, I brought my niece Ruby Ella to see your baby. Ruby Ella's going to live with me. I thought it would be nice for you to know each other."

Ruby Ella tucked Good-Time Joe way up there into the

secret place. Whenever she thought of him it was only as the lovely boy coming someday to take her to the picture show. She did with him what Mama told her to do about home when she missed it. "Look at new things when looking back hurts. Look ahead and hope." Mama and home and that boy were now part of something far away, far out beyond her reach, high out in the sky.

Still, unbidden, a vision of going to the picture show with him formed like a dream. There was the town beyond Noonday where the picture show was; there was the yellow car gliding down the street. It was dark. The town lights showed on the faces of people waiting for the picture show to open. The car stopped. She stepped out, not as she was now, barefoot and wearing an old cotton dress, but more grown up, wearing city clothes and shoes and stockings. The boy helped her out of the car. And there they were. The dream stayed way off somewhere, high, floating like a cloud in the sky.

The children did what Mama told them to do in the letter. They explored new things, searched out all the places Mama knew as a girl.

The yellow car sticking out from Pokeen's refused to retreat into her never-mores. She couldn't quiet this mysterious stirring, this exhilaration. It was as if she had suddenly become eighteen instead of just-passed fifteen. She knew an immense happiness, light and gay, flying like a banner in the sky. It made her run. She was aware of one sober thought. Deep in her heart she hoped he hadn't seen her in her bare feet. She wanted him to remember her as she was that morning, in her city clothes.

Beside her, Jesse was chirruping about something he wanted her to write in the letter to Mama. Every day after school he wanted to tell Mama about it. A long afternoon stretched before them. Aunt Lelia had to serve a late grown-up party at Abernathy's. Poor Jesse. She swept him into her arms, and ran on with him jogging against her. Ahead of them, waiting in its mystery, its strange silence broken only by sudden piercing shrieks of birds, lay the peaceful and cool grey-white cypress swamp.

Behind them the soft silent yellow car glided to roll beside them and stop. Joe leaned across the yellow leather of the seat and opened the door.

"Ruby Ella, what are you doing down old swamp road?"

She stepped into the car and sunk down into its softness. Joe Time reached over Jesse and closed the door. She couldn't answer. She knew she should get right out of that car, but she was suddenly very tired. Her excitement had burned her down like the finished wick in Aunt Lelia's lantern.

"Are you meeting someone down here?" he asked sharply.

She shook her head.

"Did you think you might run into me, or am I imagining things, Ruby Ella?" The hopefulness in his voice reminded her of Jesse. Taking her chin in his hand, he lifted her head. She had been staring at the incongruous appearance of her dusty feet on the clean yellow mat of the floor. He pressed her head into the leather so that she had to look into his eyes. She was terribly aware of his moving closer. It was incredible that she was sitting there in a skimpy dress that spanned her across the front and was too short. She moved Jesse to cover her knees.

"Come *on,* Ruby Ella," Jesse urged pettyishly.

"We have to go."

Joe Time snapped the handle, and held the door open. The sound awakened a sharp fear: she might never sit close to him again. Wanting to stay, she slid from the seat. Jesse walked ahead down the road toward their secret place. "Wait, Jesse." Joe was leaning over the door looking at her.

"I didn't even know you came down here."

"I do when I stay over. Sometimes I drive down just to look at it. I guess you've seen it by moonlight."

"No, but it must be lovely. Some night Aunt Lelia's going to bring us all down in the wagon to look for Jeddy's swampfire light. Have you ever seen it?"

He pressed his lips together. "Lots of times. Would you come with me some night to look for it?"

She had the feeling that he hadn't seen it, but that he would like to. "I wouldn't be allowed. But you could come with us in the wagon. I would love you to come." From somewhere she found the hope that Aunt Lelia wouldn't mind his being with all of them.

"Do you think you'd be allowed to go to the picture show with me?"

"I could ask Aunt Lelia. It might be all right if I took Jesse." She knew it wouldn't be all right, but a hope was growing that she could talk Aunt Lelia into letting her if...

"Well, maybe you *are* too young," skeptically, as if he thought before that she was, then was thinking maybe she wasn't, but now saw that she was.

She tossed her head. "I could probably go tonight. Aunt Lelia's serving a party."

He leaned close, placing his hands on her shoulders. "Ruby Ella, one time up north I saw a girl I knew but had never dated. I said, 'How about you'all going to the show with me?'" His hands dug insistently into her shoulders, as if his fingers tried to feel the bones. "When I got to her house she was standing on the porch with her whole family ready for me to take them. Do you understand what I'm trying to tell you, Ruby Ella?"

"Sure I do. It would cost an awful lot of money to take them all."

His eyebrows shot up, making lines across his forehead. Deep in his eyes lay a glint like laughter. Drawing her to him, he held her until she could feel the buttons of his shirt pressing into her chest. "Listen to me, Ruby Ella, haven't you ever been alone with a boy, other than your brothers?"

"Boys used to walk home from school with me."

"Did any of them come into the house when your mother wasn't home?"

"They weren't allowed."

His arms held her lightly. "Then you've never been alone with a boy, close?" he whispered, "a boy that wanted to be alone with you like I do?"

She shook her head.

Releasing her suddenly, he grabbed both of her hands. "Maybe we'd better go to the picture show tonight. You take Jesse out to your Aunt Madelaine's. Meet me here as soon as it gets dark, will you?"

She nodded.

He let her go, and slid back across the seat. "You sure are pretty, Ruby Ella," emphatically. Behind her she heard the car start, knew it was backing quietly. When she looked back it was gone.

Jesse was standing at the tree, waiting for her to take the big towel and the sulphur powder from the pocketbook. The first time they were there he sat on a scorpion and had since been careful where he sat. She wrote the letter. He fell asleep with his head in her lap. Sitting on the cypress-needle pad, her back pressed o the tree, she looked up through the spindly branches to the sky. Her dream hung like a kite with a string: she could pull it close, or release it. It could go higher and higher, out of reach, forever, or . . .

"Ruby Ella, why can't I go to the frogging party with the boys? Lutie Mae says the preacher had Doodle making frogging forks for *all* the boys, that he already had my initials on one."

"Because you're too little, Jesse. You might fall in." She placed her arms around him. "It'll be dark and spooky."

Starting to cry, he rubbed his eyes. "Then let's go see the boys. You promised Lutie Mae we'd take Mama's letter for them to read."

Aunt Madelaine admitted that lots of little boys were going to the frogging party. Jesse had never heard Pinkney's songs, and the preacher had arranged for him to sing all Trunk Brewster's swamp songs to scare them before they left the church for the lake. She would fix a costume for Jesse. The boys promised not to let him out of their sight. "Now, Ruby Ella, you show up at Lutie Mae's for the girl-party."

"Yes'm, Aunt Madelaine." But she had a lost feeling. She didn't want to be with girls. Jesse was so tickled to be going frogging, he threw his arms around her neck.

She walked slowly to Aunt Lelia's house. For a long time she worked with her hair. Finally she wound the braids high on her head to form an oval crown like Mama's. She got out her black city dress and tried it on, put on stockings and her black city shoes.

She sat on the back porch looking toward Dallas, out

over the low hills. The great orange sun was sinking fast into the sky skimmed with long grey-black clouds.

She was dressed up; she could go to the girl-party. She took off her shoes, pulled off her stockings and put them into her big pocket book. She stood on the warped front porch looking down Evening Road toward the church, but her bare feet turned the other way. She ran toward the swamp.

The yellow car was luminous in the moonlight. She could see it shining deep in the cypress, silvered as the trees and the still water. She could see Good-Time Joe's white shirt, bright, near the tree.

"That you, Ruby Ella? Come here. I think I see the swampfire light."

"Silly, you couldn't see it unless the night was pitch black." She leaned against the tree, pulled her stockings from the bag swinging at her side and slipped one over a bare foot. He put his arm around her waist to brace her.

"I think we could see it if we stood close together and looked real hard," he was laughing way back in his throat.

She pushed her back firmly against the tree, trying to keep her balance on one foot on the slippery needles while she got her shoes. He pulled her, grabbed at her so suddenly she dropped the shoes, and the strap of the bag slid down her arm. She snatched it back. "If we're going to look for it, I've got to put on my shoes. Scorpions come out thick at night."

He lifted her chin. "I got something for you in town, Ruby Ella, a keepsake to..."

"They're deadly poisonous," trying to slip one foot into a shoe. He pressed her close. "We'd better go, or we'll miss the first part of the show." Her voice trembled.

Laughing, he kissed her, lightly, barely touching her lips, and rested the side of his face against hers. "I thought you liked me, Ruby Ella. You're acting as if you don't." He sounded hurt, lonely, like Jesse. Her arms slipped around him, as if of their own accord, an action apart from her mind which was confused. Closing her eyes, she tried to collect thoughts that darted frantically. A sentence came back. She pushed him.

"Let's go to the picture show, Good-Time Joe."

He caught her, scraping her shoulder against the rough bark of the tree. She tugged. "I'm trying to tell you something, Ruby Ella. Please listen to me. Oh, come on, you don't want to go to the show. It's a spook show, for little kids. You knew we weren't going..."

She heard what he said, but she kept listening to be sure she'd heard right. Her thoughts stopped wavering, and her fingers searched the top of her purse.

He held her. "Ruby Ella, please let me talk to you," urgently.

She ducked, twisting away from him. Her fingers closed over the bead head of the pin. She drew it from the leather, cramping her fingers so it wouldn't slip. "Scorpion." Her voice reached a high crescendo as she jabbed the pin straight down to his seat.

Run, Ruby Ella, run like the wind. Don't fall down. She started to run, the hat pin still clenched in her hand, Mama's big purse banging at her side, her shoes still back on the cypress needles.

She ran, her loosened braids flying out behind her, tears streaming down her face. As she broke out of the swamp shadows into the field lying grey in the pale moonlight, she let go a wild shriek as she knew an immense freedom. At the same time, deep inside, she knew she would never feel free in the same lightness of that morning again in her life. It was gone, like childhood, flying away somewhere high in the sky, a banner waving free.

Chapter 24

THE SWAMP OF JEDDY'S SORROW

Olivia Flower, rocking Oriole's baby on her flowery front porch, watched the tall, thin leathery brown mule. Minus the black sun-shades, he could be an old Texas steer. The mule dragged down the road, his great ears straight up, loose flesh wobbling. Pinkney, his hair the same shade as the bleached boards of the wagon, humped on the high seat. Under that seat, wrapped in old cotton-boll bags, would be his banjo, and the cobweb-wrinkled paper sack that carried jars and bottles back and forth between her house and Aaron's.

Old hypocrite. Don't tell her Aaron didn't know whose wine, homemade bread and butter pickles and jellies he consumed. Shut himself off from the whole family because they didn't see much sense in fighting Drew when he came back after a stint at the base near their town equipped with papers that proved him to be a descendent of David Brewster who died at Shilog. Aaron raved. "He isn't as much Brewster as Cecile was." Dark-eyed, dark-haired Cecile, last daughter of Ruth and Aaron of Virginia, had caused almost a half century of whisperings to cease when she came straight out in her will demanding that none of her descendents marry LeFleurs, designating descendents of the dashing Jacques.

Oh, she didn't blame Aaron for ducking the Historical Society women who plagued him, nor the real estate people who poked at him endlessly, and the builders who offered him unbelievable sums for his last acres separated from Noonday by the apartments Drew built. The town was growing. The Historical Society, and rightly, wanted the first house preserved. The real estate people wanted to build more apartments. How Aaron had chased Clay! Clay was only interested in the history, and wrote fine articles that had appeared in the newspaper.

Everyone wanted or needed something. Abraham wanted a fine new church, a school for the children who had to trudge clear up to town. All of Noonday wanted Evening Road paved, wanted water and electric lines extended.

The mule made it to her bush-concealed circular drive, and stopped in front of her steps. Pinkney reached for the paper sack and crawled down.

"Well, Pinkney, so you came back again?"

"Yes'm, Miz Olivia, Mister Aaron needed weedin' out. The coops need cleanin'."

"How is the old buzzard?"

"The historic women pestering him to death. He tole me, 'Pinkney, go upstairs, toss scalding water. That'll flatten their feathers.'"

"He can be vitreous." She pushed forward a chair with her foot. "Sit down, Pinkney. You've been gone a long time. Tell me about it."

"I'd dearly love to set, Miz Olivia, but I promised Abraham to sing spook songs at the boys's Hollows' Eve party before they go froggin'. I would drank a cup of coffee. And I tole Lutie Mae I'd sing after for the girls' party. She and Willow and Aretha giving the girl-party. Abraham said to tell you that should take care of the outhouses this year."

"I'm relieved to hear that. Last year I spent the evening sitting in mine with a lantern. The next morning, Oriole's little brother—now mercifully in Shreveport—tore up here to report to me that it got away in the night and was in the swamp."

He nodded. "Every year since I can remember."

"Oriole told me Lutie Mae and Doodle were back. What happened? They were living it up with Sal Brewster at Garrett's funeral."

"I was right sorry to miss Garrett's service. Well, Miz Drew, she sold the Dallas house. Lutie Mae tole me Drew, he never came back. She came over here."

"Sal Brewster moved over here? What on earth for?"

"Colleck rents on the apartments, I guess. Lutie Mae says she ain't got any for a long time. Miz Olivia, you goin' volunteer to pick over at the experimental farm in Dallas this year?"

"Little late, isn't it?"

"No'm, Abraham says not for Mister Carlisle. Tole Abraham he'd pay double for every picker from Noonday."

She nodded. "And he'll make them deposit every cent for the new church fund." Oriole's baby started squalling.

"Yes'm, he already tole me I couldn't keep any if I pick. That Abraham got his fingers in more fires."

"Well, you're not going. You're too old to pick, and so am I." She stuck her finger in the baby's mouth.

"I guess rightly I am. Where'd you get that white baby at?"

"Sssh. He isn't white; he's sickly. You know this is Oriole's baby. Oriole's been helping me since Madelaine got Arlie's boys."

Pinkney put on his narrow, steel-rimmed glasses to peer down into her lap, squinted. "Another Ainsley," shaking his head.

"Pinkney. You want Oriole to hear you?" Lifting the child, she stared at its features.

He shrugged. "Noonday's divided on it. Half say Ainsley, half blame that nice Time boy."

"Well, it isn't Joe Time, I can assure you. No one knows that better than I do. He never went near Oriole until her folks left her. He's a lonely soul. Drives down to look at the swamp. I often walk down to talk to him." Leaning toward the door, she yelled, "Oriole, coffee, please."

"I'm not saying Oriole couldn't have walked down to talk to him once or twice." Pinkney looked thoughtful. "No, her folks knew it was Ainsley," he whispered, one eye on the door, "that's how come they had to leave. They wouldn't take the check to Adam's fo' cashin', so Pokeen done it for them. Why, Ainsley paid them to go to Shre'po't, and they foiled him. They was too righteous to take Oriole and the baby."

"They weren't being righteous, they were cruel. She's little more than a child. Poor Oriole."

He was still thinking it out. "Well, Noonday divided on it, but I seen too many of them Ainsley babies to be doubtful."

Oriole, a big girl in an oversized black dress given to her by Olivia when she needed it, shoved open the door with her high-heeled shoe, and, tottering on the heels, wended a perilous trip with the coffee tray around cats and flower pots to the table. She smiled at Pinkney.

"Yo' all right, Pinkney?"

"Yes, thanky, Oriole. Yo' goin' move to Shrev'po't?"

"Yo' crazy, Pinkney? My folks don' want me, but I'm leavin' when the baby gets bettah. I'm goin' down Naw Leans, but I ain't goin' by way of Shre'po't. I'm jest biding my time." She stood in the doorway watching a blue Cadillac sweep into the drive to grind to a leaf-flinging stop behind Pinkney's wagon. Her eyes narrowed at the car. "Some folks gets and some folks gets left. I'll bring another cup, Miz Flower."

Olivia reached over the baby to hold both hands out to Sal Brewster. Sal placed a plastic bag on the floor and dropped into a wicker chair.

"If you don't mind, Olivia, I'd like you to plant these violets for me. I couldn't think what to do with them... They're from my father's farm in Illinois."

Olivia eyed the bag gingerly. "All right, Sal. This is Pinkney, my brother Aaron's man."

Sal turned, eyes suddenly glowing. "Are you the Pinkney who sings the ballads? Bimby Brewster just told me you wouldn't let Pokeen record them. Now, you ought to do that, Pinkney. You're the only one who knows all of them. Bimby told me how lovely they are, how beautifully you sing them. You ought to do it so people can hear them after you're gone."

"Is Mister Bimby over here now?"

"Sure, he's cleaning the station Boyd and Josh are going to open."

Pinkney stared at her. "Why, I seen that white boy up there. I never... Yo' mean..." his eyes were flooding; his mouth moved considerably. "Yo' mean Mister Boyd and Joshua both comin' back? Lawdy." He blinked. "I told Pokeen, I know every song old Trunk sang, but I can't write down a letter."

"You don't need to write, Pinkney. You just take your banjo into the record studio, and sit down beside a machine and sing. It imprints the sound of your voice and the words and music. You know, sort of like a victrola record only... He wants to make records, and sell them. You might make a lot of money."

"Well, I guess I could sometime. I'm working' fo' Abraham tonight. He could use the money on the new church. I don' need money, but I would rightly like the ballads kept goin'. I keep lookin' fo' a little boy what could listen to me and learn 'em like I learned 'em, but..." He placed his hand softly on her glove. "Should I know you, Miz Lady, ma'am?"

"No, you shouldn't, Pinkney, or your boss would kill you for talking to me. I'm Mrs. Drew Brewster, or was..."

He peered at her, then reached slowly into his pocket and got out his steel rimmed glasses and studied her. "Lawdy. Well, thanky, ma'am." He turned to leave, remembered the paper sack and handed it to Olivia. "Mister Aaron's piggles and presarves, please, ma'am."

"And wine, Pinkney?" Holding the baby in one arm, she took the bag to the door and yelled, "Oriole, bring all that stuff we packed for Pinkney last month, and Oriole, put a mess of that chicken you're frying on top."

With the baby clutched in one arm, she walked down the steps with him, went around the departing wagon to the pump, scraped leaves with her shoe, laid the thick mat of violets there, patted black dirt around it, walked back to Sal, and handed her a penny out of the pot.

"Stay and eat with me, Sal. Tell me about it."

Sipping coffee, Sal watched the frail baby. "Lutie Mae says that's Bert Ainsley's baby, that Bert ought to be put away before..."

The candles in Olivia LeFleur Brewster's New Orleans crystal chandelier burned low. The reflections of Olivia Flower and Sal Brewster shimmered in shadow upon the rubbed front of the altar brought over from Mississippi by Olivia Brewster and which now served to hold pots of delicate plants kept indoors.

Olivia slowly placed her wine glass on the crocheted doily. "You're brave, Sal, to want to face Aaron. I'm going with you." She stood up. "We'll stop by Clay's. He'll know what to do."

It was moonlight when they left the darkened house. Oriole bumped down the road, the baby in one arm, a sack of food in the other. The lantern dangling from her hand glowed on the mimosa trees that surrounded Olivia's house, separating it from the fields.

Olivia looked back. "I hope I still have an outhouse when I come home. Abraham's supposed to be handling Halloween."

Sal glanced up at the sky. "Pinkney said his big toe predicted a storm tonight."

"Then you can count on it."

The moon was white. The wind had risen, stirring the trees and the almost overpowering scents of blooms in the yard. A yellow convertible shot past them up swamp road toward Pokeen's to swing right, past the quiet station and disappear into the great live oaks of Evening Road.

"That was Joe Time," Olivia said. "Oh, Lord, and here comes Bert Ainsley, headed with a bottle for the swamp. I hope Oriole has thrown down the lock." A figure in white stumbled past them. "I'm more than thankful Abraham has seen to the children tonight."

Joe Time's headlights picked out Ruby Ella huddled on the steps of Lelia LeFleur's house. He got out, leaving the car door open. The dash lights shone, illuminating tears in her eyes.

"Go away, Good-Time Joe."

"I am going away, Ruby Ella. That's what I was trying to tell you down in the swamp. In a few minutes I'm going to drive out this road, and I won't come back until you write and tell me you are old enough to marry me." Leaning over, he dropped into her lap a small box in which lay a little ruby encircled with pearls, a ring he had bought in town for her that afternoon. He wanted her to have something to remember him by.

"Don't come near me, Good-Time Joe."

Stricken, he backed away. "Whatever you think of me, think of me saying that I've never said this to another girl in my life, never knew how. I love you, Ruby Ella. I want you to stay as you are. The ring is to remind you, to keep you safe for me. Do you understand, Ruby Ella?"

He swallowed. He wanted to remember her like that, pigtails awry, eyes wide and innocent, but not filled with tears. He'd never known anyone like her, but she was still a child.

She leaned far forward, staring at him, and brushed at her eyes with the back of her hand. "What about Oriole, Good-Time Joe?"

"Now, listen, Ruby Ella, Oriole and I are good friends, but we didn't become friends until she needed a friend. Go ask her. Ask Lutie Mae, she knows." Looking at her, he stepped to the car. He didn't really want to do what he was going to do, but ever since that first day he'd met her, he knew. And today down on Old Swamp Road, he knew for sure. He just wanted to keep right on driving with her there beside him. He slid under the wheel. "And stop calling me that. I'm not having a very good time." She started to get up. "No, don't come over here. Sit there. Watch me go. I'm having a hard enough time." He hung his head. He wanted to tell her the whole thing, but he couldn't. How could he say, Ruby Ella, I never had a mother or father to teach me to be gentle, to recognize goodness when I found it. I made my own way. Sure, I have a flashy car; salesmen are supposed to, but I'm not bad. You couldn't explain things like that to a child like she was. He would someday. Someday he would tell her how her arms around him swept away the lonely years, how they showed him what life might really hold.

"Joe, I'm sorry, I..."

He stepped on the starter. "Think of me now and then, Ruby Ella. Write to me. I'll send you my address, and you write. I'm going to get my territory switched. You will write, won't you?"

She nodded, holding the ring box in both hands, looking up at him.

He closed the door, taking away the light. She was only a small shadow now, outlined by the headlights. "And, Ruby Ella, hang on to that hatpin, will you?"

She nodded. He drove away fast, heading out Evening

Road toward the macadam. He knew that it was the hardest thing he had ever done in his life, yet the kindest. He felt that he wanted to put his head down on the steering wheel and cry.

Ruby Ella jumped up, stood watching the beam of headlights trace the dirt road, pick out shacks, stubbly fields, saw the twin tail lights fade. You can't call someone back after they'd gone. She'd already learned that. You had to look ahead and hope. She sat down on the step, opened the box. A little red flame flashed, then a mist crossed over the moon. She slipped the ring on her middle finger. It fit. She left it there, and put the box in her purse. She sat thinking about what he had said. Why, he was like Jesse; he was lonely. She'd felt that about him all along. She nodded. He was like her, too. With her hand pressed to her chest, she sat watching the fast moving white mist flowing northward over the moon, her bare toes digging into the dirt. The wind rose, swaying the trees, rolling them fiercely. It was going to rain. And her shoes. She'd left her shoes down in the swamp, there by the tree. She swung her purse under the steps, ran inside to catch up one of Lelia's lanterns, lighted it, and raced across the drying cotton fields toward the swamp.

Brewster nervously watched the church door. Wizards, hobos, clowns, spooks, rabbits, great black cats, gypsy boys in bandannas and gold earrings, until finally Terence came in his black Zorro cape hat and mask. They had gotten the costume at Adam's so Brewster could recognize Terence if he could sneak away from the party he was supposed to go to. He had insisted upon coming. Brewster wanted him, but he didn't like no one knowing where Terence was. He had been responsible for Terence to his uncle and to Aunt Lelia too many times in the past. But Terence always won. Nice as he was, much as he liked him, Terence had to have his way, or he blackmailed you into giving it to him. Reaching out into the aisle, he tugged at the black Zorro cape.

"Psst, Terence." Giggling, Terence slipped down on the board seat beside him.

His uncle Abraham, Raven and Doodle were passing out

the last of the icepick-sharp frogging forks. Lutie Mae had wrapped flour sacks around the ends so none of the boys would get hurt. The sacks were to hold frogs. They were one fork short. Brewster told Doodle he'd share his with Zorro. At the front of the room, under the yellow glow of the bare bulb hanging on a cord from the high ceiling, Pinkney waited on a straight chair, the banjo resting on his right knee, the neck even with his shoulder. He closed his eyes, dropped back his head. The high sweet pitch of his voice sent chills running down Brewster's back:

> *They run off into the swamp,*
> *Did Laurel and Jeddy Black,*
> *While Baby Raven sobbed.*
> *Wantin' his moma back...*

How mournfully the chords rang out through the room, quieting the boys until no sound except the beginning wind blended with the songs. Brewster listened to the familiar verses, to the high voice so much like Abram's. He could see the swing back in the dark and smelly hall in East St. Louis. A tear formed under his mask. He had to grit his teeth and make himself think about the song, a far yesterday, instead of dwelling on old Abram and Leah, yet, he yearned. He hadn't heard the songs since...

Abraham had them all lined up at the road, ready to cross at the great live oak to the lake. Terence grabbed Brewster's arm.

"Now, boy, did you see him go? When I grow up I'm going to sell records, and have a yellow convertible just like that." He tugged at Brewster's arm. "What if your uncle does want us to frog at the lake? He'll never miss you with all those other kids to watch. Come on, we can be down in the swamp and back before he calls you all in." They were going to fry froglegs and sing.

"Now, listen, Terence, I told you..."

"I'm going to tell Lelia you made me come; that you came to the house and forced me to come."

"Terence, when are you going to grow up?" The others had crossed. Lanterns and flashlights bobbed through the field like giant fireflies. They didn't have a light. Creeping past Doodle's house, Brewster took Terence's arm. "Now, you've been wanting to hear Pinkney's songs for a long time. You didn't hear many in the church. Wouldn't you like to stand for awhile and listen? He's going to do all different songs for the girls, not spooky."

"No, I wouldn't. I've never seen the swamp close, either, and I've lived here all my life. You don't understand what it's like to be sickly and babied. Sometimes I think I'll choke, I get so mad." He tugged at Brewster.

Brewster held back, listening as Pinkney struck the first chords inside Doodle's window.

Hush, little baby, don' yo' cry,
Uncle Jacques's got fine, big house in Texas...

Reluctantly, Brewster turned away. "Terence, it's going to rain. If you get soaked, both Aunt Lelia and Uncle Abraham will be after me."

They crept down the dust road past Madelaine's house, dark now, past the ghostly tall long-needle pine, and made the turn into Old Swamp Road. Brewster held Terence's arm as a mist rolled fast over the moon, and the wind rose, clacking the great fence of dead cypress lining the road.

"Now, Terence, this is Old Swamp Road. There's the swamp on your left. The road runs clear down to Oriole's where it turns to pass Miss Olivia Flower's house, and on up to Pokeen's, and Adam's store. Now, you know what the swamp looks like, you ready to go back?"

"We just got here." Terence's teeth were chattering so loud Brewster could hear them, and it wasn't cold. "How far back does the swamp go?"

"I don't know. Parts of it have been left alone forever. Lutie Mae, who came up out of it, says it goes clear to Louisiana. Doodle says it never ends. Raven knows. For generations, his family has searched it for traces of Jeddy and Laurel Black. You come on now, and someday he'll take us around part of it in his rowboat. He goes in often, has even when he was littler than us."

"Brewster, do you believe all that old stuff?"

"It's all true; it's history. Jeddy Black ran off into the

swamp after Aaron Brewster of Virginia was trampled by his wild steers. All Brewsters remember hearing about it forever. Ask your mother, or Adam, or Miss Flower. All Brewster's remember about Jeddy Black. He came as a child from Virginia with them, and your mother was a Brewster."

"Gee, my mother ought to know, but she never cared much about old stuff."

The wind tore in great sweeps, lashing the trees, tossing Terence's Zorro cape wildly. Now they were walking on the damp earth beside the swamp. A great gnarled cypress rose up eerily beside them. Mist and clouds swept past the moon, covering, uncovering it, sending out phosphorescent glows that would briefly light up the trees. Brewster tightened as across the fields far ahead of them a dark figure outlined by a lantern's light ran toward the other end of swamp road. A piercing shriek rent the night. The boys ran together, bumping.

"Geemy!" Terence yelled, grabbing Brewster's frogging fork. The sack fell off and blew toward the swamp.

Trying to catch him, Brewster yelled, "That was only a bird screaming. They do it all the time. Give me that fork. It's sharp. If you fall, it might kill you."

Grabbing him, Terence hung on. "If that was a bird, who's that down there with that crazy-turning lantern?" Now a white form had joined the black, eerily outlined in the glow of the wheeling lantern.

"It's big kids Halloweening. They drag outhouses down to the swamp."

They both froze as a frightened and terrified shriek sounded out above the wind.

Terence said shakily. "If that wasn't human, I'm not Terence Abernathy."

Brewster stood still listening. It didn't sound like kids playing. "It sounds like a girl. You stay here, Terence. Don't you move. I'll come back for you." He was already running with Terence hanging on to his arm.

"Brewster, if you leave me alone in this swamp, I'll tell my mother you dragged me..." panting.

The white form shimmered in the lantern's glow.

"Terence, honest, it *is* just kids playing. We might get hurt. Look, there comes another one running from the other way. See, look at that lantern swinging."

They were close enough now to hear the sounds of scuffling. They were already in the melee. Something struck the side of Brewster's head as he caught a whiff of whiskey smell. Terence was pulling him, dragging him. He tried to clear his head. That black figure was jumping up and down. He had to get Terence home safely. That wasn't kids. Those two big ones were grown people, and that man was white. Cutting in toward the drying cotton field, he held Terence's hand.

"I know who it was," Terence's voice was shaking. "If my mother ever finds out you brought me down here where he..."

"You just forget it, Terence, I'm going to get you home before something bad happens to you. I just hope we make it before the rain hits." Big drops were beginning to slash at them. Inside, he felt half-sick. That black woman had grabbed his frogging fork. Both boys froze as a voice cried up from the swamp.

"I always thought someday I'd kill yo'!"

Then, in terror, the boys raced toward Evening Road.

Chapter 25

MIMOSA FOLDS HER LEAVES FOR NIGHT

Clay Justice stood with his hands clasped on the window sill of his apartment overlooking Aaron's house. A damp wind stirred the trees that hid Aaron's chicken enclosure. He knew Pinkney peddled Aaron's eggs, that the chickens were concealed in the dense hollow of bushes and hackberry trees, but he'd never seen the top of a coop, or the flutter of a wing. He'd heard the chickens. He'd seen the thin relic of a man come out of the thicket bent under the weight of egg crates. He saw him many times tottering across the sweep of lawn pushing a hand mower, or walking the grassy last acres bent against the wind, followed by the dog Buck, trailed by Comanche, the grey cat, tail straight up—a lonely entourage until Pinkney would return from his mysterious travels. Pinkney was the only human Aaron suffered on his land, those broad last acres of the dwindling Brewster Plantation. Olivia had told him of the lean years, how Aaron had had to sell off to the growing town, how his father before him had let go acre by acre until most of the town was built upon land that had once belonged to Brewsters and LeFleurs.

Lighting a cigarette, he stared down at the house which was revealed by moonlight, then darkened by the clouds rolling up from the south. Proud, the house looked, gallant, with the small light glowing from the summerhouse kitchen—a last soldier on the tightening battlefield. Silently, Clay was proud too, of Aaron and of Olivia. It was sufficient to be near them. He asked nothing more. That made up for his years of loneliness.

Clay had seen the old house for the first time at the end of a long journey southward to Shiloh where he sat beside the marked grave of David Brewster, on to Vicksburg where he wandered the now peaceful hilly battlefield, looked over the river, and asked about the Plantation, South Wind, the name that since his childhood had enthralled him when his mother told him the history handed down to her. He drove a back road to all that remained of the once fabulous plantation so vividly described by Lila Brewster who had stayed there for a short time during the Civil War with her distraught mother and an older sister. The mother and sister died later during the influenza epidemic that swept Chicago.

An old negro told him that according to older folks, the Brewsters and their slaves had moved on to Texas, to a place a wandering preacher had recently told him was the town Noonday, once the Noonday Plantation. He didn't know where it was. Clay spent some time clearing out an old cemetery there along the river, reset the ancient wrought iron fence around it, and headed out for Texas. He wasn't sure then what he would do if he found his relatives. He just wanted to see them... to know...

The day he stopped in the bois d'arc lined lane and got out of the car to examine the pale green wrinkled apples on the ground, stooped over, he saw the house, the soft red of the sun touching the grey planks. Long afterward, when he had his job on the paper in the town above Noonday, Drew came to put Aaron through the agonizing battle for the land that had been in Brewster hands for generations, cotton land and grazing land for which his ancestors fought Indians and wars to hold. Throughout that court battle, Clay had listened intently for some absolute proof that this man did truly descend from David Brewster. He knew in his heart that if David Brewster had had a son to another wife, his mother had never known it. From what he had heard of David, he doubted it. Still, he kept quiet. It wasn't easy, but the proof Drew brought with him seemed unquestionable. There had been times during that court that Clay doubted his own history told over and over to him by his mother. Later, he moved into one of Drew's apartments, not that he approved Drew's claim, nor the building Aaron would hate, but because they were comfortable and air-conditioned, and apartments were hard to find in the town.

Clay had been horrified to see city equipment rip out that

fenceline of trees to pave a street once a lane with no destination other than the Brewster house. He asked the mayor to replant the bois d'arc trees. The Historical Society got into the fight. Too late. The loss of them left the house exposed, bare and shabby. That, and Drew, put the anger into Aaron. From then on he evaded friends, relatives, real estate men, the women from the Historical Society so bent on nothing more eating into the richest of their local treasures. He had seen Aaron duck into the barn or run brittley for the chicken thicket. Clay deeply regretted the historical articles he'd had published in his paper. He hadn't meant them as an affront to Aaron, but as an accolade. Many times since he was to wonder if most of Drew's family knowledge hadn't come directly from the articles. It was not until he accidently met Abraham many years ago that he found in Abraham a wealth of Brewster history. He found the wandering preacher who had told the old negro back in Mississippi about Noonday. They spent many pleasant hours fishing the lake while Abraham told how he had traveled back to South Wind, over into Alabama, followed the same trail the Brewsters had taken from Virginia up into Appomattox County where descendents of Brewsters still lived. He had almost fallen into the lake when Abraham told him of the old records kept back there as keepsakes. He urged Abraham to write to them to borrow the records...

His buzzer sounded.

He rarely had callers. Then he smiled to himself. It was Halloween, and he hadn't bought any treats. He pressed the buzzer, and waited. Heels sounded across the hall floor. He opened the door.

"Sal," involuntarily, painfully. He hadn't seen her since Garrett's funeral. "And Olivia. Come in. I was just going to light the fire and make coffee."

Ashes made a small sound tumbling down in the grate. Outside, the wind rolled the trees. He sat with his head lowered. It hadn't been easy for Sal to tell him this. Now he glanced up. Olivia, who had remained silent, sat back in her chair studying them. Sal stared into the fireplace.

Her voice was soft. "If you've known all along Drew falsified those papers, why did you wait, Clay?"

"Don't you know?"

Olivia nodded her head sagely. She leaned forward. "I suspected it the instant we walked into this room." She made a pleased *humping* sound. "If you thought you were giving Sal time to get out of Texas to join Drew, you were wrong. She wrote to him when she put the house on the market..."

Sal didn't even look up. "Olivia, please..."

Olivia went right on. "Drew got a Mexican divorce."

Now Clay wasn't listening. He just looked at Sal. The rain beat against the windows, the side of the building. Olivia wandered over to stand there and look out.

Finally Olivia turned. "Clay, get out your proof. Aaron goes to bed with the chickens, so we'd better get on over there."

Clay went to the cabinet and drew out the stack of old ledgers and the tied bundle of letters Abraham had carried around to bring down to him.

"As I said, Drew just didn't sound true. When I went up to Chicago to check that first time all I learned was that he didn't get his job in the records department until after he was in camp down here. Recently, I went back for proof that David Brewster's children were both girls. There was no record of his earlier marriage, if there was one. I wanted to look into every possibility, although I knew David had married shortly after he set up his law practise there. By that time the records department had got interested and were doing their own checking, and a thorough job they did of it. I didn't tell them about Drew's case down here, but they were beginning to nose around. I hurried back to have it out with Drew, but he was gone." He handed the ledgers to Olivia. "These came from Virginia. Old Abraham remembered his father telling him that Adam Brewster wrote letters of family history to the dead son, Charles. These are the letters mailed to Charles. They were preserved by relatives still living in the old Brewster Plantation in Virginia. They entrusted them to Abraham who brought them to me. Some of the ledgers are old slave inspection records."

"Well, then, who was Drew?" Olivia asked both of them.

Clay answered. "He was a Chicago Brewster, and his family background has been traced far beyond the Civil War. He did not even remotely come down from David Brewster."

"No offense to you, Sal, but I'm glad." Olivia beamed at both of them.

The wind pitted the sharp rain into the thin skin of Clay's coat as he pressed the button and waited. He heard the bell ring as if from some deep distance, not musical chimes or a modern buzzer like in the apartments, but an old fashioned doorbell. He heard Aaron's footsteps crossing the floor, which was stone, he decided from the sound.

The lock slid raspingly as the old man opened the door. "Pinkney, where the hell..." He had a can opener in one hand, and with the other braced the door against the wind. The big collie edged up close, and the cat waited, tail straight up. On Aaron's face was the most scathing look he'd ever seen. "What do you want?" his caustic voice scraped the words.

Clay couldn't determine the color of his eyes, only their fierce intensity, their bitterness. He wondered that they didn't blink—the shaggy ends of the brows dug into them. The long white hair wasn't soft. In the courthouse, and across the distance from his apartment window it fluffed like the top of a blown dandelion. It was strong and bushy, and out from it the large ears glowed transparent crimson from the dim electric bulb behind him. Weathered skin taut over the crook of the large nose and the high bones of the cheeks pulled the thin mouth into a malefic grimace. His withered frame bowed forward as a tree leans to the windward, yet the defiant tilt of his head on the fragile neck gave the effect of his standing unbendingly erect. He wore heavy field boots, an unironed plaid shirt and tan cavalry-twill pants held up by a belt that might have been cut from an old Sam Brown, the raw edges showing where it barely caught in the buckle.

He heard Clay out, and then shut the door and slid the latch. He didn't slam it, he simply closed it and walked back across the stone floor deep into the house. Clay waited. The wind was turning, whipping in from the north, and stirring up into the moisture-heavy clouds that had boiled up from the south all evening. Ducking against the wind, drawing his wet-weather coat around him, he went to the car for Olivia and Sal.

When Aaron returned to admit them, he wore a necktie of some ancient vintage, oddly tied, and a coat.

Clay steered into Olivia's drive.

Olivia stopped with her hand on the door handle. "I was proud of Aaron tonight. Sure you won't spend the night with me, Sal? I can't blame you. This house predates the apartments by some years and conveniences. When the legal side is settled, I'll take one of the apartments."

"We might get stuck, Sal, but if you want to see the swamp during a storm, this is the time, and I'm with you even if I have to wade out." Clay backed into Olivia's drive and headed out the other way.

Parked near the great dead cypress, he turned the headlights out across the tossing black water. Moss and limbs tossed furiously. Cypress needles padded the hood with the rain. Lightning flashes brilliantly displayed the white trees that stretched far into the distance like a great tumbled wall.

Her hand lay in his. "I can't understand why you don't tell them who you are, Clay. They like you. It wouldn't be like..."

He stared straight ahead.

"I thought you resembled Boyd. I see him a lot. Your eyes didn't though, and tonight when I read old Adam's description of David's wife in a letter to Charles, I thought of your eyes."

"And you guessed. If I am that transparent, I'm surprised Olivia didn't."

"If she did, she won't let on until you tell them."

"Someday I will, after Aaron's bitterness has worn off."

"You're afraid they'll think that you want... I know you don't. They have little enough left. That's what I tried to tell

Drew even when I thought he really did belong to the family. But, you're lonely, Clay, and they are your people."

"What are your plans, Sal? I'm more interested in what you are going to do."

"I don't know yet, but I do know this—I won't leave until everything is straightened out, until Aaron has everything back... Clay, isn't that a lantern out there? I've been looking at it." Leaning over, she wiped at the mist-coated window with her glove. "Clay. Oh, Clay, it isn't a girl..." She threw open the car door and ran toward the tree.

Clay righted the lantern, then pulled Sal to her feet. "God! Who could have done this?"

"But Clay, it's Arlie's child, Ruby Ella, her beautiful child! What can we do?"

"Pokeen's phone is closest."

"I can't leave her here in this rain, Clay."

"We daren't move her. This is murder, Sal. Oh, honey, I'm sorry. Don't cry so..."

Chapter 26

FLIGHT

Grinning, looking wondrously at each other, Lutie Mae and Doodle waited at Abraham's house for Raven who was to return with Aretha. When he came in, soaked through from driving all the drenched froggers to their homes, Lutie Mae threw her arms around his neck.

"Raven, you're my people! I'm your cousin. All your children are Pip Doodle's cousins."

Raven held her hand. "Well, Lutie Mae, I'm happy. How do you know?"

"Abraham and Pinkney figured it out. Pinkney, when he sang for the girls, sang songs I remembered. I knew I didn't learn them in Noonday, 'cause I've been singing them all my life. Abraham says the only way I could know them was that I'd come straight down the line from Laurel and Jeddy Black. Why, I'da known long ago had I heard the Jeddy Black song!"

"Oh, Rever'nd Abraham, I didn't know Brewster was asleep. Here I've been yellin' and talkin' and laughin' up my own happiness, and ... He isn't in there?"

"No, I just looked again to be sure. I haven't exactly seen him since the church, but there were so many boys..." His eyes fretful, Abraham leaned to the window to look down the road.

"You want Doodle to look for him?"

"No." Hesitantly. "He'll come in."

"Then we all better go home. Night, Cousin Raven, night, Aretha. Oh, I'm just that happy! But I guess we all is wore out. Now, Doodle, you cover Pip Doodle's head real good so he don't get wet..."

Olivia sat on her porch, a wet cat under her chair, a cup of coffee in her hand. The storm had lasted three days, had beaten limbs and leaves upon the heads bowed for Ruby Ella and Oriole's baby. Pokeen said Oriole came running up there just before the storm hit, her baby wrapped in a coat. She was hysterical and the baby was in convulsions. He rushed her up to the hospital, and stayed with her because she had no one. Bimby had been recording Pinkney's songs when Clay burst in dragging Sal, both of them drenched and just about in shock. Sal went with Bimby to the apartments to change before stopping for Abraham to go with her into Dallas to get Arlie. Abraham didn't think he could get Arlie out, but he did. And Lelia was so grief-stricken, so remorseful that she hadn't taken Ruby Ella with her to Abernathy's that night. When she went to work, she didn't know little Jesse would be in on the frogging party. She thought he was too small to go.

And poor Oriole. She'd made her come home with her after they buried the baby. They sat in the kitchen.

"If I'd been home, if I'd heard Ruby Ella scream out, yo' know I'd killed Bert Ainsley to save her. Yo' know that, Miz Olivia."

"How do you know it was Bert Ainsley, Oriole? Half the town says it was Joe Time."

Oriole's head snapped up and her eyes met Olivia's. "Yo' know Joe Time never killed an ant. He's too tender and kind. Bert Ainsley, he caught her and then he run out across the swamp and I'll bet they never find him. Done a lot of rotten things, but he never killed nobody before."

Olivia studied Oriole's face. She had a feeling Oriole knew more than she was telling, and she'd kept that hunch ever since. You could never tell with Oriole.

"They've been out there all day in boats, Oriole. And Raven's helping. If anyone can find him, Raven can."

The police had searched the town ever since Claire Ainsley told them Bert hadn't come home Halloween night. Joe Time had been driven back from Texarkana in his own car by a ranger. After Sal brought Arlie to Noonday, she took Olivia to jail to see the broken Joe. He cried, told them about the ring. No, there was no one they could call for him;

he didn't have anybody. He sat there and told them what he said to Ruby Ella when he left her. He had stopped for the night in Texarkana and called his boss in Chicago asking for a transfer, a different territory, and the police seemed to think that clinched his case, that it was open and shut. She and Sal had rushed to the jeweler who sold Joe the ring. Joe had told him he was buying the ring, not for an engagement ring, but for a little girl he would marry when she grew up. She hoped they called the jeweler because he would speak well for Joe.

But she was frightened for Joe. Even Lelia felt that it had to be him. His fancy car, his lighthearted manner, his city look had given an impression to most of the people in Noonday who wouldn't step forward and speak about Bert Ainsley, and most of the town children had seen Joe's car tear past the church. The police had prints of his car deep in the swamp road, but all other marks had been washed away by the storm. Nothing had been found but Ruby Ella, her shoes, and Lelia's lantern. Her purse had not been found. No one in Noonday could remember ever seeing her without that big shoulder-bag purse.

Oriole had looked at her. "Maybe he drowned? Would they find him, if he drowned? Would he float to the top?"

Was that fear in Oriole's eyes? Terror? or just fierce anger that she'd not been home to save Ruby Ella? Or was it simply sorrow over her baby?

"I don't know, Oriole. Lots of people have disappeared into that swamp and were never seen again."

"Would it prove he killed Ruby Ella if they found him? Or if they didn't?"

"I don't know, Oriole. The police will decide who killed her."

"How will they know for sure? Maybe somebody killed Bert Ainsley, then what would they do, the police?"

"I don't know, Oriole."

And now Oriole was packing. She had nothing to hold her in Noonday, no folks, and no sick baby.

"You can work for me as long as you want to, Oriole."

"Thank you kindly, Miz Olivia, but I want to go down

Naw Leans, get me a job. I want to see how other folks live. I want nice clothes and nice eats. I want it to be like I never heard of Noonday and it never heard of me. I want to forget Noonday. That's what I want."

The skin of the girl's face had pulled tight; her eyes narrow and glittering. "I'm through with this place, fo'ever."

Bitter? Heartsick? You could never tell about Oriole.

"I hope you find peace and happiness, Oriole."

"Happiness, Miz Olivia, yo' crazy? What's happiness? I never know it; yo' think I'd know it, had I it?" How tense Oriole's shoulder had been under her hand.

"Oriole, they might call on you to testify."

"What fo'? I wasn't here. The hospital can say that, and so can Pokeen." Quick words, spilling out...

"You might be needed, Oriole, to say something good for Joe Time."

Oriole's head snapped up. She should have told Oriole how bad it looked for Joe, that every good word would be needed. Over half the town thought Joe Time had fathered that sickly baby. Now, Olivia stewed. The coffee was bitter. When she placed the cup in the saucer, the kitten mewed.

"Yes, I know you're hungry. I suppose I should eat too." She stood up.

A small figure trudged into the drive. She walked to the steps, staring. The walk was that of a shrunken, finished little old man with a job to do, and he was hunched down with the burden of it. He came, dragged a storm-battered mimosa limb to the steps and laid it at her feet. He stood there, Ruby Ella's long black shoulder-bag purse stringing to the ground to rest on his bare toes. He stood, his arms hanging to his sides, his small hands stretched out to her, his head thrown back, his great blue-grey eyes streaming tears, pleading with her. *Dear God, does this child think I have the power to bring back Ruby Ella, to give her back to him?*

"Jesse." Dropping to her knees, she enfolded him into her arms, and carried him to the chair and sat rocking back and forth, patting his head while her mind ran through the house searching for some treasure to give him, some comforting thing to hold. The kitten, mewing, wrapped itself around her ankles, coaxing. She reached down, picked it up and dropped it in his lap.

If I had Bert Ainsley within arms reach, I would kill him myself. I would beat him and drag him to the swamp's edge and shove him in. She rocked, and stewed.

She knew by the excited voices, and the yells, and the motor starting down by the swampedge.

"Jesse, that kitty is hungry. Now do you think we should go in to the kitchen and feed it? Do you think we could eat some lunch?"

Carrying him and the kitten in a tight bunch with Ruby Ella's purse banging her leg and knocking over flower pots, she made it inside the door before the black police truck swept up out of the swamp toward Evening Road. *Let him be alive to clear that Time boy,* she gritted through closed teeth. *Let him stay alive that long.* Then she looked down at Jesse who had told Arlie and Lelia that Joe Time had met Ruby Ella in the swamp that afternoon. Pinkney had come down and told her that. She was heartsick...

The kitchen was hot from the heat-blasting wood stove. Oriole wiped her face on her sleeve and reached for another pan. As fast as Miss Olivia flipped the too-sweet smelling cakes from the layer pans, Miss Sal spread the icing Oriole had mixed.

"Now, Oriole," Miss Olivia reminded her, "you get those pans clean. I don't want ants in my cupboard again. You're not in any hurry."

Something fiery flared up in Oriole's chest. With a dripping hand, she snatched her water glass from the windowsill and swallowed fast to douse the words she almost blurted. *Oh, I'm in more hurry than you ladies know. I ain't stickin' 'round here 'crim'nating myself into jail, not for Bert Ainsley.* "Yes'm, Miz Olivia," she answered solemnly.

Yo' so inst'rst in me, Miz Olivia, yo'd see I gets outa here, 'stead of worryin' I stick around to save Good-Time Joe. With what folks think about me, I'd get him in deepah. She knew it. One question from a policeman, if she wasn't alert—and she wasn't, she knew—and it'd blurt right out. She was a dead give-away of herself like when the new preacher came. She looked right into those sad eyes and listened to that soft voice, and like a sinner confessing in tongues blurted, "What good church do me, Rever'nd? Steeped as I am in sin?"

"Now, Sister Oriole, we're all sinners born..." And then afterward, gently, "Oriole, your baby ought to be baptised. Please let me baptise him."

"When he's bettah, I get him named down in Naw Leans." Now the poor little thing would never make it to heaven, but it didn't matter, she wouldn't either. Rotten Bert Ainsley. She took those pearl earrings that he got her into the mess with in the first place in town to the jewelery store.

"Why, girl, I couldn't give you ten dollars on them. They aren't worth ten cents."

"Yo' crazy, Mistah? They're real pearl and diamonds."

And she'd put her hand to her mouth because she almost blurted out to him that Bert Ainsley said they were real and when Miss Claire found out she'd taken them, she would end up in jail. Rotten Bert Ainsley. *Now, Oriole, I tell Miss Claire where her pearl and diamonds went, you'll go to jail.* Liar. Edging close to her all the time. Getting her to baby-sit with his sister up above the highway so he could take his sister out to a nightclub. At least there she got paid for baby-sitting. She needed that money after Miss Claire let her go.

"You'll have to go back to the cotton, Oriole. Don't cry. It isn't your fault. Bert's so crazy with drink he's after anyone in a skirt. And you did so well as a picker. You were the best picker we had." Poor little Miss Claire. If she only knew it, she was better off without him.

His sister. She'd gone to Mister Adam. "Mister Adam, how's Mistah Ainsley's sister up to the highway? I hear she's poorly."

"Someone's pulling your leg, Oriole. The only sister Bert Ainsley ever had died ten years ago."

Then her family found out. "Yo' layin' around with Bert Ainsley instead of baby-sitting like you tole us?"

"Papa, I do baby-sit. I'll tell yo' the address. I'll go up there with you."

"Well, Oriole, I'll tell you somethin'. You're goin' to be

baby-sittin' for yourself one these days, then don't come squallin' to me."

Now the baby was dead. If she hadn't run out there when she heard Ruby Ella scream... How'd she know Ruby Ella was already done for? She saw her layin' there, and she tossed the poor baby to the ground and lit into Bert, let that poor baby get soaking wet and scared to death and maybe trampled by those boys that come running in, and she'd grabbed that frogging fork. She still didn't know Ruby Ella was dead when she dragged that rotten hulk of a Bert Ainsley over and shoved him down under that cypress hole. She'd like to tell the police. She was dying to tell someone. Everybody ought to know. But she was scared. She was so scared when she found that Ruby Ella was dead, she almost died herself. Then when the baby went into that awful shaking and making funny noises, all she could think to do was run for Pokeen.

Well, she didn't have to be scared. She was going down to New Oreans now. Miss Sal had cleared her way, not meaning to, but she had. She was taking Miss Olivia over to Dallas and Miss Olivia couldn't watch Oriole go. She got five dollars for the toaster Bert had given her. *A 'lectric toaster down here and no 'lectricity in Noonday. Yo' crazy, Bert?* All the other gifts she'd hidden away were now sold. She had enough money. She would hitch a ride into Dallas, and get a bus to New Orleans. She was too smart to go through town, let somebody catch her leaving. Only thing was: if they were really friendly-like, she could ride clear to Dallas with Miss Olivia and Miss Sal. She smiled down at Miss Sal as she folded waxed paper around one of the cakes.

"I'm sorry about your baby, Oriole," Sal said.

Oriole wiped her eyes on the tea towel. "I sho' do miss him," she said truthfully.

Miss Olivia pulled on her gloves. "I never in the world would have started these cakes if I'd known, Sal." She was taking the cakes up to Lelia's, to Madelaine's, and one on out to the preacher's.

Oriole studied the women thoughtfully. If she told the police, and went to jail, could Miss Sal work it to get her out of jail like she was getting Arlie out? She was a slick worker, all right... But it wasn't worth the chance.

"I should have called up at Adam's, Olivia. He would have sent someone down. I was just so excited after I talked to Arlie's Miss Toliver and she said she would help, then I called the lawyer..."

"You knew I'd go, Sal. I'm so glad you could get the appointment for tomorrow instead of Monday. Joe Time's hearing is set for Monday, and it seems I'm just about the only one in Noonday who will put in a good word for him." She tossed a hopeful glance Oriole's way, but Oriole let on she didn't get it. "Now, Oriole," picking up her purse, "you don't need to rush the work while I'm gone. Just do your regular work." Oriole eyed the purse swinging on her arm. "Oh, you want me to pay you now?" Suspiciously. "You'll need it before I get back?"

More than you know, Miss Olivia. 'Cause I won't be here when you get back. I'll be long gone. "Yes'm, Miss Olivia, please."

"All right, but remember, Pokeen's paid in full, and he was considerate. Now, if you have extra time, please iron those curtains I dampened. I was going to do them this afternoon."

Oriole watched the long sleek blue Cadillac smoothing out the drive. They ought to know she wasn't crazy enough to stick around. Slamming the irons on the stove-top, she flew for the ironing board. She'd do every lick of work Miss Olivia paid her to do if it took all night, then she'd go. Everything she was taking along was ready in her paper sack. If it wouldn't attract attention, she'd set a match to her shack and go off in glory.

Raven leaned out from the jammed pickup, holding the map he'd drawn for Abraham. He talked louder than usual, nervously.

"You sure you know where to turn, Abraham? Get into that right hand lane at the big intersection at Bill's station. It'll head you straight for Carlisle's." Abraham nodded, glancing at the troubled faces in the rear end of the pickup.

They were all tense since Raven told them that he'd seen a frogging fork in Bert Ainsley's chest.

Last year when they left for Noonday Cotton Picking Day at Carlisle's Ranch, it was just like a picnic. They were to work Saturday. The proceeds of their work would be deposited toward the building fund for the new church. They were leaving this afternoon to start picking at daybreak tomorrow. Abraham had to stay to hold prayer meeting. He and Brewster would drive over in Bessie the next morning. Folding the sheet of lined tablet paper Raven had given him, he nodded.

He stood in the middle of the road watching the pickup and the big truck jammed with men and boys pull away. They would come back more evenly distributed with Bessie's added space. He made his way slowly up to the porch and sat down. No one in Noonday felt cheerful. The dreadful tragedy had touched every one of them. No one who ever laid eyes on Ruby Ella and little Jesse—one thought of them as always together—could help feeling sick all over. Brewster was always quiet. That was his way. But normally he had a healthy appetite. Since the night Bimby knocked at their door with the terrible word, Brewster had hardly eaten a bite of food, and Abraham couldn't remember him saying a word unless Abraham asked him something. On the last night of the storm, he woke up to see Brewster standing in the doorway, just staring while the wind blew at the final few drops of rain, beat out the last of its bitterness.

Brewster was more than troubled. He watched him now, got up from the chair and watched him walk right through puddles and mud he would normally jump over. Dropping back into the chair, he tried to recall the night of the frogging party. There were over forty boys, all except Brewster in strange Halloween attire. Brewster didn't want a costume. He bought a nickle mask. Every penny he could save went into his school fund with the railroad pension checks. He had his heart set on going to a fine preparatory school, had it picked out over in Mississippi, studied hard toward that end. He hadn't been late or missed one day of school since he came to Noonday. "I'm going to keep my record clean. I'm going to be a credit to mother." To Leah.

He studied hard on it: he should have some recollection of Brewster down at the lake, but he didn't. He couldn't remember seeing him or hearing his voice after the group crossed the street, yet on other outings, Brewster had always helped with the smaller boys. He might have stayed behind to hear the rest of Pinkney's songs at the girl-party. That was it. He stayed behind listening to the songs Abram used to sing to him. It troubled Brewster, took him back to East St. Louis, to the lost years when he had Abram and Leah. Thus encouraged, he stepped inside to warm the coffee and to cut a large slice of the cake Miss Olivia Flower had dropped off for them.

Brewster came too quietly inside, sat down with his books in his lap. He shook his head at the cake, just sipped the coffee, staring at Abraham with solemn eyes. "I want to talk to you about Halloween night. About the swamp. I was down there. It wasn't Joe Time. His car wasn't there. Do you remember? We were standing beside the road when he passed. All the little kids would remember seeing that car. We waited to cross."

Abraham nodded. He did remember that car shooting past. He could tell Brewster didn't know that Bert Ainsley had been found, didn't know about the frogging fork. Gently, he pushed the piece of cake toward the boy, watched the relief on the boy's face as the story spilled out.

"Now, Brewster, it doesn't sound to me as if you were down there alone." Getting up, he busied himself at the stove, lighted the fire under the blackeyed peas. He didn't turn around. "Can you manage another piece of cake?"

"I sure can. I haven't been able to swallow since Ruby Ella was found. I'd give my life to go back into that night and save her. But I saw the white man. I smelled the whiskey. I thought they were Halloween frolicking."

"Did you bump into the man or the woman?"

"I'm not sure. Something hit me."

"The woman wore black. You're sure it wasn't Ruby Ella?"

"She was much bigger than Rudy Ella. I didn't see Ruby Ella. If I had, if I'd known she was there... Two lanterns were there. One burning low near that big cypress. The other was brighter and in the middle of the road. That was the reason I was sure Joe's car wasn't there."

"And this white man and the woman were fighting?"

"Yes. She was screaming. That's why we... *I* ran to them. Then I saw he was white, and smelled the whiskey. I didn't think it was anything serious. She cursed. But some people sound like that when it isn't serious. I heard a lot of it when we lived back in the apartment in East St. Louis. At first, I thought it was big kids throwing outhouses in the swamp."

"Brewster, who was with you?" Brewster just stared at him. "And this was all before the storm hit?"

"It was starting to rain when we... Afterward."

"Did you hear anything else?"

"Yes, I heard Oriole's baby crying. We were pretty close to her place, but it was dark."

"You mean Oriole's house was dark?"

Brewster nodded.

Brewster was asleep when Abraham came back from the prayer meeting. It hadn't been a large meeting, just women and children, and the older men who hadn't gone over to Carlisle's. Inside the flickering lamp-lit room, he heard the sound of the boy's exhausted sleep. Outside, somewhere high in the dark sky, a nightbird cried. The lonesome sound came into the room. He blew out the lamp, and sat on the kitchen chair. That was Brewster's frogging fork in Bert Ainsley. Almost every man and boy in Noonday had a frogging fork, but these had been special. Doodle put the boys' initials on the handles. They had been short one fork, he remembered. The men were hoping that an outsider had stolen it. Closing his eyes, he remembered the boy with the nervous walk, the boy in the black cape. *Terence.* Pushing his feet around, he searched for his shoes.

"Why, Reverend Cork, Lelia isn't here this time of night. She's been much too upset to even work dinner hour. Terence?" she frowned. "No, I couldn't wake him. He's been dreadfully ill ever since Halloween night. He was caught in the storm on his way from a party in town. It was nice of you to stop. I'll tell him in the morning, but now I must go. I have my hands full without Lelia."

"Mrs. Abernathy, tell Terence that Brewster and I will stop by here in the morning. You be sure to tell him that, please, ma'am."

"Reverend Cork, is something wrong?"

He hesitated, then shook his head.

Blowing out the lamp, Abraham lay open-eyed, staring into the black night. One small star got through the thickness of the live oaks to blink solemnly at him. He would go to Oriole's early, before he got Brewster up. The minute Adam opened the store, he'd call Clay. Clay would know what to do, and would go with them to the police station. He wished that he had walked on up to the apartments last night, but his feet had bothered him. He had considered driving Bessie since he had the key and would be using it... No, he wouldn't be using it. He and Brewster would not be going to Carlisle's to pick cotton.

As he let the outbuilding door close, the splint-leg mockingbird Brewster had mended in the spring spoke sweetly down to him from his searching on a limb. Now full grown, the bird was doing well with his stiff repaired leg. He had taken the boy out shooting. Brewster could hit a can halfway across a field, but he couldn't bring himself to shoot a bird. Abraham felt that he could have explained all this to Rosey, but that he couldn't to a strange policeman. It was going to be hard enough to tell Brewster that they had to go straight to Adam's and call Mister Carlisle to tell Raven and Doodle that they weren't coming. He stood thoughtfully inhaling the morning scent rising from the leaf-covered path. He braced himself in the morning chill, preparing the words for the police. He rehearsed, his breath slipping soundlessly from his lips and frosting white in the uncolored air like the smoke from the chimney where he had coffee and grits warming and eggs ready to fry when he got Brewster up.

It was still night in the west, deep black down the horizon. Here in the middle it was waiting, no color. The leaves of the oaks were still black. The massive trees grew under and around his stilt-built house, the thick limbs almost concealing the grey planks and the steep corrugated roof. The smoke was diffused by the leaves. The entire circle of the house and the trees were a grey cloud. It didn't look like a good sign.

To the east, quite a few miles east, the unseen sun was beginning to mention morning by laying a pale orange line behind the still-black fence of swamp cypress. A light glowed in Oriole's shanty. With Miss Olivia in Dallas, Oriole would be going over to straighten the house. Oriole was like the silky girl up in Little Rock. He had never been able to reach her, to get through to her, but now he had to.

An uneven orange-yellow circle shot shimmering rays upward, tinting the sky. Clouds stood out black above the swamp, suspended, hanging out in space. He studied the sky, trying to sort out warning or benediction until the red faded, oranged, became too varied to be called a red sky. The sun was just rising into the regular fall sky haze of yesterday's cotton seed smoke, smoke from burned leaves and of wood fires now stretching as far across the morning as he could see.

Instantly behind him to the west on the black lake, as if having just received some unheard secret signal, hundreds of wild geese and ducks rose up, made their announcements, swung into businesslike formations and headed southeastward where the marshes waited. The new day wind stirred Doodle's finished but unplowed cornfield. The rain-grey stalks, now dried, scratched against the cold Bessie. If they had been going into Dallas as they had planned, he would have already started the motor, warming it. Sighing, he watched the light go out in Oriole's shanty. She would be going to Miss Olivia's house now. He went in the back door. He'd get his coat and walk over and talk to her.

Brewster was sleepily pulling on the overalls he was wearing to pick cotton. Abraham shook his head. "Put on your school pants, Brewster. You know what we must do today."

"Yes, Uncle."

Abraham cracked the eggs. It was good to see the boy eat.

He didn't feel hungry this morning. Glancing at the clock, he walked to the front door. A dark figure tottering on high heels passed the great live oak in front of Raven's. He ran out into the road. It was Oriole, carrying a brown paper sack. She went on past Raven's, headed for the macadam road.

"Brewster, Brewster, never mind changing. Hurry!" Snatching the key Doodle left on the table, he pushed the boy out the door.

Bessie gasped, chugged, sputtered and died. Holding the choke, he pressed the starter, pushed the pedal to the floor, turned the wheels sharply to pull crazily out into Evening Road. Through the traffic spinning down the macadam, he saw her standing on the other side. Just as he pulled up to the stop sign, a small blue car picked her up and sped off toward Dallas. He felt a chilling sweat as he watched the narrow, heavily traveled road. Bessie gulped unsteadily as he waited for an opening. Seeing a hole, he darted across.

Hanging on, and leaning out, Brewster watched the blue car. Abraham drove carefully, with a horror that he'd have to stop suddenly. He had borrowed Bessie often enough to know that when she was cold, she would stall. The cars from the city were steady. From behind, cars darted around them. One small car kept poking in and out to shoot forward at a place where the road curved. A large truck swept around the bend and pounded toward it. There wasn't room for him to shoot forward to let the car in. With a quick prayer that the driver would pull in behind the car ahead, he shot for the precipitous shoulder. The truck tires screamed as the driver hit the brake. With a smear of rubber, the blue car slammed into the space. Abraham rocked along the shoulder until he could pull back into traffic. The blue car had disappeared around the curve.

The road was rising. It curved, then straightened to sweep over the high railroad crossing. The blue car was out of sight. Abraham was four cars from the railroad crossing when the whistle sounded. The automatic signal began blinking back and forth to the ringing of the bell. The cars ahead of him shot across the high fill. Abraham glanced at Brewster, then slammed to a stop behind the signal box. Brewster jumped over the gate and raced to the tracks to peer under the revolving wheels.

He tore back to the truck. "He let her out at the corner, right at Bill's station. I could see the car and her black dress."

They made it to the station just in time to see Oriole totter around the building. Her paper sack was propped against the cold drink machine. When she came around the station, her eyes narrowed at the sight of Bessie. Abraham handed her a bottle of lemon pop.

"Yo' all right, Rever'nd?" Eyes slitted, she saw Brewster grinning and waving from the truck.

"Come on over, Oriole, see Brewster. We're on our way down to Carlisle's to pick. Yo' pickin' today, Oriole?"

She studied him over the pop bottle, a suspicious glint in her eyes. "I thought it was jest men and boys."

Brewster stepped down and helped her into the seat. She tried to draw back. "I was headin' down Naw Leans."

"Well, Oriole, you came a long distance out of your way. You should have struck out through town. Now, the quickest would be for you to ride down to Carlisle's with us. I could drop Brewster off to start, and take you on out to the south road."

"Yo' do that fo' me, Rever'nd? Go all that ou'ta yo' way?"

"Sure, Oriole, don't we have to help one another?"

They chugged along the southeast road. "Uncle says you picked more cotton than any two men the last two or three times."

"Yo' heard that, Rever'nd?"

"Sure, Oriole. Everyone knows you're worth more than three men the way you pick."

"Yo' want I should pick today?"

Chapter 27

THE SEARCH FOR SINGING RIVER

It was spring. Around the big houses Abraham passed, and dotting the old graveyard, forsythia and daffodil lay golden upon the new green grass. Great mounds of azaleas in myriad shades of red, in pink and white clustered against pale green fringed mimosa leaves, red bud and deep-color flowering plum.

Shifting the journals, he walked between Garrett and Ruby Ella's stones. The city wreath was there. Every trip Joe Time made here he brought one over from Dallas, always identical—an immense circle of minute and dainty white flowers with a center of dark red rosebuds. Abraham always looked for it, and hoped that it wouldn't be there. It wasn't right for a young man to brood that way. Joe talked about changing his territory, but he never did.

Moving on, he looked down upon markers with wind-worn names: Laurel Hill, Mary Anne. George. Edward. Trunk and Zilpah Brewster. Abram. Leah. He crossed to the other side. Aaron and Ruth Brewster. Adam and Olivia Brewster. Jacques and Antoinette LeFleur, many more. He crossed back over to his own side. Oner and Amelia LeFleur... The long years.

The south wind pushed at his back. Old longings stirred. He glanced down at his feet. The bunion bandages that had stood out white and glaring from the holes in his shoes as he walked from the hospital steps were dusted over. His feet felt better. He wanted them in good shape. Brewster would want to walk the woods again when he got home from Mississippi where he was in school. He was proud of Brewster. But the house had been empty and dreary. He had known a lostness ever since that first trip when he took Brewster over to see that the school was all that Brewster expected it to be, hoped that it was. He could see them all at the depot that evening. Brewster wore a new long-pants suit with a jacket. He stood, a new imitation leather suitcase at his side, talking with Terence.

Bless Terence. Bless Lelia for showing Terence he had the courage to step forward when he did, to step right up there and say, "I was with Brewster. I recognized Bert Ainsley and Oriole. I knew Oriole's voice." It was manly and good the way he answered all those questions. The Abernathys sat in pride of their son, of his manliness.

Straightening, Abraham stepped right out, anxious to get the mail. It had been too early when he passed Adam's store on the way to the hospital for his treatment. While his bandages were still clean, he had stopped by the apartment to see Sal and Clay and the new baby, and to drop in on Miss Olivia.

Ahead of him, beyond the store, the road looked bare. The gaping holes left when the big trees were removed had been filled. The paving machinery was quiet. A rain-crow cried. The grinding wouldn't start again until Monday, and not then if it rained. Adam saw him coming up the steps, and reached into the slot.

"You're going to be disappointed, Abraham, have a lonely summer. On this card Brewster says he'd like to stay on for special classes if it's all right with you," handing him the card and an envelope addressed in the precise handwriting of the young preacher who had relieved him when he took Brewster to Mississippi the first time. He glanced at it.

"Sit down, Abraham. I just put on a pot of coffee. I wish you wouldn't walk up there every day. You should have bought Lelia's mule."

"I thought about it when the Abernathys moved to Dallas, but when Pinkney bought Lelia's house, she threw in the mule. You know, all that money Bimby made for Pinkney couldn't fill the empty spot left when his old mule died."

Adam carried his cup over and stood in the doorway. "So Sal named the boy Robert Brewster Justice. I like that. And it made me feel good to see those two marry, two lonely people like them."

They were silent, remembering. Abraham saw Sal, smiling, saw Miss Olivia walk into the church on old Aaron's arm, and pass the pew where he sat with Pinkney. It did make you feel warm.

Getting up, he rinsed his cup, and picked up the ledgers. From next door the strains of one of Bimby's blues records reached out across the morning. And the red ends of Joe Time's new car stuck out behind Pokeen's. He strolled in. Joe looked bad. "You coming over, Joe?"

"Yes, Abraham. But first, I'm headed down to have lunch with Arlie and Josh. Why don't you come along? I'll be taking Arlie to the cemetery."

They turned at the barriers, into Swamp Road. Evening Road was closed. Pinkney and the others living between the church and Adam's store had to use back roads. By the time the paving was finished, Boyd's new pumps would be in. Doodle would be through working on the church, and ready to go to work for Boyd.

Joe swung into the drive at Miss Olivia's old house. She hadn't taken one plant with her to the apartment, said she wanted Arlie and Josh to enjoy them. The pots and kettles had been lifted to stand in tiers on the old church benches he'd given Josh in trade for the fine Catholic altar that had come from Mississippi in the wagon with Olivia LeFleur Brewster. Doodle and Raven had put a new floor on the porch, and new pillars, painted white. Chairs were lined up, six on each side. By day cats slept on them. In the evenings, the family and whoever stopped by, often Abraham, usually Madelaine on her way home from Miss Olivia's apartment, would sit there listening to the music from Pokeen's.

Olivia had been dubious about Joshua buying her house so close to the swamp, but his light heart and kindness had gradually urged Arlie up out of her darkness. She could look out upon the grey shack where she was born, the fields she had worked with her family. She had mourned Ruby Ella. Even Jesse realized the hardness of it for her. On the day she stood before him to be married to Joshua, Jesse had marched up the aisle to stand with them, holding her hand. She looked fine now running to greet them.

"You come right in and eat with us, Abraham. Lutie Mae says all the building going on over there and the road noise have taken your appetite."

Placing the ledgers on the back seat, he followed them into the house.

Leaving, Abraham stood for a minute looking at the ledgers on the red leather seat. He left them there, and walked slowly toward the swamp. Someone had torn down Oriole's shanty. An old Virginia rail fence that went back no one remembered how far, had been repaired to line the road clear around to Madelaine's. The road, carrying heavy traffic now, had been leveled. The old scars were gone.

He sat down under the big cypress, leaned back to let his eyes follow the swiftly traveling mists moving northward. He was going to miss Brewster this summer. He read his card over and over. Then he drew out the letter from the new young preacher.

Dear Reverend Cork:
I was most impressed with your Noonday, and the plans for the new church. I have now finished my studies, and will be free at any time to take over whenever you go to visit Brewster.
Respectfully, John Colborn.

Abraham glanced over the letter to his feet. The new bandages were dark now, almost blackened by the soil of swamp road. It would be hard to visualize those wayworn shoes with their slivered holes on the new polished-cypress floor. It was impossible to imagine his green and frayed frock coat beside that beautiful altar. He couldn't see himself standing in that lighted vestibule pulling the satin rope now attached to the old slave bell Aaron sent down with Pinkney, or walking past the hand-hewn shining magnolia pews to stand under the crystal chandelier that Arlie and Joshua insisted upon donating to the church when they moved into Miss Olivia's house. Doodle had wired it so that it now held sheer twisted light globes.

He matched the old church, felt at home passing the grey benches in the room where the narrow windows gave so grudgingly the light, where the dim bulb stringing over his book allowed little more light than the lanterns had. Now, that new young preacher, with his polished shoes and sermons...

Above him, somewhere high, up beyond the mists, geese yipped. It had been a long time since he'd been able to heed that call. They were going north...

Joe's red car turned out of the drive. He would be taking Arlie to the cemetery. They would be gone for an hour or so, then Joe, in his pattern, would drive down old swamp road, park, and sit staring out over the water. Joe was too young to live like that. Far better if he followed a new and different road. Unfolding the preacher's letter, he wrote the number on the envelope. Getting up stiffly, he walked up to Adam's, got dimes and quarters, and stepped into the phone booth.

By the time he got back to the swamp, Joe was parked in his usual place. He got out to hand Abraham the ledgers.

"You forgot these, Abraham. I looked them over. These were Ruby Ella's people?"

"Yes. A long time ago I promised to return these ledgers. I could mail them, but I want to see it all again. I want to see that wide river. I thought I'd walk over to Vicksburg, wander down to South Wind, have a little visit with Brewster, then follow the Natchez Trace, go on to New Orleans." He looked straight at Joe. "Head out to Alabama, go all the way, follow the route." Joe was listening, his eyes studying the tall cypress above them. "Go all the way up into Virginia." He clutched his right foot in his hand. "I'll make it. I'll walk slowly. Now and then I'll get a ride. What I'd really like would be to run into some friend who is headed that way, someone interested in seeing places he's never seen."

Joe stooped down, his eyes laughing. "Come on, you old rascal. I'm taking you home. It's too damp for you to be standing around here. You can make a pot of coffee."

"I thought I'd leave right after church tomorrow..."

That night a restless wind walked across Texas, stirring

the leaves, scratching limbs against the house. Abraham lay in the soft feather bed watching leaf-shadows on his old gladstone waiting in the corner of the room. Pushing back the quilt, he walked to the window and stood looking at the black fence of tall pines lining the western sky. A narrow, tilted moon hung reflected upon the lake, outlining a dinghy, illuminated for a moment a duckblind never built.

The morning was fresh with a south wind blowing. He pulled the satin bell-cord. The sound, strangely familiar, echoed through the new church. His footsteps padded across the new floor. In the front row, Jesse sat with Pinkney who held his banjo across the knees of a new grey suit. If his record sales had not been so great, the church would not be so fine.

Abraham looked at all of them—Lutie Mae, Doodle, Pip Doodle, Arlie, Joshua, the boys. Raven and Aretha with Jib and the girls. The Johnsons. Pokeen and his girl. Ivory, Little Ivory, Johnny, Madelaine. They sang the first hymn. Jesse, who was learning from Pinkney, watched his fingers on the banjo.

Now, in these last few minutes, Abraham tried to think if he was needed. There was still the school. He hadn't been able to bring himself to stand before that school board to ask for it. There, that was a job for the new preacher. He was better qualified to ask for that. He tried to think if he had helped them, if he had done any good. He had told them of their fine heritage. They had wanted the wiring, and they had it. They had wanted Evening Road paved. They were getting it. Many fine oaks had bowed to the earth-moving equipment. They were out in the open now, exposed. Townspeople would use their short cut to Dallas, probably even buses that now used the south road. Each man's conduct under this new scrutiny rested within himself.

He was not going to say goodbye. He talked of their new exposure, the new eyes that would see them in passing. They were listening. Some eyes strayed upward to the sparkling chandelier. Some gazed toward the lake where fish jumped. Some looked at him.

Of them all, only Pinkney looked at him in any way differently than they had always listened to his sermons. Pinkney leaned forward. Finally, he reached into his vest to pull out his steel-rimmed glasses. He studied Abraham's face. It was time for Pinkney's solo. He carried his banjo up to the chair that had been placed between the altar and the windows. He struck a chord. It was not the planned song. Jesse's eyes narrowed quizzically. If Brewster were there, he would have recognized the old slave tune of farewell.

As Abraham walked slowly toward the new vestibule he saw the red car pass and stop under the great live oak in front of Raven's.

It was past noon. They had all rushed to their homes. Noonday lay quiet. Over the lake a small duck skimmed.

Everything ended too soon. His eyes pinched, remembering what he might have said to Arlie long ago in Dallas, what he should have said to Oriole. He saw again that long look that passed between him and Pinkney at the church door, felt again that age-dried hand. Why did he always wish too late that he'd held a hand tighter? Did all men feel their failures? their incapabilities? Did they cry as he cried now glancing back into the little room that Lelia had entered long ago carrying the sleep-blessed Brewster?

His gladstone waited on the porch. The westering sun picked out a rusted buckle that glittered briefly over the black hook-handle umbrella, the duck gun. Picking up the bag, he walked down the wooden steps into the road, looked hard at the lake and raised his hand in a hail. He stepped right out toward the waiting red car.